Robert Goddard's first novel, *Past Caring*, was an instant bestseller. Since then, his books have captivated readers worldwide with their edge-of-the-seat pace and their labyrinthine plotting. He has won awards in the UK, the US and across Europe and his books have been translated into over thirty languages. In 2019, he won the Crime Writers' Association's highest accolade, the Diamond Dagger, for a lifetime achievement in Crime Writing.

KT-154-118

www.penguin.co.uk

4 4 0073477 6

ONE FALSE MOVE

Robert Goddard

CORGI BOOKS

TRANSWORLD PUBLISHERS
61–63 Uxbridge Road, London W5 5SA
www.penguin.co.uk

Transworld is part of the Penguin Random House group of companies
whose addresses can be found at global.penguinrandomhouse.com

Penguin
Random House
UK

First published in Great Britain in 2019 by Bantam Press
an imprint of Transworld Publishers
Corgi edition published 2019

A CIP catalogue record for this book
is available from the British Library.

ISBN
9780552172615 (B format)
9780552176828 (A format)

Typeset in 11/13.75pt Times NR MT by Jouve (UK), Milton Keynes.
Printed and bound in Great Britain by Clays Ltd, Elcograf S.p.A.

Penguin Random House is committed to a sustainable
future for our business, our readers and our planet. This book
is made from Forest Stewardship Council® certified paper.

MIX
Paper from
responsible sources
FSC® C018179

1 3 5 7 9 10 8 6 4 2

ONE FALSE MOVE

OPENING GAME

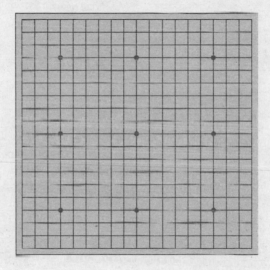

CARL SAID I WAS ABSOLUTELY THE RIGHT PERSON FOR THIS JOB. I think he meant it. He didn't actually say it was a job for a woman, but I could tell that's what he thought. The target was probably male and probably young. It goes with the territory. So, send me.

I wanted to go. I leapt at the chance, in fact. Not just because it promised to put my career back on track after my transfer to London, but because it really was fascinating. Who was this guy? And yes, like Carl, I felt sure all along it *was* a guy. When I was shown what he could do, I *wanted* to talk to him. I *wanted* to understand. We could exploit his abilities to put Venstrom ahead of the competition. Of course. That was always the commercial calculation. But beyond that, how he did what he did was an irresistible and unfathomable mystery.

Carl didn't know what he was getting us into, of course. He couldn't. No one could. There's nothing to warn you when you cross an invisible line. But the other side soon starts to feel different. And, in this case, not so very long after different . . . dangerous.

*

So, this is what happened beyond that line. This is what happened as it happened. This is how I got to where I am.

* * *

Monday October 7

I LINGER OVER BREAKFAST. THERE'S NO HURRY. THE HOTEL'S quiet, ticking over this early in the week, this late in the season. The weather's mostly grey, but silvery light keeps piercing the clouds over the sea. There's no wind. I gaze out through the high windows of the restaurant and see a couple of bulk carriers moving slowly out beyond St Anthony Head, heading to or from Falmouth. The view here in St Mawes is serene and beautiful, the sea tranquillizingly still. I catch myself thinking how nice it would be to be here on holiday and how much nicer again to be here on holiday with the right person.

I used to think I knew who the right person was. Now I haven't a clue. And I'm not on holiday either. It's just me here, with a job to do. I sip my coffee and check my phone.

No alert yet. He isn't playing. But he will be. Soon.

All we know for certain about our mystery man is that the IP address of the computer he's using leads to Conrad Vogler of Admiral's Reach, Upper Castle Road, St Mawes, Cornwall. And all we know about Conrad Vogler is his directorship of a company called Conmari Ltd, nature of business unspecified, and his date of birth, July 2, 1970, which makes him too old to be an obvious candidate. The other director of Conmari Ltd is Marianne Vogler, presumably his wife. The company name seems to be a tacky pairing of Conrad and Marianne, which doesn't make me warm to them. But a super-geek son of theirs could well be our guy. We're betting on that.

The Voglers don't have much of a presence in the virtual world, in fact none at all, which could make some people suspicious. Venstrom has grown as huge and successful as it has by offering people solutions to problems they didn't know they had, by selling them goods and games and all the vital ingredients of the virtual lives we lead. So, to me and my colleagues, who don't just like but need to know as much as we can about our customers, the disconnected are either dinosaurs or people with something to hide. And somehow the Voglers don't come across as dinosaurs.

I took a look at Admiral's Reach straight after I arrived yesterday evening. Modern, white-walled, slate-roofed, with plenty of glass and steel, all hard angles and blank surfaces, set in a big, gently sloping plot a little way up the hill from St Mawes Castle. Most of the windows were lit. There was a big four-wheel-drive pulled up in front of the garage. Someone was evidently at home.

I didn't try my luck then. Our guy never plays at night. He's a daytime only player. If I'm just going to show up at the Voglers' door – and I can't think of any other way to approach them – I want it to be while he's online. It'll be more difficult for them to deny it then. I'll have something to show them.

I put my toe in the water with an email before leaving London, inviting Conmari Ltd to contact us for some free website design advice. No response. Which leaves nothing for it but the face-to-face approach. Carl didn't give me any bright ideas about how to pitch it. I think I'm just going to have to charm my way in and see where we go from there.

I'm a bit nervous. And I'm very curious. I suppose, most of all, I'm excited. I've just no idea what I'm going to find.

My phone beeps just after ten. He's on. And so am I.

I don't want to turn up so close to him starting to play that he'll make a connection, so I leave the hotel and walk past the harbour, rehearsing a whole load of ways I can introduce the subject without alarming him. The ferry from Falmouth is docking. A few late holidaymakers are clambering off and climbing the steps to the quay. No one gives me a second glance.

I'm wearing a navy blue trouser-suit and white blouse under my mac. I look like I mean business. I've applied a touch more make-up than usual. Nothing obvious, though. Just enough to make me difficult to turn away.

This isn't necessarily my only chance. But it might be my best one. I plan to make the most of it.

I walk down the curving drive to the front door of the house. The 4WD's gone and there's a battered Fiat parked in its place. The grounds are terraced, falling away towards Lower Castle Road. I'm imagining a panoramic deck and big sea-facing windows on the next level down. There's not much to see on this side of the house. I check my phone. He's still on. His sessions generally last an hour or two. I ring the doorbell and wonder just what kind of reception I'm going to get.

Half a minute or so passes. The door opens. A woman in jeans and a T-shirt looks out at me. She's too young to be Marianne Vogler. My money's on her being the cleaner. When she speaks, it's with a local accent. And I don't have the Voglers down as local.

'Hello,' she says.

'I'm looking for Mr or Mrs Vogler.'

'They're out.'

'Ah. Right.' That isn't necessarily bad news. 'Is, er, any other member of the family at home?'

'It's just Mr and Mrs Vogler who live here.' That isn't quite an answer to my question, I notice. 'You can leave a message if you want.'

'Right. Thanks. My name's Nevinson. Nicole Nevinson. Can you give Mr and Mrs Vogler my card?' I hand one over. She glances down at it. 'I contacted them recently about a business opportunity. And I happened to be in the area, so . . .'

She looks unimpressed. I can't really blame her. 'I'll tell 'em you called.' A tight smile. She starts to close the door.

'Lovely house,' I say brightly.

'Yeah.'

'I bet the views from the front are amazing.'

She frowns. 'They are.' But it's obvious there isn't going to be an invitation to take a look. 'I've got to get back to work.'

'Of course. But . . .'

'Yeah?'

'When do you think Mr and Mrs Vogler will be back?'

'Dunno for sure. But Mrs Vogler will probably be here this afternoon.'

'OK.' I smile. 'I'll try then.'

'OK.'

The door closes. I walk slowly back up the drive, asking myself whether that was a total screw-up or just a minor setback. I can try again this afternoon. I'll have to. I check my phone. He's still on. And Kyra has texted me the GPS report. He's in St Mawes. Most likely, I reckon, inside Admiral's Reach. I glance back at the house from the road, then head off towards the castle.

I wander round the galleries and trinket shops. I drink another coffee. I have an early lunch and try to put my plans in order. There's a lot riding on this. Though, since Venstrom's resources are massive, I really should be able to make an offer that's too good to refuse. The rest is just . . . presentation.

He stops playing while I'm having lunch, so I decide to go back to the house. Even though he's no longer online, I have enough to go on.

A few spits of rain are in the air as I walk along Lower Castle Road. There are houses and cottages to my left, facing the sea. To my right are high-hedged banks bordering the gardens of the big houses in Upper Castle Road, one of them Admiral's Reach.

There are steps up to back gates concealed by undergrowth. I wonder which one might lead to Admiral's Reach and whether it's worth going up to take a look.

Suddenly a young man appears, jogging down the nearest flight of steps. He's tall and slim, with a mop of dark hair and a pale, narrow face. He's dressed in jeans, T-shirt and retro corduroy jacket and is carrying a bulging leather shoulder-bag. I notice how long his fingers are as he pushes one hand through his hair.

9

Is he my guy? I look at him as he turns and strides off in the direction I came from, back into town. I don't have long to think about it. But he ticks all the boxes. Age, sex, appearance. The consensus, based on his online behaviour, has always been that he'd turn out to be someone like this. *Yes.* I follow, ten metres or so back. Carl's last words to me as I left his office last Friday were, 'Good luck.' Well, I've just got lucky. This is my guy. I'm sure of it.

He walks fast, head nodding, maybe in time to music on his earphones. He looks relaxed and contented, in a world of his own. He's certainly got no idea he's being followed. I could overtake and try to engage him, but just for now, I'm going to play it cool. I'm going to see where he's going.

The answer turns out to be the harbour. The Falmouth ferry's in and he means to catch it. He already has a ticket. I have to spend a few minutes buying one at the booth on the quay while he goes down the steps and boards. But the ticket man tells me not to worry. 'You've got plenty of time.'

He's right. I may be in a hurry, but no one else is. The boat fills slowly, then we cast off. My guy sits in the cabin, near the stern. I sit opposite him. I try to look as if I'm gazing past him out to sea as we clear the quay. But actually I'm studying him intently.

Dreamy eyes, a high forehead and those long fingers I noticed up the road. Age? Early twenties, I'd guess, but there's something about him that makes me feel he could be slightly older than he looks.

He's obviously a regular on this trip. He gives the ferryman a card to swipe and they seem to recognize each other. As the boat noses out of the harbour, he opens his shoulder-bag and takes out a box of some kind. It's quite small, hinged on one side. He opens it out on his knee. There's a grid pattern on its face. I think I know what it is. A few seconds later I'm sure.

He takes a small draw-string bag out of his pocket and starts lifting out tiny counters, some black, some white, which he places alternately on the grid.

It's a pocket-sized Go board. The counters are magnetic Go stones. He's playing Go with himself, laying the stones out on the intersections of the grid at lightning speed, his brow furrowed in concentration.

I knew nothing about Go before Carl called me in and told me about what our guy had been doing. I don't know a whole lot now, except the few basic rules. The game's about surrounding and controlling territory. Its apparent simplicity disguises a fearsome complexity, with the possible permutations of positions exceeding the total number of atoms in the visible universe – according to Wikipedia. It originated in China a few thousand years ago. It's got that east Asian Zen feeling about it. It's not really my kind of thing.

But that's not the point. The point is that Venstrom's online Go-playing program adjusts to the ability of each player, all the way up from beginner to expert, even though it can beat the very best with ease. Except this one player. Except *this* guy. Our programmers have upgraded the system just for him. Yet he still keeps up. He doesn't always win. But he often does. And that's enough for us. Because at the level we've taken him to he shouldn't be able to. He *really* shouldn't be able to.

How does he do it? That's the question the whole tech

world would want the answer to. *If* they knew about him. But so far only we know. He's our secret. He's our prize. If we can reel him in.

If *I* can reel him in.

I wonder why he's using a physical pocket set rather than playing on his phone. Is it because he doesn't want to leave too much of a trail? Although he's already left enough of one to get our attention. He just doesn't know that yet.

I also wonder where he's going and why. I could go over and sit next to him, try to strike up a conversation, ask a few dumb questions about Go, see where that leads. But I reckon it's better to hold off for now, better to find out as much as I can about him before I make a move.

As the ferry chugs out across the estuary, some of the passengers peer around, scanning the waves for seals, pointing enthusiastically when they think they've spotted one. My guy isn't interested. His eyes and his mind are fixed on the Go board, the tip of his tongue squeezed between his lips as his fingers dip in and out of the bag containing the stones. It looks like a pattern's already emerging on the board. Maybe it's a game he's running through again to see where he made a vital slip, or his opponent did. Maybe he's just freewheeling in some way.

We're crossing the estuary now, with Falmouth Docks ahead of us. The cloud's thickening. It's started to rain. Passengers begin to desert the open deck and bunch in the cabin. My guy frowns slightly in irritation as someone jogs his knee. But the magnetic stones on his Go board stay firmly fixed in place.

The Docks, with their wharves and warehouses and oil tanks, drift past. Then we head in towards a pier in the centre of Falmouth. A change in the sound of the boat's engine as it throttles back tells him we're about to arrive. He clears the Go board with a swipe of his long fingers, slips the bag of stones back into his pocket and snaps the board shut as the ferry edges in to a flight of steps down from the pier.

He's faster than most of the passengers, so he's among the first off. I have to apologize to several people as I jostle to keep up with him. He takes the steps two at a time and is away along the pier.

He's still in that unsuspecting world of his own, though, earphones in, mind elsewhere. I don't have to be any kind of surveillance expert to follow him.

He turns right into the main street at the end of the pier. Almost immediately he crosses the road and dives into a health food shop called Bean Feast. I tag along behind. There's a café on the first floor. He heads upstairs and so do I.

The café's nice, quiet and appetizingly scented, all ground coffee and cinnamon toast, with a partial view of the pier from the street-facing windows. My guy approaches the counter, pulling out his earphones as he goes. There are two girls serving. One of them gives him a grimace that's obviously meant sarcastically before she breaks into a grin. She's brightly dressed, small and slim, with lively, beaming features and hair that's blond where it hasn't been dyed lime green.

'You're late, Joc,' she complains good-naturedly.

'Sorry, Zip,' he responds in a slow, soft, slightly dreamy voice. 'Lost track of time.'

'When did you ever keep track of it?'

'When I last needed to, I s'pose.'

'Had lunch?'

'Nah. But Mum'll do me tea. I'll be fine. Just popped in to say hi. Oh, and I'll have a ginseng to go.'

'I'll come to the Stars. Usual time?'

'We might overrun.'

Zip rolls her eyes at that and starts preparing the ginseng. I do a slow turn and go back down the stairs, where I linger until Joe, as I now know he's called, comes down with his takeaway ginseng and wanders back out of the shop.

He turns left and heads uphill, following the street that runs parallel with the waterfront. I keep pace with him. I've got his girlfriend, her name too, plus her place of work. He can't revert to total anonymity now.

The narrow street opens out, with views across the estuary, partially obscured by a thin curtain of rain. A raised pavement takes us along a terrace of Victorian or maybe Georgian villas. He's got his earphones back in now, but he pulls them out when he reaches the gate of a house that's a bit bigger than most of its neighbours, with an extra floor and imposing bay windows and a basement. The paintwork's overdue for a touch-up, though, including on the sign that reads *Tideways Guest House, AA listed, all rooms en-suite*.

Joe pushes his way in through the gate, pauses to pet a black-and-white cat that comes out of the porch to meet him, then goes into the house.

I stand outside in the street, pondering my next move. But it's obvious what I need to do.

First I check something, though. I get out my phone and call up the Falmouth Go Club website I tracked down before leaving London. *Yes.* Monday night is club night, like I remembered, venue the snug bar of the Seven Stars. That's where Joe's going this evening. Me too.

14

I wait five minutes. Then I go and ring the front doorbell.

The woman who answers is middle-aged, in her fifties probably. She's a together kind of person, dressed in jeans and a sweater, but neatly turned out, black hair streaked with grey, attractive, youthful good looks overlaid with a few creases and wrinkles. Her eyes are grey-brown and, I don't know, maybe just a little sad.

I ask if she's got a room. She smiles. 'I have, lovely. How long are you thinking of?'

'Not sure. A few days at least.'

'No problem. Would you like to take a look?'

'Yes. Thanks.'

'No luggage?' she asks as we step into the hall.

'I've left it somewhere else for the moment.'

'Fair enough. This way.'

There's a door standing open in the hall through which I glimpse a small dining room done out in reasonable style. We go up two flights of stairs to the second floor. She explains the first-floor front room's taken but the next one up is free, with a sea view. She quotes a rate of £75 per night, bed and breakfast. I say that sounds fine.

It's not luxury, but the room's OK, clean and comfortable. The bathroom's a pleasant surprise, even if it is on the small side. I don't waste much time saying I'll take it.

'How long have you run this place?' I ask, trying to sound friendly and casual.

'Longer than I care to remember,' she says with a smile.

'It's very nice.'

'Glad you think so. Best thing I ever got out of my husband, that's for sure. Now, I will need a credit card number. Maybe we can go downstairs and sort it out.'

'Sure.'

We go down to a small room at the back of the house that's fitted out as an office. She swipes my credit card and it's all done. I ask if there's any parking. She says I may be able to find a space in the road at the back. It's first come first served. She gives me a pair of keys on a ring. One's for the room, the other the front door. Then she reels off a few recommendations of places to eat in the evening. She's friendly and helpful. I wonder if she'd be less friendly and helpful if she knew I might be about to change her son's life. And hers with it. I doubt she knows what Joe's capable of. It's all going to come as quite a shock – when it comes.

Which should be sooner rather than later now I'm under the same roof as Joe. I hurry back to the pier, but there's forty minutes to wait for the next ferry to St Mawes, so I go back into Bean Feast and have a coffee and a slice of cake. Zip serves me. The café's quieter now and she has time to chat, which she seems happy to do. She asks me if I'm on holiday. I dodge that question and ask if she's always lived in Falmouth.

'Yeah. Born and bred.'

'It's beautiful,' I say. 'The sea. The countryside.'

'Right. But it's not exactly at the centre of things, is it? I sometimes think I should get out of Cornwall. You know, like, see the world. Or more of it, anyway.'

'Good idea.'

'Tell that to my boyfriend.'

Maybe I will, I don't say.

The ferry's still not in when I get back to the pier. The rain's more or less stopped, so I'm able to stand at the far end and watch for it from there while I phone Carl to tell him we've got our man and I plan to talk to him this evening.

Carl sounds pleased. So he should. 'Where does this leave us with the Voglers?' he asks.

'Maybe nowhere,' I reply. 'It looks like Joe just works for them or something like that. He uses their computer to play on.'

'Why not his own? Why the Voglers'?'

'I haven't a clue.' That's not quite true. I suspect Joe feels he needs to hide his ability. Maybe he knows it makes him a target for the likes of us. But does that mean he hides his ability from the other members of the Falmouth Go Club as well? From Zip? From his mother?

'Maybe it doesn't matter,' says Carl. 'Just offer him whatever it takes, Nicole. You follow? We can't risk someone else cashing in on his talents.'

'I follow, Carl.' Oh yeah, I follow all right. Carl wants this done fast. Patience isn't one of his strengths. Nor is subtlety. I guess he's looking to me to supply just enough of both. And that's exactly what I intend to do.

I collect as much as I need for a few days at Tideways from the hotel in St Mawes, but I keep the room on in case the Vogler angle turns out to be important, though for the moment I'll just leave them guessing about the reason for my visit this morning.

Then I set off on the long drive up the estuary, over the King Harry car ferry and back down to Falmouth. I squeeze the car into a spot round the back of Tideways and let myself into the house, bags in hand.

I meet Joe coming down the stairs as I reach the second landing. I don't know if anyone's staying on the top floor. Maybe it's Joe's private domain. I smile and say hello.

'Oh, hi,' he says, smiling back at me. And it's a great smile, warm and open. 'Mum said you booked in earlier.'

He helps me through the door of my room with my bags. He seems so ordinary in so many ways, but I know he's anything but. I introduce myself.

'Good to meet you, Nicole,' he says. 'I'm Joe.'

'Didn't I see you on the ferry from St Mawes earlier?' I ask.

'Maybe.' He scratches his head. 'Was I that noticeable?' It looks like the idea worries him slightly.

'Only because you were playing Go.'

He frowns at me. 'You a Go player?'

'Not exactly. I had a boyfriend once who played and was always promising to teach me but never did.'

'You'd probably hate it.'

'Maybe. But it would've been nice to find out.'

'Well, if you get any spare time while you're here, I could teach you the basics.' But I can tell he doesn't think that's actually going to happen. He assumes I'm just making conversation. 'Better dash. Enjoy your stay.'

Off he goes then, down the stairs at a soft-footed, loose-limbed lope.

I close the door behind him and unpack a few essentials. The Falmouth Go Club sessions start at six, according to their website. Which means I just have time to shower and trawl through my incoming emails before I set off.

Falmouth's quiet now the shops have closed. The Seven Stars is an old pub tucked in next to what was once the post office in the centre of town. The front bar is a narrow, mellow-wooded taproom, with various mellow regulars drinking their fill and swapping opinions. It's not obvious territory for a woman my age on her own, though I'm made to feel welcome almost because of that.

'I'm here for the Go,' I tell the barman as I order a sparkling water.

He looks surprised. 'They're in the back,' he says, gesturing with his thumb to the snug bar behind him, where I can see a couple of men sitting at a table with a Go board set up between them. 'They'll certainly be pleased to see you.'

He doesn't expand on the remark, but as I make my way round to the other bar, he calls to someone in there. 'New recruit for you, Jerry.'

By the time I make it into the snug a beanpole of a man, bald, bespectacled and bright-eyed, with a whippet-eager look to him, has sprung out of his chair. 'Hello,' he says with a grin. 'We welcome beginners.'

'You're assuming she *is* a beginner,' says the guy he's playing. He's younger than Jerry, an Anglo-Asian man in his mid-thirties, well dressed in a casual style and good-looking with it. He has attractive eyes and a hovering, mischievous smile. 'I'm Roger Lam,' he says. The voice is cultured and confident. 'I'm relatively new here myself.'

'Hi, I'm Nicole. I *am* a beginner, actually. Well, not even that really. I'm just curious about the game.'

'That's a good way to start.'

'I'm Jeremy Inkpen,' Jerry interrupts, shaking my hand. 'Club secretary.'

'Hi. Pleased to meet you.'

'So, what interests you about Go, Nicole?' Roger asks.

I rehash the story about the non-existent Go-playing boyfriend, then mention that the son of my landlady plays the game.

'Ah,' says Roger. 'Joe Roberts. Now, he is a reason to be interested in Go.'

I'm not absolutely sure how to take that and Jeremy

looks puzzled too, as if he's just learnt something he'd previously been unaware of. 'Joe is quite a good player.'

'Thanks to your tutelage, Jerry,' says Roger with a thin smile.

'Well, I . . .'

'You're probably wondering how many members we have,' Roger continues. 'Not enough would be Jerry's answer, I'm sure.'

'We usually get half a dozen or so in on nights like this,' says Jerry defensively. 'It's still rather early.'

A man greeted by them as Walter arrives at that point. Roger adroitly suggests Walter and Jerry pair off for a game while he shows me the way round a Go board. Jerry looks as though he's aware he's been outmanoeuvred. I get the distinct feeling there aren't any female members of this club.

We sit down. Roger sips some whisky from his glass. He smiles at me over the wooden board. It's empty, with the stones stored in readiness in two tubs. 'I'm a stranger in these parts myself,' he says. 'Guest lecturer for a term at the university. I was delighted to discover there was a Go club in town. This gives me my weekly fix.'

'What got you into the game?'

'I grew up in Hong Kong. Go's bigger than chess there.'

'And what do you like about it?'

'Oh, the subtlety, I suppose. And losing a Go game is much less painful than losing at chess. It just creeps up on you. It's almost as beautiful as winning.'

He gives me the black stones and runs through the rules. He gives me an advantage of five stones, which he positions for me. Then we start playing. He's soon gently explaining the mistakes I'm making. I don't even notice he's about to capture one of my stones until he points it out to me. Not that I'm paying much attention. I'm putting more effort into squeezing Roger for information.

'How good a player is Joe?'

'Hard to say.'

'Really? Can't you just . . . tell?'

'You'd think so, wouldn't you? Joe's certainly the best player in the club, though just how good he really is . . . is difficult to gauge.'

'Why?'

Roger frowns, considering the question. 'Because he's modest, I suppose. And he plays modestly. He doesn't seem to enjoy winning much. That is, he doesn't seem to enjoy beating an opponent. He's a little too . . . gentle.'

'Sounds like just the kind of opponent I need.'

'Then stick around. He's sure to be in at some point. But if you're going to play Joe . . .'

'Yes?'

He taps the board. 'You need to concentrate.' Has he noticed I'm more interested in Joe than the intricacies of Go? Not sure. He's friendly. But he's nobody's fool.

It's another forty-five minutes before Joe shows up. Two other players have arrived by then, middle-aged men with slightly quirky looks, who seem delighted to see me. Joe, on the other hand, is just surprised to see me. He wasn't expecting our brief conversation about Go to lead to this.

Roger's explained the rule of liberty and the ko rule to me by then, though I haven't really taken them in. I think he knows this and his suggestion that I'm ready for a game with Joe is obviously mischievous. Joe's reluctant, but can't get out of it and turns out to be rather a good teacher.

He sips orange juice and nibbles peanuts while he plays. He smiles a lot too, at me and at the board. I ask him between the tactical insights what he loves most about the game.

'It's the game with the fewest rules and the most possibilities,' he replies.

'Is that why it was the last game computers outdid humans in?' It's a difficult question for him to answer truthfully. But he doesn't know I know that.

'You should ask Roger about that. He was in the audience at the Four Seasons Hotel in Seoul when AlphaGo beat Lee Sedol.'

'It's true,' says Roger, who's pottering around, watching the other games. He's overheard what Joe said. 'The poor guy looked like a train had hit him when he went three-nil down.'

'A technological train *had* hit him,' says Joe. 'But he won the fourth game.'

'A fluke.'

'Can you fluke a win against a computer?'

'Anyway, he wouldn't get even one now. Three years is like light years in computer development. AlphaGo Zero's taken it to a whole new level.'

I watch Joe carefully as he responds to that. 'Logically, you must be right.'

'How are you enjoying the tutorial, Nicole?' Roger asks.

'It's fascinating,' I reply, just a little too quickly. Joe catches my eye. I can't read the expression in his gaze. But I get the feeling *he* can read *me*. Like a book.

'Why don't you take a break, Nicole?' he suggests. 'Watch Roger and me play. Did you bring a clock, Rog?'

'I did.'

'Twenty minutes each?'

'Why not?'

I let Roger sit down and watch as they set themselves up with a timer clock, then start playing. The stones move quickly, more quickly than I can properly follow. As we approach the twenty-minute mark, Joe suddenly resigns with a smile and a handshake.

Roger suggests best of three and Joe agrees. He wins the second game with spectacular ease well within the allotted time, which leaves Roger shaking his head in disbelief. But Roger wins the decider, to his apparent bemusement. 'Bad day, Joe?' he asks. 'You're really up and down tonight.'

'I probably need a smoke.' Joe gets up. 'I'll be back soon, guys.'

Off he goes, leaving Roger shaking his head.

'What's wrong?' I ask.

'Nothing really. But that second game was . . . pure poetry. Like he . . . forgot himself.'

'What do you mean?'

'Just that.' Roger frowns. 'Forgot to hold himself back.'

I excuse myself and head for the ladies. When I come out, Joe's still not back, so I step outside and find him sitting at one of the picnic tables in front of the pub, puffing at a roll-up cigarette. It's turned cold. The air's damp and misty. But that doesn't seem to bother Joe.

'Hi,' he says guardedly.

'You were unlucky to lose in there,' I respond, unsure quite how subtle or unsubtle to be.

He smiles at me. 'How would you know?'

'Well, I wouldn't, of course, but Roger seemed to think—'

'What do you want, Nicole?'

'Sorry?'

'I bet you never really had a boyfriend who played Go.'

'What makes you say that?'

'Intuition. Go's good for that. You develop a sense of what'll work and what won't. Of what's real and what isn't.'

'What are you saying, Joe?'

'I'm saying the time's come to level with me. What's this all about? You see me on the ferry. You book into Tideways. You turn up here. You don't seriously think I'm going to buy your story, do you? I mean, come on.'

I hesitate. I was thinking of leaving this until tomorrow. Now I haven't got any choice. It has to be now. It has to be here. I sit down next to him. 'I'm with Venstrom Computers, Joe.'

'Who?'

'Venstrom Computers.' I hand him one of my cards. I virtually have to force it between his fingers to make him take it. 'We developed the *gridforest* Go-playing system you've been showing yourself to be a match for these past few months.'

'I don't know anything about *gridforest*.'

'That's not what our game experts say. They say you've worked your way up to the top level and just keep on winning. Which really shouldn't be possible. Man against computer? That was supposed to have been settled in the computer's favour three years ago.'

'An online gaming program can't be compared to something as powerful as AlphaGo.'

'Oh, but it can. We've enhanced *gridforest* just for you, Joe. It's beyond AlphaGo now. Which puts it way beyond the capabilities of any human Go player. Except you.'

'I haven't been playing *gridforest*.'

'Yes, you have. On the Voglers' computer.'

Joe says nothing for a long time. He takes a last drag on his cigarette and stubs it out. Then he looks at me, though I can't see his eyes. They're buried in shadow. 'You followed me from St Mawes,' he says quietly. It isn't a question.

'We just want to know how you do it, Joe. How do you beat the computer?'

'Fuck,' he says under his breath.

'It's a simple question – a genuine question.'

'That kind of tracking of an IP address is illegal, isn't it, Nicole?' he asks.

'It's a grey area.'

'I think that's why I love Go. There are no grey stones. Only black and white.'

'Just tell me how you do it.'

'Maybe you've run into someone who's using a stronger program – testing their computer against yours.'

'Ours is the best.'

'You can't know that.'

'We have people who *can* know that. And that's what they've told me.'

'How long have you worked for Venstrom?'

'Does it matter?'

'They say women have a hard time getting on in the tech industry. Have you found it hard?'

I don't want to think too much about that right now, so I ignore the question. 'We can offer you whatever you want, Joe. You can basically name your price.'

'Maybe I don't have a price.'

'It doesn't have to be money. Silicon Valley is made for someone like you. It'd be a complete change of life. For Zip as well if you like.'

'You've spoken to Zip?'

'I had coffee at Bean Feast this afternoon. We chatted about this and that.'

25

'Her name's Karen. Only her friends call her Zip.'

'I'm sorry about the subterfuge. There didn't seem to be any other way to track you down.'

'Who said I wanted to be tracked down?'

'You must have known it would happen, considering what you've been doing.'

'Go is just—' Joe breaks off. 'Shit.'

I turn and see Zip heading towards us across the square in front of the pub. She's huddled up in a duffel coat and the green strands of her hair have taken on a weird kind of turquoise in the lamplight. She doesn't look as surprised to see me with Joe as I might have expected. I wonder if she recognizes me.

But she does. 'Hello,' she says. 'Again.'

Joe jumps up from the table and intercepts her. 'Let's split,' he says.

'You've never had enough already?' she says incredulously.

'I have tonight. Let's go back to yours.'

'I fancied a drink.'

'I'll buy you one in the Ladder.'

'Maybe we can talk in the morning, Joe,' I say, standing up as well.

'Yeah, maybe.'

With that he grabs Zip's arm and pilots her back across the square. She looks back at me quizzically as she goes. Joe doesn't look back at all.

I watch them cross the road and disappear into a block of shadow next to Lloyds Bank. I wait a couple of minutes, then go after them.

Next to the bank is a steep flight of steps, climbing into the darkness above. Jacob's Ladder, the sign says. I guess there's a pub at the top named after the steps. But I reckon

26

going up to see if they're in it is a mistake. I'll have to let Joe get used to the idea that he's no longer anonymous before I spell out in more detail what we can offer him. He'll come round in the end. I'm sure of it.

My coat's still in the Seven Stars, so I have to go back and fetch it. Jeremy Inkpen is standing outside when I arrive, half-drunk pint of beer in hand.

'Wondered what had become of you,' he says, the lamplight forming pools on the lenses of his glasses as he beams at me. 'Where's Joe?'

'Decided to call it a night.'

'Early for him to do that.'

'His girlfriend came by.'

'She usually does.'

'I think I'll call it a night myself.'

'That's a pity. How long are you in Falmouth?'

'Not sure.'

'I do walking tours of Falmouth for the tourists. All the principal sites. I could do one just for you . . . if you like.' I suddenly realize Jerry's asking me out. God knows what he's hoping might come of it. 'Bespoke, you could say.'

'Well, that's very kind, but I'm not sure I'll have time.'

'The town has a fascinating history. Were you over by Jacob's Ladder?'

'Er, yes.'

'Built by Jacob Hamblen in 1791 so he could go to and fro between his house up top and his business down here on The Moor. One hundred and eleven steps in all.'

'Really?'

'There's lots more to show you besides that.'

'Yes, well, as I say . . .'

'I run a photography business in Arwenack Street.

Why don't you look in when you're passing?' I think he's decided to settle for that and I'm happy to as well.

'I'll make a point of it.'

He smiles at me with an expression of earnest goodwill. I feel a slight pang of regret. He knows what I'm really saying, poor guy. Then he adds, almost desperately, as if hoping it might interest me, 'Joe's dad was a nasty piece of work. Joe and his mother are well off without him.'

'Is that right? You knew him, did you?'

'I did. But . . . I shouldn't really speak ill of the dead.'

'You just have.'

'Yes. Sorry. Forgot myself. Are you sure you won't stay for some more Go? Or maybe just a drink?'

'No.' I give him what I hope works as a letting-down-gently smile. 'I won't, thanks.'

The night's still and quiet. I walk up the hill towards Tideways with lights twinkling at me from the opposite shore across an invisible gulf of water. I catch a drift of cigar smoke in the air as I turn in through the gate. There's a man standing near the porch, barely visible in the shadows. I might have missed him altogether but for the smoke and the glow of his cigar-end.

'Hello,' I say cautiously.

'Evening,' he responds. I can't really see his face or what he's wearing and it's hard to put an age on him. Sixty, maybe. His voice is gravelly but rich-toned. 'You must be the new arrival.'

'You're a guest here yourself?'

'Of long standing. I live on the top floor. Grand night, isn't it?'

'A bit cold for standing around.'

'You think so? I like cold nights. They clear the mind.'

'I expect the cigar helps.'

'It does. Liz – Mrs Roberts – won't allow smoking on the premises. So, I'm banished out here. But I like it.'

'Well, enjoy the rest of your cigar.'

'Thanks.'

I move past him and go into the house. I feel suddenly tired. This kind of work isn't covered by my job description. But if it goes well I should get a whole new job description – and a salary to match – in the not too distant future. Joe was right. Women do have a hard time of it in the tech industry, as I can personally testify. But this is my big chance to change that. I'm not going to let it slip.

I go up to my room and phone Carl. He answers straight away. I imagine him in his Thames-side apartment, gazing out at the city as he speaks. I can hear slow, ballad-like music in the background. It should be calming. But he doesn't sound calm.

'Tell me you've got our guy on side, Nicole.'

'Nearly. He just needs time to think about it.'

'Well, don't give him too much time. Make it clear what's on the table.'

'I think he already knows.'

'Then what's the problem? If I could do what he does I'd be writing my own cheque in a hurry.' So he would. But then Carl has always been hasty.

'It's possible he's running a rival program on us.'

'Bullshit. There's no rival to *gridforest*.'

'What if there is?'

'Then we'll buy it out would be my guess. Billy's fully committed to this.' The backing of our remote but somehow omnipresent boss, Billy Swarther, the king of computer gaming, is vital to everything we do. But it's a two-edged sword. If he backs you, you'd better make sure you succeed.

Carl and I both know that. 'A signed-up hyper-genius would be a big coup for you and me both, Nicole. So, is that what we're looking at here? What's your instinct?'

'I think he's the real thing, Carl.'

'Then reel him in. Any way you can.'

It must sound easy to Carl. And maybe it will be. Tomorrow will tell.

Tuesday October 8

I SLEPT BETTER THAN I HAVE IN A LONG TIME, WHICH SEEMS ridiculous really, with so much riding on what today holds. I hope Joe turns out to be more materialistic than he seemed last night. Alternatively, I hope Zip – or Karen – can talk him round. She did say she wanted out of Falmouth, after all, and Silicon Valley's definitely that.

I clear a few emails, then go down to breakfast. I wonder if I'll run into Cigar Man from last night, but there's no sign of him in the dining room. A woman's there to take my order. She's homely and friendly and recommends the sausages on the grounds they come from her cousin's farm. There's one other guest, eating muesli and reading the *Guardian*. She's wearing a grey trouser-suit and looks quite serious, with short blonde-tinted grey hair and a severe, sharp-nosed face. She's older than me, but in good shape.

We're sitting at adjacent tables and soon start chatting. Ursula, as she's called, turns out to be less serious and more loquacious than she appears. She's been staying here for more than a week now, working on what she refers to as 'VAT issues' at the Docks. I assume she's with HMRC. I'm more or less obliged to introduce myself and explain that I'm trying to interest a local corporate client in a groundbreaking new Venstrom system. As cover stories go, it sounds plausible as I trot it out.

'I met another guest last night,' I say after Hazel – as Ursula addresses her – delivers my scrambled eggs and one sausage. 'He was smoking a cigar out front when I came in.'

'Ah,' says Ursula. 'That'll be Mr Forrester. He lives on the top floor. I believe he caters for himself up there. A driving instructor. You'll see his car around town. And parked round the back. Forrester School of Motoring. Except there is no school. He's a one-man band.'

'You've picked up a lot in just over a week.'

'Well, Falmouth's a smaller town than I'm used to. And I'm stuck here on my own while this assignment lasts.' She smiles. 'Can't help noticing things.'

'I met Mrs Roberts' son when I arrived. Joe. Seems very bright.'

'He does, doesn't he? Could really go places if he wanted to.' She holds her smile a second longer than strictly necessary. I wonder if she actually knows how apt the remark is. Then I dismiss the idea as absurd. She's just making conversation.

My phone beeps at that moment. I check who the message is from. I don't recognize the number. But I open it anyway.

Can we meet in half hour? We need to talk. Don't want to come to Tideways. Can do Prince of Wales Pier. Urgent. Karen Kliskey.

Karen Kliskey. The girlfriend. She wants to talk. I think for all of about half a second before texting back. See you there.

Ursula's still smiling at me. 'You're never alone with a phone, are you?'

*

The weather's brighter than yesterday, with gleams of sunlight that glisten on the grey-slated rooftops of the town and the wave-crests out to sea. It's colder too, with a keen edge to the breeze.

Prince of Wales Pier is where the St Mawes ferry runs from. It's handy for Bean Feast, of course. Maybe I'm catching Karen just before she starts work. She's waiting for me at the end of the pier, leaning against a bollard and tapping at her phone, which she puts away smartly when she sees me coming. Her skin's pale, almost transparent, in the sharp light.

'Are you for real, Nicole?' she asks straight away, holding up my card. 'Venstrom Computers. Silicon Valley. There's a picture of your head office on your website. Looks a bit like an egg-carton.'

'Yes, I'm for real, Karen. And I have the authority to make Joe a very generous offer if he'll agree to what I've proposed.'

'I thought Go was just a game.'

'Well, it is, of course. But there are games . . . and games.'

'Joe's told me what he's been doing. Beating the computer and all that. Is it really such a big deal?'

'It's an enormous deal. He shouldn't be able to do that. The Go world champion certainly can't.'

She frowns. 'No?'

'No.'

She chews her lower lip for a moment, then says, 'Would he have to go to California?'

'Not necessarily. California would come to him if he insists on it. But doesn't he want to go? Don't you?'

'I'd be part of this?'

'If you're part of Joe's life, then why wouldn't you be?'

'He's nervous.'

'What of?'

'The change, I s'pose.'

'But it would be exciting. For both of you. There's a big world out there, Karen.'

She sighs. 'Joe's always been . . . different. I know that. I mean, different in a loveable way. But . . . there's part of him that's way beyond me. The part that can beat computers at Go for a start.'

'But he needs you to keep him grounded.'

'Does he?'

I nod. 'I suspect so, yes.'

'How does he do it, Nicole?'

'That's what we want to find out.'

'I'm not sure he'll be able to tell you.'

'He may not have to. Our researchers can figure it out when they see him in action.'

'No one at that Go club ever said he was . . . a genius.'

'I get the feeling he hasn't let them see just how good he is.'

'Yeah.' She looks thoughtful. 'That's Joe all over.'

'Where is he now?'

'Where he always goes when he needs to think.'

'And where's that?'

'Look, he just told me to tell you he'll contact you when he's decided what he wants to do. You won't get anything out of him if you badger him. I can tell you that from experience.'

'How long d'you think he needs to think?'

She shrugs. 'How long is a piece of string? You'll just have to wait.'

'Do you know why he only plays on the Voglers' computer, Karen?'

'Not really.' For the first time, I get the feeling Karen

may not be telling me the truth. She probably does know why. I can probably take a guess myself. Joe has never wanted his talents to be recognized for some reason. But they have been. They were always going to be in the end. I guess that's what he's struggling to come to terms with.

'You shouldn't let him walk away from this, Karen. It's a golden opportunity.'

'Joe's not a money-oriented person. You need to understand that.'

'What about you?'

Her gaze tightens slightly. 'More than Joe, for sure.'

'There you are then.'

'You might have to buy him out of his contract with Conrad Vogler.'

'His *contract*? What exactly does he do for the guy?'

'Financial analysis.'

'What kind of financial analysis?'

Another shrug. 'Haven't a clue. Way over my head.'

I smile at her. 'I somehow doubt that.'

'All I'm saying is you might have to make a deal with Vogler if you want to . . . make a deal with Joe.'

I nod. 'Understood. Don't worry. I'll sort everything out. If money's the problem, my company has the solution.'

'That sounds nice.'

'It will be for you and Joe, Karen. Believe me.'

I think Karen does believe me. And I believe her that the best way to bring Joe round to seeing things my way is to give him the time he needs to think everything through. Carl won't be so patient, of course, but he may have no choice in the matter. Knowing when not to force the pace is a talent I'm pretty sure I have more of than him. He's just going to have to let me decide how to play this. If

I play it right, it'll turn out to be a golden opportunity for me as well as Joe and Karen.

I walk down the main shopping street and stop for coffee. Unusually, I have time on my hands. I'm even up to date with my emails. And Kyra confirms Joe isn't playing this morning. No surprise there. Joe isn't playing because Joe's thinking.

I leave the café and walk on. Shortly after the street takes a kink round King Charles Church I spot a photography shop ahead of me. Falmouth Photographic. It's got an old-fashioned look about it. I'm not sure Jeremy Inkpen has been keeping up with the digital world. One window's full of framed photographs of sailing craft around Falmouth: barges, yachts, coasters. They're not actually sepia-tinted, but they might as well be. The other window's given over to happy couple and baby pictures.

I'm planning to walk straight on, but I haven't allowed for how slack business is. Jeremy's out of the door, grinning at me, before I've made it past. He's holding an old camera in his hand and is fiddling with the winding lever. It looks like I've caught him in mid-repair.

'Nicole,' he says, his grin broadening. 'Good morning.'

'Morning,' I say as brightly as I can manage.

'Are you coming in?'

'Well, I . . .'

'Please do. It's fairly quiet at the moment. I can show you round.'

I'm soon inside. The shop's not very big, so being 'shown round' doesn't threaten to be too arduous. Jeremy witters about inheriting the business from his father. He shows me pictures on the wall of a couple of dead ringers for himself who turn out to be his father and grandfather. Then there are the antique cameras to be admired, the miniature studio and the digital equipment which he insists keeps him bang up to date. There's still a darkroom, though, and a general air of anachronism.

'Changed your mind about the town tour?' he asks hopefully.

'I really don't think I'll have time, Jerry.'

'That's a pity.'

'In fact—'

'I'm glad to have seen you this morning, Nicole. I wanted to ask you to forget what I said last night about Joe's father. Er, well, whatever it was I did say, that is. I can't exactly recall. I might have had a little too much to drink. Or maybe I was intoxicated for some other reason.'

I'm not quite sure what to say to that. What I eventually come up with is, 'I can't remember you mentioning him.'

He smiles and nods his head in appreciation. 'Charlie Roberts wasn't such a bad fellow, at least when he was sober. He just lacked business sense. And luck, I suppose. We all need that.'

'We certainly do.'

'Actually, I have a picture of him here somewhere.' He casts his gaze around the innumerable framed portraits and period views the walls of the shop are adorned with. 'There it is.' He points.

I step closer and peer at the photograph. It shows two men standing by the foundations of some waterside building in suits and hard hats. A banner behind them bears the words *Carrick Haven Phase One*.

'That's Charlie.' Jeremy extends a finger past my nose. It lands on the older and tubbier of the two men. Charlie Roberts is fortyish, paunchy, round-faced and mustachioed, grinning broadly with the air of a schoolboy who's just got away with something. He doesn't look much like Joe.

His companion is a slighter, slimmer man with a graver expression, even though he's also smiling. There's something cautious about the smile, though, something provisional. There's nothing larky about him, as there is about Charlie. His eyes as they meet the camera's gaze have a hardness to them.

'What was Carrick Haven?' I ask casually.

'A development of waterside apartments up near the yacht marina. Wrong place, wrong time, unfortunately. Charlie sank his money into it just as the property market crashed in the late eighties. More or less wiped him out. I mean, he went on, with various schemes, but they never came to anything. No one was surprised to hear he was up to his neck in debt when he died.'

'And when was that?'

'October 1994. Drove his car into Stithians Reservoir and drowned. Suicide was rumoured, but he'd been drinking and it was a misty night. It's not actually difficult to get into trouble on that road. Although as to why he was *on* that road . . .'

'How old was Joe then?'

'Oh, he'd have been just a babe in arms. Far too young for him to have any memories of his father. Although he can always ask Charlie's ex-partner about him if he wants to, of course, since I gather he does work for the man in some capacity.'

Suddenly I'm hanging on Jeremy's every word. 'Joe works for Charlie's ex-partner?'

'So I'm told.'

'Are we talking about the other guy in this photograph?'

'Yes. Conrad Vogler. That's him. He owns a big house

over in St Mawes. He's done very well for himself. In fact, everything started to go right for him around the time Charlie died. Ironic, really, considering what Charlie did for him.'

'And what was that?'

'Well, he gave him a start in this country. Conrad fled Rhodesia, as it then was, to avoid military service in the late seventies. Charlie took him on. It's funny how life turns out. Charlie's star sank. Conrad's rose. And went on rising.'

'Is Vogler still in the building business?'

'I couldn't really tell you *what* business he's in. But living in one of the priciest houses in St Mawes suggests it's certainly profitable. Nothing's cheap over there. I've asked Joe, out of curiosity, but all he says is that Vogler's . . . "an investor". In what, you may well ask.'

'Did Charlie Roberts play Go?'

Jeremy smiles thinly. 'Hardly. Charlie was too busy playing fast and loose to indulge in board games. Joe doesn't take after him in any way at all. In fact—' He breaks off suddenly.

'What?'

'Nothing.' He shakes his head energetically. 'Nothing at all.'

Then, somewhat to Jeremy's surprise, it appears, a customer comes in and the prospect of making a sale distracts Jeremy, allowing me to slip away.

I explore the town a bit more. It's funny to have leisure imposed on me by circumstances. I'm not really used to having time to kill and, to be honest, I don't really like it. I enjoy the buzz of being busy all the time. Maybe I *need* the buzz. Standing out on the breezy headland at Pendennis Point, I realize just how much I've been using work to distract me from the mess that led me to return to London in the first place.

As I'm walking back into the centre past the Docks, my phone rings. Carl's my first thought. But no. It's an unrecognized number. I take the call.

'Hi, Nicole,' says Joe in his soft, careful voice.

'Karen told me you needed time to think.'

'Yeah. Well, I've thought.'

'And?'

'I'll be out of town this afternoon. But you've got a car, haven't you?'

'Yes.'

'Then you can pick me up on the King Harry ferry. Five twenty sailing from the Trelissick side.'

'OK. But—'

'You'll be there?'

'Yes. Of course. I'll—'

He's gone.

Five hours later, I'm in the queue of cars on the hairpin lane down to the King Harry car ferry. It's a cool grey late afternoon. The woods on the opposite shore running down to the water's edge look like the jungle along a South American river. But this is the Fal and we're in Cornwall. It's also the rush hour, or what passes for it round here. There are cars and vans stacked up behind me as far as I can see.

And suddenly there's Joe. I catch sight of him on the ferry as it reaches the slipway and lowers its ramp. He's standing on the narrow viewing deck next to the pilot's cabin. He leans against the railings and watches as the vehicles start rumbling off the boat.

After the last of them has driven past me and headed

off uphill, boarding begins. As I drive on, I see Joe descending the steps to the car deck. He's carrying his shoulder-bag with him. He nods to me as he walks round to where I've pulled up behind a Transit van, and climbs in beside me.

'I wish you'd stayed away,' is the first thing he says.

'You must've known we wouldn't watch you beating the computer and just let it go.'

'Why not? It's supposed to be a game.'

'We monitor everything, Joe. In the interests of all our millions of customers.' I wince as I give him that particular piece of corporate bullshit and he lets me see he knows I don't believe it. 'Your record . . . was too good to ignore.'

'I don't always win.'

'But sometimes you do. That's the point. At the level you've taken it to, so I'm told, you really shouldn't be able to win even once.'

'What exactly are Venstrom offering me?'

'Whatever you ask for, basically, in return for exclusive cooperation. The plan would be to incorporate your technique in the *gridforest* program and produce a new generation of machines. The possibilities are limitless. For you as well as us.'

The ferry is full now. The gates close and we move slowly away from the shore.

'Where are we going, Joe?'

'Let's not get into that yet. Mind if I smoke?'

I'm about to object, but I can't afford to piss him off. 'No. You can—'

'Do whatever I like so long as I sign up for whatever Venstrom want out of me?' He smiles grimly as he looks at me. 'Does that sound as shitty to you as it does to me, Nicole?'

'We just want to know how you do it, Joe.'

'Remember what I told you about ko?'

'Ko? Er, yes. That is . . .' He and Roger both mentioned the ko rule during my tutorial in the Seven Stars, but I wasn't really concentrating. I certainly can't recall now what it's about. I sigh. 'Not exactly.'

The ticket man appears at the window. As I open it, Joe hands me a plastic card. 'Use this. It works on here as well as the St Mawes ferry.'

'There's no need. Honestly.'

He smirks. 'It's my treat.'

'OK.' I give the card to the ticket man. He swipes it and I pass it back to Joe.

'You're going to make me rich, aren't you, Nicole?'

'Venstrom will. If that's what you want to be.'

'So, I can afford to be generous. Now, back to ko.'

He takes out his foldable miniature Go board, opens it up on his lap and starts to arrange several stones on the grid. I look down at them.

'Black has just played there' – he points to the black stone in the middle of the group – 'capturing the white stone that was there' – now he points to the empty

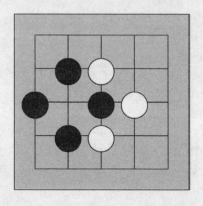

intersection next to it – 'but white can immediately capture the black stone by reoccupying the space. Yes?'

It certainly appears to be true. I nod. 'Yes.'

'No. Because of the second of the two rules of Go. Which is?'

I look at him helplessly. 'I've forgotten.'

'I doubt it. I doubt you ever knew it in the first place. And you can't forget what you never knew, can you?'

He has me there. 'No, Joe. You can't.'

'The second rule of Go states that stones on the board can never repeat a previous position. So, white can't reoccupy the space because that would take us back to where we were before.' He moves the stones, illustrating the point. 'And that would lead to an endless repetition of captures and recaptures. So, white must play elsewhere. You see?'

'Yes. I do.'

'But do you see the beauty of it? Go mirrors life. You can't stand still. Every move you make changes everything else, however fractionally. Ko is derived from a Buddhist word meaning eternity. And we don't get to experience eternity in this life.'

'No. We don't.'

'D'you see what I'm saying?'

As he looks at me with his big, brown, contemplative eyes, I suddenly think I do see what he's saying. 'You can't go back to how it was before I saw you leaving Admiral's Reach yesterday even if you want to.'

He nods. 'No. I fucking can't.' He sounds angry but reconciled all at the same time. He drops the stones back in their bag and puts away the board. We're approaching the Roseland shore now. Car engines are being started around us. A deck-hand is readying himself by the gate.

'Are you going to tell me where we're going now, Joe?'

'Follow the St Mawes road. And listen. I'm going to tell you what my terms are.'

'OK.'

The metal ramp scrapes up the slipway as the ferry comes to a rest. The deck-hand opens the gate and waves us off.

Joe doesn't speak until we're driving up the hill past the queue of vehicles waiting to board. Then he says, 'I want anonymity. A change of name. So no one except you and a select few at Venstrom know who I really am or where I come from.'

Carl's been operating on a strictly need to know basis so far. I suspect he'll be happy to indulge Joe on this one. It may even suit him. 'I'm sure we can do that, Joe, but—'

'Don't ask me why.' He sounds very serious about that.

'OK. I won't ask.'

'Second condition. There needs to be generous compensation for Conrad.'

'Conrad Vogler?'

'Yes. He'll be losing my services.'

'And what exactly are those services?'

'He pays me to study financial data on companies worldwide and calculate which ones he should invest in.'

'And your analysis has worked out profitably for him?'

'I guess so. He hasn't complained. It's not analysis, though. It's synthesis. A different approach.'

'What does that mean?'

'It means seeing in a whole bunch of data the potential for a company to transform itself a year or two down the road. It means seeing the big picture.'

'Is that how you've become so good at Go? Seeing the big picture?'

'I see things other people don't, Nicole. They're things

that are obvious to me. It's taken me a long time to understand they're not obvious to anyone else. A computer's
basic characteristic is efficiency. It calculates how to win
a particular game and follows that method. It basically
ignores its opponent. But there's never only one way to
win. Not if you can see far enough ahead.'

'And you're better at that than a computer?'

'Sometimes, yes.'

'Sometimes is good enough for us. Any more
conditions?'

'We're on our way to see Conrad now. I told him we
needed to talk through something important. I didn't tell
him what it was. Or that I was bringing you. He'll be surprised. And he won't be happy. He'll be even unhappier if
you tell him I've been using his computer to play Go and
that's what's brought me to Venstrom's attention. So,
third condition. Nothing about tracing me via him. You
got it?'

'Sure.'

'It won't play well for me *or* you if he gets the idea you've
been tracking activity on his system.'

'Secretive character, is he?'

'He likes his privacy. And he has clients who like their
privacy too. I don't know the details of his business. I
don't want to know. Neither should you.'

'Why not? Is it . . . illegal?'

Joe looks exasperated with me. 'Just don't go there,
Nicole, OK?'

'OK.' I glance towards the estuary that stretches, gleaming silver, towards Falmouth and the horizon, beyond the
fields we're speeding past. 'I'm sure we can satisfy Mr
Vogler.'

'He'll hold out for a good deal.'

'And he'll get one. We want to make this transition as smooth as possible for you, Joe. There's really nothing to worry about.'

Joe says nothing to that. But it doesn't sound to me like the silence of conviction.

To be honest, I'm not convinced either.

A quiet evening is settling over St Mawes as I pull down into the driveway of Admiral's Reach. The giant four-wheeler I assume belongs to Vogler is parked in front of the garage. I park beside it.

'Let me do the talking to start with,' Joe says as we get out of the car.

I don't argue. We go to the door and Joe rings the bell.

It's opened by a busty, blonde-haired middle-aged woman with the leathery skin of a sun-worshipper. She's wearing clothes that are too young for her: low-cut T-shirt, tight jeans slashed at the knees. 'Hi, Joe,' she says, flashing him a gleaming smile. Then she looks at me. 'Who's your friend?'

'Nicole Nevinson,' says Joe. 'Nicole, this is Marianne Vogler.'

'Nevinson?' Marianne frowns at me. 'Didn't you leave your card earlier?'

'Yes. I did.'

Joe shoots a glance at me. I haven't mentioned my encounter with the cleaner. 'I told Conrad I'd be round,' he continues. 'I've brought Nicole to explain what we've got in mind.'

Marianne's frown doesn't go away. 'Well, Con's expecting you all right. But Nicole here will be a surprise. And you know he doesn't like surprises.'

Joe shrugs. 'Not much I can do about that.'

'Well, come on in. Con's in the lounge. D'you want a drink?'

'Don't mind a beer.'

'Great. Nicole? Glass of wine?'

I don't really want one, but I reckon it might smooth my path if I accept. 'Thanks. White, please.'

'Chardonnay? Sauvignon?'

'Er, Sauvignon, please.'

'Coming up. Go on through.'

Marianne peels off towards a vast white marble kitchen while Joe leads me through a big dining room with a glass-topped table to an even bigger lounge, which gives on to a decked balcony over the lower part of the house. The doors are open and Vogler's prowling around outside, barking into a phone. The sea behind him is a blue-grey mass stretching to the horizon.

He's put on a lot of weight since he posed with Charlie Roberts at Carrick Haven thirty-odd years ago. He's round-bellied and bull-shouldered, casually dressed in cashmere sweater, striped shirt and roomy trousers. His face is sort of swollen. He's ruddy-complexioned, with grey-black hair and a close-cropped beard.

Joe raises one hand in cautious greeting as Vogler turns towards us in his phone-prowl. He looks at Joe, then at me. Is he smiling or scowling? It's hard to tell. He makes a give-me-a-minute signal and turns away again.

He's still on the balcony when Marianne comes in with the drinks. We sit down and she leaves us to wait. Joe looks about as awkward as I feel, shrugging at me between pulls on the bottle.

Then Vogler comes into the room, which instantly

seems to shrink around him. Joe springs up. I stand. We're introduced.

'Venstrom Computers,' says Vogler with a glance at Joe. His voice is low-pitched, with just a hint of his southern African origins. 'Was it you who emailed me recently, Nicole?'

'Er, yes.'

'They contacted me a while back,' says Joe.

'About what?' Vogler couldn't look more suspicious if he tried.

'A sort of job offer.'

'And you mentioned working for me?'

'Well, I might've mentioned . . . Conmari Ltd.'

'We did a bit of digging without telling Joe,' I chip in, trying to deflect any blame from Joe.

'What were you digging for?'

'Well, we . . .' It seems pretty obvious leaving the talking to Joe isn't going to get us anywhere. 'We want to offer Joe a job. It's a great opportunity for him. But it would involve leaving Falmouth . . . and leaving your employment.'

'Leaving my employment?' He says that as if it's not so much unexpected as inconceivable.

'Would you like me to explain more fully?'

'Yeah.' Vogler pulls the balcony doors shut and turns round to face me. 'Why don't you do that?'

'Mind if I sit down?'

'No. Let's all sit down, why don't we?'

We do that, gathering in an uneasy circle in the polar vastness of faintly squeaky white leather. Vogler grabs a tumbler of whisky from some side-table where he left it and takes a swig or two while I hear myself deliver a jargon-laden account of the exciting future in computer gaming program development we have in mind for Joe, who stares into space while I speak. Meanwhile Vogler squirms and grimaces, losing the battle to stay silent when I finally mention Go.

'Go?' He looks at each of us in turn with a mixture of bafflement and disgruntlement. 'You're talking about a fucking board game?'

'Indeed,' I say emolliently. 'But Joe's particular expertise makes him an ideal recruit for our research department.'

'Because he's good at Go?'

'He's more than good, Mr Vogler.'

Vogler glares at Joe. 'What have you been playing at?' I don't think he intends the pun.

Joe looks abashed. 'I just, er, do a little online Go . . . from time to time.'

'*What?*'

Joe shrugs. 'It doesn't do any harm.'

Vogler gapes. It's obvious he thinks it's done a lot of harm. 'For fuck's sake . . .'

'Mr Vogler,' I say, still trying to sound ultra-reasonable. 'I've no idea what exactly Joe does for you. He's been very discreet about it. But you can't really mean to stand in his way, can you? I realize it may be inconvenient, but—'

'We had a deal, Joe.' Vogler isn't listening to me any more.

Joe gives another helpless shrug. 'This sounds like a better deal.'

Vogler stares darkly at him. He goes on staring as I say, 'I'm authorized to offer a very generous package to compensate you for the loss of Joe's services, Mr Vogler.'

Vogler's head swivels towards me. 'Pretty fucking difficult when you don't know the value of those services, I'd say.'

'You tell me. You put a figure on what you'd expect.'

At last, Vogler pauses for thought. Joe chips in with, 'Venstrom's resources are pretty close to infinite, Con.'

Vogler goes on thinking. Eventually, he says, 'You're set on this, are you, Joe?'

Joe nods. 'I'd like to see what there is for me in the tech industry, yeah.'

'A fucking fortune, I should imagine.' Vogler sounds almost philosophical now. He turns to me. 'You're seriously inviting me to name my price, Ms Nevinson?'

'As a starting point, yes.'

He relaxes back in his chair. 'All right. I get the picture. Joe's outgrown me. I need to let him move on. And I need to let you cut me a fat cheque.'

'You could put it like that, yes.'

'Tell you what. I think you and I need to discuss this in private, Nicole.' First it was Nicole. Then it was Ms Nevinson. Now, a few seconds later, it's Nicole again. It's hard to know where you are with this guy. 'Let's go into the study. You OK for half an hour or so, Joe?'

'Sure. I can . . . run through a few things on the computer.'

'For a little longer, anyway, hey?' Vogler smiles ruefully. 'OK. You get busy with that while Nicole and I talk turkey.'

'Cool.' Joe stands up and heads out of the room, bound for wherever the computer he uses is located.

Once he's gone, Vogler smiles affably at me. 'This way,' he says. We stand up and head off to the study, which is out of the lounge and down a short passage.

It's smaller than the lounge, but still large for a study. Nor does it look as if Vogler actually does much studying in it. There's no computer, no papers, no files, no nothing really apart from a big, gleamingly lacquered desk, a buttoned-leather swivel-chair behind it, another, smaller chair, a strikingly orderly bookcase and some framed nautical charts on the walls.

Vogler closes the door behind us as we enter and heads for the big chair behind the desk. He passes one of the windows, which looks on to the drive, glancing out as he does so. He pulls up.

'That your car out front, Nicole?' he asks.

'Yes.'

'Looks like you've got a problem with one of your tyres.'

'Really?'

'Yeah. Take a look.' He points through the window and I step past him to see what he's talking about.

Suddenly, he grabs me. I'm shoved up against the wall next to the window with my left arm bent up painfully behind me. But I can't cry out because his other hand is over my mouth, clamping it shut. The pain in my shoulder increases as he levers my wrist further and further beyond the vertical. I feel his breath on my neck and smell the whisky he's been drinking. The weight of his body is pressing me into the wall, making it difficult for me to breathe. He's far too strong for me. He knows it, I know it. I'm frightened. More frightened than I've been in a very long time.

'Listen to me, Ms Nevinson,' he hisses in my ear. 'If you want to leave here with your shoulder still in its socket, you'll nod in agreement when I tell you how this is going to go down. Joe isn't leaving my employment. Venstrom aren't taking him on. You're going to go back to London and explain to your bosses that it was all one big fucking misunderstanding. Joe's not the real thing. He's no use to them. Sell it any way you fucking like. But sell it. Otherwise Joe will suffer and his mother will suffer and, when I track you down, you'll suffer too. Along with *your* mother. And any siblings you turn out to have. Don't make the mistake of thinking I don't mean any of this. I mean every fucking word. And I have the means to do it. You got me?'

I nod helplessly. There's nothing else I can do.

'So, I'm going to take my hand away from your mouth and you're not going to cry out. You're not going to say a single fucking thing. Is that clear?'

I nod. All I want is to be out of his grip and out of his house.

He withdraws his hand. I say nothing. My heart's pounding. My breathing is fast and shallow. If I did speak, I'm not sure it would sound like me.

'We're going to tell Joe we have the basis for an agreement and then you're going to tell him tomorrow it's all off following consultation with Head Office. Are we clear?'

I nod again.

Then his free hand closes around my bottom. He squeezes. 'Good girl,' he says sneeringly.

You bastard, I think. But I don't say anything. I don't say anything at all.

'Shall we go and wait for Joe in the lounge, Nicole? I'll ask Marianne to join us and we can chat about property values in St Mawes and Silicon Valley architecture. You can finish your wine. Maybe have another glass. We'll all play nicey-nicey for now. Best all round, I reckon. You with me on that?'

I swallow hard and turn slowly round to face him. His face is hard, like baked clay. His eyes are cold, like iced water.

'You can speak now,' he says quietly. 'You can say you agree to our deal. You know that's the only way this can go that equates to a result for you. The alternative? You don't want to go there. You seriously don't.' He stares at me for a silent moment. Then he says, 'Well?'

'I agree,' I say hoarsely.

He nods. Then he smiles. 'Thought you would. Shall we go?'

The next half hour or so is a blur. Marianne did join us. There was a conversation of sorts. Vogler told her he'd explain what we'd agreed after Joe and I left. Joe came back into the room. Vogler smiled a lot and assured Joe there'd be no problem. I went to the loo at some point and stared at myself in the mirror, wondering how Joe and Marianne could fail to notice how different I was from the confident, lucid woman who'd first walked into the house. But fail to notice they did. Maybe I was putting on a better act than I knew. Maybe they just weren't paying attention. I don't know.

As we drive away from the house, my grip on the steering-wheel disguises the tremor in my hands. Joe's relaxed and contented, talking about how much better the encounter with Vogler went than he expected.

'He was really mature about it, don't you think?' he asks.

'He, ah, drove a hard bargain,' I reply, which I realize as I say it is actually me giving myself room to back out of the situation.

But that's not apparent to Joe. How can it be? 'I'd expect him to,' he says. 'He's that kind of guy.'

'I'll, er, have to run the figures past my boss tomorrow morning.'

'What did he ask for?' Joe's grinning. He's actually enjoying himself. Vogler doing a deal. Joe using that as the starting point for a deal of his own. It's become a game to him. A cheap rush compared with Go. But a rush even so. He has no idea, of course, unlike me, what kind of a man his employer really is. We're both way out of our depth. But I know it and he doesn't.

'I can't get into that, Joe.'

'No? That's kind of disappointing.'

'Sorry. But . . .'

'Are you OK, Nicole?' At last, he has noticed something. 'You look . . . stressed.'

'It's been a long day.'

'Has it?'

'Feels like it, anyway.'

'Once you get the OK for your deal with Con, I'll put Mum in the picture.'

'How will she . . . react?'

'She won't want me to leave Falmouth. But she's always going on about me needing to better myself, so I guess she'll be pleased once she's thought it through.'

'Good.' I take the next bend too fast, fail to hold my line and have to pull in sharply to avoid a car coming in the opposite direction. There's a moment when I actually think we're going to clip wings. But we don't. The other driver blares his horn.

'Are you sure you're OK, Nicole?' asks Joe. 'That was close.'

'Sorry.' I blink and try to force myself to hold everything together. 'I'm tired, that's all. Just . . . tired.'

Somehow, we make it back to Falmouth. I drop Joe on the main road skirting the edge of town. He says he'll walk from there to Karen's flat. I drive down to the back of Tideways and park awkwardly, way out from the kerb, behind Mr Forrester's School of Motoring car. I don't go straight into the house, though. I cross over to the Green-bank Hotel on the water's edge and drink several G&Ts at the bar. The alcohol hits my system. The stress ebbs. My hand steadies. My pulse stops racing. Anger starts to surface. Who the fucking hell does Vogler think he is? But that takes me nowhere. What am I actually going to do about him? Why's he so desperate to retain Joe's services? What sort of business is he in? How do I get out of this mess? And what do I say – to Joe, to Carl, to Billy in the end? They're the key questions.

And tomorrow I'm going to have to find some answers.

I head straight up to my room at Tideways. I don't see the note that's been slipped under the door until I come back out of the bathroom. I sit down on the bed and unfold it.

Ms Nevinson: Roger Lam came by earlier hoping to speak to you. Asked if you could ring him on 07285588766. Liz

Roger? What does Roger want? A date? I'm certainly in demand. Just a pity I don't really want to be.

In the end, though, a friendly voice may be just what I need to hear. I call him.

And he's just as friendly – just as normal – as I hoped. 'Oh, hi, Nicole. Glad you called. Look, I don't know what your schedule's like, but I have a free day tomorrow and . . . well, the thing is my work at the university means I have the use of a boat when no one else on the marine biology team needs it, which tomorrow they don't. The weather forecast's good, so I was planning to take a little pleasure cruise up the estuary. It won't be much fun on my own. Would you like to join me?'

'I'm not sure—'

'Carrick Roads is a fascinating ecosystem. And there's

a decent pub halfway up where we can have lunch. You'd enjoy it, I promise.'

The way I feel at the moment he has to be right. I wasn't expecting him to get in touch, though. It sounds like I might have made more of an impression on him than I thought. Which wouldn't necessarily be such a bad thing. But I've really no idea what tomorrow holds. I have to say no.

But I don't. 'It sounds great, Roger. It's just . . . I may not be able to make it.'

'That'd be a shame.'

'Maybe . . . I could phone you in the morning.'

'OK. Or just show up at Pendennis Marina at ten. We've got a berth close to the Maritime Museum.'

'Well . . .'

'Say you'll try, anyway.'

'OK. I'll try.'

'Great. Hope to see you tomorrow. And wrap up well. Fine or not, it can be chilly out on the water.'

He rings off. A day out, away from all this, is more appealing than Roger can possibly imagine. Maybe I will go. Maybe I just will.

I stare at my phone, knowing I should call Carl now and brief him on the problem we've run into. But I can't bring myself to. I feel tired, drained by how badly wrong the visit to Vogler went.

I lie back on the bed and stare at the rose moulding above the lamp in the middle of the ceiling.

A couple of hours later, I jolt awake and realize I'm still lying there, fully dressed. The gin's worn off and I feel miserable. I pull off my clothes, turn off the light and climb into bed.

Wednesday October 9

I WAKE EARLY. ROGER'S RIGHT ABOUT THE WEATHER. THE DAWN'S pearly grey and pink, with mist lifting from the estuary. I lower the window and breathe in pure, clean air.

I decide to phone Carl straight away. I catch him jogging on the Embankment, which doesn't put him in the best of moods. And his mood only gets worse when I tell him we've struck a major snag with Conrad Vogler. I don't want to admit Vogler threatened me. Carl might think I'm exaggerating, covering up for not being able to talk him round. But he has to know there's a problem.

'What d'you mean he doesn't care about the money?' I sense Carl is having a lot of trouble not shouting. And the only reason he's holding back is he doesn't want to be overheard by other joggers.

'Joe's been advising him on stocks and shares. He doesn't think he can afford to lose his expertise.'

'For Christ's sake, Nicole, Joe's a free agent. We don't actually owe Mr Vogler a single fucking penny if his employee prefers to become our employee. Did you tell him that?'

'It wouldn't have helped, Carl, believe me.'

'But you made it clear we were willing to be generous – generous to a fault?'

'Yes. I made it clear.'

'Then what's wrong with him?'

'I don't know. He's just not willing to play ball.'

'I thought you could handle this, Nicole, I truly did.' The reproach was never going to be long in coming. Carl always needs to blame someone for failures – including his own.

'He's not a man you can negotiate with, Carl. You haven't met him. He's . . . threatening.'

'*Threatening?*'

'He said if we didn't drop this, Joe and his mother might . . . suffer.'

'Are you serious?'

'He is.'

'Bullshit. I know his type. He's all bluff and bluster. He's watched too many gangster movies. You can't believe everything a guy like that says.'

'I believed him.'

'Well, Nicole . . .' Carl considers his next remark for a good long while. Then he says, 'You've done a good job with the boy, but this sounds like something I need to deal with. Man to man. You get me?'

I get him. 'I don't think that'll work with Vogler, Carl.'

'We'll see. You got a number for him?'

I have. Vogler pressed a Conmari Ltd card into my hand at Admiral's Reach while we were, in his terminology, playing nicey-nicey in Joe's presence. I read out the number.

Carl logs it on his phone.

'But—'

Too late for any more objections. Carl's gone. Along

with most of the kudos I was hoping to get out of this mission.

Shit.

I shower and go down to breakfast. Ursula's there again, chatty as before, but, mercifully, pressed for time. 'Got a meeting first thing,' she says as she bustles off, leaving me to drink coffee, check emails and wonder how Carl's conversation with Vogler is going. There's no way he can win Vogler round, of course. I know that. It was only to preserve what's left of my reputation that I didn't tell Carl how I knew that for a certainty.

Then Carl calls back. The ring tone of the phone actually makes me jump. As I listen to what he has to say, I start to feel sick.

'Vogler's a bit of a dinosaur, Nicole. Totally unreconstructed. I can see how you'd have trouble with him. Maybe it was my fault for sending you. I think he reckoned having a woman pitch the deal to him was some kind of affront. Anyhow, we traded a few insults, then he started to take things seriously. Bottom line is he's going to mull the situation over and let me have his terms within twenty-four hours.'

'His terms?'

'His compensation figure for letting Joe go. It'll be inflated, of course. We'll knock him down a bit just to look respectable. But we'll do a deal. That's the point. Whatever we have to bung Vogler's way is worth it to get Joe, right?'

'Right,' I say numbly. I'm not sure for the moment I can actually believe what I'm hearing.

'All you have to do is keep Joe sweet until Vogler's happy. Then we can ship Joe up here and the seriously exciting part of this project can kick off.'

'Right,' I say again.

'Think you can manage that?' The sarcasm in the question's impossible to miss.

'I can manage that, Carl, yes,' I say slowly and deliberately.

'Great. More when I have some, then.'

He's gone. I turn the phone off. Not to sleep mode. Just off. Completely. I've had enough. And for the moment I can't take any more.

I meet Liz in the hall as I head for my room.

'Enjoying your stay?' she asks brightly.

'Yes thanks,' I reply, trying to match her brightness.

'Looks like it's going to be a nice day. Better make the most of it.'

I can't think of anything to say to that. I just smile and nod and start up the stairs.

I'm fed up with every way this has gone wrong. Vogler's easy recourse to violence; Carl's equally easy assumption that he can succeed where I've failed; worst of all, the fact that he seems to be right.

I should care more, but just for the moment all I can think is, *Stuff them.* I need a break from circling round all this in my head.

I walk down through the town to the National Maritime Museum. There's a marina on the harbour side of the building. I wander out on to the pontoon, wondering if I'll spot Roger before he spots me.

Then, there he is, waving at me from one of the cross-pontoons. He looks smart, almost athletic, in jeans and a guernsey. He signals to the gate into the section of the marina where he's moored and strides along to meet me there.

'It's great you could make it, Nicole,' he says, opening the gate.

I smile. 'It sounded too good to pass on.'

'Well, it's not often the tide, the weather and my time-table cooperate to this degree.' He gestures at the calm sea and the blue sky, in which the clouds are just benign puffs of cottonwool. 'Come and see the *Egret*.'

He leads me back to the berth where the university's boat is waiting. It's a classy motor-launch, with a forward cabin and nice wood detailing. He hops aboard and gives me a hand as I join him.

'Not bad, eh?'

'Lovely.'

'So, game for a trip up river?'

'Absolutely.'

'There's coffee in the thermos. Help yourself.'

I do, and the coffee tastes good, as Roger backs away from the pontoon and heads out into the estuary. I watch the town recede behind us and feel just some of my anger recede with it.

'When you get out on the river, it gives you a sort of perspective on everything you're involved in on land,' Roger says reflectively as he takes us out into the channel leading between the docks and the opposite headland. 'I seem to see things more clearly when I'm afloat.'

'Really? Well, I could do with some of that.'

'Problems?'

'Just a few. But none I want to talk about.'

He chuckles. 'Understood. We'll just let the river work its magic.'

*

And that turns out to be exactly what the river does. As we cruise gently up the estuary, the serenity of the surroundings begins to seep into me. The trees grow low to the water's edge. The fields are small and rounded, the inlets silvery and inviting.

We pass a couple of sail-powered oyster dredgers and a tourist boat coming down from Truro. Nothing moves quickly or noisily. The river leads us slowly on.

The estuary is more extensive than I'd have imagined. I see the King Harry ferry crossing ahead of us and, beyond it, tankers moored in the river, 'waiting for an uptick in the oil business', according to Roger. Their hulls loom over us like cliffs as we cruise past them.

Thanks to the state of the tide, Roger explains, we can take a look at the upper reaches of the river that are so often mudbound. He seems quite excited at the prospect.

The banks close in as we follow the river's meanders. The woods are thick around us now. Signs of habitation are few. But there's one plain stone cottage sitting close to the water that Roger points out to me. The undergrowth around it is thick and tangled. There's an adjacent barn with a hole in its roof. I guess the place is unoccupied.

'The cottage is accessible by water for only a couple of hours around high tide,' says Roger. 'By road . . . well, there's just a rough track for a mile or so from the nearest road. I walked along to it once, just to see what there was, having seen it several times from the river.'

'What did you find?'

'Nothing much. It's maintained to some degree and furnished, as far as I could see. No idea who owns it. Kolonn Drogh, it's called. Cornish for broken heart.'

'That sounds sad.'

'It does, doesn't it? What the story is I don't know. Joe might, but . . .'

'Joe Roberts?'

'Yes. I saw him here a few weeks ago, gazing out at the river from the field above the house. There.' He points to a weed-choked meadow behind the cottage. 'He didn't see me. I had some students with me at the time. He paid us no attention at all. When I mentioned it to him later, he said he might – might, mind you – have been walking in the area. But I don't know. You can never really tell with Joe.' Roger smiles. 'That's one of the things that makes him so good at Go. There's a pattern to what he does, to the plays he makes. You know there is. But you can't see what it is until, suddenly . . .'

'You've lost?'

'Well, let's just say you realize you're likelier to lose than you thought you were a few seconds earlier. It's not a pleasant realization.' He laughs. 'Though I've gotten used to it.'

'Do you know Conrad Vogler, Roger?'

He looks round at me sharply, eyebrows arched in surprise. 'Joe works for him, I'm told. *You* know him?'

'No. Jeremy mentioned him, actually. He showed me a photograph of Joe's father. Conrad Vogler was in the photograph with him.'

'Jeremy? Ah well, he seems to enjoy digging up nuggets of local history. He's mentioned Vogler's partnership with Joe's father to me as well. Though I must say I'm impressed by how quickly you've picked all this up.'

'I can't seem to stop people telling me things.'

'No.' He nods. 'Evidently not.'

We've drifted past Kolonn Drogh now. The creek stretches on ahead, the water glistening in the low-angled sun. Roger studies his watch.

'Time to turn back, I'm afraid,' he announces. 'Otherwise we'll pass the point of no return.' He grins. 'Tidally speaking, that is.'

We cruise back down the river and round into Restronguet Creek, where we tie up at the quay beside the thatch-roofed Pandora Inn. It's warm enough to sit outside with our drinks and we stay out there for lunch. The setting's ridiculously picturesque. That and Roger's company do a good job of helping me forget the disaster my trip to Cornwall's turned into. At least for a few hours, it doesn't really seem to matter.

Roger talks about Hong Kong and marine biology and Go, which he still can't quite believe I'm interested in. 'If you didn't grow up with it, I'm not sure how you ever really get to grips with it. My father introduced me to it, just as his father introduced him to it and his father before him.'

'How does that apply to the other members of the club?'

'Oh, they all have their own story.'

'What's Joe's story?'

'Ah, well, Joe's different, naturally. I gather he was something of a chess prodigy. But then, according to Jeremy, someone told him Go was more difficult than chess. It's not strictly true, though Go's certainly more complex in its strategic possibilities. Anyway, once Joe tried it, he was hooked. Apparently. And now he's . . .'

I look at Roger enquiringly. 'Yes?'

'Now he's very good.'

'Just very good? Or better than that?'

Roger sits back in his chair and gazes out across the still, twinkling water of the creek. 'I'm not sure exactly. As far as Go is concerned, Joe is an enigma. By design, I sense. But then . . .' He looks back at me. 'We all have our secrets, don't we?'

It's mid-afternoon when we leave the Pandora. The weather's still fine, though turning cool. As we cruise south towards Falmouth, I can't stop my mind focusing on the problems that are waiting for me there. Roger seems to notice the sombre turn in my mood.

'If there's any help you need while you're here, Nicole – with anything, really – you only have to ask, you know.'

'That's kind. But . . . I can cope.' What I've told him about why I'm in Falmouth amounts to little more than the cover story I gave Ursula. But I'm not sure he quite believes flogging a new Venstrom system is all there is to it.

'I don't doubt it. But sometimes there's an easier way of doing things that's only obvious to a neutral observer.'

We smile at each other. 'I'll bear the offer in mind.'

'Do.' He nods ahead. 'Your boss come down to check up on you, Nicole?'

I follow his gaze. There's a sleek-hulled super-yacht moored ahead of us off Castle Point, at the entrance to St Mawes Harbour, all silvery steel and tinted glass. It wasn't there when we left this morning.

I laugh at Roger's suggestion. 'My boss doesn't own anything like that.'

'Really? Isn't Billy Swarther in the multi-billionaire bracket?'

'I meant my boss in London. I guess Billy might own something like that. But it's likelier to be moored in the Bahamas than Carrick Roads.'

'Who does own it, I wonder,' Roger muses. 'Someone extremely rich, that's for sure.'

'Well, if you get an invitation to go aboard, I'll be happy to tag along.'

'And I'll be happy to ask you to. I've really enjoyed today.' He smiles at me warmly and, as far as I can tell, genuinely.

'Me too.' Which is also genuine.

But reality awaits on dry land. Roger's heading home. I'm heading back to Tideways. We part and I walk up through the crowds in the centre of town alone, wondering what kind of answer Carl might have had by now from Vogler.

I'm hardly through the door at Tideways before I realize something's wrong. Hazel the waitress is there with Ursula, talking in an anxious gabble. I catch the word 'hospital' and guess there's been some kind of accident. They confirm that as soon as they see me.

'Liz has been in a car accident,' Ursula explains. 'Hazel's just been telling me about it.'

'They've had to operate,' says Hazel, wringing her hands. 'We don't really know how bad it is.'

'Apparently,' Ursula goes on, 'she was driving back along the by-pass when she lost control going down the hill towards the roundabout at the edge of town. It's quite a steep slope on that section. She ploughed into a lorry.'

'Brakes must have failed,' says Hazel.

'Or maybe she was ill,' suggests Ursula. 'We just don't know.'

'My God, this is awful,' is all I can say. But it's not all I think. In my mind I hear Vogler's voice. *Joe will suffer and his mother will suffer and, when I track you down, you'll suffer too.* Is this what he meant when he told Carl he'd give him his response within twenty-four hours? Or am I being paranoid?

'It might not be as bad as it sounds,' says Ursula consolingly. 'We haven't got any details.'

'Where's Joe?'

'At the hospital,' says Hazel. 'He phoned me from there.'

'I'm afraid there's nothing to be done except wait for news,' says Ursula.

'I've got to see to some things,' says Hazel abstractedly. 'She'd want everything to carry on as normal.'

'We're fine, Hazel.' Ursula smiles at her. 'Isn't that right, Nicole?'

I nod in agreement and Hazel bustles off down the stairs to the family flat in the basement, leaving Ursula and me staring at each other in bemusement.

'Terrible turn of events,' she remarks after a brief silence.

'Yes,' is all I can say to that.

'You look a bit shaken up, if you don't mind me saying.'

I notice my hands are shaking and I wonder if Ursula's noticed too. If so, she must be wondering why I'm reacting like this to an accident affecting someone I hardly know. 'It's, er, quite a shock.'

'I thought of phoning the hospital, but I suspect they'll tell me nothing.'

'I have to sit down,' I say. I stumble into the dining room and take the nearest chair.

'This has really knocked you, Nicole.' Ursula's frowning down at me. I can see her mind working through the possibilities, none of which can make much sense to her.

'I think I need to find out how badly Liz is injured.' My voice sounds slightly quavery. 'And how exactly it happened.'

67

'You'd probably have to go to the hospital to stand much chance of learning what her condition is.'

I take a calming breath. 'I'll do that, then.'

'You don't look in any state to drive.'

'I'll manage.'

'No need. I'll drive.' She fixes me with a decisive look. 'I'm anxious myself, goodness knows. Let's just go and see what we can find out, eh? It's better to be doing something than sitting around here wondering.'

I nod numbly. 'That sounds good.'

Ursula reckons the part of the roundabout where Liz crashed will still be cordoned off, so the traffic will be a nightmare, with the rush hour well under way. But she knows a route that doesn't touch the by-pass until later.

It seems to work. We're soon out of Falmouth, heading north, none too fast, but faster than the southbound traffic, which is badly clogged. Ursula asks a few questions that I can tell are designed to elicit an explanation from me for my reaction to the news. Liz Roberts is just my landlady, after all. I deflect her as best I can with some stuff about what a nice woman Liz is. True, of course, but it's not enough. Ursula knows it and I know she knows it.

My phone rings twice during the journey. It's Carl both times. I don't answer. Ursula notices that too. She must be very curious about my behaviour.

Treliske Hospital is on the outskirts of Truro. The car park, when we finally get there, looks full, with cars circling hopefully.

Ursula pulls into the set-down bay. 'You go and find out what you can while I look for a space,' she says. 'I'll catch up with you in there.'

'OK.' I jump out and head for the entrance, relieved she isn't coming with me. I'd rather face Joe alone.

The directions they give me at main reception take me eventually to a ward where Liz is due to be transferred after surgery. No one can give me any details of her condition, nor any clear idea of how long it's likely to be before she arrives there. The ward sister suggests I wait for news in a nearby seating area. As for Joe, she knows nothing about where he might be.

The corridor leading to the seating area is a backwater in the generally busy hospital. It looks to be deserted as I approach. But, turning a corner, I see there's one person sitting there alone, staring into space.

It isn't Joe.

'Mr Forrester,' I say, genuinely surprised, as well as uncertain, just for the moment, that it really is him. I didn't see much of him when we spoke outside Tideways on Monday night.

He looks up and gives me a quizzical glance. 'Miss Nevinson,' he says. He's wearing a rumpled suit and tie. His grey hair hangs over his forehead forlornly. He looks older than I first thought. Closer to seventy than sixty, I reckon. There's something travel-worn about his weathered features. His expression is sorrowful but philosophical. His eyes are wary. 'What are you doing here?'

'I came to see how Liz – Mrs Roberts – is.'

'That's good of you.'

'Is there any news?'

'Part of the driver's door pierced her lung. She lost quite a lot of blood. But she's strong. She should be all right. Eventually, anyway. She's going to be laid up here for a while.'

'How did you hear about it?'

'Joe phoned me.'

'And where is Joe?'

'Outside somewhere. Having a smoke, I expect. Or just breathing some non-hospital air. There was no point him staying here. When they do transfer Liz, she won't be conscious.'

'But you stayed.'

'Yes.' He smiles awkwardly. 'Not sure why, really.'

'I think I might try and find Joe.'

'You seem to have got to know him quite well in the short time you've been in Falmouth.'

'I went along to his Go club.'

'And then you offered him some kind of job.'

'He told you that?'

'It cropped up while we were sitting here.'

'Well, that doesn't matter much in the circumstances, does it? His mother's recovery is all that's important.'

'Of course.' Forrester's gaze is discomforting. He seems able to see inside me. 'Although it'll be important at some point to establish exactly what happened.'

'Hazel said she lost control of her car on the by-pass running down into Falmouth.'

'Liz isn't somebody who loses control, Miss Nevinson.'

'Please. It's Nicole.'

'OK. I'm Duncan. Thing is, Nicole, when I went out to the roundabout where it happened, I noticed there weren't any skid marks. That suggests brake failure to me.'

'I guess so.'

'But Liz has her car serviced regularly by the garage I recommend my learners to use. So, brake failure really isn't very likely.'

'What, then?'

'I don't know.'

70

'Any idea which direction Joe went in?' I'm eager to change the subject, little good though I suspect it'll do me. Forrester's on to something. And he doesn't strike me as the sort of man who'll be happy to drop it. 'The grounds look pretty extensive.'

'He won't have gone far.'

'OK. I'll see if I can track him down.'

'Tell him nothing's changed here.'

'I will.' I turn to go.

'Oh, Nicole—'

'Yes?'

'Have you spoken to Conrad Vogler about this job you've offered Joe?'

'Well . . . yes.'

'How did he react to the prospect of losing Joe's services?'

'He seemed . . . resigned, I suppose.'

'I see.' Forrester's expression doesn't alter. But it's obvious he's unconvinced. 'Well, always a man of business, Mr Vogler.'

'Yes. Exactly. Now I really—'

'It's OK, Nicole. Don't let me hold you up.'

It's getting chilly outside as dusk falls. I check one way for Joe, then another, before I finally spot him in a small garden area, where he's sitting on a bench. I'm surprised, but somehow not, to see he's playing Go.

He looks up as I approach. 'Nicole. Didn't expect to see you.'

I sit down beside him. 'Duncan said I'd find you out here.'

'Has something happened in there?' he asks, suddenly anxious.

71

'No. Your mother's in good hands.'

'Like you know that for a fact?' He sets the Go board down carefully on the bench beside him. 'Sorry.' He holds up one hand in apology. 'Bit stressed.'

'Does Go help?'

'Always.'

'Who's winning?'

'This game? Not sure yet. Ke Jie lost from this position against AlphaGo.'

'Can you win?'

'Maybe.'

'You have a remarkable ability, Joe. You're quite possibly unique.'

'I'd trade that for Mum making a complete recovery.'

'I'm sure she will.'

'Couldn't have happened at a worse time. How will I tell her now I'm leaving Falmouth?'

'It may not be a coincidence.'

He looks sharply at me. 'Come again?'

'There's something I have to tell you.' I swallow hard. 'About Conrad Vogler.'

'What about him?'

'Maybe I should have mentioned it when we left Admiral's Reach last night, but I, er . . . didn't really take it seriously.' *Didn't I? Didn't I really?* 'While we were alone, in his study, Vogler told me he wasn't prepared to let you go and that I had to withdraw Venstrom's offer. If I didn't . . .'

'Yeah? If you didn't?'

'He'd make you – and your mother – suffer.'

Joe's face twists in disbelief. 'He said that?'

I nod. 'He threatened me too, but . . .'

'Why didn't you tell me?'

'I thought he was bluffing.'

'Bluffing? Christ.' Joe bows his head and rubs his fingers up and down his forehead. 'Con wouldn't hurt Mum, would he? I mean, I just do a job for him. I just analyse stocks.'

'Maybe you analyse stocks like you play Go – better than anyone else.'

'But that's crazy. I mean, I know Con comes over as a bit of a tough guy, but he wouldn't, seriously he wouldn't, sabotage Mum's car just to . . . keep me working for him. Would he?'

'You know him better than I do, Joe.'

'He worked with my father. Mum's always said Dad should never have trusted him. I don't exactly *trust* him myself. I just get paid to do a job. That's all it is, Nicole. A fucking job. I'm not his slave.'

'I'm sure he'll deny having anything to do with your mother's accident. And maybe that's all it was. An accident. Although Duncan seems to think there's something suspicious about it. So . . .'

'Shit,' Joe mutters.

'We could take you all away, Joe. You, Karen *and* your mother. Out of Vogler's reach. Venstrom could arrange that.'

'You talk like we need to go into a witness protection programme.'

'The alternative is to turn Venstrom down and go on doing what Vogler wants you to do for him. For the rest of your life. Or until he's finished with you.'

'And pretend I don't know what he did to my mother?'

'We can't be sure he did anything. I assume the police are looking at the car. If it was tampered with, they'll find out.'

'Doesn't that depend how expertly it was tampered with? It'll be weeks before we know, anyway.' Joe shakes his head dolefully. Then his phone pings. He looks at it. 'Duncan. Mum's arrived on the ward.' He jumps up, scooping up the Go stones and folding his board shut.

'I'm sure she's going to be all right, Joe,' I say, aware of how platitudinous that must sound.

He looks down at me. 'I'd rather you didn't come in with me, Nicole.'

'OK.'

'I'm trying really hard not to blame you for this.'

There's a reproachful edge to his voice and I can't summon a response. I just try not to flinch.

'If you hadn't come looking for me . . .'

He doesn't seem to want to finish the sentence and I don't want him to either.

'I'll see you later.'

He heads for the hospital side-entrance then, slightly hunched as he strides along.

I watch him disappear into the building and wonder just where we go from here.

Then, quite suddenly, I'm aware of Ursula standing a few feet away from me.

'God. Ursula. I didn't see you there.'

'Neither did Joe. Or, if he did, he didn't look at me long enough to recognize me.'

'He's gone to see Liz. They've just transferred her on to a ward after surgery. He's a bit . . . distracted.'

'Understandably.'

'Duncan Forrester's here as well.'

'I know. I parked near his car.'

'We should—'

'Leave them to it?'

I smile uncertainly. 'Something like that.' I'm beginning to wonder how long Ursula's been within earshot.

And then she tells me. 'I have to make a confession, Nicole. I listened to your conversation with Joe. That probably sounds terrible. But I didn't like to interrupt. And then . . .'

'And then?'

'I realized you and I might be able to do each other a favour.'

'I'm sorry?'

'We share a problem.'

'We do?'

'Conrad Vogler. It's possible we can share a solution as well.'

'I can't imagine what you mean.'

'I'd be happy to explain. Why don't we talk in my car? It's getting cold out here.'

There's no arguing with that. The sky's darkening. The air's growing chill. But I'm suspicious and she knows it.

'A super-yacht moored off Castle Point this afternoon,' she says, with no obvious relevance, as we walk away together. 'Massive thing. The owner probably thinks it's beautiful. To my eye it's rather ugly.'

'I saw it earlier.'

'You did? Well, you know what I mean, then. I suppose it's too much to expect such people to possess good taste in addition to great wealth. Especially when you consider how they came by that wealth.'

'You talk as if you know the owner.'

'I feel as if I do in some ways, though I've never actually

75

met him. He and Conrad Vogler, on the other hand, are well acquainted.'

'They are?'

'From what I overheard, Venstrom want to offer Joe a job. To exploit his talent at Go for . . . what, programming a superior gaming system? Something like that, anyway. They sent you down here to sound him out. Is that basically it?'

'I'm not sure I want to discuss this with you, Ursula. I'm not sure it's any of your business.'

'Ordinarily, it wouldn't be. But Vogler's the overlap on our Venn diagram.'

'If you say so.'

'I do. Now tell me, what's made Duncan Forrester suspicious about Liz's car crash?'

'The lack of skid marks at the scene.'

'Doesn't that suggest brake failure? Like Hazel said.'

'He reckons Liz's car is too well maintained for that to be plausible.'

'Well, I'd back him to know, wouldn't you? Here we are.'

Ursula's parked in what isn't actually a bay at all, rather a striped-off triangle under a pine tree. Forrester's driving school car is more neatly parked a few bays away.

We get in. As the doors close, the sounds of the evening are suddenly cut off. There are only our voices now, talking quietly in the gathering darkness.

'I really do work for HMRC,' Ursula says once we're settled. 'At any rate, an agency of HMRC. But VAT isn't my priority. Conrad Vogler is.'

'If you're going to tell me he's fiddling his income tax, I won't be surprised.'

'It's a little more serious than that. What I'm about to say is highly confidential. It can go no further. You understand?'

I nod.

'Vogler acts as money launderer for an organized crime syndicate called the Clearing House. They're basically problem-solvers for lower-level organizations who need to get things done in places where they have no presence or influence of their own. Hence the name. Vogler's role is to turn the payments the Clearing House receives into legitimate assets and make a profit while he's doing it.

'That's where Joe comes in. I'm sure he's no idea who Vogler's clients are. There's no reason why he should suspect his employer is up to his neck in international crime. Besides, that's not how he functions, is it? Stocks and shares. Go. Both are games to Joe. Games he's good at winning. He doesn't want to look too deeply into things. He's brilliant at what he does. But he's also content with what he does. Creative. But not inquisitive.'

Ursula pauses, as if waiting for me to comment. But until I understand where we're going, she's going to get nothing more out of me.

'The source of the money Vogler handles for the Clearing House is hidden in a labyrinth of offshore shell companies. The trades Joe works on abide by all the rules, though the calls he makes are certainly unorthodox. They're also hugely profitable. Which explains, I think we can assume, why Vogler's as reluctant to lose his services as Venstrom are eager to acquire them. Joe's obviously a genius. As such he's irreplaceable. An organization like the Clearing House doesn't tolerate failure. And a fall in the profits Vogler's generating for them would definitely count as failure. So, you see, Vogler simply can't afford to act like a normal employer and let Joe go. As you've discovered. And as Joe's discovered now too.

'I'm part of a small team that's been trying to pin something on Vogler for a long time. But he's clever *and* careful. He has no electronic or written communications with the Clearing House that we can trace. It all seems to be done face to face. What we need – what we can't proceed without – is hard evidence. And I think you can help us get it.'

A silence falls. I have no idea what she can be about to suggest. In the end, it seems she requires me to ask. 'How?'

'The super-yacht's called the *Dymas*. It belongs to Andreas Kremer, a high roller in the Clearing House. He's basically their CFO. It looks to me like he's coming down for a meeting with Vogler. Probably tomorrow. Kremer will fly in. The *Dymas* comes complete with a helipad. The meeting will be on board, I suspect, so they can talk freely in a secure environment. Of course, if we could eavesdrop on that conversation, we might well get the kind of hard evidence we need.'

'But you can't.'

'Not as it stands. And we have very little time to act. This is a rare opportunity. I don't want to let it slip. I'm hoping you'll agree to help. You've had dealings with Vogler. You have every reason to talk to him again. Intercept him in St Mawes tomorrow on his way to the quay, which is where he'll be picked up by launch. Engage him in conversation. After what's happened to Liz that won't be difficult. In fact, he'll probably be expecting some kind of approach from you, so he won't be suspicious.'

'What exactly do you want me to do?'

'Plant a listening device on him. It's very small. And light. Fabric-adhesive on one side to attach itself to the inside of a cuff or a lapel. Get close enough to him, make sure he's paying attention to what you're saying, not what you're doing with your hands, and it should be possible.'

'Why don't you do it yourself?'

'Because the micro-transmitter has a limited range, so I'll need to be out on the water when the time comes in a Customs launch, as close to the boat as we can get without attracting attention. I can't be in two places at once. So, it has to be you or it won't work.'

'You're serious, aren't you?'

'Absolutely. This could be the break you need too. Think about it. A recording of Vogler's meeting with Kremer should give us more than enough to bring charges against him. Once he's in custody, he'll be out of Joe's life. We get whatever he's ultimately willing to tell us about the Clearing House plus the disruption to their activities the loss of their money launderer is bound to cause them. You get your game-programming genius. It's win-win.'

'Unless he catches me in the act, that is.'

'If you can't manage it when the time comes, or decide it's just too risky, I'll quite understand. But if you *can* manage it . . .'

'You're asking a lot.'

'Perhaps. But ask yourself how else you're going to extricate Joe from Vogler's clutches. He'll never have the nerve to leave now he believes Vogler targeted his mother. This is our chance, Nicole. Kremer coming here is a godsend. We have to take advantage of it.'

'*You* have to.'

'I'd say you'd be wise too as well, Nicole. There's nothing to say Vogler won't target Karen next. Or you. And besides, I assume saving the day where Joe's concerned will win you a lot of brownie points at Venstrom. You have to think of your career as well.'

'It won't do your career any harm either.'

'True. But you're much better placed to pull this off than I am. And like I said before, you don't have to go through with it if you reckon it's going to go wrong. Won't you at least look at the device and see whether you think it's feasible?'

'You've got it with you?'

'No. It's at Tideways. We can go back there now. We may as well. I get the feeling Joe doesn't want you sitting by his mother's bedside with him, don't you?'

'I—' My phone pings. It's Carl. I consider blanking him again, but he's going to get seriously narked if I go on doing that. 'I have to take this,' I explain to Ursula, climbing out of the car.

'Sure,' is all she says.

I slam the door behind me and walk far enough away from the car to be sure she can't hear what I'm saying. I end up standing next to Forrester's car. *Rise to the Test with the Forrester School of Motoring* reads the message on the passenger door. I raise my phone to my ear.

'Hi, Carl.'

'I haven't heard from you all day, Nicole. What's going on?'

'I was waiting to hear from you about Vogler's response.'

'He's gone quiet.'

'Not exactly.'

'What d'you mean?'

'Joe's mother has been injured in a car crash.'

'Sorry to hear that. What's it got to do with us?'

'Her brakes may have been tampered with.'

'What? Are you suggesting Vogler tampered with them?'

'Maybe.'

'Christ, Nicole, that's crazy. You need to pull yourself

80

together. Joe's mother prangs her car and suddenly you're wetting your knickers. I thought you could handle this. I was obviously wrong.'

I tell myself firmly not to get angry. I'm just going to let Carl know exactly where we stand. 'Joe thinks Vogler's responsible. So, he isn't going to risk any further repercussions. Which means he won't come and work for us. *That's* what we've got to handle.'

'Fucking hell. This was supposed to be simple. How have you managed to lose control of the situation so totally?'

'Because it's a much more complex situation than we ever knew. And I think Vogler *has* given us his answer. You just don't want to believe it. And neither do I. But we might have to.'

'Bullshit.' There's a pause. I can almost hear him thinking. Then: 'All right. I'm coming down there to sort this, since you obviously can't. I'll take an early train tomorrow. I'll have Kyra book me into the same hotel as you in St Mawes. You can pick me up from Truro. Think you can manage that?' He doesn't wait for an answer. 'I'll let you know my arrival time in the morning. And Nicole . . .'

'Yes?'

'Do nothing until I get there. OK?'

Again, he doesn't wait for an answer. Which is probably just as well. Because I've already decided what to do. And it isn't nothing.

I get back into Ursula's car. 'Everything all right?' she asks neutrally.

'I'll do it,' I hear myself say.

What I really mean is that I'll put myself in a position where I can do it, even though I suspect in the end I'll reckon it's too difficult or dangerous to pull off. Ursula probably realizes that, though she doesn't say so.

The roads are quieter on the drive back to Falmouth. Neither of us speaks. It's as if we don't want to risk getting to know each other too well. I ask myself whether I wouldn't be wiser doing as Carl wants and letting him find out for himself that Vogler isn't negotiating with us in any genuine sense. But then the chance to nail Vogler would slip through our fingers, Joe would be left working for a man he now has good cause to fear and Carl would ensure I took the blame for its all going wrong. Career-ending? Not far short, I reckon. 'Fuck,' I mutter.

'What did you say?' asks Ursula.

'Nothing,' I assure her.

Like she said, the bug she wants me to plant on Vogler is small, no bigger or heavier than a five pence piece. I can see how it could be placed inconspicuously inside a cuff or collar or pocket. What I can't see is how Vogler could fail to notice me doing it. And I don't like to imagine what the consequences of being caught in the act might be. But Ursula keeps reassuring me I don't have to go through with it unless the circumstances are right.

'Remember, you don't have to do it when it comes to the point, Nicole. And you shouldn't, if you think it's not going to work. It's not in your interests or mine for him to realize what we're trying to do. Better to walk away in that case. Much better. No one will blame you.'

I'm not sure about that. Maybe I will. 'What time do you think this meeting will happen?'

'I don't know. Obviously we'll have to wait for Kremer's helicopter to arrive. And then we'll have to wait for Vogler to set off for the boat. We'll keep in touch by text.'

It sounds as if Carl may have to whistle for that lift from Truro. Annoying him will be worth it, though, if this plan delivers what Ursula hopes for. And if not, well, he can't be much more pissed off with me than he already is.

The rest of the evening hangs heavy. I plan to spend the night at the hotel in St Mawes rather than Tideways, so I can be ready to move as soon as Ursula says, but I don't want to draw any attention to myself, so I leave my departure as late as possible.

When my phone rings I assume it's Carl again. But I'm wrong.

'Hi, Karen.'

'You know about Liz, right? Joe says you were at the hospital earlier.'

'Yes. I was there.'

'Joe's on his way back here now. Liz is "comfortable", apparently. He thinks she's going to be OK. But he says this changes everything. You know what he means, don't you?'

'Yes. I know.'

'It can't be true, can it?' I'm not sure how much Joe has told her and I can't afford to guess. 'I mean, it's totally insane.'

'We probably shouldn't discuss this on the phone, Karen.'

'Joe never would've talked to you if he'd known it could lead to something like this. I wouldn't have either.'

'You can blame me if it helps.'

'I would if it did.'

'I'm sorry. I really am.'

'You should be.'

'Why don't we talk again tomorrow?'

'Why? What's going to change?'

It's a good question. She hangs up and leaves it with me, unanswered.

An hour or so later, while I'm packing an overnight bag, there's a knock on the door. I assume it's Ursula. But I'm wrong again.

Duncan Forrester looks grave but calm. Maybe it's his default expression. 'I thought I should tell you Liz is doing quite well. She's groggy, of course, after the operation, but all the indicators are good, apparently.'

'Thanks for letting me know,' I say limply.

He frowns slightly. 'I thought you'd come back in after we spoke.'

'I got the feeling Joe preferred me not to.'

'Ah. Right.'

'Did Liz . . . say anything about the accident?'

'To suggest it wasn't an accident, you mean?'

'I didn't mean that, necessarily. But . . .'

'She confirmed her brakes failed. Completely. She tried changing down, but that didn't slow her down enough before she reached the roundabout. That was about it. She was very tired. It was all she could do to tell me that much. I'll see if she remembers anything else tomorrow.'

'Such as?'

'Anything . . . suspicious.'

'Accidents do happen, Duncan.'

'Yeah. That's what they said when her husband ploughed into Stithians Reservoir.'

'What do you mean?'

'I expect you know what I mean, Nicole. Goodnight.'

*

Forrester's left me with plenty to think about as I set off for St Mawes. Vogler was Charlie Roberts' partner. Now he's Joe Roberts' boss. Charlie died in a car crash. Liz has nearly gone the same way. It looks like Vogler isn't a man to be crossed.

So, what do I do? Leave well alone? Keep my head down? Take the positives out of the situation? Christ, I would if there were any. But I don't need an appraisal interview to tell me this is my last chance to go anywhere at Venstrom. And the thought of giving in to a man like Vogler is sickening.

I hold the bug in my hand and weigh the odds. If I don't take this chance, I'm going to regret it. And if I do take it . . .

You never know until you know.

Thursday October 10

I GET A MESSAGE FROM CARL WHILE I'M HAVING BREAKFAST. On train from Paddington. Arrive Truro 1154. See you there. He doesn't actually ask for a reply and I don't send one. Maybe he'll see me there. Maybe he won't.

A few minutes later, I see, sliding across the grey skyline, a helicopter approaching the moored bulk of the *Dymas*. As I watch it land at the stern of the boat, my phone pings and it's a message from Ursula. Are you seeing what I'm seeing? I text back I am. She responds Be ready. I tell her OK.

I don't know if Vogler will be collected straight away, but I play safe by walking along to the quay. Nothing's moving on the *Dymas* at the moment, though I can make out the shape of the helicopter sitting on its deck. I buy a coffee at the St Mawes Hotel just beyond the quay and sit outside, cool though it is. This way I can hardly miss the launch – or Vogler. I work through my emails. The morning begins to slip by. I have a second coffee.

Suddenly, Vogler appears. There's no sign of the launch yet. But he's striding along the road from the direction of Admiral's Reach, looking very smart in a navy blue suit, white shirt and red and white striped tie. He's carrying a slim briefcase. I wonder what Ursula would give for a glimpse of the contents. He looks like a businessman on his way to an important meeting – which is just what he is, I suppose.

'Good morning,' I call to him.

He stops and stares at me, then slowly walks up to my table. 'What are you doing here, Nicole?'

'Killing time. Join me for a coffee?'

'No. Unlike you, apparently, I have work to do.'

'You've got a moment to sit down, haven't you?'

He glances once towards the *Dymas*, appears to decide he can spend a few minutes finding out what I want and sits down, stowing the briefcase at his feet. The chairs are close. Our knees are nearly touching and I smile at him in a way intended to persuade a man like him that I acknowledge his dominance and might even find it attractive.

'Apparently you've been talking to my boss, Carl Hinkley.'

'Oh, him? Yeah, we had a chat. Got to say, Nicole, he sounded a bit of a prat.'

'Well, prat or not, he calls the shots, which is why I'm at a bit of a loose end. He's told me to let him handle negotiations with you.'

'Ah, those precious negotiations. I told you the score Tuesday night. Nothing's changed. As far as Carl Hinkley goes, I'm giving you a chance to make the situation clear to him. And as for Joe . . .'

'He had some bad news yesterday.'

'I know. I've told him to take all the time he needs while his mother's laid up. Dreadful business.'

I need to act. I need to plant it now. But how? 'I've been thinking about our discussion, Conrad.'

'You can call me Con. Everyone does. What have you been thinking?'

'That I do understand your position. Completely.'

'Good.'

'But still I'm wondering . . . if there isn't room for compromise.'

'Did I sound like I was willing to compromise?'

'No, Con, you didn't. But then I never got the chance to spell out exactly what I was willing to offer, on a personal basis.'

'Personal?'

I lean towards him, willing him to lean towards me. He doesn't. 'An extra inducement that might persuade you to consider sharing Joe's expertise with us.'

'And what would that be?' He's smiling now, enjoying the game, not quite sure whether to take me seriously or not. There's never going to be a compromise, of course, but that wouldn't necessarily stop Vogler accepting whatever I offered him in pursuit of one.

I hold his gaze. 'Anything you wanted that I could make available.'

'Really? Anything?' He props one elbow on the table and draws closer.

Vogler's phone pings. He ignores it. But out of the corner of my eye I can see something moving out at sea – moving fast. I can't hear it yet, but I think I know what it is. My phone pings then as well. And I also ignore it.

'We both seem to be in demand, Nicole.'

'It's probably Carl. He can wait.'

'Not sure my caller can.' He glances towards the harbour. His eyes narrow. He's judging how long he can loiter here with me.

His tie's sagging over the edge of the table. It's only

inches from my grasp. I touch his forearm and he looks at me slyly. 'I might have misread you, Nicole.'

'Never judge a book by its cover.'

'I have to go, I really do.'

'You could call me later.'

'Maybe I will.' He stretches down for his briefcase, accentuating the sag of his tie. This is it. Now or never.

And it's now. I press the bug on behind his tie, high enough to be partly concealed by the sewn fold. It holds. But he senses the movement.

'What . . . ?'

'Sorry.' I smile. 'I spilt some coffee earlier. Didn't want you getting your tie stained.' The table has a wobble. When it caused some coffee to slop out of my cup earlier, I was miffed. Funny how things work out.

He smiles back at me, genuinely grateful, as far as I can tell. 'I've got to go.' I can hear the rumble of the launch's motor now. I can see the wake thrown up behind it as it heads into the harbour. 'But I'll be in touch.'

'I'll look forward to it.'

'Tell Carl from me I prefer dealing with you.'

'I will.'

He's off then, striding across the road towards the quay. The launch is slowing as it takes a wide loop round the sea wall.

I can't quite believe it's happened. But it has. I don't want to think about how Vogler will react if he finds it. He'll know for sure it was me. But before then, with any luck, Ursula will have given the go-ahead for his arrest.

I check my phone. The message was from Ursula, as I suspected. Launch left. I text back It worked. The reply is more or less instantaneous. Well done.

I signal the waitress for the bill. It's time I was moving.

It seems I'll be able to collect Carl at Truro station after all. And there's nothing I can do here. What I could do I've already done. And the consequences? I'll know soon enough.

I don't go back to the hotel. I go straight to my car and drive out of town, heading for the King Harry ferry. I feel nervous, but also elated. Vogler had this coming.

I keep glancing at my phone, hoping for a message from Ursula. None arrives. I reassure myself it could take a while before she can tell me anything useful and, until then, there's nothing for her to say. But she could at least tell me the micro-transmitter's working. She must know that by now.

But still there's nothing.

I reach Truro station with ten minutes in hand. The train's on time according to the information screen. I wait in my car.

The train pulls in. The forecourt's suddenly busy with taxis and cars leaving. Carl's one of the last passengers to emerge from the station. He's on his phone. What with that and his shaven head, soft jacket, distressed jeans and smart tote bag, he looks conspicuously metropolitan.

He stops some way short of my car to finish his call, then flashes me a smile before tossing his bag on to the rear seat and climbing in beside me.

'Christ knows how you can travel west from London for so long and still be on dry land,' he complains. 'But here I am.'

'At least the train wasn't late,' I remark as I start to reverse out of the bay.

'Hold on a mo, Nicole. Where are we going?'

I stop. 'The hotel in St Mawes?'

'That depends. I've just been talking to friend Vogler.'

'*What?*'

'No need to look so surprised. I told you he was going to get back to me.'

I can hardly tell Carl why I'm actually astonished Vogler's been in touch with him. 'Who actually phoned who?' I ask suspiciously.

'Does it matter? Point is, he's very much up for a deal.'

'He is?'

'One hundred per cent. He's a businessman, Nicole, I told you.'

'He's ruthless, Carl. *I* told *you*.'

'It's just an act. You've let this . . . coincidental car accident . . . cloud your judgement.'

'Is that what you think?'

'It's where the evidence is pointing. Listen. Vogler's tied up for the rest of today. But he's invited us out to dinner tomorrow night with him and his wife. Some Michelin-starred place just up the coast. We'll seal the deal over champagne and caviar. How does that sound?'

'Incredible.' Literally, I'm tempted to add.

'We're obviously going to have to stretch the budget to get him out of Joe's life. But I need to know we're getting the real deal with Joe. His record speaks for itself, of course, but Billy wants proof that it's *his* record, that Joe isn't fronting for someone else – one of our competitors, for instance. So, I've downloaded a newly upgraded version of *gridforest*. I want to watch Joe play against it. *Physically* watch, I mean. I need you to arrange that. Before we meet Vogler, obviously.'

'I'm not sure that's going to be possible.'

'Why the hell not? He should surely be able to understand we want to see what we're getting for our money.'

'His mother's in hospital, Carl. She's lucky to be alive. He's pretty distracted at the moment.'

'Well, *un*distract him. Phone him now.'

'*Now?*'

'Yes. Or give me his number and I'll phone him. Chop chop, Nicole. I'm done with messing about.'

Sometimes there's no reasoning with Carl. I call Joe's number. '*The person you are calling is not available.*' I let Carl hear the message. He's not impressed.

'What about the girlfriend you mentioned? Try her.'

That pretty much seems to be an order. I call Karen. She does answer.

'What d'you want, Nicole? I'm at work.'

'I'm trying to reach Joe. It's urgent.'

'He's at mine. Asleep, probably. He was up most of the night.'

'It'd be in his best interests if I could speak to him, Karen.'

'I bet.'

'Would you mind if I called round there?'

She thinks a long time before responding, after a heavy sigh. 'I guess not.'

'Can you give me the address?'

'OK. But I'll try and let him know you're coming. So, if he's not there, you'll know he doesn't reckon speaking to you *is* in his best interests.'

'Understood.'

'Thirteen Waterloo Road. Flat C.'

'Thanks.'

'Joe and I are planning to visit Liz this evening, Nicole. I don't want him upset before we go.'

93

'I won't upset him.'

'That's a promise, is it?'

'Yes.' But it's a pretty disingenuous promise. I can't guarantee Carl won't do some upsetting all on his own.

13 Waterloo Road looks like it was once a workshop, even though it's part of a residential terrace. A side-gate leads to a yard where a rear extension has been built. That's Flat C. The door's at the top of a short flight of steps.

I hang back as Carl climbs the steps, checking my phone for a message from Ursula. There's still no news from her, which is starting to nibble at my nerves. Carl's doing nothing for my peace of mind either. He's so convinced he's got every base covered I'm tempted to think he might actually be right. But the rational part of my brain keeps insisting he couldn't be more wrong.

He gives the bell a lot of pressing and adds a few raps on the door. Eventually, a sash window diagonally opposite us slides down and a bleary-eyed Joe stares out. It doesn't look as though Karen got through to him.

'Nicole,' he says hoarsely. 'What's going on?'

'Can we have a word, Joe?'

'Who's your friend?'

'Carl Hinkley,' Carl chips in. 'I'm Nicole's boss.' Nice of him to make that clear.

Joe's expression gives nothing away. Maybe it's his Go face. 'Hold on,' he says, with little enthusiasm. 'I'll let you in.'

It takes Joe a couple of minutes actually to open the door. He's wearing jeans and a hoodie. There's none of the normal brightness in his eyes. He looks like he needs more of the sleep we presumably woke him from.

The flat itself is small but quirkily colourful. Karen seems to like lilac and yellow, potted plants and swirly lampshades. Joe takes us into the lounge, where there's an aroma of joss stick and a great many cushions, on one of which a full-size Go board is standing, with a game apparently in progress.

Carl doesn't fail to notice it. 'You've got our attention in a big way, Joe,' he says, nodding at the board. 'You know that, don't you?'

'S'pose so,' is all Joe manages by way of response.

'How's Liz?' I ask.

'Recovering OK, according to the doctor. But . . . she's not going to be up and about for a while yet.' There's less expressiveness in his voice than usual. He's weighed down by the uncertainties of what has happened.

'Sorry to hear about her accident,' says Carl.

'Thanks,' says Joe, who doesn't sound as if he really believes Carl's sorry about anything. 'We're not actually sure it was an accident.'

'Take my advice and you'll steer clear of conspiracy theories.'

'Because conspiracies never happen, right?'

'Look, Joe, I've spoken to Conrad Vogler. We can agree terms with him. I'm confident of that. We can get you out from under.'

Joe looks across at me. 'Are you confident, Nicole?'

'It's possible everything Vogler's said and done is designed to get the best price, Joe. It's possible he's just a very tough negotiator.'

Carl shoots me an appreciative glance. 'Exactly. My understanding is you'd be happy to leave your job with Vogler, Joe, and join us to explore the exciting applications of your very particular ability.'

Joe slumps down on the couch and gazes up dubiously at Carl. 'They've taken AlphaGo way beyond board games, into areas that would actually benefit humanity like protein folding. Would that be part of the deal?'

'Absolutely. There are no limits to where we can go with this.'

'Great.' There's no conviction in Joe's tone. He doesn't quite believe this is going to come off.

'I know what you're thinking,' says Carl, sitting down next to Joe and beaming at him confidently. 'What about Vogler? Well, leave him to us. We're going to strike terms tomorrow evening. Don't worry. It's going to happen.'

Joe looks at me again. 'You buy that, Nicole?'

I can't lie to Joe. But I can't contradict Carl either. 'It looks like there's a price he may be willing to settle for.'

'Which will involve a substantial financial commitment by Venstrom,' Carl goes on. 'And I've got to tell you, Joe, we have to be sure you can deliver before we make that commitment.'

'Deliver?' Joe looks bemused by Carl's choice of word.

'I need to see you hold your own against the computer with my own eyes.'

'You think I'm faking it?'

'The people who matter need to be certain you're the genuine article.'

Joe shakes his head. 'Incredible.'

'I'm sure you understand our position.'

'Yeah.' Joe glances at me. He isn't angry. He almost seems to pity me. 'I understand.' He's still looking at me. 'Nicole, could the . . . "accident" . . . really just be a negotiating ploy?'

'Maybe.'

He shakes his head. 'I can't take the risk. Not after what's happened to Mum.'

'But the police will be able to prove one way or the

other whether it really was an accident or not,' says Carl. 'If it was, you'll be happy to go with us, right?'

Joe shrugs. 'I guess.'

'Then what do you lose by giving us a . . . demonstration of your abilities?'

Joe frowns at him. 'What exactly do you want me to do?'

'Play an upgraded version of *gridforest* I've got on my laptop. Nicole and I will be in the room with you. And the game will be viewed by our specialists in Palo Alto.'

'Maybe you've upgraded it beyond my ability level.'

'I seriously doubt that.'

'But if I flunk it, the deal's off?'

'Well . . .'

Joe smiles. He seems amused by Carl's presumptuousness. There's an arrogance buried beneath his diffidence. The arrogance of someone who knows what he's truly capable of. 'When?' he asks simply.

'California's eight hours behind. Tomorrow afternoon would be good. That'll give me time to set it up with them. Let's say two o'clock. Don't worry. They won't mind starting early.'

'Two suits me.'

'Good.'

'Come to Tideways. We'll do it there.'

I suddenly realize Joe is relieved. We've given him back control. Go is his element. He can't think his way out of the position we've put him in with Vogler. But maybe he can play his way out.

'Sounds like it'll be interesting,' he says with the ghost of a smile.

Carl seems pleased with himself when we leave and it's very obvious why. He's well on his way, as he sees it, to sorting out the mess. I say as little as possible. I'm angry as well as confused. Carl can't be handling this better than me. Yet apparently he is. Something's definitely wrong. But I can't figure out what it is.

News from Ursula would make me feel better. But all I get, when I stop at Tideways and go in to tell Hazel I won't be staying there that night – mercifully persuading Carl to wait in the car – is news *of* her.

'Miss Kendall's left. Short notice. I know. Liz wouldn't be pleased.'

'*Left?*'

'Called back to head office in London, so she said.'

I'm so dumbstruck I can see Hazel wondering what there is between Ursula and me. I say no more and make an exit, pausing out by the front gate to phone Ursula. But I just get voicemail. I leave a message – 'Call me' – then head for the car.

'Cheer up, Nicole,' Carl greets me. 'Everything seems to be panning out just perfectly.'

I manage a stiff smile and keep my thoughts to myself.

Carl chatters about office goings-on while we drive out of Falmouth. Fortunately, he doesn't seem to require much of a contribution to the conversation from me. My mind whirls round the ifs and maybes of the situation to no avail.

I feel a surge of relief when Ursula actually does call back. We're waiting in the queue for the King Harry ferry when it happens. With a quick 'I've got to take this' to Carl, I jump out of the car and move a safe distance away.

'What's happening, Ursula? I've just been to Tideways.'

'Ah. You know I've had to go back to London, then. I'm in transit as we speak.'

'But what about—'

'Let's not get into specifics on the phone, Nicole. Suffice to say I'm going to submit the results we got for evaluation. Hence my trip.'

'There *were* results, then?'

'I can't say any more. Just sit tight and I'll be in touch.'

'But how long—'

'As soon as possible. You can rely on that. We both have an interest in moving this forward without delay.'

'Yeah. But I'm the one stuck—'

'Sorry. Got to go. Speak soon.'

She's gone.

I hurry back to the car. The ferry's in and the first vehicles are driving past us.

'Thought I might have to take the wheel myself,' Carl complains.

'I'm here now.'

'Physically, yeah.' He taps me on the temple, which I find incredibly annoying. 'We could do with your brain coming to the party as well, though. Who was that you were gassing to?'

'No one,' I murmur in reply as I start the car.

'Seemed urgent.'

'Well, it wasn't. So that's all right, isn't it?'

Carl makes a face at me. 'If you say so.'

The evening isn't much fun, to put it mildly. It's close to torture, in fact. Carl's full of optimistic predictions about what Joe's going to do for Venstrom and hence for our careers. More specifically, *his* career.

We both end up drinking too much before, during *and* after dinner, though for different reasons. I slip out of the hotel after telling Carl I'm off to bed and walk along by the harbour. I wonder if Vogler really is going to do a deal. He frightens me almost as much as he angers me. But has Carl actually managed to read him better than I have? And why did Ursula leave town so abruptly? Something isn't right.

I walk as far as the stretch of Lower Castle Road where I first spotted Joe on Monday. I can see the house lights of Admiral's Reach above me through the undergrowth. I go up the steps Joe came down that morning. The shadows are inkily black at the top. I tread carefully as I follow a path to the left.

I nearly collide with a gate, find the latch by feel and press it gingerly down. It opens to my push.

The path continues on the other side. There's light ahead, flooding down across a sloping lawn.

I linger in the overhang of some bushes, careful not to step into the light. The house is above me, lights blazing in virtually every room, most of them uncurtained. But I can't see anyone.

Then a figure does move. A door slides open and Marianne walks out on to the decked balcony. She's sloppily dressed in loose trousers and a fleece and she's carrying a tumbler in one hand. She leans on the railings and looks down towards me. She takes a deep swallow from the tumbler. I hear ice clink against the glass. Then she arches her neck and stares up into the darkness of the sky.

There's a shout from inside the house. Her name, I think. She glances behind her. Then she drains the tumbler and throws it down on to the terrace below the balcony, where it smashes explosively, making me jump with surprise.

There's another shout from inside the house. She tosses her head and walks back in.

I stay for another few minutes. But nothing else happens. The show's over.

It looks like I'm not the only one angry with Conrad Vogler.

Friday October 11

THE FIRST THING I SEE, WHEN I LOOK OUT OF THE WINDOW OF my room, is Carl in jogging kit, stretching his thigh muscles on a bench a little way up the road that leads out of the village. He's already just about completed his morning exercise programme, while I feel fuzzy-headed and stiff-limbed, unable to think about much beyond strong black coffee.

But Carl has no intention of letting me ease into the day. About twenty minutes later, while I'm still drying my hair after a shower, the phone rings. It's Carl, calling from his room.

'You up for breakfast, Nicole?'

'Go ahead without me.'

'OK. But here's a heads up. I had a Skype conference with Bruno last night.' Bruno Feltz – Venstrom's head of technical operations. Carl Skyped him last night? After all that beer, wine and brandy? Amazing. And why, anyway? As far as I know, he spoke to someone in Bruno's department setting everything up earlier in the evening. 'We're definitely on for two o'clock this afternoon. It's all set.'

'Great.'

'You could sound more enthusiastic.'

'I'm really looking forward to it, Carl.'

'Good. Because I'll need you to be on top form for that *and* our dinner with the Voglers. They're picking us up at seven. Got anything glam you can put on?'

'It won't come down to how I'm dressed.'

'How long does a game of Go actually last?' The question, popping into his head, mercifully distracts him from the subject of what I'm going to wear.

'Joe normally wraps up his online games within a couple of hours.'

'As long as that?' He sounds as if he was hoping for a lot less. 'He'll win, though, won't he?'

'I don't know. Besides, it's not the result that matters. It's how he measures up.'

'He'd better be as good as we think he is.'

'It's the computer that says he's good, not us.'

'This is a big day, Nicole. You do appreciate that, don't you?'

'Stop worrying, Carl. Everything's going to be fine.'

I say it to get him off the line. As for believing it . . .

I haven't a clue what's going to happen today.

It's not until I go down to breakfast an hour or so later that I realize the *Dymas* is no longer anchored off Castle Point. It's gone, vanished like some kind of mirage. And with it, presumably, Andreas Kremer. Whatever needed to be settled between him and Vogler has been.

Why that should worry me as much as it does I'm not sure. It feels, I suppose, like yet another piece in the puzzle I don't understand. More disturbing in its way is the sensation I have that I may be no more than a piece in the puzzle myself, moved and manipulated by others for reasons I can't begin to comprehend.

We reach Falmouth at midday and have a long but light working lunch at the Greenbank Hotel. Carl's on edge, cautioning me to be on the look-out for signs that Joe's trying to rig the game. How I'd spot any such signs he doesn't explain. But, since I'm certain Joe won't try to rig anything, I just nod obligingly to shut him up.

We walk over to Tideways half an hour before the game's due to begin. Hazel's there, cheered by a recent telephone conversation with Liz – 'She sounded well and said she was feeling pretty good considering' – but Joe hasn't arrived yet. He's told her he's using the dining room this afternoon, though, which sounds promising. Carl and I settle ourselves in there and wait. Carl establishes the link with Bruno's team in Palo Alto. There's a run-through of how the computer's moves will display themselves on the screen. Then they wait too.

Joe ambles in with only about five minutes to spare, running his fingers through his hair and looking ridiculously relaxed. I say how pleased I am to hear Liz is doing well and he gives me a distant smile. 'She's doing OK, yeah.' He sounds different from how he normally does. He sounds as if he's speaking to me from some place far away.

Carl starts outlining how we'll proceed, but Joe cuts him short. 'We'll play this out on a proper board if it's all the same to you.' Or even if it isn't, his tone implies. 'I've brought Rog along to move for the computer.'

As if on cue, Roger Lam walks in, carrying a briefcase. He takes out a folded Go board, two pots of stones and a special timer clock. He sets them down on one of the tables and unfolds the board. I introduce him to Carl, who looks put out by this unexpected turn of events.

'Don't worry,' says Roger. 'Joe's explained the situation to me. I'm just going to make sure we stick to the rules and get a legitimate result.'

'What are you implying?' Carl responds snappishly.

'Nothing at all. But I understand you want to see Joe play a *physical* game of Go. Isn't that right?'

'Yeah, but—'

'Well, here we are, then.'

'Do you know what's at stake ... Roger?' Carl asks suspiciously.

'I think so.' Roger glances at me. 'I was quite surprised when Joe told me about Venstrom's interest in his talents, but I was more than happy to help him out this afternoon. In fact, I'll be fascinated to see what happens. You too, I imagine, Nicole.'

I give him a rueful smile. 'I'm sorry I couldn't be completely frank with you, Roger.'

'Is there a problem your end, Carl?' Bruno cuts in on the computer audio. *'We're past time for commencement.'*

'No, there's no problem,' Carl responds in a fluster.

'We're happy for Joe to play Black.'

Joe smiles. 'I'm happy for *gridforest* to play Black.'

Carl gapes around helplessly. 'What's the difference?'

'Black has the advantage of playing first,' says Roger. 'Compensated for under Chinese rules with a komi of seven and a half points or six and a half under Japanese rules. Chinese rules suit us. Which suits *gridforest*?'

'Whatever,' says Bruno, sounding impatient.

'OK. Chinese rules it is. And a time limit of two hours. Agreed?'

'Agreed.'

Roger sits down at the table, positions the bowls of stones and the clock and carefully squares up the board.

Joe sits opposite him. He leans back and pushes his hair clear of his forehead. He lets out a long, slow breath. 'OK,' he says softly.

'Are we good to go?' asks Bruno.

Roger looks enquiringly at Joe. Joe nods. 'Yes,' says Roger. Then he smiles. He at least, it seems, is enjoying himself. 'Let battle commence.'

The computer stands on a table next to the one at which Joe and Roger are sitting. Its screen is angled so both Roger and Joe can see it, though Joe appears to pay it no attention whatsoever. He concentrates on the board and, for substantial stretches of time, the ceiling above his head, bending his long neck back to gaze upwards. Roger moves twice as Black – once on the board, once on the screen – and once as White, on the screen only.

The clock is actually two clocks in a single case, each controlled by a push button. After *gridforest* moves, Roger presses the button on his side, stopping his clock and starting Joe's. After Joe moves, he presses the button on his side. And so on.

The game begins in a strange kind of semi-religious hush. Carl and I just sit and watch. Joe says nothing. Neither does Roger. Joe and *gridforest* start by occupying two corners of the board each. Then two of the corners start to be filled in. Neither player seems to hurry or hesitate. The pattern's lost on Carl and me, of course. It might be orthodox, it might be daringly different. We just don't know. And only a student of Roger's pursed lips and raised eyebrows would be able to deduce what he makes of it.

Play slows after half an hour or so. By now there's a bunching of stones in one corner. I'd love to know what the balance of advantage is, but I can't ask. Joe looks calm and confident. Roger is, well, rapt is the only word, I think. He starts to be slightly more expressive from this point on, though, smiling or shaking his head, often at the same time. But it doesn't seem as if he's impressed by one side's play as against the other.

Carl's having trouble containing himself. He whispers in my ear, 'Who's winning?' and all I can whisper back is, 'Haven't a clue.'

That's not strictly true, of course. The clues are there, in black and white stones, slowly gathering on the board. But we aren't equipped to interpret them.

Suddenly, while *gridforest* is pondering its eightieth or so move, the door opens and Duncan Forrester walks in. He pulls up in surprise when he sees what's happening. Joe looks over his shoulder at him, but I can't see the expression on his face. The expression on Forrester's face is . . . disappointment, I think. 'Excuse me,' he says quietly. Then he turns and slips out of the room.

'*Move,*' Bruno announces impatiently down the line from California. *Gridforest* has moved. But Roger hasn't reacted.

'Sorry,' he apologizes at once. He peers at the screen, then makes the move on the board and re-starts Joe's clock.

Joe looks troubled as he turns back to the board. He mutters something I can't catch.

I don't understand what's occurred between him and Forrester. But something has. I jump up and follow Forrester out into the hall, closing the dining room door carefully behind me.

Forrester's just standing there, staring at a drab framed print of a maritime scene that hangs on the wall. He turns and looks at me. 'It's getting serious, I see,' he says in an undertone.

'Venstrom can open up a whole host of opportunities for Joe, Duncan.'

'I'm sure that's true.'

'But you don't approve?'

'It's got nothing to do with me, has it?'

'Actually, I get the feeling it has.'

'It's Joe's decision.'

'We think he may be a genius – a uniquely talented individual. He could guide a team that transforms the way humans and computers interact. With all the concern there is about AI and what it portends for the future of mankind . . .'

'It'd be a crime to neglect Joe's ability?'

'Yes. I think it would.'

'Well, there are crimes and then there are crimes, aren't there? Liz told me something interesting last night. She crashed on her way back from Asda at Penryn. Crossing the car park with her trolley after leaving the store, she saw someone she recognized. A guy called Frank Scaddan. He worked for her late husband. Tough sort of a character. No stranger to the police. His brother runs a dodgy car repair business. Not your natural mid-afternoon Asda shopper, I'd have said.'

'You think he sabotaged Liz's car?'

'Well, he'd know how to. And working for Charlie Roberts means he worked for Conrad Vogler as well. Maybe he's gone on working for him.'

'Maybe. But that's all supposition, isn't it?'

'It is if that's all you want it to be.' He looks at me for a long moment, then says, 'Forget I mentioned it. I've got to go. I have a lesson at three.'

With that he turns and walks straight out of the front door.

When I go back into the dining room, it's immediately obvious something has changed in Joe's mood. He's wandering around the tables, muttering to himself. Roger looks up at me and shrugs.

'What did the old guy say?' asks Carl.

I shake my head. 'Nothing. He just wanted to let Joe know his mother's doing well.'

'Then what's the problem?'

'Joe can take as long as he likes over any move within the overall time limit,' says Roger.

'Is that what he's doing – deliberating over his next move?'

'How's it looking, Rog?' Joe asks suddenly in mid-wander.

'Is he allowed to ask a question like that?' Carl puts in before Roger can reply. 'Bruno?'

'*Why not? If he can win with a little help from his friend, maybe we'll hire his friend as well.*'

'I can't help Joe win,' says Roger. 'As for how it's looking, not good for White, if I'm honest.'

Joe chuckles. 'Not good as in terminally bad?'

'I certainly don't see any chances for you.'

'Black's shoulder hit at forty-seven was quite something, wasn't it?'

'As it's turned out, yes.'

'But that's all *gridforest* thinks about, Rog. The long term. The whole board. How *everything's* going to turn out.'

'How do you combat that?'

'It computes the best route to victory from every position as it arises. Best meaning most efficient, most certain. But there's never only one route, is there? There are short cuts and work-arounds. Computers are never quite so hot when it comes to those. And besides . . .' Joe's voice tails off.

'Besides what?' Roger prompts.

'Sometimes you can just see more clearly than anyone else. Than any*thing* else.'

'You mean *you* can.'

'It's like I'm . . . above the board . . . looking down. Like I'm watching the stones moving through all the possible variations. Through all the alternative futures flowing from that moment.'

'All of them?'

'All of them that matter.'

'You're jawing away a lot of time, Joe,' puts in Bruno.

Joe leans against the back of his chair and looks down at the board. 'How would you play from here, Rog?'

'Damage limitation. And hope my opponent slips up.'

'Which isn't much of a hope, with this opponent.'

'You don't have to carry on if you don't want to, Joe,' I say, feeling suddenly sorry for him.

'What?' Carl glares at me.

'Well, he doesn't.'

'As per our agreement, he damn well does.'

'And he's going to.' Joe smiles at Carl. 'Relax. Just sit back and watch the fun.' He slides into his chair and pushes his hair back.

He places a white stone on the board almost immediately and then, for the next half an hour or more, he and *gridforest* both keep up a fast pace, the moves

111

following each other in a rhythm of clock presses and stone placements.

Then both sides slow down. Joe thinks more. So does *gridforest* – apparently. During one of *gridforest*'s thinking periods, Roger says to Joe, quietly, almost reflectively, 'I don't understand quite how you've done it, Joe, but you've created some possibilities I've only just noticed. I thought you'd have to attack at the bottom to compensate for your weakness in the centre, but you stuck with the centre and move one twenty-six now looks . . . inspired.'

'Just neat, Rog. Very neat, maybe. I'd have lost the option if I'd waited any longer.'

'But how did you—'

'*Move*,' Bruno cuts in.

'Sorry.'

They continue in silence. The stones are arrayed across the board in clumps and lines and zigzags now. I get the feeling we're at the crisis of the game, though I couldn't tell you how or why or even where on the board the vital manoeuvre is likely to occur.

Move 204. Joe makes it, positioning his white stone on the board with his long, slender fingers. Then he smiles and stands up. 'That'll do it,' he says, as if stating the blindingly obvious.

'Double sente,' murmurs Roger appreciatively. 'And you're not going to take the ko, are you?'

'Why should I?'

Roger smiles. 'Why indeed?'

'I need some air.'

I'm not sure whether Joe actually means he's going outside, but that turns out to be just what he has in mind. He leaves the room without a backward glance.

Carl stares after him. 'Where the hell is he going?'

'You heard him,' says Roger. 'He needs some air.'

'Is he coming back?'

'I don't think so.'

'What's going on? Has he conceded the game?'

'Technically, maybe. But actually . . .'

'Yeah? Actually what?'

'*Gridforest* can't catch him. He's closed off the upper right. The score's about even on the board, but there's no way Black can pay the komi.'

'What the fuck does that mean?'

'It means Joe's got the better of your computer.'

'Looks like his friend's right according to our provisional analysis,' puts in Bruno.

'He could have stayed and forced a resignation,' says Roger wonderingly. 'Why didn't he?'

'How big a deal is this?' asks Carl, though surely he must realize it's as big as it gets. Maybe he's just in shock. I know I am.

'We didn't hold gridforest back, Carl,' says Bruno. *'The machine gave it everything.'*

'Then . . .'

'What we've seen shouldn't be possible.'

'But it is.' The words come slowly out of my mouth.

'Amazing.' Roger shakes his head in disbelief. 'That is just . . . quite simply . . . unbelievable.' He stands up and steps back from the table. Then he pulls out his phone and takes a photograph of the board.

'How did this happen, Bruno?' Carl asks, clearly bewildered. We hoped Joe would win, of course. We might even have expected him to. But, now he has, we can't absorb the reality of it.

'*Gridforest's algorithm is solid gold, Carl. Its predictive powers are way beyond human reach. It could play the Go world champion a hundred times and win one hundred to zero.'*

'But we just saw it lose.'

'So we did.'

'How do you explain that?'

'I don't. I mean, we'll check for glitches, but there's no way it's down to a technical problem this end.'

'Then what is it down to?'

'Some kind of billion to one quirk in the way Joe's brain works would be my guess.'

'How much has the *gridforest* program cost to develop?' Roger cuts in.

'That's confidential,' Bruno replies.

'North of twenty million dollars?'

'Like I—'

'Never mind. A lot, I assume we can agree. One hell of a lot. And all that algorithmic power you bought couldn't win this one game against Joe Roberts sitting in his mother's guesthouse in Falmouth.'

'Well, it kinda . . . looks that way.'

'So, it all changes here, doesn't it?'

'What d'you mean?' asks Carl. But I think I know what Roger means.

'Joe's life. It's about to be turned upside down.'

'Kind of, I suppose. But in a good way. He's going to be famous. And extremely rich.'

'Famous. And extremely rich. I suppose that says it all.' Roger starts clearing the board, loading the stones back into their pots.

'Shouldn't you go after Joe, Carl?' asks Bruno. *'He's just become a very precious commodity. We don't need to see any more from this end.'*

114

'Yeah. Of course.' Carl looks at me in sudden panic. 'We need to find him.'

Carl is almost running as he leaves the room. Roger smiles sympathetically at me as I hurry after him.

Carl reaches the street way ahead of me and, glancing to his right, evidently catches sight of Joe, because he heads off at a jog.

When I make it out through the front gate, I can see Joe ambling in the distance, with Carl closing on him.

'Not exactly playing it cool, is he?' says Roger, walking out from the house behind me, briefcase in hand.

'There's a lot riding on this.'

'You can say that again. Though whether for Venstrom Computers . . .'

'What do you mean?'

'Shall we go after them?'

'Yeah.' We start walking, fast but not as fast as Carl's moving. He's at Joe's shoulder now. Joe stops and turns to face him.

'Joe's ability marks him out from the rest of humanity, Nicole. I doubt Venstrom will be allowed to cordon him off as some kind of corporate commodity.'

'Won't that be up to Joe?'

'I'm not sure very much about Joe's future will be up to Joe.'

'That sounds awful.'

'Maybe he should have thrown the game.'

'But he didn't.'

'No. And now he has to live with the consequences. He'll need help. Are you going to give it to him?'

'I'll try.'

'Well, that's more than Carl will, I'm sure.'

'I'm sorry about him.'

'He is a prick, isn't he?'

I smile. 'I'm afraid so.'

We draw level with Carl and Joe. Carl's talking rapidly, gabbling through some encomium to the wonders of Venstrom's Palo Alto campus and the facilities Joe will have the run of. Joe's smoking one of his roll-ups and gazing in puzzlement at Carl, as if he can't quite understand the words he's hearing.

'That was a wonderful thing you did back there, Joe,' Roger cuts in.

'Go's just a game, Rog,' Joe replies with a self-deprecating shrug.

'It's a game that's going to open up a world of opportunities for you.'

'So Carl's just been telling me – I think.'

'We should get some kind of preliminary engagement agreement hammered out for you as soon as we can, Joe,' says Carl.

'I thought you had to speak to Con first.'

'We'll square him tonight. Then there'll be nothing to hold us up.'

'Why the rush?' Roger enquires disingenuously. We all know why, of course.

Carl rounds on him. 'What's it to you?'

'Look, I'm just wondering if Joe shouldn't take advice before getting into bed with you guys.'

'It's OK, Rog,' says Joe emolliently. 'We can get together tomorrow if that's what you want, Carl.'

Carl beams. 'That'd be great.'

'Want to come to my flat?' says Roger. Carl's beam fades.

'Yeah,' says Joe. 'That'd be cool. You can make sure I don't sign anything I shouldn't then. Zip's not working tomorrow, so she could be there too. And maybe . . . Well, we'll see.' Does he have it in mind to invite someone else? I'm not sure. But, if so, I wonder who that might be. 'How about eleven o'clock?'

Carl nods in instant agreement. He's obviously decided objecting to Roger's presence may antagonize Joe. And he wants to avoid that at all costs. 'Eleven will be fine.'

'Fifty-two Wood Lane,' says Roger. 'Apartment two.'

I smile at Roger, wanting to make it clear I'm more than happy for him to host the meeting – and look out for Joe's interests. 'We'll be there.'

'OK,' says Roger. He takes a deep breath, as if still shocked by what he's seen his young friend is capable of. 'Well, any chance I can buy you a drink, Joe? I certainly need one. And you deserve one.'

'Only if we go via Bean Feast.'

'No problem.'

They head off down the hill into the centre of town then, leaving Carl and me to walk back to Tideways and collect his laptop. He's much less talkative now, perhaps sensing I don't necessarily approve of the hard sell he's given Joe.

'Maybe we should give him more time to think his priorities through,' I venture.

'And maybe you should join the Samaritans or something.'

'I'm sorry?'

'We need to sign Joe up, Nicole. Without delay. And certainly without agonizing over his state of mind. All that matters is what that mind of his can do for us. For the future of our company. You saw what I saw. He's a

117

fucking phenomenon. And he has to be *our* fucking phenomenon.'

'We won't be driving a hard bargain with Vogler, then?'

'What do *you* think?'

And that's all the answer I get.

Until, an hour later, we're sitting on the King Harry ferry, rumbling across the Fal on our way back to St Mawes and our dinner date with the Voglers.

'Change of plan, Nicole,' Carl says suddenly, breaking a lengthy silence. 'I'll see the Voglers on my own. You can sit this out.'

'Why?'

'I don't want you bringing a negative attitude to the discussion.'

'Negative attitude? I don't know what—'

'I can't trust you to toe the party line, Nicole. It's as simple as that.'

'That's ridiculous.'

'This has to be handled right. And you've mishandled Vogler every step of the way. So, I don't want you there. Got it?'

'Vogler will be expecting me.'

'All he cares about is the bottom line. Venting about Joe's delicate sensibilities will just get in the way.'

'I have no intention of *venting* about anything.'

'Good. But you're still not coming. And Vogler will get over your absence in double quick time when I start offering him serious money. I promise you that.'

'Listen, Carl, I—'

'No, you listen. I'm here to do a job. And I'll do it a whole lot better without you around. Got it?'

*

118

Carl's a fully paid up shit. He wants all of this for himself now he realizes just how big it's going to be. I know exactly how his tiny mind is working.

He doesn't know how my mind's working, though. Being told I don't have to sit down to dinner with the Voglers isn't exactly catastrophic news from my point of view. I was worried about how I was going to handle Conrad Vogler. And how he was going to handle me. I have no idea what Ursula got from the bug I planted on him or whether he found it. I haven't given Carl the slightest inkling of what Ursula told me about Vogler's organized crime connections, which means I know – but Carl doesn't – that Vogler has more to lose by letting Joe go than Carl can possibly imagine.

In the end, though, Vogler surely can't stop Joe's talents being exploited by the wider world. They're just too extraordinary for some kind of accommodation not to be reached. In many ways, Venstrom Computers isn't so very different from the Clearing House. They're both in business to solve problems.

Besides, if Ursula can nail Vogler, I'll have the last laugh on Carl by sparing Venstrom the expense of any deal he strikes. Then I'll be the one smelling of roses.

Maybe it's all going to turn out well for me after all.

I keep hoping for news from Ursula, but she doesn't call. The afternoon fades into evening. I stay out of the way when seven o'clock comes round and see nothing of Carl's departure with the Voglers. I'm left to guess how they'll react to news of my absence.

But a phone call to my room about half an hour after Carl was due to be collected sheds a different light on what's happened. Marianne Vogler is on the line.

'Con spoke to Carl earlier and heard you wouldn't be joining us this evening, Nicole. He decided in that case it should just be two boys together. I think he was afraid I might cramp their style. And that would never do, would it? Anyhow, I'm here at Admiral's Reach with the ingredients for a tasty supper and the run of the wine cellar, so . . . why don't you join me?'

This I certainly didn't expect. And for the moment I've no idea how to respond.

'Actually,' Marianne continues, 'I'm glad we've got the chance to meet. Y'know, just the two of us. I know you understand the difficulties losing Joe will cause us and I have a proposition I want to try out on you before I put it to Con. Or to Carl, come to that. Sometimes women just see through problems more clearly than men, don't they? Well, that's my experience. So, why don't we get together? Plus we can drink some seriously good wine. What d'you say?'

What I find myself saying is yes. I know it's safer to stay well away from Marianne Vogler. But something about her proposition is just too tempting to resist. Outflanking Carl would be seriously satisfying. Maybe Marianne and I really can come to a better arrangement than anything he and her husband can cook up. I've got to find out what she has in mind.

I'm at Admiral's Reach half an hour later. There's soft music playing. The rooms are delicately lit. Marianne is quite plainly but elegantly dressed in a black top and trousers. She obviously doesn't think anything tight or revealing is worth bothering with for female company.

She seemed half drunk when I last saw her, but though

she's wafting about with a glass of white wine in her hand she comes across now as sober and focused. We go into the kitchen. There's a puzzling lack of any obvious sign of a meal being prepared, but I suppose there'll be something to eat in due course. I join her in a glass of wine and we sit down at a large table, where there's a laptop open with papers scattered around it. The papers look like invoices and balance sheets, but I can't be seen paying them much attention.

'When Con said you were opting out this evening,' Marianne says after we've clinked glasses, 'I was afraid you were ill. But you look fine.'

'I am.'

'Sidelined by Carl, then? I mean, I've never met the guy, but I bet he wants to take all the credit for whatever deal we do with Venstrom.'

I smile. 'Something like that.'

'Yeah. That's men for you.'

'Your husband excepted, presumably.'

'Oh, no. If Con had his way, I'd do nothing but cook his meals and pander to his sexual whims. Just a pity I have a better head for money than he does.'

'Is that what your proposition's about, Marianne? Money?'

'Every proposition in this world is about money, Nicole. Or sex. Or both. But, yes, this one is just about money.'

'Venstrom are willing to compensate you very generously.'

'I'm sure they are. But how much do you know about what exactly you'd be compensating us *for*?'

'Well, the loss of Joe's services as a stocks analyst.'

'Just that? It sounds so ordinary.'

'I'm sure he's very good at it.'

121

'Oh, he is. And we need him to be. As I think you're well aware.'

'I don't quite know what you mean.'

'Come on, Nicole. Let's be honest. You decided to play dirty, didn't you? By planting a bug on Con yesterday morning you took this to a whole new level.'

Shit. This isn't how I saw this going. She knows. *They* know. I frown as genuinely as I can manage. 'I've no idea what you're talking about, Marianne. A bug?'

'It means you – or whoever was listening in – knows what was said in the meeting Con was on his way to when you met him. I suppose that makes you think you can blackmail us into letting you have Joe for free. Definitely a good deal for Venstrom. But a bad deal for us. Very bad.'

'This is all . . .'

'What? A misunderstanding? Don't waste your breath denying it. No one else could have planted it. No one else had any reason to.'

'I planted nothing.'

'You plan to stick to that line?'

'It's the truth. You can believe it or not as you please. Now, I think I'll be going.'

I stand up. Suddenly, I'm aware of being slightly unsteady on my feet. But, still, I don't believe there's anything Marianne can do to stop me leaving. I'm anxious, but not yet frightened.

Then I see a man standing in the kitchen doorway. He's squarely built and muscular, dressed in jeans and a leather biker's jacket. He has close-cropped greying hair, a raw-boned face and cold blue-grey eyes that are studying me intently. He's chewing gum with a slow methodical rhythm of the jaw.

'Sit down, Nicole,' says Marianne.

The man takes a couple of steps towards me. He goes on staring at me.

I get the feeling refusal would be a serious mistake. I lower myself back into the chair.

'Frank's going to stay with us while we talk this through, Nicole,' says Marianne, topping up her wine glass. *Frank*. It has to be Frank Scaddan, the guy Forrester told me about. Shit, shit, shit. 'And you're going to answer my questions. If not, Frank will force you to. Don't make him do that. Please. I don't enjoy that kind of thing. He does. But I don't. And you certainly won't. OK?'

I glance round at Scaddan. Marianne's not bluffing. I tell myself how stupid I've been to return to this house after what happened last time. But here I am. With no good options. 'OK,' I murmur.

'Let's start with Joe. Why do Venstrom want him so badly?'

'He's a games-playing genius. He can help us revolutionize our computer gaming programs.'

'So, this is just about making money out of online gaming?'

'Well, there's lots to be made.'

'How do you know he's a genius?'

'He's proved it.'

'How?'

'He, er . . .'

Marianne nods faintly to Scaddan, who steps still closer and lays one hand heavily on the crown of my head. The downward pressure is bearable – for now. *'How?'*

'He beat our best computer program in a demonstration game of Go this afternoon.'

'So?'

'That shouldn't be possible.'

'But he did it?'

'Yes.'

'How many other people could do that?'

'No one we know of.'

'The world Go champion, maybe?'

'Not even him.'

'How did Joe do it?'

'We don't know. He just . . . did.'

'Like he just makes money for us out of companies we've never heard of on the other side of the world.'

'I guess.'

'How unusual does that make him?'

'Unique. A one-off. A phenomenon.'

'So everyone will want a piece of him.'

'I suppose they will.'

'But they'll have to go through Venstrom to get that piece. And they'll have to pay for it. They'll have to pay big.'

I nod awkwardly. The weight of Scaddan's hand makes it difficult actually to move my head. 'Yes.'

'And you're greedy. You don't want to share any of that with us. So you decide to dig up some dirt on us – on our business – so you can freeze us out.'

'Your husband didn't leave us much alternative.'

'Have you heard the recording, Nicole?'

'No.'

Another nod. And Scaddan pulls my head back so far I actually think my spine's going to snap. I cry out. And he stops. But he holds my head where it is, leaving me looking up into his ice-blue eyes.

'I haven't heard the recording,' I gasp.

'Sure?'

'*I haven't heard it.*'

'Has Carl?'

'No.'

'Someone higher up the Venstrom food chain, then?'

'No one at Venstrom.'

'That doesn't make any sense, Nicole. Who's got the recording?'

I don't want to betray Ursula to these people. But I think I may have to.

Scaddan relaxes his grip and I'm able to raise my head and look at Marianne again. For the moment, I just don't know what to say – what I *can* say – that will get me out of this situation.

Suddenly, Scaddan loops something round my neck and draws it tight against my windpipe. I choke and raise my hand to try to release it. It's a thin leather strap. But I can't prise my fingers beneath it.

'Stop struggling and answer the question, Nicole,' says Marianne, staring straight at me. 'Who's got the recording?'

I choke again. Scaddan loosens the strap by just enough to let me speak. When I do, my voice is hoarse and cracking. 'HMRC,' I manage to say.

'*What?*'

'HMRC. The tax authorities.'

Marianne looks as if I couldn't have told her anything worse. 'Fuck,' she says quietly.

'Ursula Kendall,' says Scaddan. It's the first time he's actually spoken. His voice is flat and hard. 'The woman staying at Tideways.'

'Ursula Kendall has the recording.' Marianne looks enquiringly at me. 'Is that right, Nicole?'

'Yes.'

'She left town yesterday,' says Scaddan.

Marianne takes a deep swallow of wine and glances away for a moment. Then she sighs and returns her gaze to me. 'You put the taxman on our tail, Nicole? Is that what you did?'

'She was already investigating you. The bug was her idea. But . . .'

'It suited you to help her gather evidence against us?'

'Yes.'

'And now she's scuttled back to London with it and dealing with Venstrom is basically irrelevant because we're going to have the Fraud Squad banging on our door.'

'Not necessarily. I mean . . .'

'It depends what's on the recording. Is that what you mean? Well, enough is the answer. More than enough for Ms Kendall's purposes.'

'I can't—'

'Help us out of the mess you've landed us in?' Marianne shakes her head sadly. 'No, I'm sure you can't. And this means—' She breaks off. 'I told you we might end up in a situation like this, Frank. Well, here we are. Remember what I said we'd have to do about it?'

'I remember,' says Scaddan.

'Take her to the cupboard in the hall.'

Scaddan jerks me up from the chair. I'm forced to stand simply in order to avoid being strangled. And I'm well aware that he's quite strong enough to choke me to death if he wants to. Or if Marianne tells him to.

'Move,' is all he says, the word rasped in my ear.

We set off out of the kitchen into the hall. I have to walk rapidly to avoid being bowled over. Our route leads

126

ultimately to the front door. But we're not going to reach the front door. There's a closed door ahead on our left. Marianne overtakes us and opens it.

Scaddan pushes me into a narrow, shelved space and whips the strap away from round my neck. I glimpse mops, cloths, brushes, a vacuum cleaner, a pile of old newspapers and stacks of spare light bulbs. Then the door slams behind me and I hear a key turn in the lock.

I'm in the dark. It's not completely dark, though. There's light seeping under the door. 'You can't keep me here,' I shout. But they can, of course. They very much can.

'Shut up,' Marianne shouts back. 'Our cleaner will let you out in the morning. I don't want to hear any more from you. If I do, I'll get Frank to tie you up and tape your mouth shut. OK?'

I'm terrified *and* ashamed. I'm trapped and I'm helpless and it's my own stupid fault, which only makes it worse. How did I allow this to happen? It doesn't really matter. I'm here. And Marianne is calling the shots. So, I say nothing.

Neither does Marianne, other than something to Scaddan I don't catch. They move away. I hear footsteps heading in different directions. The front door opens and closes. But there's still someone – Marianne, I assume – in the house. There are muffled movements at some distance. I strain my ears, but I can't make out anything distinctly.

Long periods of silence follow, when my own breathing and heartbeat are all I hear, broken by occasional sounds from some way off. Then the light goes out in the hall and the darkness is total. I hear the front door open and close again, followed by the beeps of an alarm. They've both gone now. I'm alone.

I try to force the door open, but it's solidly constructed. All I get for my efforts is a bruised shoulder.

Looking into the keyhole, I can see the key is still in the lock. Feeling around on one of the shelves, I find a roll of fuse wire. I slide a sheet of newspaper under the door, then fashion the wire into something I can push into the hole to dislodge the key, hoping it'll fall on to the paper, though even then I'm pretty sure I won't be able to pull it back under the door, which is very nearly flush with the floor.

Not that it matters. The fuse wire, even wound round on itself, isn't stiff enough. The key stays exactly where it is.

I can only guess what the time is. My phone's in my handbag. And my handbag's in the kitchen. At least, it *was* in the kitchen. I slump down on the floor of the cupboard, push the vacuum cleaner to one side and lean my head back against the wall. There's nothing I can do. Absolutely nothing. It's a bleakly comforting thought. The cleaner will come in the morning and let me out. All I have to do is wait.

Then the thought occurs to me that Marianne may only have said what she needed to in order to shut me up. Maybe she'll cancel the cleaner's visit. And tomorrow's Saturday, so maybe the cleaner isn't due to come anyway. Besides, Marianne may intend to return before then. I don't know where she and Scaddan have gone or why. I don't know what her plan is. But she has one. And I don't.

Pummel my brain as much as I like, there's not a single thing I can do.

Except wait.

*

I must have fallen asleep. My neck aches when I jolt awake. There was a noise. Breaking glass, maybe? I can't be sure I didn't dream it.

Then the alarm starts to beep. Someone's moving. I hear soft, hurrying footsteps. The light of a torchbeam flashes past the door. The alarm goes on beeping. It can't be Marianne. She would have switched on a light and deactivated the alarm by now. Then who?

Suddenly, the alarm bell starts ringing. Loudly.

And just as suddenly, it stops.

A minute or so passes. Then the torchbeam's back. It comes to rest on the newspaper I slid under the door earlier. Whoever the intruder is, they're very close by.

I have to take this chance in case I don't get another. I scramble to my feet. 'Hello?' I call.

There's no answer. There's no sound from the other side of the door at all.

'Hello?'

Still nothing.

'Please. Let me out.'

Then the torchbeam moves away. I rattle the handle and thump on the door. But the beam doesn't return.

Has the intruder gone? I don't think so. I can't hear anything, but I sense there's someone in the house. Minutes slowly pass. Maybe half an hour in the end. I try a few more thumps on the door. Nothing happens.

Eventually, I sit back down on the floor. I start to wonder who the intruder can be. What's brought them here? It's too much of a coincidence to believe this is a standard burglary. If it is, how were they able to turn the alarm off? Do I know them? Have they recognized my voice?

There's no flash of the torchbeam to warn me when it

happens. The key turns in the lock. That's all I hear. A click of the lock being released. Nothing else.

I jump up, turn the handle and fling the door open.

I see nothing. There's a sound, far off in the house. I head for the front door and flick the switch I find on the wall near it.

I'm dazzled at first by the brilliance of the hall lamp. I stand by the front door, heart pounding, breath racing. Slowly, my eyesight adjusts. But there's nothing to see.

My first instinct is to get as far away from Admiral's Reach as I can as quickly as I can. Then I remember my handbag's in the kitchen, with my phone inside. I don't know if it's still there. But I have to find out.

I walk cautiously along to the kitchen, switching on every light as I come to it. I keep expecting to see someone ahead of me. But I don't.

I do see my handbag, though. It's just where I left it, on the chair next to the one I sat in.

I grab the handbag and check for the phone. It's gone. Marianne must have taken it. I left it on, so she'll have access to everything about me. Shit, shit, shit.

But at least I'm out of the cupboard. And she hasn't taken my car key. I loop the handbag over my shoulder and head back along the hall.

I can't stop expecting the intruder to step suddenly into my path. But nothing happens. I reach the door. It opens when I turn the latch.

The night's cool and quiet. It's dark on the driveway. The light from the hall is enough to see my car by, though. I try to ignore the deep shadows beyond and around it. I try to put the intruder out of mind. If they'd meant to harm me, they'd surely have done it inside the house.

I run for the car, pressing the key to open the doors as

I go. I leap in, find the ignition after several fumbles and start up. I hit reverse and pull back across the drive. There's a crunch as the rear wing strikes the wall next to the garage, but I don't care. I swerve round and accelerate up the drive.

Then I'm out on to the road and heading away from Admiral's Reach. Fast.

It's nearly two o'clock when I pull into the village car park. St Mawes is deeply quiet. The air's still and chill. I hurry across to the hotel entrance and find the door locked. I press a button for the night porter, who eventually appears and lets me in.

'Hope you had an enjoyable evening,' he says, which he must assume I've had given the time.

But I've got no energy to spare for idle conversation. 'Is Mr Hinkley back?'

The porter looks surprised when he checks. 'Er, no. No, he isn't actually.'

'I'll be able to make calls from the phone in my room, won't I?'

'Er, yes.' Clearly, the question puzzles him. 'Are you all right? You look, er . . .'

'I'm fine. Thanks for the key.'

I head straight up to my room and call Carl from the bedside phone. No answer. Straight to voicemail. Why isn't he back? Where in God's name is he? I call him again. Same result.

Then I call the Venstrom security helpline – the number's on my company ID card – and cancel all access to my phone. It's off anyway, the guy there tells me. But that only means Marianne's finished delving into my texts, emails and call log. There's a system for tracking the phone, he reminds me, but only if the phone's active. Somehow I don't think it's going to be active again now.

I sit on the bed, surrounded by anonymous hotel furniture and decorations. Should I call the police? It'll be difficult to prove Scaddan assaulted me or Marianne locked me in a cupboard. I haven't got any physical evidence for what happened apart from a red mark round my neck that's probably fading already. I have visions of a deadpan police officer noting down everything I say and believing me less and less with every word I utter.

Where *is* Carl? I realize I don't even know the name of the restaurant Vogler was taking him to. Not that it matters. There isn't going to be anyone there to answer the phone in the middle of the night.

I double-lock the door of the room and put a chair against it, which is crazy, but makes me feel slightly better. I turn on the television, just to break the silence with mindless normality. I lie back on the bed. I try to work out, calmly and logically, what the best thing to do is. But the effort only takes me in a circle.

It's a circle from which there seems to be no exit. My brain isn't working properly. Everything's a fog. Everything's—

Saturday October 12

MORNING LIGHT, SEEPING THROUGH THE CURTAINS, WAKES ME.
I'm still lying on the bed, fully dressed. My neck's sore, my
throat's dry and my head aches. When I look at my watch, I
see it's nearly eight o'clock. I can't believe I've slept so long.

I gulp down some water and call Carl on the bedside
phone. Voicemail again. Then I call reception.

'Is Mr Hinkley back?'

There's a pause. Then: 'No. Er, he doesn't seem to have
come in last night at all.'

'Has he called?'

'Not . . . as far as I know.'

'Can you check?'

'Hold on.' A delay. Voices in the background. Then:
'No. Mr Hinkley hasn't been in touch. Is there a
problem?'

'I don't know.' But actually I do. I'm sure there *is* a
problem. And I'm going to have to do something about it.

I decide I can't think without a shower and some food.
Hot water powering down over me feels good. And I realize how hungry and dehydrated I am as I work my way

133

through apple juice, muesli and bacon and eggs. Breakfast among the other guests, with a watery sun glistening softly on a still blue sea beyond the windows, restores some perspective to my thoughts. But those thoughts still take me nowhere.

Carl and I have an appointment at Roger's flat in Falmouth at eleven o'clock. I wonder, almost in desperation, if Roger or Joe has heard from him. It's possible he's tried to contact me, of course. There may be a simple explanation for his absence from the hotel. And, if he's left a message on my phone, he may believe I know what it is. That doesn't explain his failure to answer his own phone, though. I just don't know what to think.

I have to wait until I'm back in my room before I can call Roger or Joe. Then, when I'm just about to, I realize I don't have their numbers any more. *They're on my phone.* God, I'm lost without it. I can't even phone Kyra on the general office number to see if she's heard anything from Carl because it's Saturday.

So, I call Venstrom Security again and tell them I'm worried about Carl because I haven't heard from him. They *don't* sound worried. But they say they'll try to contact him.

Next I call my mother and my sister Evie. Neither answers, which is a relief, really. I leave messages for them saying my phone's been stolen, but they're not to worry and I'll be in touch with a new number soon. Notifying other people will have to wait.

Then I call Tideways, hoping Joe might be there. But Hazel, who answers, says he isn't. And she doesn't have his number. Or Karen's. She suggests I ask Liz, though she's not sure how easy it is to speak to her at the hospital.

I'm not even going to try. I need to move and be doing something, so I decide to head for Falmouth. But something deters me from driving there, some half-formed fear that Scaddan will follow me and force me off the road somewhere between here and the King Harry ferry. I opt for the passenger ferry instead. There's safety in numbers.

Onboard, everyone else looks relaxed and carefree. I don't feel either. I can't fit what's happening into a pattern I understand. Everything's confused. Nothing's certain.

When the ferry reaches Prince of Wales Pier, I'm first off. I check Bean Feast, but Karen has the day off, just like Joe said. From there I hurry round to Jacob's Ladder and climb the long flight of steps up to Waterloo Road.

As I pant along towards number 13, I see a police car ahead of me, stationary in the middle of the road between the rows of parked vehicles. There are a couple of officers on the pavement. One of them's escorting a man to the car. I suddenly realize it's Joe. He doesn't see me. He looks straight ahead, head bowed.

The policeman checks he doesn't bang his head as he loads him into the back of the car. Then he jumps in the front and they pull away. Another car, parked at the kerbside, with no police markings, pulls out and follows. They turn right at the corner and are out of my sight.

When I reach number 13, I see Karen standing in the gateway that leads to the yard at the back of the house. She's wearing jeans and trainers, but above the waist what looks like a pyjama jacket. She's talking animatedly on her phone. When she spots me, she grimaces.

'I basically don't know what to do,' I hear her say as I approach. She holds up a hand, stalling me. 'Yeah. If you can ... OK ... It's all crazy stuff, but ... Exactly ...

'OK . . . Yeah . . . Anyone you recommend . . . I'll wait to hear . . . OK. 'Bye for now.'

She rings off. Her face is grey and tight with tension. 'What's happened?' is all I can ask.

'Joe's been arrested,' she says numbly.

'Arrested?'

'Well, taken in for questioning. But if he hadn't gone they would've arrested him. The plain clothes guy was very clear about that.'

'On what charge?'

'Dunno exactly. Involvement in tax evasion and money laundering, I think the detective said. It didn't make any sense. It's something to do with Conrad Vogler, though. I do know that. The detective mentioned him.' Karen shakes her head. She looks close to tears. 'Joe should never have worked for that guy. I wanted him to quit. But . . . he enjoyed what Vogler had him doing and . . .'

'He was good at it?'

'This is all to do with you somehow, isn't it?' Anger flares suddenly in her eyes. 'If you hadn't come down here looking for Joe . . .'

'I've been trying to get Joe away from Vogler, Karen. This is the last thing I'd have wanted to happen.'

'Why are you here now, then? How come you turn up just as the police take him away?'

'I came to check if our meeting with Joe this morning was still going ahead.'

'Well, it isn't now, is it?'

'No. Obviously. But—'

'Anyway, why didn't you just phone?'

'My phone's . . . broken. I . . . dropped it in the bath.'

Karen looks at me as if she doesn't believe me. I can't really blame her.

'And I can't seem to contact Carl.'

'Your boss from Venstrom?'

'Yes. That's him.'

'What d'you mean you can't contact him?'

I shrug helplessly. 'Just that.'

'Aren't you staying in the same hotel?'

'He's disappeared, Karen, if you want to know the truth. I've no idea where he is. That's one of the reasons I came here. I thought Joe might have heard from him.'

'No. There's been nothing.' She frowns. 'This is all getting seriously weird. Your boss isn't the only one who's suddenly hard to find. When he realized the police meant to take him in, Joe told me to phone Duncan and get his advice on what to do.'

'Duncan Forrester?'

'Yeah. Joe trusts him. Anyway, Duncan wasn't answering his mobile, so I phoned Tideways. Hazel said he'd gone away for a few days. No idea where or why. And this is a guy who never normally goes anywhere.'

'Who were you speaking to just now?'

'Roger Lam. I reckoned he was the next best bloke to try. He said he'd see what he could find out. Ask some of his uni contacts if they know a solicitor who can get the police to drop all this money laundering crap. I mean, Joe isn't a criminal. They must be able to see that.'

'They're probably just trying to build a case against Vogler.' It's the most optimistic thought that's come to me.

'That's what Rog said. Christ, I hope you're both right. Joe and me were supposed to be visiting Liz this afternoon. What am I going to say to her?'

'Maybe you should wait to hear more from Roger.'

'Wait? You say that like it's easy to do.'

'I know it's not, Karen.' I want to hug her, but I'm afraid

she'll burst into tears. 'Look, why don't I call Roger and see if he and I can make any sense of this?'

'OK. Why not?'

'Can I use your phone?'

'Sure.' She hands it over. 'His number's logged in. I'll go and finish getting dressed.'

She turns and walks through to the rear of the house, heading for her flat. There's an anxious slump to her shoulders I haven't seen before.

I walk out on to the pavement and dial Roger's number. He picks up straight away. 'Sorry, Karen, I haven't—'

'It's not Karen, Roger. This is Nicole. I've borrowed her phone.'

'Nicole? Are you with her? She should have said.'

'I've only just got here. I was in time to see Joe being driven away, but not in time to speak to him.'

'This is a terrible shock for Joe and Karen, obviously, and a serious problem for you and Carl, but—'

'Have you heard from Carl?'

'Me? No. Why . . .'

'I'm having trouble tracking him down.'

'Really? I thought you were staying at the same hotel.'

I can't let myself get sucked into explaining about Carl going missing, so I change tack. 'Apparently you told Karen you thought this might be more about Vogler than Joe.'

'Well, it probably is. Vogler's obviously a crook. In fact . . .'

'What?'

'It's likely the police have already arrested him. Or tried to. They'll need to get on with searching his house before he has a chance to destroy any evidence. With any luck, they just see Joe as their most valuable witness.'

'How can we find out if that's really the way their minds are working?'

'Well, I was thinking of going over to St Mawes and seeing if there's a police presence at the Vogler house. I'm hoping to get a call back from a solicitor who's been recommended to me before too long, but meanwhile I may as well check out the lie of the land over there.' He pauses, then says, 'Want to come along?'

I agree to go with Roger only partly because checking out Admiral's Reach is the most logical thing to do. The other part is all to do with my state of mind. I still don't have any sense of being in control of events and, right now, I reckon it's safer to spend as little time as possible on my own.

When I go up to the flat, I find the door open. Karen's sitting on the edge of the couch, staring into space. She hasn't actually finished dressing, as she said she would. She's still wearing the pyjama top. She nods faintly as I lay her phone on the cushion beside her.

'I have to go, Karen,' I say, feeling bad about leaving her as she is but seeing no alternative.

'It's OK,' she responds in a distant voice.

'Roger's on the track of a good solicitor. There's every chance the police just want to pump Joe for information they can use against Vogler.'

'Hope so.'

'This is going to turn out all right, Karen, I know it is.'

She looks at me with dismal scepticism. 'You don't know any such thing. And neither do I.'

I leave Karen's flat in a hurry. I reckon I've just about got time to buy a basic pay-as-you-go phone before I head for

139

the ferry to meet Roger. On my way towards the top of Jacob's Ladder, though, I see Duncan Forrester's car coming slowly round the corner from the next street. For a moment, I wonder if there's been some misunderstanding and he hasn't left town after all. I step into the road and flag him down.

But, as he pulls in, I see the driver isn't Forrester, though he does look quite like him, only a bit thinner and balder. He winds down the window and frowns at me. 'What's the problem?'

'Sorry. I thought you were Duncan.'

'Are you a pupil of his?'

'No. Just . . . a friend. D'you know where he is?'

'Nah. I'm just covering his lessons for him. He calls me in from time to time. He's out of town. That's all I know.'

'How long for?'

'A few days, he said, maybe longer. Not an easy bloke to pin down, Dunc, if you know what I mean. But the money's useful, so I'm not complaining. Now, I'd better be moving. There's a nervous learner waiting for me round the corner.'

With that, and a leery grin, he drives on.

Roger's waiting for me on the pier. There's something in his smile that radiates confidence. And God knows I need an infusion of that at the moment.

'I've heard from the solicitor,' he announces after kissing me lightly on the cheek. 'Nick Brown. From Truro. He says he'll contact the police right away and have them ask Joe if he's happy to be represented by him on my recommendation. I imagine Joe will agree.'

'Venstrom will cover the cost,' I assure him.

'Thanks. I thought you'd say that. Well, hoped, I suppose.

Now, look, when I sketched out the circumstances for him, Brown's first thought was the same as ours. The police are probably trying to frighten Joe into giving them evidence to use against Vogler. If he does, he'll be in the clear. And there's really no reason why he shouldn't, is there?'

'Misguided loyalty, maybe?'

'Brown should be able to talk him out of that. Meanwhile, what's with Carl? How can you have lost touch with him?'

My answer takes us past the arrival and departure of the ferry. It's chilly out on the water and, positioning ourselves in the bow, under the wheelhouse, we're out of earshot of most of the other passengers. I explain Carl decided to drop me from dinner with the Voglers and I haven't seen or heard from him since. I use the same story to account for the loss of my smartphone as I gave Karen and it comes over more plausibly this time as a goofy accident related to drinking too much over a solitary meal at the hotel.

I'm not exactly sure why I say nothing about my visit to Admiral's Reach last night. I suppose it's mostly because an honest account of what happened there would involve admitting to Roger that I planted a bug on Conrad Vogler to help Ursula Kendall build a tax fraud case against him. I haven't heard a word from Ursula in over twenty-four hours, though it's possible she *has* tried to contact me this morning. She, or her superiors, may have told the police to move in on Vogler, which would have led to Joe being picked up. That would begin to make sense of what's happened to him.

'Why didn't Carl want you at the dinner?' Roger asks as the ferry nears Castle Point.

'He didn't think I was sufficiently committed to persuading Joe to take up our offer.'

'And are you?'

'I suppose it struck me, during the Go match, that Joe's entire world is about to change. And maybe those changes won't be good for him. Maybe living quietly in Falmouth with Karen and playing Go just for fun is the best thing for him. After all, he hasn't made much effort to do anything else.'

'What about the good work he could do for humanity?'

'He's one person. With one life.'

'And one world-changing gift.'

'*World*-changing?'

'Joe's generation is going to have to grapple with the challenge of humankind's relationship with artificial intelligence, Nicole. The vital question is going to be how we manage AI when it surpasses the intelligence of its creators. If there are humans who can continue to compete with computers beyond that point and Joe's one of them, well, don't we have to find out how he does it, whether it can be replicated, whether it can be *taught*?'

'You're saying Joe can't be left alone? That it's not up to him?'

Roger shakes his head. 'Pretty much, yes.'

'You said yesterday you doubted Venstrom would be allowed to monopolize him.'

'I don't think there's a chance they will be.'

'So I may as well give up and go home?'

He smiles. 'Too late for that, I reckon.'

We dock at St Mawes. There's a relaxed, weekend feel about the place in the milky sunshine. Fathers and sons messing about in boats. Family groups wandering along Marine Parade. Drinkers standing outside the Victory Inn. I feel out of synch with the mood. I only wish I didn't.

Roger suggests we drive up to Admiral's Reach. 'Then we can just cruise by and see what's going on.'

That makes sense to me, so we walk over to the car park. As we near my car, I see the damage to the rear wing's worse than I thought. The light's smashed and there's quite a dent in the metalwork.

'How did that happen?' asks Roger.

'Oh, I reversed into a wall. Just wasn't thinking.'

'Well, you've had a lot on your mind.'

There's no denying that. We get in and I head for the exit.

We're most of the way there when Roger asks me to stop. He points to an elderly, well-dressed man climbing out of a big old Jag. 'I ought to have a quick word with him. Retired industrialist. He puts quite a lot of money the university's way. Including the funding for my visiting lectureship. D'you mind?'

It strikes me he'd never have noticed Roger if we'd just driven on by, but I don't argue. I pull in a couple of bays away. Roger jumps out and goes over to the man, who greets him warmly. He looks about seventy, three-piece-suited, tall and lean, bowed at the shoulders, with white hair and craggy features. They both smile a lot as they talk.

The conversation goes on longer than I expected. The old guy opens the boot of his car and shows Roger something I can't see. There are more smiles and a gale of laughter. Then, finally, they're done.

As Roger heads back towards me, the old guy looks past him and gives me a friendly nod, as if to apologize for holding me up.

'Sorry about that,' says Roger as he gets in beside me. 'He goes on a bit.'

143

The old guy's still fussing around in his boot as we drive past. 'What business was he in?' I ask.

'Shipping.' I pull out of the car park and start threading a path through the pedestrians spilling across the road. 'Listen, Nicole, do you know where Duncan Forrester's gone? Karen said he's left town.'

'I don't know any more than that.'

'Strange fellow.'

'Is he?'

'Joe's always spoken well of him, when he's spoken of him at all. I get the feeling they have some kind of father–son relationship. Well, Joe never knew his real father, of course. I've sometimes wondered if . . .' Roger doesn't finish the thought. 'The point is it makes no sense for Duncan Forrester to quit town when Liz is in hospital and Joe needs his help and advice more than at any time in his life.'

'But nevertheless he's gone.'

'Yes he has. Apparently. Did he say anything to you, when you went out to speak to him at Tideways, during the Go match, that would . . . account for it?'

'No.'

'You were gone some time.'

'He told me Liz had seen someone she recognized near her car before she crashed. Someone who might have tampered with it. A man called Scaddan. Frank Scaddan.'

'Never heard of him.'

'Apparently, he used to work for Joe's dad, Charlie Roberts. So he must have worked for Conrad Vogler as well. And Duncan suspects he still does.'

'Making him the saboteur. If there was one.'

'Yes.'

'All the more baffling then that Duncan should swan

off somewhere, leaving Joe at Vogler's mercy. And Scaddan's.'

He's right. It is baffling. Maybe I should tell him now about my ordeal at Admiral's Reach last night. But still I say nothing. I want to trust Roger, I really do. God knows I need to be able to trust someone in this whole tangle of contradictions. But is he the one? I just can't be sure.

We're through the narrowest, most congested part of the village now. I accelerate up the hill, take the bend by the castle and carry on uphill towards Admiral's Reach.

As we reach the house, I slow to a crawl. There's nothing behind me, so I pull over and stop.

'I'll take a look,' says Roger. He jumps out and peers down over the boundary hedge, then signals for me to get out too.

There are two police patrol cars and two other saloon cars parked on the drive. I hear a distant crackle of radio communication. The front door of the house is open. We both dodge back out of sight when a uniformed police officer walks out through the door, heading for one of the cars.

We get back into my car and I drive on. It's as Roger predicted. The police have come for the Voglers as well as Joe. But I strongly suspect they haven't got them.

'So,' says Roger as we head on along Upper Castle Road, 'the Voglers may very well be under arrest.' I don't tell him Marianne for one got out while the going was good. I let him reason away. 'That's if they were at home when the police arrived. We don't know *when* the police arrived, of course, but it was probably around the same time they picked up Joe. D'you think it's faintly possible Vogler got wind of what the police were planning and struck some deal with Carl that involved dashing up to London last night and getting your company's lawyers to give him protection?'

'I think you're overestimating the powers of our lawyers, Roger. And how would that help Joe anyway? He's who we're after. If we can't get him, Vogler's no use to us.'

'OK, OK. That's true. I'm just trying to account for Carl's disappearance. Where did he and Vogler go for dinner?'

'I don't know. Somewhere not far from here with a Michelin star.'

'The Driftwood. Near Portscatho. I've eaten there. It's a hotel as well as a restaurant. Let's go there now and confirm they turned up. Who knows what we might find out?'

I don't argue. Doing something is better than doing nothing. I find myself wondering if Vogler really has been arrested. Maybe Carl too, in some kind of ridiculous mix-up. Not Marianne, though. I'm certain she left Admiral's Reach last night with no intention of returning any time soon.

I follow Roger's directions up the main road for several miles, then off along narrow lanes to the coast and the Driftwood Hotel.

We park and go into Reception, where we have to do some fast talking before we're given confirmation that Conrad Vogler – a regular patron – dined in the restaurant last night. And there's not much doubt his companion was Carl. Mrs Vogler wasn't with her husband – as I already knew, of course. There's nothing else they can tell us.

We sit in the car outside and swap theories about what

146

could have happened to Carl. None of the theories are convincing – or reassuring. Roger suggests a drink will help us think. I don't argue with that. We drive down to Portscatho and sit outside the pub in the centre of the village.

My least disturbing idea remains that Carl was somehow caught up in Vogler's arrest. Roger gently points out that he'd surely have been able to talk his way out of that by now and would then have contacted me. Except he can't contact me, of course. A call on my new phone to the hotel in St Mawes swiftly establishes they've heard nothing from him, however, so we're still a long way from any kind of plausible explanation for his disappearance.

'Maybe you should inform the police,' Roger suggests at last. 'If you're seriously worried about him. Though he hasn't been gone long, so I'm not sure they'd even classify him as missing in any technical sense. Does he have a wife or girlfriend you could check with to see if he's been in touch?'

'He's not married. Beyond that, I don't really know. We're colleagues, not friends. And I've lost his number along with my phone.'

'Tricky. I—' Roger's phone rings at that point. It's Nick Brown, the solicitor. But the connection's evidently not great. Roger heads off across the village square in search of better reception. I watch him pacing up and down as he speaks, with the phone clamped to his ear.

He comes back to where I'm sitting about five minutes later. 'OK,' he begins. 'There's good news and bad news.'

'I'll take the good first,' I say. 'I could use some.'

'Right. Well, they haven't charged Joe with anything, though Brown thinks they will if he starts demanding to be released. It looks like they'll go easy on him if he agrees to cooperate and provide as much detail as he can on Vogler's activities.'

'And has he agreed?'

'That's the bad news. He wants Brown to get hold of Duncan Forrester. Which Brown can't do, of course. Joe says he isn't making any decisions until he's spoken to Duncan.'

'For God's sake.'

Roger smiles ruefully. 'He can be infuriating at times.'

'What are we going to do?'

'Find Duncan, I suppose.'

'How?'

'No idea. Except . . .'

'What?'

'We could try Kolonn Drogh. The cottage I showed you from the river. You remember I told you I'd seen Joe there once. Well, I'm just wondering if it could be some hideaway Duncan uses. I mean, I know it's a long shot, but . . .'

'Long shots are all we've got?'

Roger nods. 'Seems like it.'

'And you know how to get there?'

He nods again. 'I do.'

Back on the main road, we follow a narrow, winding lane across the peninsula to Philleigh. Just beyond the village, Roger has me turn off on to an even narrower lane with high hedges and a ridge of grass down the centre. The tarmac gives way to fractured concrete, then bare earth with plenty of puddles and deep wheel-ruts.

A band of woodland appears ahead. The track becomes muddier as we enter the shadow of the trees. I glimpse water off to our left: the weak sun glints on a finger of creek. Then, as the wood thins, there's a fence bordering a field overgrown with weeds and thorns and the roofline of the cottage, visible over the swell of the land. And a five-bar gate, closed across the track.

I pull up short of the gate. Roger jumps out, unlatches it and swings it open. I drive through and stop. The track continues ahead round a bend towards the cottage.

Twenty metres or so away, in the middle of the track, blocking the route, is a large, mud-spattered four-wheel-drive car. And I feel as if I recognize it.

Roger sees the car as well. Instead of getting back in, he walks round to talk to me through the window. 'Looks like someone's got here ahead of us,' he says, keeping his voice low.

'I'm pretty sure that's Vogler's car,' I respond.

'How sure?'

'Well, I didn't memorize the registration number, but it's the right model and colour.'

'Could be a coincidence. There are a lot of four-by-fours around here.' He pauses, then says, 'Let's take a look.'

'Is that a good idea? Maybe we should call the police.'

'We can call them if it looks like we need to.'

'OK.' I nod, take the key from the ignition and get out.

The silence of our surroundings pounces on my senses. The wood behind us seems to be holding its breath. There isn't even the hint of a breeze.

We start walking towards the 4WD. Suddenly, a pheasant bursts explosively into flight from the undergrowth. I physically jump in shock.

'Steady,' says Roger softly, touching my arm. 'It's only a bird.'

'Sorry.'

We walk on. With each step towards the 4WD, I feel

more certain it *is* Vogler's. The cottage looks empty. But someone could be watching us from one of the windows and we'd never know.

We reach the 4WD. There's a Barbour jacket thrown across the rear seat, partly obscuring some letters and papers. On one of the envelopes I can see half of an address. *Reach. Road. Mawes.* There's no doubt, then. It does belong to Vogler.

'What d'you make of this?' asks Roger, pointing to some dark red smears on the rear bumper.

I look at them. My first instinct, which I don't really want to trust, is that they're smears of blood. 'Not sure,' I reply.

'There's something under a tarpaulin in the stowage area.' Roger peers in, then jerks his head back. 'There's blood on the floor beyond the edge of the tarp. And this is blood on the bumper as well.'

'Oh, God.'

'Try the driver's door.'

I move to the front of the car and pull the door handle. It opens. I see a half-finished pack of mints lying down by the pedals. Why I notice them I'm not sure. But I do. 'It's not locked.' My voice falters as I speak the words.

'Stay there,' says Roger. He doesn't explain why he wants me to. But he doesn't have to. He opens the tailgate. Then he reaches in and lifts the tarpaulin.

I see the expression on his face twist with horror. He lets the tarpaulin fall back into place, covering what he's just seen.

I take a step towards him, but he says, 'No,' and moves quickly towards me. He's trying to shield me, I assume, from the reality of what's there. But I want to know. I *need* to know.

He pulls something out of an inside pocket of his jacket

as he closes on me. It looks at first glance like a TV remote. He's still the same concerned, protective Roger I think I know. I have no presentiment of danger. I haven't the slightest expectation that he's going to do what he does.

He jams the device into my chest. There's a jolt, followed by a bolt of pain. I'm falling. My limbs are rubbery. My muscles refuse to obey me. My brain's scrambled.

He catches me as I fall. 'I've got you,' I hear him say through a fog of pain. He kicks the driver's door wide open behind me, pulls my raincoat off and half lifts, half lowers me into the car. I'm sprawled across both seats. I think I feel him raising my feet and pushing them in after me. Then I hear the door slam shut. The muscles of my arms and legs and chest are convulsing. I can't control my movements. I can't sit up. I can't think.

The passenger door opens and he climbs in beside me. I see his face above me. He's frowning in concentration. There's no compassion in his gaze now. There's no hatred either. He's just someone doing something he's planned to do. And he's doing it to me.

He undoes the button on my cuff and pushes the sleeve of the blouse up to my elbow. I hear a sound of plastic being stretched and snapped. Then he's holding a syringe above me and pushing the needle into a phial of clear liquid. He's wearing surgical gloves. I try to squirm away from him, but I can't. I try to scream. But no sound comes.

The light changes behind him in that instant. A shadow. A blur of movement. Someone grabs him by the shoulder and wrenches him backwards, away from me. The syringe and phial slip from Roger's hands. He's pulled right out of the car, falling heavily to the ground. I hear the breath forced from his mouth by the impact.

My muscles are still twitching. I can't control them. But

151

I manage to swivel my neck just enough to see Duncan Forrester standing over Roger. Judging by the angle of his knee, he's got his boot jammed against Roger's chest. He's clutching a gun with both hands and pointing it at Roger.

He glances fleetingly at me. 'Take it easy,' he says. 'You'll feel better soon.' Then he looks back down at Roger. 'What's in the phial?'

There's no immediate answer, so Forrester presses his foot down harder. Roger groans. 'OK, OK,' he gasps. 'You win. Morphine.'

'That's not enough for a fatal dose. You must have more phials with you.'

'I do.'

'And you'd have gone on injecting her until the job was done?'

'Yes.'

'I've seen what's under the tarpaulin. Did you kill them?' *Them?* God, who's Forrester talking about?

'Not me,' Roger replies.

'Who, then?'

'Marianne, probably. Or her goon, Scaddan.'

'But not here.'

'No. We decided to move the car.'

'And set Nicole up to look as if she killed them, then drove here and killed herself.'

'The police would have settled for that in the end.'

'Why Nicole?'

'She was at Admiral's Reach last night. She must've tipped Marianne off. But she was also involved in planting a bug on Vogler. I couldn't be sure of her allegiances. Or how much she knows.' Roger couldn't be sure of *my* allegiances? What about his? Who is he working for? Who's the *we* who decided to move the car?

'But the bug was Ursula Kendall's idea,' Forrester presses on.

'I never thought she'd try something like that. She's just a glorified tax inspector. Way out of her depth.'

'So, you frame Nicole to tie off the Vogler end of things. Where does that leave Joe?'

'Safe in our hands. We couldn't let the Americans get him. He's far too valuable.' It sounds like Roger has some security service connection. And so, apparently, does Forrester.

'You'll persuade him he has to cooperate in order to get the police to drop the case against him.'

'You seem to know all about it.'

'What I know is how you've been trained.'

'Who are you?'

'No one you've ever heard of. Who's running this operation?'

'Hexter.'

'He should've been pensioned off by now.' So, Forrester knows Roger's boss, from way back, apparently.

'Well, he hasn't been.'

'Did he recruit you?'

'Yes.'

'Where?'

'Hong Kong.'

'I might've guessed.' There's no doubt, then. Forrester and Hexter are connected by something in the past.

'What are you to him?'

'A threat. But not as big a one as he is to me.' Forrester glances towards me. 'Can you move yet, Nicole?'

I try to straighten my left arm. It obeys. There are still lots of twitches and spasms, but the pain's almost gone. 'I . . . I can, yesh.' My voice is slurred. My tongue and lips feel as if I'm coming round from an injection at my dentist's.

'I need the key to your car.'

'Wha . . . what . . .'

'You have to trust me. Everything will be all right if you do that. Where's the key?'

Should I trust him? The question forms and then dissolves in my mind. Roger would have killed me if Forrester hadn't intervened. 'In . . . my pocket.' I try to reach into the pocket of my trousers. My fingers aren't working properly yet, though. I can't do it. But I can push the key out with the heel of my hand.

'Pass it to me as best you can.'

I fumble around and work my hand under the key so it's resting in my palm. Then I stretch out awkwardly in his direction. He reaches across the seat and takes it.

'I'll be back soon.' He steps cautiously to one side. 'Get up,' he says to Roger, keeping the revolver trained on him. 'Slowly.'

Roger sits up, then rises to his feet. Slowly, as instructed.

'Toss your phone and the stun gun into the car.'

Roger does as he's told and tosses them on to the seat next to me. Fleetingly, our eyes meet. I can read no sympathy in his gaze, no regret – other than regret that his plan's gone wrong.

'Walk slowly ahead of me to Nicole's car,' says Forrester.

They set off. I manage to prop myself up on one elbow and watch them go. Feeling's returning to my toes and fingers and lips now. With a struggle, I grasp the steering-wheel and pull myself up into a sitting position. My head swims for a moment, then settles. I draw a few deep breaths. I'm going to be all right. I'm alive. But as to what happens next . . .

I'm not sure how long I stay there, gazing weakly through the windscreen at the cottage, the overgrown outhouses, the grey-blue water and the sloping green fields on the other side of the river, trying hard, so very hard, not to think about what's behind me, in the back of the car.

Then Forrester returns. He opens the door on my side and looks in at me. He's no longer carrying the revolver. Instead, he has my handbag looped over his arm.

'Who are you?' I ask, my voice sounding normal again, though husky.

'You know who I am.'

'I don't think I do.'

'I've locked Lam in the boot of your car. They'll find him eventually. By then, we need to be long gone.'

'Whose bodies are behind me, under the tarpaulin?'

'Conrad Vogler and your colleague, Carl Hinkley. Both shot through the back of the head.'

Carl dead. And Conrad Vogler. My God. How *did* it come to this? 'Was it you who let me out of the cupboard at Admiral's Reach?' I can't think who else it could have been.

'Yes. I watched Marianne leave with Scaddan. I went in to see if you were OK. And to remove anything that could make things look bad for Joe. In case the house was searched.'

'It was. This morning.'

'They won't have found much. As far as I could tell, Marianne took everything important with her. Presumably because you told her HMRC had a recording of Conrad's meeting with his Clearing House boss.'

'I had no choice but to tell her.'

'I believe you.'

'How do you know about the Clearing House?'

'I know what I need to know.'

'Did Marianne really kill them? Carl? And her own husband?'

'She's not one to shrink from whatever action she judges necessary to protect herself. The recording you helped Ursula obtain made it all too likely Conrad would do a deal in return for a light sentence. The Clearing House would have done whatever they needed to do to stop that happening. And that would have included silencing Marianne. So, she decided to take the initiative by silencing Conrad. I'm afraid your friend Carl was just in the wrong place at the wrong time.' And I could have been there with him, if he hadn't cut me out of the party. Christ, what an irony. 'Over dinner Conrad had probably negotiated a payment he planned to use as getaway money. But Marianne obviously decided that didn't give her enough protection.'

'Christ.'

'Carl wouldn't have known much about it. If that's any comfort.'

'Not much. Who does Roger work for?'

'The Intelligence Services.'

'Like you used to?'

'We don't have time for a leisurely inquest, Nicole. We need to leave here. On foot. I've got a Land Rover parked on a track three fields away. Think you can make that?'

'Why don't we just call the police?'

'Because you're a marked woman now. A security risk, as the powers that be see it. That's why Lam was ordered to kill you. Do you live alone?'

It feels as if he already knows the answer. 'Yes.'

'That'll make it easy for them. Compulsory sick leave from Venstrom. A note on your file by the company doctor saying he's worried about your state of mind. Then a neighbour will find you dead in bed, with empty blister packs of painkillers scattered around the room. Suicide. If at first you don't succeed . . .'

'How do I know you're not just saying these things to frighten me?' And he *is* frightening me. Mostly because I believe every word he's spoken.

'Without me you won't survive this, Nicole. It's lucky for you I'm not willing to let Hexter run Joe's life for him.'

'Is Joe your son?'

'He's certainly the closest I'm ever going to get to one.'

'How did you know Roger would bring me here?'

'I found Vogler's car before they did. I followed when it was moved here. I can still manage to follow people without them knowing they're being followed. In fact, I think I'm better at it than I used to be. After they left, I waited . . . to see what would happen next. My name's on the lease of this cottage. There'll have been some idea to implicate me in Vogler's death.'

'What do you use this place for?'

'I keep it on for old times' sake. What age are you? Thirty?'

'Thirty-two.'

'Too young, even so, to understand. It's stupid, really. Human nature.' He smiles and shakes his head. 'It can't be helped. There's nothing I can do to stop them using the connection against me. What's vital now is for us to get a long way away from here. Then we can decide what action to take.'

'Action?'

'We have two choices. Run and keep on running. Or turn and fight. Like I told you, I'm not prepared to let Hexter take control of Joe's life. So, for me, it's turn and fight. What's it to be for you?'

'What are you talking about? I'm not running *or* fighting.'

'You have to. If not, they *will* come for you. And I won't be around to save you next time. The life you led before today?' He shakes his head. He looks genuinely sorry for me. 'That's gone, Nicole. Gone for ever.'

'That's ridiculous. It can't be as bad as you say.'

'But it is.'

'Venstrom's a powerful multinational company. They'll protect me.' I don't believe that even as I say it.

'No one will protect you. No one can. Not even me.'

'What are you offering me, then?'

'Your only chance. If you don't want to take it, I'll leave you here and go my own way. Do you want me to do that?'

I can't seem to frame a reply. I just look at him. And he looks at me.

Then he says, 'Only I can't wait for an answer any longer. You have to decide. Now.'

I don't know what to think. Everything seems to have changed in the blink of an eye. All I know for certain is that I have to make a decision. And it has to be the right one.

When I climb out of the 4WD, Forrester puts his hand under my elbow to steady me, but I tell him I'm fine to walk. It's strange how fast and how clearly the brain works when it has to. Carl's dead. Vogler's dead. And I'd be dead now too, but for Duncan Forrester and whatever secret links him to Roger's boss. Hexter. Was he the man Roger spoke to in the car park at St Mawes? Was that the moment my death was sanctioned as part of an official cover-up? How calm, how casual it all was. He looked at me. A single glance. *Nice-looking young woman*, he may have thought. *Not long for this world, though.*

But here I am. Still in the world. Still alive. For now.

'I don't know whether I can do this, Duncan,' I say, relieved I can be honest with him.

'Only one way to find out.'

'I think I have to see the bodies before we go.'

'You should spare yourself that. It's not pretty.'

'That's why I *shouldn't* spare myself. Because I'm guessing life isn't going to be pretty from here on. And I have to be sure. I have to understand what we're doing is . . . real.'

'It's real.'

'Then show me.'

He nods. 'OK.'

'And then we go.'

And then we go. Out of one life. Into another.

MIDDLE GAME

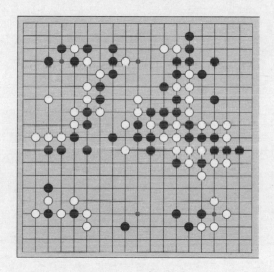

I WAS IN FORRESTER'S WORLD, WHETHER I WANTED TO BE OR not. His and Hexter's. But it was a world I knew nothing about.

Until he told me.

* * *

There are many milestones in life, Nicole. One of them is the first time someone you trust betrays you.

Hexter went beyond betrayal, though. He tried to kill me. And my reputation. He tried to *destroy* me.

He almost succeeded. He still might. Now we're up against one another again. After all these years. After believing it was over.

But this isn't over. I'm not sure now, looking back, it ever could have been.

You need to understand what happened between us. You need to hear something I've never told anyone before.

The truth. About Hexter and me. All of it. The whole damn thing.

Old habits die hard. I'm not going to tell you any more than I have to about my time in the Service. I had an aptitude for the work. It suited my analytical mind and my

163

self-contained nature. I was reliable. I was thorough. I was right for it.

There was no meteoric rise up the hierarchy for me, though. Compared with Clive Hexter, who joined around the same time as me, I was an amateur at playing the preferment game. Hexter had a sort of magical sheen. You never doubted him. He always knew how to get what he wanted. Promotion. Admiration. The best out of any situation. He had the touch.

Women loved him, even though they couldn't trust him, or maybe *because* they couldn't trust him. Actually, though, everyone who met him fell in love with him to some extent. And that's a great gift to have in the intelligence world.

If there was an exception to the general rule of Hexter worship it was me. I was never convinced he was the genuine article. But he ended up being my departmental boss, so I had no choice about working with him. And ironically we chalked up quite a few operational successes together.

Hexter had an insight into Far East problems thanks to studying Chinese and Japanese at Cambridge, which meant he was in high demand when China started to engage with the wider world. My field was eastern Europe, so we didn't always work in harness. But in the summer of 1975 we were in Helsinki together, hunting for intelligence crumbs on the fringes of the CSCE negotiations – the Conference on Security and Cooperation in Europe. With the NATO and Warsaw Pact countries all represented, it was a rare opportunity to probe for weaknesses.

In my diplomatic cover role overseeing day-to-day security for the British delegation, I liaised with Tahvo Norrback of the Finnish Foreign Ministry. A good man. We hit it off together. But poor old Tahvo liked his drink and had a tendency to get into trouble when he'd had one too many. He had a file of sensitive documents stolen from him in a bar one night. Luckily, the thief was a local chancer rather than a KGB agent, so he only wanted to be paid to hand them back. But Tahvo couldn't afford what he was demanding. I put up the cash from departmental contingency funds and we handled the exchange so we got the documents *and* kept the money. It was a neat night's work.

When Hexter got to hear about it, he reckoned I should have secured the file and used it to blackmail Norrback for whatever we could get out of him. My argument was that I'd earned Norrback's undying gratitude by getting him out of a hole and that would give us much more in the long run. Hexter suspected I hadn't told him what I was planning because I knew he'd have insisted I do it his way. He was right, of course.

But I was right too. Norrback cut down on the booze and got promoted to a senior position in the Finnish Foreign Ministry. Which gave us a valuable contact in the Baltic world when Gorbachev started to loosen things up in the Soviet Union. Hexter never thanked me for that. But C, the boss we all answered to, certainly did.

1989 was the year everything changed. And it was very nearly the year I died. Some in the Service were cock-a-hoop about the difficulties engulfing the Soviet Union and China. The Soviets had pulled out of Afghanistan with their tails between their legs and the Chinese were struggling to cope with student protesters filling Tiananmen Square and demanding liberalization. It wasn't anything like as obvious then as it is now how it was all going to turn out.

But Deng Xiaoping was made of sterner stuff than

Gorbachev, so maybe we should have known. Overnight on the third and fourth of June, the People's Liberation Army cleared the square. More than two thousand protesters dead, seven thousand wounded. Just like that. Normal service resumed in the People's Republic.

Hexter was in Hong Kong when Tiananmen unravelled and I was sent out to help him handle the British side of Operation Yellowbird: a scheme we sponsored to smuggle fugitive dissidents out of China, mostly via Hong Kong. Obviously, we wanted to be the first to question them, though we spent most of our time trying to coordinate the various escape plans. And when we were able to sit down with them, they basically told the same story. They hadn't seen the crackdown coming. They simply hadn't understood how ruthless Deng was capable of being.

One episode stands out from those hot summer weeks I spent with Hexter in Hong Kong. There was a dissident called Chen Shufan we were particularly keen to get out. Lots of rumours attached themselves to him. He was a prime mover in the student uprising, but he was also a nephew of Deng's regular bridge partner. The word was he knew things we needed to know and that we wouldn't regret helping him, whatever the cost.

And the cost was high. More than fifty thousand dollars in smugglers' fees. But it was all for nothing. Somehow the PLA patrols got wind of where he was going to be lifted from. Chen Shufan ended up dead in the surf on a Guangdong beach. Someone had talked. After that Hexter reckoned Yellowbird wasn't worth investing in. He recommended we pull out.

We were waiting for a ruling from London on that point when, instead, we were summoned home for reassignment.

It was early September and C had a highly sensitive job for us to which my relationship with Norrback was vital.

The course of the rest of my life was set as we sat round a conference table in Century House on Friday the eighth of September. I had no idea what was being set in train. I hadn't a clue. Only one man really understood what was likely to transpire. And even he may not have anticipated how far it would reach.

The backdrop to all this was the weakening of the Soviets' hold on eastern Europe. East Germans had been sneaking out to the west via Hungary for months. Now information had reached us that Hungary's border with Austria was going to be thrown open completely on the eleventh of September, which was the following Monday. The consensus was that this was the beginning of the end for the Soviet bloc régimes. If they couldn't or wouldn't hold their people, then they were finished.

The key was Gorbachev. He'd seen what had happened in Beijing and was appalled by it. He wasn't going to send the Red Army in to restore order. And that guaranteed *dis*order.

The long and the short of it was this. The Berlin Wall hadn't fallen yet. The balance of power in Europe hadn't yet ceased to be viable. And our political masters weren't keen on seeing the house of cards come down for fear of the unpredictable consequences. A reunited Germany. A disintegrating eastern bloc. A collapsing USSR. They didn't like the sound of that. And that made it impossible to ignore an overture that had been received from one Viktor Slavsky, a Politburo member under Brezhnev and Andropov and thought to be a prime mover in opposition to Gorbachev.

Slavsky wanted to talk, in secret, on neutral ground, about how NATO would react in certain circumstances he didn't care to specify but weren't hard to guess: Gorbachev's violent removal from the scene. To my amazement, he was being taken seriously at the highest levels. And the future he might be able to engineer appealed to our risk-averse leaders.

But he required assurances that if there was a new government it would be recognized and treated favourably. The Americans, the British and the French were willing to consider going along with this – unofficially, of course. A retired British politician known and trusted by Slavsky had been settled on as a go-between. It's best I don't name him. Let's call him X. Hexter and I were to accompany him to a meeting with Slavsky where it was hoped an agreement would be arrived at. Along for the ride would be an observer from the CIA and one from the French equivalent, the DGSE. Everything would be deniable and ultra top secret.

A Finnish venue was Slavsky's idea. He obviously wanted the shortest and least detectable journey possible. That's where Norrback came in. Could he be persuaded to host such a meeting? Yes was the answer, with clearance from the Finnish government based on scrupulously not knowing the purpose of the gathering.

I didn't like any of this. We were in the process of winning the Cold War and suddenly we weren't happy about the unpredictability of what would follow. We were hooked on the stability of the East–West face-off. We didn't want it to end. Better the devil you know, in the final analysis. That was the attitude, in London, Paris *and* Washington.

The Austro-Hungarian border opened on cue on the eleventh and thousands flooded across. We all watched the scenes on our televisions in amazement. It was really happening. And Gorbachev didn't do a thing to stop it.

I had a heart-to-heart with Hexter about what we were planning a few days later. I put it to him that encouraging Slavsky and his fellow conspirators in Moscow would preserve the very system we were supposed to be in business to destroy. We were going against the grain of our own history. And we were betraying all those hopeful liberals in eastern Europe while we were about it.

'Ours not to reason why, old boy,' was his initial response. But he was happy to expand on that. The Bush administration wanted to prevent denuclearization in Europe and that meant preventing German reunification. Bush's priority was preservation of the status quo. As for Thatcher and Mitterrand, they had their personal memories of war to stiffen their opposition to stitching the two Germanies back together.

Remember, this was *before* the Berlin Wall came down. This was *before* all the changes that swept through eastern Europe came to be seen as inevitable. If you're given a choice between stability, even one based on mutually assured destruction, and *in*stability, with nothing certain and very little controllable, what *is* the truly responsible course of action? Who knows what I'd have decided in their place?

But I wasn't in their place. I was just a humble facilitator. So, off to Helsinki we went. There was always Hexter's clinching argument to cling to. If Gorbachev was likely to be toppled, we shouldn't waste the opportunity to take the measure of those plotting against him.

Norrback had inherited a large house on Kulosaari, an

island-suburb of Helsinki, and it was there we went on Friday the twenty-second of September. The British embassy didn't even know we were in Finland. We were operating on need-to-know. And no one needed to know. We had an interpreter with us, of course, plus X, our retired politician. That was it.

Henri Bourdil from DGSE joined us that evening. Peter Curtis, the CIA's man, turned up the following morning. They were both fluent in Russian. Slavsky arrived a few hours later, accompanied by an interpreter of his own and an assistant. They were a tense, tight-lipped trio. Slavsky came across as standard issue hard-bitten Communist party man, reared on Stalinist principles, to whom *glasnost* and *perestroika* must have been absolute anathema. He was taking a big risk. We all knew that.

How the group had crossed the border without detection from the Soviet side was unclear. They must have had help from someone senior in the Soviet air force. Norrback had cleared the way for their unmarked plane to land at a small airfield west of Helsinki.

Norrback wasn't going to be party to any of the discussions. In fact, he was planning to be absent most of the time. He'd never been told the exact purpose of the meeting, nor had he asked.

But he'd guessed anyway, as he told me when we were alone together. 'You want things to stay as they are, don't you? You want the last forty years to go on for another forty.'

'It's not what *I* want, Tahvo,' I objected.

'No. But it's why you're here.'

'I'm just doing my job.'

170

'Some job. I get the feeling you're planning a funeral. But you're not quite sure who's being buried.'

I brushed his comment off, but it stayed in my mind the whole time we were there. I don't think he knew just how right he was. Until later.

The weekend was a round of earnest discussions in the drawing room and breathers in the garden. Slavsky dwelt on nuts and bolts. Could X guarantee tacit support for a replacement regime? How soon after a takeover would the necessary recognitions be forthcoming? What would be tolerated with regard to the treatment of those removed from office? What arrangements could be made for financial assistance in the medium term?

X preferred to deal in generalities and Slavsky had to press him hard for specific commitments. It seemed to Hexter, as we shared a late-night whisky on Saturday, that X hadn't given as much as Slavsky had hoped for, though whether that would make the difference between going ahead with the coup and not . . .

'Second-guessing the Russians is like looking at a fog-bank through binoculars,' Hexter joked. 'All you get is a closer view of fog.'

'Do you think they might actually kill Gorbachev?' It was a question that had been seriously bothering me.

'Not if they want swift recognition. No, no. Slavsky and his co-conspirators don't intend to kill anyone if they can avoid it. Just . . . crush a few dreams.'

So, that was the business we were in. Crushing dreams. I didn't sleep well that night.

Next morning, X sprang a surprise. He'd received a fax, which he'd already delivered to Slavsky. He didn't say

171

who it was from or what it said. But Slavsky seemed satisfied. Discussion went ahead in a noticeably less tense atmosphere. Less tense on the part of Slavsky and X, that is. Curtis and Bourdil both wanted to know more about the fax. But X wouldn't tell them.

'Sub-contracting this operation to you Brits didn't involve us being cut out of the loop,' Curtis complained as he, Bourdil, Hexter and I conferred in the garden. 'What the hell's going on?' And Bourdil said much the same, in a French accent.

We couldn't enlighten them, but, apart from emphasizing they'd be reporting this development to their governments, there wasn't much they could do without scuppering the outcome of the meeting, which they didn't have the authority to do. X himself told us the less we knew the better.

There was a final wrap-up session during which Slavsky vented some of his contempt for Gorbachev and his outrage about what was happening to his country before we downed shots of vodka with varying degrees of enthusiasm and said our farewells.

Before leaving in the car Norrback had laid on, Slavsky enveloped X in a bear-hug. There was no doubt they understood one another perfectly. A deal had been done.

'I'll be keeping a close eye on the ticker tape when we get back to HQ,' Hexter said to me in an undertone as the car headed away along the drive. 'I reckon there could be some interesting developments in Moscow in the days ahead.'

I couldn't summon a reply. I'd done what I'd been told to do. But I didn't like it. I'd been in the Service sixteen years and I'd never had such a feeling of . . . moral contamination.

'Don't look so miserable,' said Hexter. 'Remember, this wasn't our choice.'

'You can say that again.'

'I probably will. When we know what the consequences are.'

Ah, the consequences.

I didn't want to think too much about what those were going to be as the party broke up. Curtis and Bourdil went their separate ways, then we left with X, heading for the Airport Hilton. We weren't due to fly back to London until the following morning. Norrback shot me a glance as he saw us off that spoke volumes. He didn't think we had anything to be proud of and he barely acknowledged X's effusive thanks.

'Bit of a cold fish, our host,' X remarked as we drove away.

'That's the Finns for you,' said Hexter. And X laughed. But I didn't.

And none of us was laughing an hour later, when the news reached us.

It came in a phone call from Norrback. Slavsky's plane had blown up shortly after clearing the Finnish coast. Completely destroyed. No possibility of survivors. Wreckage scattered across the sea. 'I am sorry,' he said. And there really wasn't anything else he could say.

Hexter was surprised, but not shocked. 'The KGB hasn't lost its teeth, then. What a waste of time and effort – and life, of course.'

The KGB's responsibility seemed clear. We reckoned they must have sent agents into Finland to plant a bomb on the plane while Slavsky was busy conferring with us. Detonating it just after the plane had cleared the coast suggested they wanted to minimize the recovery of evidence. Slavsky had friends in high places. But he had enemies too. And now they had struck.

We notified HQ and watched the coverage on the TV news. The commentary was in Finnish, of course, but we got the gist. A private plane with four people on board had taken off from Torbacka airfield late that afternoon, booked destination the Åland Islands, and exploded over the sea south-west of Helsinki. But the plane's route suggested they weren't actually going to the Åland Islands at all. Staff at the airfield said the four had spoken to each other in Russian. It was all very mysterious.

Except to us. When we broke the news to X, he reacted as if this was a possibility he had foreseen all along. 'Disappointing. Very disappointing.' As to what would happen now Slavsky's coup was stillborn, all he said was, 'We shall just have to trust to luck, gentlemen. Maybe this was a falling-out amongst plotters. Maybe they'll still go ahead.'

Hexter and I agreed that was whistling in the wind. The conspirators would go to ground now. Gorbachev was safe. For the time being, anyway.

I can't pretend I was altogether sorry. I mean, I was sorry Slavsky and his companions had died, obviously, but I'd been unhappy about the whole project. Part of me was relieved the KGB had given us a way out of a deal that could have turned seriously sour.

We flew back to London the following morning, straight into a vigorous debriefing at Century House. C was livid about what had happened, though it seemed to me he was angrier with our political masters for putting us in such a position than with us for failing to anticipate how it might end. The conclusion was that officially we'd never met Slavsky. The Americans and the French signed up to that as well. No one had gone to Helsinki to meet anyone. There'd been no contact of any kind.

Fortunately, the fax X had handed to Slavsky had been destroyed in the explosion. X himself had no formal government standing. And I was able to confirm Norrback had never known the reason for the meeting – a meeting everyone who'd attended it now agreed had never actually taken place. A small piece of history had ceased to exist.

'I spent last weekend quietly at home,' Hexter said to me over coffee. 'And I happen to know you did too.'

We moved on and were happy to do so. The world moved on too. Gorbachev was rapturously received by the crowds when he attended East Germany's fortieth anniversary celebrations. 'Gorby, Gorby, Gorby,' they chanted. They couldn't get enough of him. And while he was there he put a stop to Honecker's plan to stage a Tiananmen Square of his own a few days later. The Stasi was forced to let protesters have their say. There was to be no bloodshed. And without bloodshed – or the threat of it – there was no control.

Honecker disappeared into retirement a week or so later. The ground was shifting beneath our feet. And on the ninth of November, the first cracks appeared in the Berlin Wall. Thousands of East Germans crossed into West Germany that night. The Iron Curtain had opened.

And it could never be closed. What Slavsky and his co-conspirators had hoped to prevent had come to pass. Nothing would ever be the same again.

Politicians adapt more quickly than most. It goes with the job, I suppose. There were no votes to be won by mourning the loss of Cold War stability when our TV screens were filled every night with pictures of ecstatic young Germans tearing down the Berlin Wall. Whatever reservations our leaders had were stifled. They embraced the future. And no one – absolutely no one – wanted to hear anything that suggested they'd ever tried to stop that future in its tracks. Our abortive mission to Helsinki became an unmentioned, in fact unmentionable, subject.

I kept my head down and Hexter went back to Hong Kong to tie up the loose ends of Operation Yellowbird. 'Out of harm's way,' as he put it. He didn't take me with him, as I'd hoped. Instead, I was dispatched to Rome, to dig up whatever I could about the Andreotti government's attitude to the changes sweeping eastern Europe.

It wasn't much of a mission. Italy didn't call the shots, in NATO or the EU – the European Community, as it was then. So nobody really cared what they thought. But it was categorized as useful background information and, as Hexter said to me, Rome was a congenial place to lie low while my involvement with Slavsky slipped further and further out of our masters' minds. 'Treat it as a holiday,' he advised. 'You deserve one.'

My cover was checking security at the British Visa Office, which involved my putting in a few token appearances there and not much else. Otherwise, I was left to my own devices. I didn't get the feeling anyone was impatiently awaiting my report back in London. I was, for the time being, a forgotten man.

I had the use of an apartment near the Piazza Navona. It was tiny, with eccentric plumbing, and was wedged under the roof at the top of a crumbling old building in a winding little alley off Via dei Coronari.

I could have grouched around the city feeling sorry for myself, I suppose, but, actually, as the weeks passed and days of torrential rain alternated with days of diamond-sharp light, I slipped into one of the most contented passages of my life. Autumn in Rome, with little work to do and plenty of time to do it in. What wasn't there to like?

My only contact on government policy was a boozy old senator and former minister who turned out to be good for nothing except drinking at my expense. Before I gave up on him, though, he mentioned his niece was employed as an English interpreter in the Prime Minister's office in Palazzo Chigi and could arrange a guided tour of the building if I was interested. I think that was his way of telling me I wasn't going to get anything useful out of him.

Never look a gift horse in the mouth. I didn't need a guided tour of Palazzo Chigi, of course. But an interpreter in the Prime Minister's office? You never know what might come of that. So I called her. And, after I'd had the tour, I called her again to thank her.

I think I was already in love with Cinzia Bianconi by the time we had our first actual date. She was beautiful and elegant, in the Italian way, and I could happily have listened to her speaking her softly accented brand of English all day, especially if I could gaze into her sloe-coloured eyes while I was about it. She was lovely. And my life had been short of loveliness for far too long.

We soon began an affair. Cinzia lived in Prati with her parents, who couldn't be told anything about me because they were still hoping she'd be reconciled with her husband, whom she'd abandoned in Milan. Rinaldo was a dullard with a violent streak, according to Cinzia. There was no prospect of her going back to him and divorce was her intention, but it was going to take some time to accustom *Mamma e Papà* to the idea. And springing me on them wouldn't help.

Where I figured in Cinzia's future was hard to say and certainly we never looked much further ahead than the following week. Dinner. The cinema, with Cinzia whispering translations of the dialogue to me. Long afternoons in my apartment. Slow walks through Rome by night. They were the coordinates of our relationship. I was happy. She was happy. *We* were happy. And I just wanted it to go on for ever.

Soon, I was hardly bothering to keep up much of a pretence of doing what I'd been sent to Rome to do. But nobody back in London seemed to care. I was my own boss. And the only opinion I cared about was Cinzia's.

The affairs of the outside world faded into relative insignificance. I followed them as far as I did on the World Service and in the pages of the *Herald Tribune*. Kohl was working for German reunification. The régime in Czechoslovakia was tottering. There were rumblings in Romania. Events were playing out very much as Slavsky – and others who'd never admit as much – had feared they would.

*

I remember reading one *Herald Tribune* article in particular sitting in the December sunshine outside a *caffè* in Piazza Farnese. Cinzia was going to cook supper at my apartment that evening and I'd just bought some vegetables at the market in Campo de' Fiori. They were in a bag on the chair beside me. I remember all the particularities of the scene, even though there was no reason to at the time. The reason came later. The significance of what I read was another week away from dawning on me.

The article was about a surprise visit to Beijing by Bush's senior representatives, Scowcroft and Eagleburger. The stated reason for the visit was to brief the Chinese on a recent NATO summit, but an end to China's post-Tiananmen quarantine was also mooted. The two men met all the senior figures and had a cosy chat with Deng Xiaoping. It sounded to the *Herald Tribune* as if Bush was going soft on the Chinese. It sounded that way to me too.

I didn't really care, though. They could all play their cards in the game of *realpolitik* and take their winnings or bear their losses as events dictated. I wanted no part of it.

But what I wanted or didn't want was supremely irrelevant. I *was* part of it. I could never be otherwise. I was deluding myself in thinking my carefree existence in Rome could just drift pleasurably on. I wasn't there because I'd been forgotten. I was there because that was where they wanted me to be. Because that was where they knew they could find me. When the time came.

And it wasn't long in coming. The following Saturday, Cinzia and I saw a film and went for supper afterwards at a cosy little restaurant. She'd been distracted all afternoon and eventually told me why. She'd heard from a friend that Rinaldo had been sacked from his job and had left Milan, saying he was going back to Rome. That wasn't good news, of course, but I tried to reassure her he probably wasn't going to contact her. But she wasn't reassured and, suddenly, late in the meal, she looked out of the window and thought she saw Rinaldo watching us from the other side of the street.

I didn't see him myself. He dodged out of sight as soon as Cinzia spotted him. It occurred to me she was so worried she might actually have imagined he was there, though I didn't suggest that to her. She called him *uno mostro* – a monster. I had him down as something less forbidding. I was confident I could handle him if I needed to.

Cinzia always went home on Saturday nights to spend Sunday with her parents. It was expected, as part of an unspoken bargain that meant they never asked where she was, or who with, during the week. Normally, she took the Metro, but she was so spooked by the Rinaldo business that I put her in a taxi.

I took a few precautions walking home that night: some double-backs and detours intended to flush out anyone who might be following me. No one was. I hadn't expected there would be. I wasn't worried. Yet.

I had an early Sunday morning routine of taking a run along the riverside. Down by the Tiber at dawn, away from the traffic – those runs are one of my happiest memories of Rome. I used to follow the east bank from Ponte Sant'Angelo round to Ponte Sisto, then the west bank back to Sant'Angelo.

By the time I crossed Ponte Sant'Angelo at the end of the run, the novelty-sellers and tourists were already out.

I did my best to ignore them. In my mind, I was still down by the river.

Suddenly, a man was standing in front of me, shouting and jabbing his finger. He was thirtyish, dark-skinned, with a lot of greasy black hair and a few days' growth of beard. He was wearing jeans and a leather jacket. He could have stepped straight out of any Roman crowd. As to what he was shouting, my Italian wasn't good enough to keep pace with his words, but I caught enough of them – *bastardo, intruso, adultero* – to get the message. And he mentioned Cinzia by name several times, so there wasn't any doubt who he was.

He shoved me violently enough at one point to upset a street trader's display of Gucci handbags, which sparked a lot of shouting and gesticulating from the salesman as well. Several of the other traders seemed inclined to join in, at which point Rinaldo lost interest and hurried off, shouting a few parting threats and insults at me as he left.

I headed back to my apartment, worrying about what I'd tell Cinzia and how we were going to cope with what I'd now mentally categorized as the Rinaldo problem. Life clearly wasn't quite as free and easy as I'd allowed myself to believe. There's always a serpent in paradise.

The disturbing question was how Rinaldo had known where to find me. He hadn't followed me the night before, I felt certain. Was it just a coincidence? I wasn't buying that. What *was* the explanation, then?

I began to wonder if he could have spoken to some friend of Cinzia's and learnt from her about our relationship. It was possible Cinzia had let slip that I worked, at least in theory, at the British Visa Office. Could someone there have given Rinaldo my address? They certainly shouldn't have. But . . .

I gave the apartment building a thorough recce before going in. There was no sign of Rinaldo. But, strangely, someone was keeping a watch on the entrance, from a nearby doorway. He was nothing like as inconspicuous as he thought he was. But, then, he wasn't trained for that kind of thing.

'What the hell are you doing here, Tahvo?' The question, posed when I was close enough to touch his shoulder and he still hadn't noticed me, made him start violently.

I smiled. I was actually pleased to see him, however unexpected the visit. But Norrback didn't smile back. He looked deadly serious. 'I guess it's good news you don't know why I'm here. *If* you don't know.'

I assured him I didn't. Then I asked how he'd found out where I lived. He'd called in a favour with someone at the Finnish embassy, apparently, who'd spoken to someone at the British embassy on his behalf. He wouldn't name names.

'I'm supposed to be in Brussels for talks about Finland joining the European Community. I will need to be back there tomorrow. None of this' – by *this* he seemed to mean the effort of travelling to Rome to see me – 'has been easy to arrange.'

'So, why *have* you arranged it?'

'Are you sure you don't know?'

'I'm sure.'

'And I can trust you, can't I?'

'You know you can.'

'Yes. I know.' But he didn't look as if he knew.

'What's the matter, Tahvo?'

'I'm not sure. But if I'm right . . . for you, a lot.'

'D'you want to come up to my flat for a chat?'

'No. I'd rather talk . . . in the open.' That sounded worrying. And the way he glanced past me and then over his shoulder wasn't any less worrying.

'I really need to take a shower. I've been running.'

'OK. I'll wait down here.'

'You may as well wait in my flat.'

'No.' He licked his lips nervously. 'I'd prefer . . . not.'

I looked at him long and hard then. There was clearly something wrong. Something *very* wrong. 'Forget the shower, Tahvo. Just tell me what's going on.'

'You haven't heard?'

'Heard *what*?'

'Curtis is dead. Hit by a car while jogging in Washington on Thursday. Bourdil is dead too. A heart attack, so they say. While swimming. In Paris. Yesterday morning.'

'My God. Really? Both of them?'

Norrback nodded. 'Both.'

'That can't—'

Norrback nodded again. 'No. It can't, can it?'

There was a lot to take in and none of it was good. It was asking a lot to believe Curtis and Bourdil's deaths weren't linked in some way. But, if they were, then I was linked to them too. 'I haven't heard anything about this,' was all I could say for the moment.

'Why are *you* in Rome, my friend?'

'Oh, some two-bit assignment.'

'Which someone else could easily have done?'

'Sure. But . . .'

'Are you keeping in touch with the news?'

'Sort of.'

'Read about Scowcroft and Eagleburger going to Beijing last week?'

'Yeah. What of it?'

'I think it's all connected. Curtis. Bourdil. You. Hexter. And China.'

'What d'you mean?'

'Kissinger was in China earlier in the autumn as well. Did you know that?'

'What if he was?'

He glanced around nervously again. 'Let's go somewhere else. I'd like . . . space around us.'

Space around us? He was beginning to sound paranoid. I led him by the quickest route through to Piazza Navona. But the Befana Christmas market had started up that weekend. The piazza's wide open spaces had been filled with stalls selling nativity scenes, toys, decorations and refreshments. There weren't many people about at that hour, however. And none of them paid us any attention.

I bought a cup of mulled wine to keep myself warm and bought Norrback one as well. He swallowed his first mouthfuls like someone badly in need of a stiff drink.

'What do you think's going on, Tahvo?' I asked as we moved towards the quieter end of the piazza.

'You follow the news,' he said, speaking so softly I had to crane my head to hear him clearly. 'A non-Communist government in Czechoslovakia. Violence on the streets in Bucharest. The Berlin Wall crumbling. German reunification a real possibility. The Soviet Union has lost control of its empire. Sounds good, yes?'

'To me, certainly.'

'But not to the people who backed Slavsky.'

'No one's admitting to having done that, Tahvo.'

'No. But they did. You know that. So, ask yourself this. Who benefited most from Slavsky's death?'

'Gorbachev, I suppose. Maybe without even knowing it.'

'How about the Chinese?'

'The *Chinese*?'

'They were condemned by everybody after Tiananmen. The US banned arms sales to China and forced the World Bank to suspend loans to them. Now all that looks like being reversed. Why?'

'You're going to tell me the answer has something to do with Slavsky?'

'Slavsky heeded the lesson of Tiananmen. Cracking down is the only way for a totalitarian regime to survive. Liberalization is death. And liberalization is Gorbachev's path. Thanks to Slavsky's plane blowing up, he never got the chance to end *glasnost*. The result? A weaker Soviet Union. Good, you say. So do I. And so does the Central Committee of the Chinese Communist Party. They've seen the Soviets as a bigger threat than the Americans for the past twenty years. That's why Mao sat down with Nixon in seventy-two. Their enemy's enemy is their friend. But that friendship went cold after Tiananmen. Now it's warmed up again. Despite the Chinese army gunning down thousands of their own people . . . and maybe blowing Slavsky out of the sky.'

So this was it. Norrback was suggesting the Chinese had planted the bomb on Slavsky's plane and sabotaged the coup he was planning. They didn't want Gorbachev to be stopped from pursuing policies they regarded as disastrous for the Soviet Union – because the Soviet Union was their enemy. 'The Chinese had no way of knowing about

185

Slavsky's trip to Helsinki, Tahvo,' I objected. 'Barely *anyone* knew about it.'

Norrback's voice dropped still further as he responded. 'Then one of the few who knew must have told them.'

I considered the implications of what he'd said for a few queasy seconds. 'Are you serious?'

'Think about it. If they knew, they had – and still have – evidence that the British, French and American governments were willing to back a coup against Gorbachev. How would that look now? How would all those east Europeans cheering a liberal future react to the discovery that their supposed defenders in the west were plotting to take that future away from them?' It was a question that didn't need an answer. It would be a disaster. Careers would end. Governments would fall. 'The threat of revealing such evidence buys a lot of normalization of relations, my friend. Like the kind we saw in Beijing last week. A lot of smiles. A lot of handshakes. A lot of big fat loans. A lot of kiss and make up and let's be friends.'

I stopped walking and turned to face Norrback. 'You're saying someone betrayed us, Tahvo. Who?'

'Someone who knew *before* the meeting why it was being held.'

'And who was present at the meeting?'

'Yes. For the timing of the explosion. There needed to be a warning Slavsky was leaving.'

'I get the feeling you don't suspect Curtis or Bourdil.'

'No. I think they were killed because they could corroborate the Chinese claims if they were made public.'

'That goes for me too.'

'Yes. It does. Have you ever told anyone I guessed why you were meeting Slavsky?'

'Not a soul.'

'Then I'm betting I'm safe. But you're not, my friend. You got me out of a heap of trouble back in seventy-five. I was grateful then and I'm grateful now. That's why I came to Rome. To warn you.'

'How can you be sure I'm not the traitor?'

'I know you too well. And you're here, out of the action, which looks to me like you're being set up. Plus . . . you don't speak Chinese, do you?'

'Barely a word.'

'Know someone who does?'

I did, of course. Hexter. But I wasn't quite ready to tell Norrback that. Though his expression suggested I didn't actually need to.

'I took my own precautions during your meeting with Slavsky,' he went on. 'I wasn't happy with what was going on. I needed to be sure I wasn't being dragged into something that could come back and bite me. So, I recorded all incoming and outgoing telephone calls. Just to see who was saying what to who.' He reached into his coat and pulled out a pocket tape player, with a single earphone dangling from it. 'Press *Play* when you're ready,' he said, handing me the machine. 'Outgoing call to a car phone number, late afternoon, Sunday September twenty-fourth. Just around the time Slavsky left.'

I put the earphone in and looked at Norrback. He nodded. Then I pressed *Play*.

It was just a few minutes of two men talking in Chinese. I couldn't understand any of it. Neither mentioned Slavsky, as far as I could tell. But that hardly mattered. Because I was more or less certain I recognized one of the voices. It had a different intonation in Chinese. But still it was familiar.

187

'Is it Hexter's voice?' he asked.

I nodded. 'I think so, yes.'

'How sure are you?'

'I can't be absolutely certain. But . . . it sounds like him to me.'

Norrback sighed. 'There it is, then.'

'What are they saying?'

'I don't know.'

'Surely you've had it translated.'

'No! Who could I trust to translate it? And it doesn't really matter what the actual words spoken mean. You *know* what it means.'

Yes. I knew. We both knew. 'You're not going to let me have a copy of that tape, are you, Tahvo?'

He shook his head. 'If I did, I'd be in as much danger as you are.'

'Maybe you shouldn't have let me hear it.'

'Maybe. But you know the truth now. This way, you have a chance. I couldn't deny you that.'

'Thanks.' I meant it. Norrback had taken a risk coming to me. I couldn't blame him for shying away from a still bigger risk.

'I'll be back in Helsinki by Wednesday. If you need to contact me, phone this number.' He pushed a folded square of paper into my hand. 'The man who'll answer is my brother Alvar. You can trust him to pass a message on to me. No one else. To be sure, ask him what our parents gave him for his twenty-first birthday.' He told me what it was. 'This is for an emergency only, you understand?'

'I understand, Tahvo. If I need to contact you, I will. Otherwise . . .'

'I hope it goes well for you, my friend. I do not know what the best thing is for you to do.'

188

'Neither do I. Yet. But I'll work it out. Keep that tape safe, won't you? And thanks again.'

We shook hands. Then he hugged me. '*Onnea*,' he murmured. It was one of the very few Finnish words I knew. He was wishing me luck. And we both knew I was going to need it.

Norrback headed south from the piazza. I watched him vanish from view and satisfied myself no one had followed him. Then I threaded my way through the Christmas market and made for my apartment.

I hadn't decided what I was going to do, but making myself scarce was the only way to start. I hadn't spent sixteen years working in the intelligence world without learning that an ability to abandon the known and familiar if the need arose was essential. I'd thought about what to do in a situation like this many times. I'd even prepared for it in a few basic ways. But even so, now it was happening, I didn't really feel prepared at all.

I was filled with rage at Hexter. But I had to stifle my rage and concentrate calmly on protecting myself. Everything I did now I had to stand back from and assess dispassionately. Every choice I made had to be the right choice. One mistake could be the end. One slip could finish me.

I stuck close to the walls of the alley as I approached the apartment building so I'd be hard to spot from an upper floor. I let myself in carefully, with no scraping of the key or slamming of the door. And I took the stairs up rather than the wheezy, clanking lift. I didn't want to advertise my arrival to anyone.

As soon as I slid the key silently into the lock on the

door of my flat, I knew there was something wrong. The double lock hadn't been engaged. If Norrback hadn't warned me, I might have written that off as carelessness on my part. Not now.

I threw the door open and launched myself in. If the intruder was still there, my only advantage was surprise.

A figure moved across my field of vision, entering the kitchen in a rush. Rinaldo. If that really was his name.

I saw him grab a knife from the table. He might have been waiting a long time for me to return. And time can undermine concentration. Whatever the reason, he wasn't as ready for me as he should have been.

I kept a heavy round ebony ruler on the lintel above the kitchen door. You can never be too careful. And Rinaldo hadn't been careful enough. The ruler was still there when I stretched up for it. I swung it down as Rinaldo turned towards me, grasping the knife.

The first blow took him on the wrist. His fingers lost their grip. The knife fell to the floor. The second, third and fourth blows were to his head. He went down. And he stayed down.

He wasn't dead. How long he'd remain unconscious I had no way of knowing, so I dragged him into the bathroom and tied him to the pedestal of the handbasin. Then I went through his pockets. There was no identification on him. But there was a nude photograph of Cinzia which looked as if it was intended to be used in some scene-setting.

The plan was to write my death off as murder by my girlfriend's cuckolded husband. That was clear. So, Cinzia was in on it too. She was the bait in the trap. What I felt for her was what she'd been instructed to make me feel. And what she felt for me was . . . nothing.

I checked as thoroughly as I could to see if Rinaldo had planted anything incriminating in the flat. I needed to move fast, but I also needed to know what I was up against.

I found it in the wobbly bureau I kept my paperwork in. A blank buff envelope I didn't recognize. Inside, a sheaf of statements for a bank account in Hong Kong in my name. There were a lot of deposits. One larger than most on the twenty-fifth of September, the day after Slavsky was killed. Neat. Very neat. To those who didn't know any better, this would look like a Chinese-funded nest egg. My reward for treacherous services rendered.

I wasn't going to leave the statements there, of course, but I knew it wouldn't make any difference. Hexter would make sure the account was discovered one way or another. And Rinaldo, having botched my murder, would be edited out of the official version of events. I'd survived, but only for now. I was going to become a hunted man. And the advantage was all with the hunters.

Rinaldo was beginning to come round when I left. I pulled the telephone wire out of the wall to make it more difficult for him to raise the alarm, but, even if he couldn't work his way free, they'd come looking for him eventually. I only had a limited amount of time to make my escape. All I took with me was a hurriedly packed shoulder-bag. For the journey I was embarking on, travelling light was going to be essential.

The ebony ruler wasn't the only thing Rinaldo had overlooked. He'd failed to find where I'd hidden my reserve passport. Not the reserve supplied by the Service, but one I'd got hold of on my own initiative as a precaution. I'd never supposed I'd actually have to use my alternative identity. But now I did. Duncan Forrester was born.

Or *re*born. The original Duncan Forrester died in a motorcycle accident in 1968, aged seventeen. He'd never held a passport. And the one I held in his name had never been used. But soon it would be.

I picked up a taxi from the rank at the northern end of Piazza Navona and made straight for Termini station. I had no particular destination in mind. Getting out of Rome as quickly as possible was my number one priority.

Six hours later, I was in Genoa. I walked out of the station into gathering darkness and an unknowable future. I could have gone on to Milan, but a busy port city full of foreigners and loners struck me as a better bet. There were plenty of onward train and ferry routes to choose from and the tangled network of piazzas, alleys and flights of steps in the old centre were ideal for getting lost. And lost was what I most needed to be.

I booked into a small, cheap hotel and spent the evening drifting from bar to bar, debating what I should do and where I should go. I had little confidence in talking my way out of the trap Hexter had sprung on me. The only hard evidence against him was in Norrback's possession and I couldn't expect Norrback to endanger himself by letting me use it. Worse still, there was the very real possibility we wouldn't be believed, with the tape dismissed as a fake and Hexter proclaimed innocent. By contrast, the bank account in my name, with all those Hong Kong dollars in it, was damning.

*

192

I hardly slept that night, tormented by uncertainty about what to do for the best and imagining revenges I was unlikely ever to be able to inflict. I'd believed Cinzia loved me. Even allowing for my reservations about him, I'd believed Hexter was loyal. They'd both betrayed me. And Hexter had betrayed his country. I'd failed utterly to see any of this coming.

I headed out before dawn and found a *caffè* not far from the hotel where there was a metered phone the owner was willing to let me use for a long-distance call, although I had to part with a deposit of a couple of thousand lire before I was allowed to dial the number.

I strongly suspected Hexter had returned to London and was probably at home, given how early it was there. But what would speaking to him achieve? What exactly was I going to say? I didn't know. All I knew was that I wanted to hear his voice when he denied what he'd done.

It rang a long time, in that Chelsea flat of his I'd never been inside. Eventually, he picked up.

'Hexter,' he announced.

'It's me,' I responded.

'Well, well. This is a surprise. Where are you?'

'Not where you want me to be.'

'I gather you've got yourself in a spot of bother. There are some serious questions for you to answer.'

'You already know the answers to those questions, Clive.'

'Why don't you come into HQ and sort it all out?'

'You tipped the Chinese off to kill Slavsky. Chen Shufan as well, I assume, when we were supposed to be bringing him over the border after Tiananmen Square. Was he going to name you as a traitor? Is that why he had to die? How many others have there been whose death warrants you've signed?'

193

'You're not making any sense.'

'Why the Chinese? Why sell out to them? How did they turn you? And when? How long have you been in their pocket?'

'Tell me where you are. I could come and meet you if it would help.'

'For the avoidance of doubt, Clive, let me tell you I intend to make you pay for what you've done.'

'It's what *you've* done that's the issue. There's been quite a flap here. Not everyone finds the accusations that have been made against you as hard to believe as I do.'

'Just tell me why you did it. Doesn't your country mean anything to you?'

'Let me give you a piece of advice, old boy. Don't threaten what you can't deliver. If you're confident of proving your innocence, come and do it. If not, disappear. I think you might have the aptitude for that. You've always struck me as somehow . . . insubstantial. The stuff of shadows, so to speak. So, slip away into those shadows. And stay there. Then no one will ever know for sure what you did or didn't do. You'll remain an officially unsettled question. I'll certainly argue there's nothing to be gained by searching for you indefinitely. How does that sound?'

'Like you're frightened of me, Clive. That's how it sounds.'

'Think about what I've said. Think about it long and hard. You won't get a better offer.'

'Is that what this is? An offer? From you to me?'

'What this is, old boy, is goodbye. Don't call again.'

He hung up then. After staring stupidly at the receiver in my hand for several moments, I hung up too.

*

I traded the balance of my deposit for a brandy-laced *doppio espresso* and sat drinking it by the bar, watching the rain fall on the cobbles outside. Another customer came in and started an animated conversation with the owner. The world shrank around me. I'd never felt more alone.

Later that day, I boarded a ferry bound for Tunis. Sailing time twenty-four hours. Long enough, I reckoned, for me to settle in my mind what I was going to do.

I couldn't win. That was the dismal truth I faced, gazing out from the stern of the ferry at its wake churning the grey Mediterranean water. I couldn't win.

But maybe I could avoid losing. In the end, Hexter's advice began to make a perverse kind of sense. If the Service was willing to back him against me, then let them. I was no stranger to solitude or misrepresentation. I could survive.

I stayed in Tunis for the next three months. But I had no wish to become a lifelong exile. Eventually, I decided it was safe to go home. I arrived on a Maltese cargo vessel, bound for Rotterdam. It stopped for bunkering at Falmouth and I got off there. I wasn't planning to stay in Falmouth. But life – the life of Duncan Forrester – turned out otherwise.

There's no need to tell you much about that life. It was – and should have remained – an unremarkable, inconspicuous existence, the kind millions of other people lead the length and breadth of the country.

I didn't think about my past much. Inevitably, though, the passage of world events reminded me of the alternative course Slavsky and those who backed him had hoped to plot. German reunification, the eastward expansion of NATO and the EU, the collapse of the Soviet Union, the slow, triumphant rise of China. It's all played out just as Hexter's masters in Beijing intended. The future, we're told, belongs to them. And maybe it does.

Probably I should never have got involved with Liz. But you can't repress emotion along with identity. It has a habit of ambushing you. I kept as distant as I could from the problems Charlie's fast-and-loose business activities caused her. But that wasn't quite distant enough.

Even if it had been, fate twists and turns in ways you can never anticipate. Of all the things Joe could excel at, why did it have to be Go? Maybe I should have studied the game sooner myself. Then I'd have known the key to victory at Go is the acquisition of territory.

That's why it's never mattered to Hexter whether I was alive or dead. I was surrounded. Therefore I was neutralized. Whether I stayed on the board, isolated and impotent, was irrelevant.

Or so he thought. So I'd have thought too. But now the stones have been swept from the board. I can't let him take Joe. What does he have in mind for him? How will he use him to serve his masters' interests?

I have to step out of the shadows. I have to face him. Maybe I should have done that thirty years ago. But it seemed to me defeat was certain. And I still think it was.

So, I retreated. I lived to fight another day.

And now that day has come.

END GAME

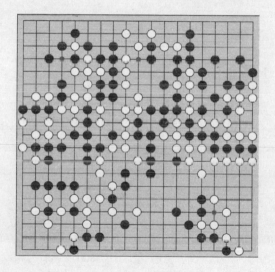

Sunday October 13

I NEVER WOULD'VE GUESSED HOW DRAINING LIVING ON YOUR nerves is. I feel exhausted in a strung-out kind of way. And I've no idea – absolutely none – whether what we're doing is our best shot in the circumstances, or won't make any difference at all in the long run. If that's the case, I'm running towards a wall. And I won't know it's there until I hit it.

Forrester isn't really equipped to reassure me. It's just not what he does. He's taciturn and self-sufficient by nature. I can see it's taken a lot out of him to tell me the story of how he ended up hiding from his past in Falmouth. Beyond that, he has plans and resources and he isn't about to give up the struggle. And he happens to be my only ally in all of this.

'Your old life is over,' he's said more than once, which, reluctantly and incredulously, I've forced myself to accept. But understanding that and living by it are two very different things. If there's a target on my back, how do I get it off?

As we hurried away from Kolonn Drogh across the fields yesterday afternoon, I was already living by different rules: Forrester's rules for survival. We hurried, but we didn't take the most direct route. We stuck to the hedge-lines. We made ourselves as inconspicuous as possible. Once we reached his borrowed Land Rover – borrowed from whom I didn't ask – he demanded I hand over my phone. It didn't do me any good to explain it was a pay-as-you-go I'd only bought that day. I'd paid by credit card and that meant it was traceable. He pulled out the SIM card and stamped it into the ground before throwing the phone into the next field.

Forrester had a stock of phones he categorized as safe for emergency use. They shared a holdall with wads of £20 and £50 notes. This little hoard was what we'd be rely-ing on in the days ahead. 'Everything electronic is our enemy, do you understand?' he said as we drove off along the lane. 'Hexter will be looking for us. And he'll be look-ing hard. We have to stay out of sight.'

'Is that actually possible?' I asked.

Forrester's answer was a long time coming. 'We'll find out, won't we?'

I guess we will. Unless I give in to temptation, go home and hand all my problems over to Venstrom to sort out. Except they wouldn't sort them out. I can't stop my mind dwelling on the sight that was waiting for me under the tarpaulin in the back of Vogler's car. Carl and Vogler, dead, hollow-eyed, with bullet-holes in their heads: exe-cuted. And I can't forget how easily and callously Roger planned to get rid of me, either. That would have been another execution. These are realities. The rest – going back to a normal life, putting all this behind me, starting afresh – is just a fantasy.

So, here we are, Forrester and I, planning some kind of

counter-attack, though what kind exactly he hasn't said. 'We'll head for London,' he announced. 'There's an old colleague there I need to speak to.'

'What can he tell you?'

'Not sure until I've spoken to him.'

'Can you trust him?'

'I think so. But I haven't seen him in thirty years. I don't know for sure if he's still with the Service. Or even alive.'

'Great.'

'No, it isn't. But we have to do what we can with what we've got.'

What Forrester hoped to get was the tape of Hexter talking in Chinese on Norrback's telephone in Helsinki in September 1989. For that he needed to speak to Norrback's brother, though the same provisos applied to the Norrbacks as they did to his old colleague. They could all be dead. Which would leave us swinging in the wind.

Still, he worked in deliberate stages. His calmness wasn't exactly infectious. But it made me feel he knew what he was doing. He related the events of thirty years ago as he drove, avoiding the trunk routes, working his way slowly east until, with night falling, we reached a pub advertising rooms on the fringes of Exmoor.

Cash up front, no questions asked. I was beginning to see how this worked. We shared a twin-bedded room. What the landlord made of our relationship I was too shattered even to wonder. We ate a meal in the bar, eyed by the locals. Forrester slipped out to make a call on one of his mobiles. To Finland.

When he came back, he said quietly, 'We're in luck. Alvar hasn't moved and he and Tahvo are both still alive and kicking. Alvar will pass my message on.'

'How long before Tahvo gets back to you?'

'Up to him. Alvar gave nothing away. But Tahvo knows I wouldn't have made contact unless it was important. He'll respond by text giving me a number to call. For that, we wait.'

'In places like this?'

He nodded. 'In places like this.'

'What if there's no text? What if Tahvo reckons it's safer after all these years to cut you adrift?'

'You think too much about the wrong things, Nicole. You can't control Norrback. Neither can I.'

'What can we control?'

'Ourselves. It's vital you don't panic or act on impulse. Marianne Vogler has your phone. So, any messages you've had on it she'll have received. That means she knows who contacts you and how frequently. Well, maybe she's not that interested now. But you have to tell your friends and relatives something that will stop them worrying about you. We don't want them going to the police.'

He's right. 'I've already told my mother and sister my phone's been stolen and I'm waiting for Venstrom to supply me with a new one, so I can't give them a new number yet. I can text my closest friends and stall them the same way. I'll explain I've borrowed the phone I'm using. Even so, Mum will start worrying if she doesn't hear from me again soon.'

'You just have to hold them off for the moment.'

'And how long is the moment?'

'I'm not sure. But every move we make has to be calculated.'

'Then you'd better tell me more about what those moves are going to be.'

'Sorry. I can't.'

'Why not?'

'Because I don't know what they are yet.'

His answer didn't help me sleep last night. Nor did the fact that he fell asleep himself in a matter of seconds, while I lay staring into the darkness, listening to his steady breathing and the burble of conversation from the bar below.

Speaking to Mum didn't help either. I pictured her as we talked, sitting by the phone – I called her on the land-line, as per Forrester's instructions – in the living room of the house in Norwich where I grew up. But I couldn't let myself think too much in case I broke down and cried. 'Everything's fine, Mum,' I assured her. 'Just hectic.'

Hectic. That's certainly one word for it.

And now we're on the move again, tracing a slow zigzag towards London through Somerset and Wiltshire as a dull, damp Sunday unfolds. Every hour, Forrester gets me to turn on the phone and check for a text from Norrback. Every hour, the answer's the same. 'Nothing.'

I ask him when and how he thinks Hexter was recruited by the Chinese, but he won't say more than he's already told me. He's trained himself so well to keep secrets it's hard to judge his mood. It doesn't seem to vary from a phlegmatic norm. He doesn't get angry or fretful. But then he doesn't get cheerful or chatty either.

'I could bear this a whole lot better if you gave a bit more, Duncan,' I complain at one point. 'I'm grateful for what you did for me at Kolonn Drogh. You saved my life. Don't think I don't appreciate that. But now I need to know why we're doing what we're doing.'

He doesn't respond, just keeps his gaze fixed on the

road ahead. And in the silence, something snaps in me. The grey, damp countryside. The unknowable future. The threat hanging over me that'll go on hanging over me as long as— Tears suddenly fill my eyes.

Forrester doesn't notice I'm crying until I pull out a tissue. He doesn't say anything, but he pulls into a field gateway a little way ahead and turns the engine off and says, 'I'm sorry.'

I blow my nose and try to sound normal. 'What are you sorry about?'

'I know you have no experience of anything like this to draw on, Nicole. And I know you'd like me to fast-track you back to your old life. But I can't. So, I'm sorry. But it is what it is. We have a chance, you and I. Whether it's a good chance or not is too soon to say.'

'What are we going to do?'

'We have to expose Hexter for what he is. There's no other way to exonerate you and me or get Joe out of his clutches.'

'What does Hexter want with Joe?'

'Not sure exactly.'

'But you think he's following orders from China?'

'Probably.'

'So, what do *they* want with Joe?'

'Nothing that'll turn out well for him. That much is certain.'

'And to stop Hexter, you need the tape?'

'Yes.'

'There's nothing else you have on him?'

'The man I'm hoping to see in London – Colin Bright – can answer that question. He never trusted Hexter. He's ten years younger than me, so he's probably still in the Service. Unless he's changed his mind about Hexter, which I doubt, he'll have been harbouring a lot of suspicions over the years. Maybe more than suspicions. He might – just might – have something we can use.'

'But the tape would be a big help.'

'It would. It *will*.'

'You really think Norrback will text you?'

'Yes. I do.'

'I hope you're right.'

'Hexter's going to offer Joe a deal. Participation in some SIS-controlled AI research project in return for getting the police off his back. He's probably already made the offer. And Joe won't have much option but to accept.'

'Where will they take him?'

'Not sure. I'm hoping Liz will give me some idea.'

'Liz? How will she know?'

'They'll have to let Joe speak to her to reassure her he's OK. Last I heard, she's due to be sent home from the hospital tomorrow. They won't want her pestering the police or going to the press. So, they'll aim to smooth things over before then. If Joe tells her he's happy to cooperate with them and will be in regular contact, I imagine she'll agree to keep quiet. But the detail of what Joe tells her may give us a clue to their intentions for him.'

'You're going to phone her?'

'Tomorrow. I can't risk contacting her prematurely. Contacting her at all is a risk.'

'She's probably worried about you as well as Joe.'

'She knows I'll do everything I can for him. And she's always known there's a lot I haven't told her about myself.'

'You think that'll stop her worrying?'

'Probably not. But there's nothing I can do about that. That goes for a lot of other things as well.'

'You could try saying something ever so slightly reassuring.'

'We'll be in London tonight. Where do you live?'

'I have an apartment near Tower Bridge.'

'Well, you can't go there. You understand that? It'll be under surveillance.'

'I understand.'

'As for those friends you mentioned, Hexter will probably have them under surveillance as well by now. Certainly your mother and sister. So, no more contact or you'll be reeled in and me with you. Pay for anything with plastic, swipe your Oyster card on a bus or linger in front of a CCTV camera, the same applies. Hexter will want to handle this quietly, so I don't think he'll have the police looking for us. But he can still bring a lot of search power to bear. Probably more than I know about. I'm not exactly up to date with the techniques. We'll stop at a superstore later and buy you some blend-in-with-the-crowd clothing. Hoodie, baseball cap, jeans, that sort of thing. You have to look as anonymous as possible. Stock up with underwear as well. We won't be loitering in launderettes. We won't be loitering anywhere.'

'Is any of this meant to be comforting?'

'I thought if you knew what our strategy was going to be, you might feel less anxious.'

'Just tell me it'll work, Duncan.'

'Nothing else will. I can guarantee that.'

He isn't lying. He isn't exaggerating. I see the truth in his gaze. His is the only way to go.

'You can bail out if you want to. I won't stop you. I *can't* stop you.'

'But surely you *should* stop me. Now I know about Norrback and Colin Bright.'

'How would I do that?'

I ponder the question for several moments. He's almost smiling at me.

'I've never killed anyone, Nicole. And I don't intend to start now.'

'How many people has Hexter killed?'

'Personally? Probably none. But if you mean how many deaths has he been responsible for . . .'

'Say I do mean that.'

'Slavsky and his team; those Chinese dissidents who never made it to Hong Kong because the military were tipped off about their escape route: they probably tot up to twenty. And that's just the ones I know about. We'd better multiply the figure by ten to take account of the scope of his very long and very treacherous career. So . . .'

'*Two hundred?*'

'Adding you to the list won't cause him a moment's hesitation.'

'Christ.' This is the truth. This is what we're up against, this old man and I.

'Are you ready to go on?'

I nod and answer softly, 'I'm ready.'

Which I'm not, really. But somehow . . . I'm going to have to be.

It's dusk by the time we cross the M25, on a minor road near Addlestone. I'm wearing my new blend-in-with-the-crowd clothing. I feel like a slightly different person as a result.

Forrester finds a privately run car park in a yard behind some shops in Brixton to stow the Land Rover for cash. We set off from there on foot. There's still been no message from Norrback.

We walk north through Lambeth, pausing to book ourselves a couple of rooms in the unlovely Consort Hotel near The Oval. The streets are damp, the traffic thin, the Consort is quiet, even if not at all cosy. It's a slow Sunday night.

Our destination is an area of terraced houses east of Waterloo station. 'I used to live round here,' Forrester volunteers as we head along Whittlesey Street. 'Colin and I were virtually neighbours. It was an easy walk to Century House. The Service has moved now, of course, to its palace beside the Thames at Vauxhall. But has Colin moved with it? That's the question.'

He stops at the door of one of the houses and rings the bell. There's a light in the downstairs front room and another light comes on in the hall. I think I can hear footsteps approaching. They're not rapid.

The door opens. A tiny, bird-like woman who could be anything between seventy and ninety looks out at us. She has blue-rinsed hair and a beady gaze. She's wearing what I think my grandmother would have called a housecoat.

Forrester smiles. Apparently, he recognizes her. 'Mrs Lane. It's good to see you.' He sounds as if he means it. 'Remember me?'

Mrs Lane peers at him for a moment. Recognition comes with a slight start and a hand to her cheek. 'My lord. It's Mr Travers.' Not Forrester, of course. I should have known. He only became Forrester when he went on the run in 1989. 'How long has it been?'

'Thirty years or more. But you haven't changed a bit.'

'Then all I can say is I must have looked a lot older than I was when we last met.' She looks at me. 'Hello, dear.' Then back at Forrester. 'Is this your daughter?'

'She's a friend.'

208

'Glad to hear that. Mr Bright said you didn't use to have any friends.'

'It's Mr Bright we're looking for, actually,' I say, giving the old lady a big smile.

'Does he still live here?' asks Forrester.

'Lord no. Moved out, oh, more than ten years ago. But he still sends me a Christmas card. Such a nice boy.'

'Does that mean you have his address?'

Mrs Lane furrows her brow thoughtfully. 'I do. But . . . he wouldn't want me handing it over just like that. Even to you.'

'Your discretion does you credit, Mrs Lane.' Forrester sounds patient and understanding. I bet he doesn't feel it. 'Maybe you have his phone number. It's really quite important I speak to him.'

'I suppose it must be, for you to turn up at my door. How did you know I was still in the land of the living?'

Forrester grins crookedly. 'I didn't. But I'd have put money on it.'

That seems to amuse the old lady. 'Tell you what I'll do,' she says. 'I'll call Mr Bright for you. Come on in.'

We enter a narrow hallway and follow Mrs Lane into the sitting room. It's small, cluttered and sparklingly clean. She offers us seats on the couch while she heads over to the phone, which stands on a low table next to an armchair.

She dials the number and looks at Forrester thoughtfully as she waits for an answer. 'Mr Bright said you left the Service,' she remarks.

'I did,' he responds.

'So—' She breaks off, then starts speaking more loudly, to the person on the other end of the line. 'It's Mavis Lane,

Mr Bright . . . Yes, I'm fine . . . I've got Mr Travers here . . . Yes. That's right. Alan Travers . . . He's here now.' She proffers the phone to Forrester. 'He wants to speak to you.'

Forrester gets up and takes the phone. By contrast with Mrs Lane, he speaks quietly into the handset, almost whispering. 'Hello, Colin . . . Yes indeed . . . I never expected you would either . . . Oh yes, it's certainly urgent . . . It does, yes . . . I've been left little choice in the matter . . . I'd much rather explain face to face . . . Anywhere you're happy with . . . OK . . . Yes . . . Got it . . . Let's say an hour from now . . . Agreed . . . 'Bye.'

Forrester puts the phone down. Mrs Lane frowns up at him from her considerable disadvantage of height. 'Are you in some kind of trouble, Mr Travers?' she asks gravely.

'Not that you need worry about, Mrs Lane.'

'It's Mr Bright I'm thinking of, to be honest. He's been very good to me.'

'We won't be causing him any trouble,' I say, hoping I sound reassuring. I stand up and smile at her.

She doesn't smile back. 'You won't be meaning to, I dare say. But what good's that if it comes anyway?'

In a gesture that surprises me, Forrester takes her hand. 'Thanks for phoning Colin, Mrs Lane.' His voice is gentle, almost regretful. 'It's been lovely to see you again, it really has. But I'm afraid we have to be going.'

We're heading for Soho. Bright's agreed to meet at a pub in Bateman Street. Forrester walks fast and would clearly prefer to walk in silence, but something's bothering me. I put it to him as we cross Hungerford Bridge.

'How can you be sure Hexter doesn't have Bright under surveillance? I mean, if he knows Bright doesn't trust him, he might've guessed you'll try to contact him.'

'Hexter would need top level approval to go after another member of the Service. And I doubt he'd relish explaining why he needed to. He has a lot of advantages over us. But he doesn't have it all his own way.'

Suddenly, Forrester pulls up. He glances behind us and moves over to the railings, then takes out his phone and turns it on.

'Anything?' I ask.

'Not yet,' he replies, switching the phone off again and burying it in his pocket.

He gazes downriver, at the illuminated outlines of the Gherkin and the Shard and the Cheese Grater, buildings that simply weren't there when he lived in London. Even Hungerford Bridge has been remodelled. I wonder for a moment how the scale of the changes that have swept in during his long absence makes him feel. Then I realize I haven't actually got a chance of guessing how Duncan Forrester – or Alan Travers – feels about anything at all.

'Come on,' he says, pushing himself away from the railings. 'I don't want to keep Colin waiting.'

Sunday night or not, the pub's crowded, with quite a few customers standing out on the pavement. We work our way through the ruck inside, entering by one door and leaving by another without Forrester giving any hint he's spotted Bright.

'No sign of him?' I ask when we're back on the street again.

Forrester just shakes his head.

'What now?'

'We—' Forrester breaks off. He looks across the road. There's a man standing in a doorway, watching us.

He crosses over to join us. He's tall and fleshy, a parka

211

hanging open over the sweat-shirted mound of his stomach. He has a round, smooth face and virtually no hair. In the sallow lamplight, he looks desperately pale. And nervous as well. Yes. More nervous even than me.

'Hello, Colin,' says Forrester.

'Hello, Alan.' They shake hands.

'Who's this?' Bright looks at me.

'Nicole,' I answer.

'Christ,' says Bright. 'You're the Venstrom woman.' He wipes his hand across his mouth.

'Good to know you're up to speed, Colin,' says Forrester.

'Wish I wasn't, really. I should have asked Mavis to tell you to fuck off.'

'Why didn't you?'

Bright shrugs. 'She detests bad language.'

Forrester nods over his shoulder. 'Why weren't you inside?'

'I was afraid I'd drink too much before you got here. I'm guessing I'll need a sober head tonight.'

'You wouldn't by any chance have wanted to be sure it was just us coming to meet you, would you?'

'There was that as well.'

'We can't talk here.'

'My flat's not far.'

'You live in Soho?'

'Going to make something of that, are you, Alan?'

'I was just wondering how easy it is to get to Vauxhall from here.'

'Easy enough, thank you very much.'

'Glad to hear it.'

Bright gives him a look that probably means more to Forrester than it does to me. Then he says, 'Follow me.'

He leads the way down Dean Street. We take a right

into Meard Street and reach the door to a small block of flats. In we go and up the stairs. Bright's seriously out of breath by the time we reach his flat on the second floor.

The place is just four rooms and a passage – I think. It's hard to be sure because most of the walls, apart from in the kitchen, are mirrored. It's as if we've stepped into a fairground entertainment. Forrester rolls his eyes at me as we follow Bright into the lounge, where the furniture gives some kind of perspective, though, thanks to the mirrors, there appears to be more of it than there actually is. Not to mention three or four versions of Bright, Forrester and me.

'Do a lot of reflecting in this room, Colin?' Forrester asks drily.

'It makes the flat look bigger,' Bright responds, a touch tetchily.

'That's a good thing, is it?'

'D'you want to give me a valuation for a quick sale? Or would you rather sit down and tell me what you want?'

We take off our coats and sit, Forrester and I on the couch, Bright perched on the edge of the cushion of one of the armchairs.

'You must have worked out what we want, Colin,' says Forrester.

'I'm not sure I have.'

'Help.'

'From me?' He looks genuinely surprised.

'How much do you know?'

'About Miss Nevinson here? Nothing, other than she's the luckless soul Venstrom sent down to Cornwall to find the Go wizard.'

'How did your colleague Roger Lam get there ahead of me?' I ask.

'The Service keeps a close eye on the computer industry. We got wind from an informant of your interest in the player who was massacring your computer at Go and decided we might have a better use for his talents than you. All we needed you to do for us was to identify him. That's what I assume, anyway. I wasn't closely involved. But I can't see any other way it could have gone. Unless . . .'

'The Chinese picked up on it from their monitoring activities,' says Forrester, finishing the thought for him. 'Go would interest them.'

Bright nods. 'So it would.'

'Did they tip Hexter's hand, d'you think?'

'You tell me. You're supposed to be the Chinese sell-out, Alan. Officially. Well, officially unofficially.'

'Excuse me, Colin,' I cut in. 'You've known Hexter is a Chinese double agent for, what, thirty years?'

Bright winces. '*Suspected*.'

'And you've done nothing about it?'

He shrugs. 'Without proof, what could I do?'

'Haven't you dug up *anything* on him?' Forrester asks.

'I need to know about you and the Go wizard first. What's the connection? When we heard about your involvement, most people didn't even know who you were – they're too young. For myself, I just couldn't make any sense of it.'

'There's no sense. It's just bad luck. I happen to be a friend of Joe's mother.'

'And but for Joe's ability at Go you'd never have stepped out of the shadows?'

'No. I never would have.'

'Maybe you should have cleared out as soon as you realized we were on Joe's trail.'

'I couldn't have done that.'

Bright's eyes narrow. 'Did he inherit his analytical genius from you, Alan? Is that it? Is Joe Roberts your son?'

Forrester sighs. 'Charlie Roberts is named as Joe's father on his birth certificate. And I've never heard you credit me with analytical genius before, Colin.'

'You should have stopped the boy drawing attention to himself,' says Bright.

'I didn't know he *was* drawing attention to himself. Until it was too late. And he wouldn't have taken any notice of me anyway. I'd have had to give him a really compelling reason, wouldn't I? Such as the truth. How d'you think that would have gone?'

'Hellish unlucky for you, having a brilliant son. Or should I say knowing the mother of a brilliant son? But aren't personal entanglements the first thing you're supposed to avoid if you want to be invisible?'

'It's easier said than done. Take it from me.'

'Oh, I don't know. I've done a good job in that regard without even needing to.' Bright smiles ruefully. 'What about you, Nicole? Married? Children? Someone waiting at home for you?'

'No to all three.'

'Just as well, given the situation you find yourself in.'

'What situation is that, as you see it?'

Bright grimaces. It looks as if he feels sorry for me. That makes two of us. 'You're a marked woman, I'm afraid. Hexter obviously decided you knew too much. I don't know who he engaged to deal with—'

'Roger Lam tried to kill me.'

Bright goes paler than ever. This news is apparently a shock to him. 'That can't be right.'

'I *was* there at the time.'

'You thought Hexter used a freelancer?' asks Forrester.

'Well, that would be . . . standard procedure.'

'He obviously had to move too fast for that to be practical.'

'Even so, it's . . .'

'A sign of desperation? Or arrogance?'

'Christ. This is serious.'

'Tell us something we don't already know.'

'You should take Nicole somewhere safe, Alan. Somewhere a long way from anywhere. You disappeared thirty years ago. Do it again. Do it for both of you. That's my advice.' And his expression tells me it's sincere advice.

'What about Joe?'

'He'll be well looked after. He's a valuable asset. No one's going to let any harm come to him.'

'I should let Hexter decide Joe's future?'

'You don't have much choice in the matter. You have nothing on your side. Well, as far as I know. Do you have anything to hurt Hexter with?'

'Maybe.'

'Really? Can you make it stick?'

'Not sure yet. I could certainly use extra ammunition.'

'And you think I can supply some?'

'Well, can you?'

'It's just a rumour.' Bright's voice has dropped close to a whisper. 'I've never been able to back it up. Chen Shufan. Remember him?'

'Of course I remember him,' Forrester replies. 'One of Operation Yellowbird's failures. Betrayed to the Chinese by Hexter, like as not.'

'And killed by a PLA patrol?' Bright glances at me. 'People's Liberation Army,' he clarifies, though actually he doesn't need to.

'That's what we heard.'

'Well, the rumour is he faked his own death with help from a sympathetic PLA officer and left China by some other route because he was convinced he wasn't going to be allowed to reach Hong Kong alive.'

'What convinced him of that?'

'Loose talk by his uncle, Deng Xiaoping's bridge partner, about how the PLA's intelligence arm had recruited a highly placed double agent either in the CIA or our own ranks here in London. Codename White Tiger. Chen believed White Tiger had a hand in Operation Yellowbird and wasn't about to let someone with his connections make it out.'

'And Chen's still alive?'

'That's the rumour.'

'Where is he?'

'Hamburg, so they say. But I spent the better part of a fortnight's annual leave scouring the city to no avail.'

Forrester furrows his brow. 'What were you hoping to get out of him, Colin?'

'A name. According to the rumour Chen has proof of who White Tiger really is. Officially that's of no interest, of course, because the working assumption is you're White Tiger – if anyone is – and out of the game since eighty-nine.'

'What sort of proof is Chen supposed to have?'

'The unspecified sort.'

'And this rumour. Where's it come from?'

'Exile circles in Taiwan.'

'Reliable?'

'It's an officially discredited source.'

'Says who?'

Bright smiles weakly. 'Roger Lam. He's our Taiwan expert.'

Forrester says nothing. I just catch a sigh from him. 'Surely it's obvious Hexter is White Tiger,' I cut in.

'Not if you believe White Tiger is probably no more than an invention of a dirty tricks unit at the Chinese Ministry of State Security,' says Bright wearily. 'That was Roger Lam's conclusion. Which found general favour.'

'Have you really no way of tracing Chen, Colin?' asks Forrester.

'I've spoken to dozens of noodle chefs who are supposed to be his first or second cousin. So far all I've got out of that is an overdose of monosodium glutamate. I think he probably knows I'm looking for him. But he doesn't want to be found. And I can't say I blame him.'

'So, there's no point pinning our hopes on Chen Shufan.'

'Definitely not. Like I told you, your wisest course of action is to drop out of sight. Permanently.'

Forrester seems to be giving the idea serious thought for a moment. Then he rouses himself and says, 'Do you know what their immediate plans are for Joe?'

'No. But I can guess. His greatest potential is in combating the latest computer-enhanced encryption techniques. So, I expect he'll be evaluated at GCHQ in the first instance.'

'I need to know for certain. I bet you could find out.'

'You do, do you?'

'I'm not ready to give up on this, Colin.'

Bright looks at me. 'Can't you talk some sense into him, Nicole?'

What is sense in our situation? I have no way of judging how far Forrester can take this. Nor where my best chances lie. I spread my arms helplessly.

'All right,' Bright concedes. 'I'll see what I can dig up.'

'Tomorrow?' Forrester presses.

'I'll do my best. But I'd feel a lot more . . . motivated . . . if you told me what you had on Hexter.'

'I'll tell you when I'm sure I can back it up.'

'And when's that likely to be?'

'I'll call you this time tomorrow night. OK?'

'OK. But do you want to give me a number where I can contact you before then? In case I have something definite for you.'

'No. I can't afford to take any unnecessary risks. You can't either. So don't go too far out on a limb for me, will you?'

'Absolutely not. An ear to the ground. That's all I can offer.'

'And it's good enough,' says Forrester. 'Thanks, Colin.'

We leave Bright's flat and walk out into Meard Street. A terrible feeling of bleakness sweeps over me. We have nothing on Hexter and we're not going to get anything on him. We won't be able to help ourselves, let alone Joe. My old life's gone and it's not coming back. I can't speak to my family or my friends. I can't go into the office. I can't go home. I can't even take a trip on the Tube. I'm lost. And my only guide is a man I barely know who may well be lost himself.

'What's wrong, Nicole?' Forrester asks. 'You're trembling.'

He's right. I am, though I wasn't aware of it. I tense my shoulders and the trembling goes away.

'Let's have a drink,' he suggests. 'We both need one.'

We go back to the pub where we met Bright. It's quieter now. I ask for a large gin and tonic. Forrester opts for whisky. We sit down in a corner.

'You're worried,' says Forrester matter-of-factly.

'Shouldn't I be?'

'Of course you should. If Norrback never makes contact and Chen Shufan stays out of sight . . .'

'We're screwed. I mean, my whole life is . . . over.'

'As you know it, yes. But if we do have to disappear permanently, like Colin said, I'll help you. OK? I'll show you how to build a new life.'

'I wasn't finished with this one.'

'It's the best I can offer.'

I believe him. 'Thanks,' I manage to say.

'You're welcome.'

'What about Joe?'

'Too soon to say.'

'If there's a rabbit you're planning to pull out of the hat at some point, you'd tell me, wouldn't you?'

'That would depend. But there's no rabbit, so the question doesn't arise.'

'You could take pity on me and lie. Tell me the situation isn't as bad as I think it is.'

'Do you want me to do that?'

'It doesn't work if I know you're lying.'

'No point, then. We're stuck with reality. Sorry.' He drains his glass. 'Let's go. Tempting as it is, staying here and getting drunk isn't a good idea.'

'What is?'

'Holding our nerve.'

'I'm not sure I'm any good at that, Duncan.'

'You're better than I expected, as a matter of fact.'

'Is that supposed to be a compliment?'

'Not sure.' He gives me a mirthless grin. 'But you can take it as one.'

Monday October 14

I WAKE TO A COMFORTLESS REALITY. I'M IN A SMALL, THIN-curtained room at the Consort Hotel, Kennington. My back aches slightly from the lumpy mattress. I grab the remote from the bedside table and try to turn the wall-mounted TV on, but I have to open the back of the remote and thumb the batteries around before it'll register. I get breakfast television, a couple of talking heads. I can't actually focus on what they're talking *about*. Blah, blah, blah, blah. I try to turn it off, but the remote's playing up again. I get out of bed and fumble around the set until I find a switch. *Off.*

The bathroom's tiny. The plastic curtain clings to me as I stand under the shower. The water won't stay at one temperature or even a fixed pressure. I feel miserable, oppressed by uncertainty.

The breakfast room is in the basement. I can't face the fry-up the waitress offers. I munch my way through some cornflakes and soggy toast. I swallow coffee that's stood too long in a stained Pyrex jug. It's wet outside. I can see a wedge of charcoal sky and slashes of rain against the window.

There's no sign of Forrester, so I knock on the door of his room as I go back to mine. No answer. *Don't go out alone.* That's what he said last night. And I said I had nowhere to go. Which was true. It still is. Christ almighty, what a mess.

I brush my teeth and look at myself long and hard in the bathroom mirror. There are bags under my eyes. My skin's grey. I don't have any volumizer for my hair. This isn't how I want to be. Already, I don't look like me.

I go to the window. It's still raining. The traffic moves slowly past. I live in London. But I don't feel as if I live in the city I'm looking out at.

Then I spot Forrester, heading along the pavement towards the hotel. He's carrying a plastic carrier-bag, filled with newspapers. He doesn't look up. He doesn't draw any attention to himself. You'd walk past him a hundred times over and never remember. He looks old and drab and . . . defeated.

Appearances can be deceptive, I tell myself. I'd better hope that's true.

I wait, expecting him to knock on my door. But several minutes pass and there's no knock.

I lose patience and go to his room. I sense him studying me through the spy-hole before he opens up.

The newspapers are strewn across the bed. He's been leafing through them.

'Looking for something?' I ask.

'Mention of a double murder in Cornwall,' he replies.

'Anything?'

'Not a word. Rather as I expected. Hexter's closed this down. That's to our advantage. His too, obviously. But it means we stay anonymous.'

'Why is it to *his* advantage?'

'It keeps Joe out of the public eye. It shuts Liz up. It gives him complete control. As he sees it.'

'I guess he's not worried about us.'

'He thinks we're powerless.'

'Well, we are, aren't we?'

Forrester gives me half a smile that makes my heart jump. 'I've heard from Norrback.'

'He still has the tape?'

'Oh yes.'

'And he's willing to give it to you?'

Forrester nods. 'Yes. I explained the tape is the only hope we have of defeating Hexter. And I got the impression Tahvo wants to see Hexter brought to justice. He's never had the nerve to try and do that himself, which is understandable enough when you consider what happened to Curtis and Bourdil. But now . . . he's old, pushing eighty, with little to lose, and we're . . . in extremis. The time has come.'

'What's the plan?'

'He's flying over from Helsinki tomorrow. His flight gets in at one thirty. He'll take the Heathrow Express to Paddington and walk down into Hyde Park. We'll meet him there and take delivery.'

'Then what?'

'I persuade Colin to help us find someone who can translate the tape. Then we take it to the top. Over Hexter's head.'

'Thirty years ago, you were afraid you wouldn't be believed. That the tape would be dismissed as a fake.'

'We'll have to make sure it isn't, won't we? Voice recognition technology has moved on a lot in those thirty years. If we can prove it's Hexter's voice, triggering the hit on Slavsky, he won't be able to talk his way out of it.'

'Well, tomorrow afternoon can't come soon enough for me.'

'I know. Until then, we have to be patient.'

'Will we stay here tonight?'

'No. We're moving on. But don't get your hopes up. We won't be going up market.'

Forrester turns out to be wrong on that last point. The Europa Hotel, Shepherd's Bush Road, is actually a step up from the Consort in comfort and cleanliness, even if it isn't any more expensive.

Forrester seems content to stay in his room and see out the day. When I tell him I'm going to have to go for a walk or I'll lose my mind, he tells me I must be careful. Keep my head down. Don't talk to anyone. Don't get involved in anything. Better still, don't go.

But I do go. Down to Hammersmith, where I mingle with the rush hour crowds near the Tube station and try to imagine feeling a normal part of London life again. I buy a few essential cosmetics in Boots that I hope will cheer me up a bit, then I go into a big, busy pub and nurse one large gin and tonic while pretending to read the *Evening Standard*. I watch three women of about my age laughing and gossiping at a nearby table. That could be me, Kathy and Sarah on a girls' night out. But it's not. I'm not part of any group. No one speaks to me. No one gives me a second glance. I'm invisible. I feel like . . . nothing.

I go back to the Europa and knock on Forrester's door.

He actually looks relieved to see me. I ask him if he was worried I wouldn't come back.

'Where else would you go?' he asks, as if genuinely

curious to know. Then, suddenly anxious, he adds, 'You haven't phoned anyone, have you?'

'No. I haven't.' I sink into the only chair. Forrester sits on the edge of the bed. 'Has anything happened?' I ask, unsure whether I really want to know the answer.

'I've spoken to Liz.' He says it casually, as if speaking to the woman he presumably once loved and maybe still does isn't so very significant.

'What did she say?'

'She's home, with Hazel and Karen looking after her. And she's heard from Joe as well as the solicitor Lam found for him. The police have dropped all charges, as we anticipated, and Joe's agreed to participate, *voluntarily*, supposedly, in a government-sponsored AI research project that's so hush-hush he can't tell her or Karen anything about it. He hasn't even said where he is at the moment, though you and I can guess. She's fretting about him, of course, but she can contact him on his phone and he sounds OK, she says. In a few days, he'll be able to tell her more. That goes for Karen too. Naturally, the solicitor recommends they do nothing to deter him from cooperating fully, "in his own best interests".' Forrester sighs. 'They have to go along with it to keep Joe out of trouble. They have no choice.'

'Where do they think you are?'

'Lying low somewhere. I told Liz I had to avoid the police because of some problems in my past, which was more or less what she'd assumed anyway. She knows I'll be in touch as and when it's safe.'

'And what about me?'

'I didn't tell Liz you were with me. The less she knows about our activities the better. As far as Conrad Vogler and your luckless colleague are concerned, they've heard nothing except that Vogler *and* Mrs Vogler have gone missing. The murders are being kept quiet. At least for now. What Hexter's planning on that front I'm not sure.'

'And what are we planning?'

'To meet Tahvo tomorrow afternoon, take charge of the tape, get it translated and see where we go from there.'

'You make it sound simple.'

'Perhaps it will be.'

'But perhaps not.'

'There's no sense meeting trouble halfway, Nicole. I've spoken to Colin as well. He says all the indications are that Joe's in Cheltenham, under close supervision by GCHQ staff. Hexter's expected to be there all week, apparently. According to Colin, he has a house in the Cotswolds, which was news to me but somehow not surprising. So it sounds like Hexter plans to keep a personal eye on Joe during his induction. That suggests he isn't unduly worried about us.'

'What does he think we're doing?'

'Running. With a view to hiding. It's what I opted to do thirty years ago, after all.'

'So, he won't see the danger from us until it's too late?'

'That's the idea. If he has a weakness, it's arrogance. He thinks I'm too frightened to make a move against him.'

'I hope you're right, Duncan, I really do.'

He looks intently at me. 'I know this isn't easy for you, Nicole. It must be strange, being in London but not being able to do any of the things you normally do or see any of the people you normally see.'

'It's way beyond strange. When I came back from California . . .' The words die in my throat. I really don't want to hear myself confiding in Forrester about my disastrous affair with Kevin Scheffer, Venstrom's chief

226

product officer, which ended with me being frozen out and sent back to London in a sort of unspecified but universally understood banishment. I remember consoling myself with the thought that in London I might be able to restore some balance to my life and rebuild my career. Christ, if only I'd known . . . 'Just tell me we won't have to keep this up for long.'

He almost smiles. 'We won't have to keep this up for long.'

Do I believe him? I'm not sure. I only know that in this moment I want to believe him. More than anything.

Tuesday October 15

I GET THROUGH THE MORNING MUCH AS I GOT THROUGH yesterday morning. I feel marginally better than yesterday, because today there's half a chance I'll start to emerge from this nightmare. Today, we rendezvous with Tahvo Norrback. And get the ammunition we need to use against Hexter.

Nothing's going to go wrong. Nothing's going to stop us.

That's what I tell myself, anyway.

Forrester drives to the underground car park beneath Hyde Park. Up in the open air, leaves are blowing across the paths with a metallic, rustling noise. The wind's cool and there aren't many people about. We head for the pony paddock on the north side of the park, near the gate where we're expecting Norrback to arrive in the next half hour or so.

Forrester's checked on the latest phone he's using that Norrback's flight has landed on time. The Heathrow Express is pretty reliable, so he should be here soon.

We stand in the shelter of some trees, giving us a good view of the gate without giving anyone a good view of us.

We don't talk much. There's nothing to say, really. We need the tape. We need Norrback. And for both we have to wait.

And wait. And wait.

It's too long. I can't say exactly when the realization begins to seep into me. But I begin to think: *He's not coming.*

He should be here by now.

But he isn't.

Forrester says nothing, but I can see he's worried. Where's Norrback? We can stare at the gate leading to Bayswater Road as long and hard as we like and will him to appear. But he isn't going to. I just know. I know and I don't want to. But I know. He isn't coming.

We can't phone him and ask what the problem is. Forrester doesn't need to tell me, though he does, that if Norrback's been waylaid in some way, we can't under any circumstances contact him without running the risk that our whereabouts will be tracked.

Of course, if Hexter has somehow got wind of our plans and had Norrback picked up, Norrback himself might have revealed where we are. It's an outside possibility, but it only makes the wind feel colder as we stand there. And maybe that's the reason Forrester finally says, 'Go to the tea room at the east end of the Serpentine and wait there. I have to give Tahvo longer, but something's obviously wrong, so it's better we split up.'

I'm not sure about that. Not by a long way. 'We should stick together.'

'It's a balance of risk, Nicole. Take these.' He hands me the keys to the Land Rover. 'And this.' He slips another phone out of his pocket and slides it into my palm. 'I'll text you on that or join you by five o'clock. If you haven't heard from me or if I haven't shown up by then, take the car and go.'

'Go where?'

'I don't know. But get out of London. Lie low somewhere.'

'I'm not going without you.'

'You have to.'

'What's gone wrong?'

'I don't know. And I've no way of finding out. But you shouldn't stay here.'

'Is Hexter on to us?'

'Hard to see how he could be. No one knew the plan, except Tahvo and us. And he wouldn't have betrayed us.'

'Are you sure of that?'

There's a flash of anger in his eyes. But he stifles it. 'Just go to the tea room, Nicole. And wait there. Please.'

So I go. The tea-room day is winding down. I sit by the big window looking out on to the lake with my coffee, watching the ducks moving on the water. Normality surrounds me like a bubble that could be pricked at any moment. I'm not sure I can take much more of this. The inaction. The uncertainty. The foreboding.

As five o'clock nears with no message on the phone, I force myself to start thinking about driving away from here alone and where I could go and what I could do. There are no answers, only questions. I feel sick with apprehension.

And then he walks in. Thank God. He doesn't move much beyond the door, just signals for me to leave. There's no one with him. Norrback hasn't come. It's just the two of us. With no tape.

All Forrester says to me as we hurry away from the tea room is, 'We have to go.'

'What's happened?' I ask.

'Nothing. That's why we have to go.'

'Where's Norrback?'

'We have to go, Nicole. We have no choice. Time's up.'

'But where can he be?'

Forrester doesn't reply. He just strides on, head down. And I follow.

'Tell me you know what we should do next,' I say as he drives out of the car park on to Park Lane.

'We have to wait on events.'

'What does that mean?'

'It means eventually Tahvo – or his brother – will explain what went wrong. Or that'll become obvious from other developments. There's nothing we can do now that won't make us conspicuous. And if Hexter has intervened, conspicuous is the last thing we need to be.'

'Can't you ask Colin Bright?'

'I haven't told him about Tahvo. And anyway I can't risk contacting him until I've got some idea of what's really going on. Our plan didn't work. We have to find out why before we try anything else. And we have to find out without giving ourselves away.'

'Meaning we just go on hiding in the Europa Hotel?'

'For the moment, yes.'

'Dear God.' The words come out of my mouth as I

contemplate long hours of solitude in my miserable room. 'I'm not sure I can do that, Duncan.'

'You have to.'

'This is driving me crazy.'

'Don't let it. Stay calm. Stay focused. We can't afford to make a single mistake.'

'But we've got nothing – absolutely nothing – to use against Hexter. We're no better off than we were three days ago.'

'We're still alive. And we're still free.'

Alive and free. I try to tell myself it's enough.

I don't tell Forrester I'm leaving the Europa that evening. I can't face another lecture from him on being careful. I walk up to Shepherd's Bush Green and use a call-box – for the first time in God knows how many years – to phone Mum. It's probably just as well she's out. Late shift at the hospital, maybe. I leave a reassuring message. 'No new number yet, but everything's fine. Don't worry. I'll call again.'

I go into a nearby cinema and watch a movie I barely follow while my mind whirls round the dangers of the situation I'm in.

I end up wondering if Forrester's telling me everything he can. Are there elements in all this he hasn't mentioned – doesn't think I need to know about? Just how badly placed are we?

I come out of the cinema into a drizzly London night. Do I walk back to the Europa and try to sleep? Do I go on trusting Forrester's every decision? I long to act on my initiative. I long to regain some form of control over what's happening to me. Take charge. Stand up for myself. Move forward. Somehow.

I hail a taxi and get in. 'Where to, luv?' the driver has to prompt me. Still I hesitate. 'You all right?'

'Yes. I'm fine. Take me to Piccadilly Circus.'

I walk up into Soho. The people moving around me make me feel safe. They don't care about me. All they're interested in is having a good time.

I reckon there's a good chance Colin Bright's at home this late on a Tuesday night. If not, I'll wait for him to return. I'll charm him into revealing as much as he knows, including what's happened to Norrback. He'll surely have heard something if Hexter had Norrback picked up at the airport. That's my plan. And it's better than nothing. By a long way.

There's a light in his window. I ring the bell for his flat. No response. I ring again. There's a crackle of static. 'It's Nicole Nevinson, Colin. Can I speak to you? It's just me.' No answer. He seems to be thinking about it. Then the door-release buzzes. I go in and climb the stairs.

He's opened his door already. It's standing ajar. I push it open, call his name and go in. The lights are on in the hall, kitchen and lounge, doubled and tripled in the mirrored walls. But I can't actually see Colin.

I go into the lounge. He isn't there. 'Colin?' I call again. No answer. The flat is silent. Now, suddenly, I'm spooked. I turn back towards the hall.

There's a figure in the doorway, blocking my exit. Frank Scaddan, the thug from Admiral's Reach. He has the same blankly menacing gaze I remember. He's chewing gum and looking at me as if he can't quite decide what to do with me.

'Hello,' he says casually. 'What brings you here?'

'Where's Colin?' I ask, trying desperately to understand how Scaddan has entered Colin Bright's world.

'Dunno. Doesn't matter. *You're* here.'

'Well, I'm leaving.' The assertion sounds hollow even to me. I advance towards him. He doesn't move.

'You're going nowhere.'

'Get out of my way.'

'Where does Bright stash his secrets? Got a safe, has he? Some hidey-hole? Must be somewhere, behind one of these fucking mirrors. I'm tired of looking. Why don't you show me?'

'I don't know what you're talking about.'

'No? Then why'd you come here?'

'None of your business.'

'My business is whatever I make it. Right now it's digging out anything Bright's squirrelled away. So, let's start with what you wanted off him. Then we can move on to where he might've put it.'

'Did Marianne send you here?' My brain is spinning. It's as hard to imagine who else could have as it is to understand *why* she should have. What the hell is going on?

'What did you come here for?'

'I don't have to explain myself to you.'

He sniggers. ''Course you do.' Then his right arm shoots towards me. I see the suddenness of the move reflected in the nearest mirror, but I'm too slow to react. The heel of his hand strikes me hard on the bridge of my nose and the next thing I know I'm lying on my back with a literally blinding pain between my eyes and heavy weights pressing down on my shoulders.

As soon as I can see again, I realize Scaddan's sitting on my ribcage, with his knees pinning my shoulders to the floor. I try to squirm free, but of course that's pointless;

he's far too strong for me. His hand closes round my throat. He forces my jaw back so it becomes difficult to breathe.

'Why are you here?' His voice has a rasping note.

'I . . . came to see Colin.'

'What about?'

'I . . . hoped he could help me.'

'What with?'

'I don't want to . . . get caught up in those murders . . . in Cornwall. I just . . . thought he could . . . keep me out of it.'

'How's big boy Bright gonna do that?'

'No idea. I just . . . didn't have anywhere else to turn.'

'Has he got some dirt on Hexter?'

Hexter? What do Scaddan and Marianne Vogler have to do with Hexter? They shouldn't even know his name. 'I don't know who—'

'Bullshit.' His grip tightens. 'You know who he is. It's why you're here.' I see something moving behind him. It's reflected in the mirror behind *me*. I can't work out what it is. Scaddan doesn't seem to notice. 'You'd better—'

Suddenly, an inverted Colin Bright swings into my field of vision. There's a click that stops Scaddan in mid-sentence. I feel him tense above me.

'I'll shoot you if I have to,' says Bright.

'You don't want to do that,' says Scaddan.

'Get off her.'

'OK. OK.'

Scaddan moves his knees away from my shoulders and stands up. I tilt my head forward and look up. Bright's holding a gun, in a way that suggests it's not something that comes naturally to him. He's pressing the barrel against Scaddan's neck, with his finger curled round the trigger. Scaddan's stopped chewing. But he doesn't look frightened or intimidated. He doesn't look as if he's lost control of the situation at all.

'What now, Col?' he asks.

'Who sent you here?'

'Can't discuss that.'

'It was Marianne Vogler,' I say, scrambling to my feet. 'It has to have been.'

'Why did she send you here?' demands Colin.

Scaddan doesn't reply. It doesn't look as if he's minded to. 'He said he was looking for . . . secrets,' I put in.

'Got a few of those, Col, I bet,' says Scaddan.

'You're going to tell me who sent you here and why.' Bright sounds frustrated that, despite having a gun in his hand, he can't seem to impose his will on Scaddan.

'No can do. Sorry. Best I can offer is to get out of your hair. Not that you've got any. But you know what I mean.'

'What secrets are you looking for?'

'Any you've got. But let's leave it for now, hey? I'll be off.'

'You're going nowhere until you've answered my questions.'

'You're not going to shoot me, Col. Not deliberately. Not in cold blood. You haven't got it in you. On the other hand, I don't want that gun going off by mistake while it's pointing at my head, so I'll just . . . leave you to it.'

Scaddan moves slowly, stepping carefully away from Bright and circling towards the door. Bright turns and tracks him with the gun, but he doesn't say anything. He doesn't tell him to stop. Because he knows Scaddan won't stop. And he also knows he won't be able to stop him.

Scaddan moves out into the hall. Bright heads after him and I follow. Scaddan doesn't look back until he

237

reaches the front door. He glances at us in the nearest mirror as he swings the door open.

Then he's gone, the door clunking shut behind him.

Bright hurries along the hall and bolts the door top and bottom. Then he peers through the spy-hole. 'He's gone,' he announces, stepping back and turning towards me.

A few seconds pass in silence as we look at each other. Bright's face is as pale as marble. He leans forward, breathing heavily. I wonder for a moment if he's going to be sick.

Then he stands upright, takes a deep breath and walks into the kitchen, where he places the gun carefully in one of the drawers. 'Sorry,' he says, sliding the drawer shut. 'That was all a bit . . . heavy.'

'Are you all right?' I ask.

He turns and looks at me. 'I should be asking you that. What happened?'

I explain briefly how I came to be in his flat, though I can't explain how Scaddan came to be there, of course.

Bright sighs. 'Scaddan must have had a key if he didn't break in, which it doesn't look as if he did. Christ. The caretaker. The management company. I can't trust anyone.'

'He asked if you had any dirt on Hexter.'

'I wish I did. Then at least I'd have some way of retaliat-ing. As it is . . .' He gives me a crumpled smile. 'Let's go and sit down. D'you want a drink? I've got gin or whisky.'

I opt for gin and we go into the lounge. Bright pours gin and just a dash of tonic into a pair of glasses and hands me one. He takes a deep swallow of his before he sits down.

I tentatively finger the area where Scaddan struck me. It feels tender.

'What happened there?' Bright asks.

'He hit me.'

'Fuck. Hold on.' He levers himself out of his chair and heads back to the kitchen. He returns with a bagful of ice, dollops a couple of lumps into each of our drinks, then wraps a small towel round the bag and hands it to me. 'That should help.'

'Thanks.' I press the bag against the bridge of my nose. And the numbing effect of the ice does help.

'Marianne Vogler's the missing wife of the late Conrad Vogler, correct?' says Bright.

'Yes.'

'Then I can only suppose Hexter's hired her to cut a few corners for him. Deal with stuff he can't put through the Service. Deal with *me*.'

'I guess so.'

'I didn't know he had me down as any kind of threat.'

'Well, it looks like he does.'

'Fucking hell.' Bright swallows some more G & T, then tops up his glass. 'I don't have the temperament for this kind of thing, I really don't.'

'I don't either.'

'No. Of course not. Sorry. I just . . . don't know what to do. Alan obviously had hopes of Norrback riding to the rescue. But that's been nixed now.'

'You know about Norrback?'

'Tahvo Norrback, seventy-eight-year-old retired Finnish civil servant, detained on arrival at Heathrow this afternoon on Hexter's orders. He must have put him on a watch list. Officially, Norrback's being questioned about facilitating money laundering for the Russian Mafia. But that'll go nowhere. You and I both know he was detained because he hosted the meeting with Viktor Slavsky in Helsinki in 1989 that ended in Slavsky's death. My guess is he was bringing something Alan hoped to use against Hexter. That must have been Hexter's guess too. Am I right?'

There seems no point denying it. I nod.

'Well, whatever it was – and I'd much rather not know – Hexter will have it now. He'll let Norrback go in a few days. Otherwise the Finns will start kicking up a fuss. But he won't be any use to Alan then, will he? He won't have what Alan needs.'

'No.' I gulp down some of my G & T and hold out my glass for a refill. 'If Hexter's intercepted Norrback . . .'

'You're screwed?'

'Pretty much.'

'*We're* screwed, in fact, since Hexter's evidently bracketed me with the enemy as well.'

'What should we do, Colin?'

'I told Alan Sunday night the best thing he could do, for you *and* himself, was disappear. Hexter's armour-plated. You'll never penetrate his defences.'

'What about you?'

'I don't know. I'll sleep on it. Does Alan know you're here?'

'No. But he may have guessed.'

'Then he'll call me at some point. You'd better stay here tonight in case Scaddan's hanging around out there. With the bolts over, we're safe for now.'

'What was Scaddan looking for, Colin?'

'Anything he could find, I imagine. Maybe Hexter thinks I've come closer to tracking down Chen Shufan than I really have. Scaddan drawing a blank will reassure him about that, but you turning up . . .' More G & T goes down. 'D'you know what I've learnt from all this, Nicole? Look after number one and leave everyone else to fight among themselves. All I want is a quiet life. Thanks to letting my suspicions about Hexter run away with themselves, that's not what I'm going to get.' Another refill. 'Ever.'

'Sorry.' Quite why I say that when I've every reason to feel sorrier for myself than for Bright I don't know, but looking at his forlorn little-boy-lost expression and the self-pity in his eyes, I do feel sorry for him.

'Thanks. You being here is a comfort in some ways, I suppose.'

'It is?'

'Well, let's face it, Nicole. You're in even worse trouble than I am.' He smiles weakly. 'More gin?'

Wednesday October 16

I DIDN'T EXPECT TO SLEEP WELL, BUT MYSTERIOUSLY I HAVE.
When Bright wakes me with a cup of tea, I'm aware of a
stiffness around the bridge of my nose. It's swollen, but
there's no pain unless I press it, and my head feels surprisingly clear.

Bright sits on the end of the bed in his bathrobe, sipping his tea and grimacing as if he's psyching himself up
to break some bad news.

'What's wrong, Colin?' I prompt him.

'Soho's never so quiet as first thing in the morning,' he
murmurs.

'Colin?'

'I have to go. I've thought about it all night. I'm just not
up to this, Nicole. Guns. People like Scaddan. I can't cope
with that kind of thing. It's not my . . . métier.'

'It's not mine either.'

'Of course it isn't. Which is why you really must persuade Alan to get you out of the firing line as well. For
myself, I'm going into self-imposed exile, which I hope
will convince Hexter I'm not a serious threat to him. My
mother lives in Canada with my sister. She's not getting

any younger. And she's not been well. I should go and see her before it's too late. Indefinite compassionate leave.' He sighs heavily. 'I should be able to swing that.'

'When will you go?'

'Oh . . . today.'

'*What?*'

'There's no time like the present.' He smiles weakly. 'Don't fool yourself, Nicole. You can't win against someone like Hexter. You can only avoid losing. If you're lucky. Which I hope you are. I've never been. Particularly. Lucky, that is. So, I have to . . . make the best of the situation I'm in.' He smiles again, a little more broadly. 'To business. Alan called last night. He knows you're here. It was a brief call. I told him you'd fill him in on what's been happening. Talking on the phone is just too risky now. If Hexter's capable of sending Scaddan after me, tapping my landline won't be a problem. Alan's waiting for you at the hotel where you've been staying. I don't know where that is and obviously I don't want to know. But you should certainly go back there. Alan's your best chance of getting out of this. Your only chance, actually.'

'Did he sound . . . angry at me?'

'No. He was his usual pragmatic self. Quite a contrast with my . . . panicky vapourings.' Bright stands up and peers at me. 'That's quite swollen. I'm sorry I . . . didn't get here sooner.'

'It wasn't your fault.'

'I'm sorry anyway. And for being so . . . useless. Tell Alan that, won't you?'

'If you want me to.'

'I think I do. Also . . .' His voice peters out. He frowns, then shrugs. 'Well, I wish you both the best of luck.'

*

It's still the rush hour when I leave the flat. I reason there's safety in numbers. The traffic's diabolical, so I decide to walk some of the way back to Shepherd's Bush. I head along Piccadilly, feeling conspicuous but knowing I'm not. I keep glancing over my shoulder in case Scaddan's following me. But there's no sign of him.

Scanning passing faces for Scaddan's leaves me unprepared, though, for the shock that's waiting as I pass the entrance to Green Park Tube station, just after the Ritz arcade. Bernice Younger, Venstrom's HR director, emerges from the crowd at the top of the steps and looks straight at me.

'Oh my God. Nicole? Is that you?' Bernice is a big, friendly, energetic woman and her smile at the sight of me is so genuine it nearly makes me cry.

I stop dead, uncertain what to do or say. She probably has tons of questions she wants to put to me. But I'm not sure I can safely answer any of them.

'Bernice,' I begin. 'I . . .'

'Where have you been? Everyone's been worried sick about you and Carl. What the hell happened to you guys? Are you OK?'

She's probably referring to the way I'm dressed. Although she may have spotted my swollen nose as well. What's happened to me more generally she wouldn't believe. 'What have the authorities told you?'

She frowns. 'All we know is that you and Carl went missing at the end of last week just after laying on that Go demonstration with Joe Roberts. We've been trying frantically to contact you ever since. Everyone wants to know where Joe is as well. We can't get any sense out of his mother. I'm on my way to a breakfast meeting with Billy. He flew over with Bruno Feltz as soon as he realized what a big thing we're on to. He's staying at the Ritz. Bruno will be there as well. They'll be massively relieved to see you, let me tell you. You'd better have a good explanation for keeping them in the dark, though.'

'I can't see them, Bernice.'

'*What?* That's crazy. Come in with me and we can sort all this out.' She steps towards me, intending, I sense, to take my hand for some motherly comfort. But I step back, bumping into someone in the process but preserving the distance between us. 'What's wrong, Nicole?'

'You don't understand. This is out of Billy's control.'

'What? What's out of Billy's control? What do you mean?'

'Carl's dead.'

Bernice grimaces with shock. 'What did you say?'

'Carl's dead. And I'm lucky to be alive myself.'

Bernice doesn't look as if she believes me. 'You're not making any sense, Nicole. Carl's dead? That can't be right. We'd surely have . . . Come and talk to Billy. We can sort this out.'

'Billy can't help me. Neither can you. I'm not sure anyone can.'

'Just come and talk, OK? Just talk. Explain what's happened.'

'No. There's nothing I can say that you'll believe. I have to go.'

'Go where?'

I don't answer. I break into a jog and run into Green Park. Bernice calls after me and starts to follow. But there's no way she's going to be able to keep up with me. I speed up along the perimeter path. Her voice grows

246

fainter. I glance back and spot her in the distance, staring after me. And I can almost see the bafflement on her face.

There was a moment I was tempted to let her usher me in to see Billy. Initially, at least, Venstrom's resources would be put at my disposal. Support would be offered. Guarantees would be given. But they'd count for nothing in the end. Venstrom can't help me. I wish they could. But I know they can't. Billy Swarther has built a multinational company by doing deals and seeing the big picture. But there's no deal to be done here. He doesn't realize it, but the truth is that, for once, he's out of his league.

I keep on running.

I pick up a taxi in Grosvenor Place and fifteen minutes later I'm back at the Europa Hotel. I encounter the landlady in the hall. She surprises me by announcing Forrester's already booked us out and gone.

I wander bemusedly back out on to the street. And Forrester pulls up beside me in the Land Rover.

'Get in,' he says. He looks even grimmer-faced than normal.

I obey and he drives away. 'Where are we going?' I ask.

'Your bag's in the back,' he replies, conspicuously failing to answer my question. 'I packed your things as neatly as I could.'

'Why didn't you wait for me to get back before booking out?'

'Needs must. There was a chance you'd be followed. But I don't think you were. Of course, if you hadn't taken off on your own in the first place . . .'

'I went to Colin Bright in search of information.'

'Get any that made the risk worthwhile, did you?' His

247

tone suggests he doubts it. And I suppose he's right. But he doesn't hammer the point home. Even when he's furious, he's able to keep a lid on it.

'They're holding Norrback on a trumped-up money laundering charge.'

'I'd already guessed it would be something like that. Hexter must have put Norrback's name on a watch list, despite not being certain Tahvo had anything on him or was in touch with me. You can't argue with the man's thoroughness. He must have the tape now. If he hasn't already destroyed it. He'll probably let Tahvo go in a few days, if only to avoid a tiff with the Finns. But there'll be nothing Tahvo can do for us then. What happened to your nose, by the way?'

The swelling hasn't escaped his eagle eye. I tell him about Scaddan. And Bright's decision to head for the hills. Also my encounter with Bernice. Only the news about Scaddan seems to surprise him. For Bright he expresses merely weary sympathy.

We're in Acton now, heading west. Out of London. I suppose. 'If you'd been more open with me, Duncan, I wouldn't have gone to Colin.'

'You *do* realize how high the stakes are that we're playing for, don't you, Nicole?'

'Of course I do,' I snap back.

'No point biting my head off.'

'Is there someone else's I can bite off?'

He concedes the point. 'I guess not.'

'Where are we going?'

'Cheltenham. Ultimately.'

'You've got nothing on Hexter now he's got the tape. And with Colin on the way out of the picture, you've no way of knowing what Hexter's planning. That's how I see it, Duncan.'

He nods. 'You see it right.'

'So what can we hope to accomplish in Cheltenham?'

'I can't leave Joe in Hexter's clutches. If Hexter's hired Marianne Vogler to do some dirty work for him, it's because his intentions go well beyond what the Service have in mind. I can only imagine what that might mean for Joe. Nothing good, that's for sure. Which only makes me more certain we have to try this.'

'Try what?'

'Joe loves Go. And he loves a challenge. I'm betting Hexter has him under fairly light supervision. He's cooperating because he has to. But he's not being held prisoner. It just wouldn't make any sense for him to run away from his minders. Though he's quick-witted enough to give them the slip if he really wants to.'

'But as things stand he doesn't want to.'

'We have to change that.'

'How? We can't contact him.'

'We can't phone him without exposing ourselves to GCHQ tracking, which will be state of the art. That's true.'

'So how can we communicate with him? If that's what you're suggesting.'

'The Falmouth club went up to a regional Go tournament in Bath earlier this year. Joe won all his games bar one. That single defeat really rankled with him. He wasn't quite sure why it had happened. He felt he'd been somehow psyched out of victory. Cheated, if you like. He told me more than once he was itching for revenge. And he didn't want to have to wait until next year's tournament to get it. What if his opponent offered him a re-match – in Cheltenham?'

249

'You think he'd jump at it?'

'I do. And if we knew where and when it was happening . . .'

'But how could we?'

'I don't know who Joe's opponent was. But Jeremy Inkpen would, I'm sure. He organized the trip and Go's a small world.' Forrester nods to the phone on the dashboard shelf. 'Give him a call on that. I've put his number in. He'll be in the shop by now. See if you can sweet-talk him into telling us who it was Joe lost to and where we can find him.'

'What reason can I give for wanting to contact this guy?'

'Think of something. Remember, Jeremy knows nothing, so you can basically make up anything you like.'

I pick up the phone and key the number. It rings. Several times. Then Jeremy Inkpen answers. I recognize his voice at once.

'Falmouth Photographic.'

'Ah, Jeremy, it's Nicole Nevinson here.'

'Nicole? This is a very pleasant surprise, I must say. I was told you'd left town.'

'I have.'

'Back to London, is it?'

'I'm afraid so. I enjoyed my few days in Falmouth, I really did.'

'You were a breath of fresh air.'

'It's kind of you to say so.'

'Rumour has it Joe Roberts has gone to work for your company. Is that true?'

'We're certainly having discussions with him.'

'Well, I suppose he must do what's best for his future. There's money in computing, after all. Far more than there is in photography, as I know to my cost. But the Go club won't be the same without Joe.'

'We're very impressed by his capabilities.'

'As you should be.'

Forrester makes a circling motion with his left hand, which I assume means he thinks I should cut to the chase. I ignore him. As far as I can. 'We want to set Joe a little test I think you may be able to help with.'

'Really?'

'I gather you all went up to Bath earlier this year for a regional Go tournament.'

'Well, quite a few of—'

'And Joe won all his games but one.'

'Yes, that's right. The one was quite a surprise, actually. But his opponent was a tricky customer.'

'D'you remember his name?'

'Lewis Martinek. Fairly notorious, actually. Go attracts more than its fair share of eccentrics. But Martinek is what you might call an eccentric's eccentric.'

'Do you happen to know how to contact him?'

'Not offhand.'

'Could you find out?'

'Well, I could phone my opposite number in Bath and ask him. I'm not sure if Martinek's actually a member of their club, but . . . is this urgent?'

'It is, rather. I'd be so grateful.'

'Mmm. Well, Nicole, since it's for you . . . I'll see what I can do.'

'I don't want to rush you. But . . .'

'I'll get back to you as soon as possible. Trust me.'

'I do, Jeremy. Thanks so very much. 'Bye for now, then.' I end the call.

'Turn the phone off,' says Forrester. We're stationary at

251

a red light. I've lost track of where we are. Ealing, maybe. Not the centre, though. Forrester's taking a winding route. As usual.

'But he's calling me back.'

'Check in ten minutes. If he's called, call him. We have to be more careful than ever now.'

I do as instructed. We drive on in silence. Ten minutes later, I check. No call. Another ten minutes later, there's been a call. I ring Falmouth Photographic.

'Ah, Nicole,' Jeremy answers brightly.

'Any news?'

'Yes. I'll text you Martinek's email address.'

'Thanks. Do you have a phone number for him?'

'Not a personal one. My friend in Bath only has a work number for Martinek. The County Records Office in Gloucester. I'll text you that as well.'

'OK. Thanks again.'

'It's a pleasure. I'm pleased to have been able to help.'

'How did Martinek manage to beat Joe, Jeremy?' I ask on an impulse. 'I mean, what was his secret?'

'As I recall, he just wouldn't stop talking.'

'Is that allowed?'

'Oh, he wasn't talking to Joe. He was talking to himself. Muttering under his breath, all the time, like some kind of incantation. It was difficult not to try and make out what he was saying. I think that was Joe's mistake. He allowed himself to be distracted. Which stopped him concentrating on the game. He should wear earplugs next time.'

'Maybe I'll suggest that.'

'Good idea. Say hello to him for me, will you?'

'I will. Though actually, on that subject, I wonder if

you could, well, keep all this under your hat. The test we have in mind won't work properly if Joe gets advance warning.'

'He'll hear nothing from me. And I won't mention it to anyone else if you'd rather I didn't.'

'I'd be grateful if we could keep it between us.'

'Consider it our little secret.'

'That's good of you, Jeremy. I do hope we can meet again at some point.'

'Me too.'

''Bye, then.'

I end the call, grimacing with guilt for leading the poor guy on, and tell Forrester what Jeremy said. By the time I've finished, the phone's pinged to signal the arrival of the text he promised. I check the information's there, then switch the phone off.

'County Records Office, Gloucester,' says Forrester after a thoughtful few moments of silence. 'I think we'll pay Mr Martinek a visit this afternoon.'

'What if he won't cooperate? What if a chance of revenge is the last thing he wants to give Joe? He might like being one up on him.'

'We'll talk him round.'

'And what if Hexter's anticipated some such move as this? Like he did with Norrback.'

'We keep probing. Eventually, we'll find a chink in his armour.'

I say nothing. I wonder if Forrester really believes what he's just said. Maybe he thinks what I think. That sooner rather than later we're going to run out of options.

And then . . .

*

Gloucester. Mid-afternoon. The city's quiet, wrapped up in itself. The County Records Office is a single-storey red-brick building at the end of a back street. The reception area's presided over by a friendly middle-aged woman. Beyond her, through an open door, I can see a search-room with people poring over old books and stacks of paper. The atmosphere is hushed and fusty.

We ask to see Lewis Martinek and have to admit it's not on Records Office business, but it is rather urgent. The receptionist makes a phone call.

'Lewis? There are two people here to see you . . . Mr Foster and Miss Nicholson . . . No. They said you don't know them . . . Urgent, apparently . . . Could you? . . . That—' It sounds like he's cut the call short.

He's not long in appearing. A tall, lanky, dark-haired guy, wearing, to my surprise, a three-piece suit with a purple hue to it. He's also wearing thin white cotton gloves, which I assume are related to document-handling. Maybe that explains his slightly stooped posture as well. His eyes dart about suspiciously before the receptionist points us out to him.

'What's this concerning?' he asks quietly, as if he has cause to be wary of unexpected visitors on non-archival business. His voice has a strange, feathery note to it.

'Joe Roberts,' says Forrester bluntly.

'What about him?'

'Interested in a rematch?'

Martinek smiles lopsidedly. 'Who are you? His agents? Turned pro, has he?'

'Could we talk about this outside?'

'Why not?' Martinek glances at the receptionist. 'Won't be long, Margaret. Go business.'

We troop out to the courtyard, where Martinek immediately lights up a cigarette. He makes no move to remove the cotton gloves and surveys us dubiously. 'Where are you from?' he asks. 'I don't recognize either of you.'

'We're friends of Joe,' I reply with a smile.

'Were you at the Bath tournament?'

'No.'

'Thought not.' He mutters something I can't catch. Numbers, I think. A date?

I frown. 'Sorry?'

He shakes his head. 'No need to be.'

'The way you beat Joe was very impressive,' says Forrester.

'How would you know? You weren't there.'

'He told us.'

'Right. So, *Mr* Roberts was impressed, was he? Good. Should've been.'

'You enjoy playing Go?' I ask hopefully.

'Enjoy? No. No more than I enjoy smoking this cigarette. But I can't give up. Too late. The teeth are in me.'

'But you relish the challenge of it?'

'Is that what we've got here? A challenge?' There's some more muttering. Numbers. I'm pretty sure of that.

'Would you like to prove beating Joe wasn't a fluke?' asks Forrester.

Martinek looks at him narrowly and slowly exhales some smoke. 'Fluke? Another word for a flounder, right? Who floundered in that sports hall in Bath April fourteen? Not me.'

'Beating him twice would nail it down, wouldn't it?'

'I'm not going to Cornwall. I don't like travelling long distances.'

255

'We're not asking you to.'

'I might have expenses, even so.'

'We could cover them.'

Martinek frowns, then smiles suddenly. 'Whose idea is this? Yours or Mr Roberts'?'

'It's slightly . . . complicated.'

'Go *is* complicated. The labyrinth without the thread.'

'What we have in—'

'Can't talk any more for now,' Martinek cuts in. 'Got a workhouse register to dig out. If you're serious, meet me in the Pelican, five thirty.'

'Where's that?'

'There's only one Pelican.'

And that, as far as Martinek is concerned, is all he needs to say. He flicks his cigarette away towards the cycle-shed and walks back through the door into the Records Office.

We head into the city centre and go into a coffee shop. I ask the barista while I'm ordering if he knows where the Pelican is. I feel fleetingly normal when he smiles engagingly at me as he answers. But normal's other people now. I'm losing touch with the condition.

'It's not far,' I report to Forrester. 'Just the other side of the cathedral.'

'Good.' Forester sips his coffee. 'I think Martinek will bite, don't you?'

'I think he's mad enough to do virtually anything. We can't rely on him.'

'We're not going to. We just need to get Joe to agree to meet him. Time and place. That'll be enough.'

I nod. But I don't know, really. Getting the tape from Norrback was a plan. This is . . . something much less.

There's a hint of desperation to it I don't want to acknowledge. And neither, I suspect, does Forrester.

The Pelican's a mellow, quiet pub. Martinek's already there when we arrive, stationed at a table remote from the bar, with a lager at his elbow and a pocket Go board just like Joe's open in front of him. The white cotton gloves have gone, only to reveal plasters round the tips of most of his fingers.

'Sharpening up?' Forrester asks as we sit down beside him.

'Reminding myself,' he answers with a smile. 'Of how I did him last time.'

'And how *was* that?' I ask, engaging him smile for smile.

'Mr Roberts has fighting spirit. He has the instincts of a winner. He lets those instincts guide him. But he's not a mathematician. I am. That's why I always keep score.'

'Somebody told me you distracted him.'

'He distracted himself.'

'We missed your victory, Mr Martinek,' says Forrester, like someone genuinely fascinated by the tactics of the game. 'We'd be very interested to see you and Joe play again.'

'Interested enough to come all this way to see me?'

'Joe's in the area. So are we. We'd like to surprise him with an offer from you of a rematch. How about it?'

'When?'

'As soon as possible.'

'Friday afternoon.'

'All right.'

'Where?'

'Cheltenham. We'll fix a venue once you've contacted

him. We can give you his phone number. But there's a condition.'

'*I* have conditions.'

'Hear ours first. You don't mention us to Joe. You say someone told you he'd been seen in Cheltenham. You got his number from Jeremy Inkpen in Falmouth. You've heard Joe's suggested your victory over him was a fluke. You're willing to give him the chance to prove that. Is he interested?'

'Are you two trying to mess with *his* head or mine?'

'What are your terms, Mr Martinek?'

Martinek takes a swallow of lager while he ponders the question. Then he says, 'Five hundred quid. Up front.'

'That's a lot. For a game of Go.'

'Maybe. But I get the feeling this isn't just a game of Go.' Martinek starts muttering then. It's definitely numbers. But I can't quite catch what they are. 'Keeping you out of it. Putting my reputation on the line. All that costs.'

'Tell you what,' says Forrester. 'We'll pay you two hundred and fifty now. The balance afterwards.'

'Whether he turns up or not? Whether he wins or loses?'

'Yes. Whether or not.'

'So, you must have a lot more than five hundred quid riding on this.'

'This isn't about money,' I put in.

'Didn't say it was,' Martinek snaps back. 'I said more than money.' He eyes me curiously. 'You got something going with Mr Roberts, have you?'

'I have the feeling you're a man who values his privacy, Mr Martinek,' Forrester says, defusing the moment.

'What if I am?'

'We value ours too. This is a confidential arrangement

as far as we're concerned. No one will ever hear from us that you were paid to approach Joe.'

'Maybe I'm happy to do it anyway.' Martinek looks suddenly offended by the idea of haggling over money.

'Maybe you are. It's just a game.'

'Not to you two. Nor to me. Nor to Mr Roberts. Just a game? People who say that are either lying or they don't know what they're talking about.'

'Do you ever play against computer programs, Mr Martinek?' I ask on impulse.

'No,' he answers decisively. 'Humans only.'

'Afraid the computer would beat you?'

'No. I'd beat a computer every time.'

'But computers have made mincemeat of world champions.'

'Only because those champions were stupid enough to agree to changes in the rules.'

'What changes?'

He takes a plastic stone from a bag and lays it on the Go board. 'There,' he says with a smile.

'What?'

'Find me a computer that can do that and I'll play it.'

'Well, obviously they can't—'

'I want to look my opponent in the eye. I want to see whether there's a tremor in his hand when he picks up a stone and lays it down. That's part of the game. That's one of the rules.'

'You'll be able to do all that if we set up a game with Joe for you,' says Forrester. 'Face to face. Eye to eye.'

'Nowhere to hide,' says Martinek, nodding grimly. 'And nowhere to run beyond the edge of the board.'

There's a brief silence. Then Forrester says, 'Do we have a deal, Mr Martinek?'

And Martinek nods. 'Give me Mr Roberts' number. And my two hundred and fifty quid. Then we'll do this.'

It's dark by the time we reach Cheltenham. We drive in past the well-signposted, fenced-off, brightly lit complex of Government Communications Headquarters. I ask Forrester if he's ever actually been inside. He says GCHQ was a smaller building on the other side of the city in his time, without specifying whether he visited it at any point.

I don't press him for an answer. And I don't ask him what he really thinks our chances are of getting to Joe through Martinek. I don't want to know.

The Belmont Hotel is just north of the town centre, opposite a building site. There's a car park round the back. Rooms are £60 a night. It's the kind of no frills place I'm beginning to recognize. We book in.

If Martinek lures Joe into meeting him over the Go board, it won't be until Friday afternoon, which leaves us tomorrow to get through as best we can. I point out to Forrester that I can't string Mum and Evie along much longer with my story about waiting for Venstrom to supply me with a phone. He agrees and hands me one of his.

'Give them this number. They can text and message you on it. But don't use it yourself after these calls and don't turn it on again in case any of their phones are bugged. That should hold the situation for a few days.'

A few days? That's our permanently rolling horizon now.

*

I make the calls. Handily, I get Evie's voicemail. But no such luck with Mum. She sounds relieved to hear from me and I soon find out why.

'Your company's contacted me, luv. A woman called Younger.'

'Bernice Younger?'

'That's it. She said they're ... concerned about you. She asked if I'd heard from you. She didn't seem to know you'd lost your phone. Aren't you going into the office at the moment?'

'Don't worry, Mum. Bernice isn't involved in this project I'm working on. It's, um, commercially sensitive, so my boss and I agreed it would be best if I dealt with most aspects of it from outside the office.'

'You make it sound a bit cloak and dagger, luv.'

'No, no. It's just a case of the left hand not knowing what the right hand's doing. I'll talk to Bernice and sort it out. Meanwhile, I *do* have a phone now. I'll give you the number. Evie's already got it.'

Have I pulled off the relaxed nothing-to-make-a-fuss-about act? As far as I can tell from Mum's increasingly chatty tone, the answer's yes. It'll only hold for so long. But it's the best I can do.

I feel completely drained after talking to Mum. I eat an ordered-in pizza, take a shower and fall asleep watching some reality show on the tiny wall-bracketed TV.

I get woken around midnight by sex taking place in the neighbouring room. It doesn't last long. But, perfunctory or not, it's human contact. And I'm running very short of that.

I think of going to see if Forrester's still up. But in the end I don't. I'm beginning to resent needing him. But

I know what I most resent is the ugly turn my life's taken this past week. If I talk to Forrester again tonight, I might start shouting at him. Or at myself. And that'll get us nowhere.

Which is where, as I edge back the curtains and peer out at the rain-smeared night, I'm very much afraid we already are.

Thursday October 17

FORRESTER PAYS ME AN EARLY CALL. IT'S BARELY LIGHT, BUT he's already been out exploring, apparently.

'I've found a good spot for Martinek to meet Joe. Costa Coffee, top of the Promenade. You can drive past it *and* you can get round the back by car as well. There are doors front, side and back. And there are plenty of shops nearby where you can pause to watch what's going on. Go take a look and see what you think. If Joe comes alone, fine. If not, we can get him into the Land Rover and away in less than a minute.'

'What if he doesn't want to come with us?'

'He'll want to come with us once I've explained everything to him. We're his escape route.'

'OK. Maybe. But . . .' My brain's still not woken up yet. 'Won't Hexter's people, if they're there . . .'

'What are they going to do in the middle of a crowded coffee shop? *If* they're there, which I'm backing Joe to ensure they aren't. He likes a challenge. He'll go for this.'

We're going to meet Martinek this evening to hear what he's heard from Joe. He suggested we just phone for an update, but naturally we opted for a face-to-face. I could see him chewing that over as he looked at us. *You two have got something to hide* was the thought written on his face. But he didn't say it. The weirdo in the purple suit and the white cotton gloves is nobody's fool.

I go and check out the Promenade branch of Costa Coffee after breakfast, as Forrester suggested. I move through the grey streets of Cheltenham town centre almost invisibly in my grungy clothes. A bruise is starting to come out over my nose, which I've camouflaged with make-up. I don't think anyone will notice it. I don't think anyone will notice me at all, in fact. It's funny. I don't really feel like myself any more. I feel like someone similar but not the same, an alternative version of Nicole Nevinson, edged out by life. It's not a good Nicole to be.

The coffee shop looks like it may once have been a bank, with a curved frontage and fancy stonework. I can see what Forrester means. There's a busy street at the front, plus a walkway round to a loading bay at the end of a service cul-de-sac that links to the next street across.

I go in and buy a *cappuccino* and a pastry. I sit down among the other customers and look around. The café's roughly L-shaped. Tables at one end can't be seen from the other. Only from the corner of the counter can you see all three doors. I can understand why Forrester thinks this is a good place for our purposes. But still there are so many things that could stop us in our tracks.

I go back to the Belmont and tell him what I think. 'If you've got something up your sleeve, Duncan,' I say, almost imploringly, 'I'd really like to hear what it is.'

But he doesn't give an inch. 'Let's just wait and see how Martinek gets on.'

'Waiting and seeing is what's killing me.'

'Then I'll take you for a drive.'

'Where to?'

'Morecote.'

'*Where?*'

'Hexter's Cotswold residence. I'm guessing he won't be home. So, why don't we take a look?'

We drive south out of Cheltenham, past Stroud and into open, rolling farmland west of Tetbury. Sunlight breaks through the clouds and makes the autumn-tinted trees glow. The reality of our situation feels remote and unreal out here.

Morecote stands in a fold of the land, with a ridge-top belt of trees behind it. It's roughly H-shaped, with a modern cross-section linking two mellower-stoned older structures. It looks like a heap of money has been spent on the place. The boundary wall's solid, the grounds extensive.

We can see the layout of the property from the footpath we've followed up from the lane where we've left the car. But trees obscure parts of the view and we're still quite a long way off.

Forrester takes a look through his binoculars, then hands them to me. 'Can you see what's written on that van?' he asks.

I train the binoculars on the house and adjust the focus. I can see the main entrance. Out front is a parking area. There's a low-slung car off to one side and, closer to the steps, a white van. The rear doors are open, though I can't see anyone loading or unloading. The sunlight on the side of the van makes it difficult to read what's written on it, but I can just about make out the words.

'Wysis Catering,' I report.

'Hexter must be planning to do some entertaining,' Forrester muses. 'Interesting.'

'Does he have a family?'

'Not sure. There was a wife. Marjorie. Children? I can't remember.'

'I don't suppose it matters.'

'Everything matters. This is a busy time for Hexter. He won't be entertaining for fun.'

'Maybe it's something his wife is organizing.'

'Maybe. And maybe we should check later on what's happening.'

I hand the binoculars back. Out here, in the fresh, clean air, with so much space around us, I suddenly feel we can talk more freely. 'Venstrom have been on to my mother, Duncan,' I say quietly. 'I smoothed things over, but . . .'

'You can't smooth them over indefinitely.'

'No. I can't.'

'Well, you won't have to for much longer.'

'That's what you said before we went to meet Norrback.'

'There's a crunch coming. Sooner rather than later.'

'Is that good news for me? Or bad?'

'I can't guarantee what the outcome will be. I can only guarantee what the outcome would've been if I'd left you in Vogler's car with Roger Lam.'

'Why have we come here, Duncan? What does Hexter's house tell us?'

'How our enemy lives.'

'Well, by the look of it.'

266

'That's right.' Forrester nods thoughtfully. 'Let's hope it's softened him up, eh?'

We're in Gloucester a good two hours before our rendezvous with Martinek. Forrester suggests we split up and meet at the Pelican. Maybe he's tired of my company. Maybe he prefers solitude. Or maybe he just thinks we'll be less conspicuous that way. 'Remember not to draw any attention to yourself,' he says as we part.

There's another possibility, of course, which comes to me as I sit in the cathedral, trying to be heartened by the beauty of the sunlight shafting through the stained glass windows. He needs to be free of me to attend to something he hasn't told me about. He's holding out on me in some way.

But, if he is, there's nothing I can do about it.

Which seems to apply to most things at the moment.

The Pelican. Once again. Same number of customers. In fact, mostly the *same* customers, I think. Including Lewis Martinek.

He's wearing a different suit. Green instead of purple. He'd be quite attractive if it weren't for his aura of weirdness. He's playing Go again on his pocket board and his lips are moving as I approach, but I can't hear what he's saying, of course. Forrester isn't here yet, though I'm not early for our appointment.

'Miss Nicholson,' he says as I sit down. 'I was thinking about you.'

'Oh yes?'

'I was thinking how lucky it is for you and Mr Foster that I value my privacy.'

'Why is that lucky for us?'

'Because it means I'll respect yours. Whereas others might . . . start digging.'

'Doesn't digging just get you in a hole?'

'Is that how you got in one?'

'Have you heard from Joe?' I ask levelly.

'Where's Mr Foster?'

'He'll be here soon.'

'Good.' He takes a sip of lager and looks down at the board.

'Are you going to tell me if you've heard from Joe?'

'I've been analysing his style. I reckon it must make him better than most at playing computers.'

'Really? Why?'

'Ah, now you're interested, aren't you? Is that because you work in the computer games industry? It would explain why you quizzed me last time about playing against a computer.'

'What I do for a living has—'

'Absolutely nothing to do with me? Right. I agree. Where *is* Mr Foster, by the way?'

'He'll be here soon.' I think I've already said that.

'I want more money.'

'What?'

'More money. Local authority archivists don't earn megabucks. And I have the distinct feeling our arrangement is about more than giving Mr Roberts the chance to beat me in a one-off game of Go. So, the price of my *discreet* cooperation has gone up. In fact, it's doubled. To a thousand pounds. Half in advance and half afterwards, as before. So that means you owe me two hundred and fifty quid, payable . . . right now.'

'We agreed terms yesterday.' Where's Forrester? Where the hell is he?

'And we're revising those terms today.'

'You can't do that.'

'Yes, I can. Mr Roberts has bitten, you see. We're on. Three o'clock, tomorrow afternoon. Venue . . . up to you. I told him I'd text the location by noon tomorrow. OK?'

There's nothing I can do. Martinek's got me exactly where he wants me. And if Forrester was here he'd have *us* exactly where he wants us. I have no choice but to agree. I nod. 'OK.'

Martinek holds out his hand. I open my shoulder-bag and turn away while I find the money envelope. I don't want him to see how much I'm carrying. I take out five fifty-pound notes and pass them across the table to him. 'Thank you,' he says. 'Fifties. Interesting. Very interesting. You're obviously not an advocate of the cashless economy, despite your occupation.' He smiles at me. And a smile, on Lewis Martinek's face, is a difficult thing to interpret. 'So, where do I meet Mr Roberts?'

I leave Martinek sipping his lager and poring over his Go problem as soon as he's confirmed he'll ask Joe to meet him in our specially selected Cheltenham branch of Costa Coffee, though I have to endure several minutes' condemnation of franchised coffee shops before we get that far. I'm worried about what might have happened to Forrester, as Martinek evidently senses. 'I hope he hasn't had some kind of accident' is his parting shot as I hurry out.

I've already decided the best thing I can do is head back to where we left the Land Rover: a side street near the Records Office. What I'll do if Forrester doesn't show up there I try not to think about.

As it turns out, I don't get that far. I go through an archway that leads to the cathedral green and suddenly hear my name being called from behind me. I glance round and there's Forrester. He doesn't even have the decency to look shamefaced.

'Where the hell have you been?' It must be obvious I'm angry.

'I let you go in ahead of me while I made sure no one was tailing Martinek.'

'And no one was?'

'No. We're still in the clear. What about Joe?'

'He's on for three o'clock tomorrow afternoon. Martinek will text him where they're to meet. But why did I have to deal with him alone, Duncan? Once you'd satisfied yourself there was no one on his tail, you should've joined us.'

'It sounds like you managed well enough without me.'

'What was this, then? A test?'

'If it was, you passed.'

'Did I? He's doubled his price, you know. I had to pay him another two hundred and fifty quid.'

'It can't be helped.'

'He's suspicious of us.'

'That can't be helped either. Will he turn up and will he keep his mouth shut?'

'Yes. I suppose.'

'Then we've got what we want out of him, haven't we? A chance to get Joe out of Hexter's clutches.' Yes, it's a chance. Though what we're going to do if we manage to pull that off . . .

Night is falling as we drive south out of Gloucester. That suits Forrester, who wants to take another look at Morecote. The idea that Hexter might be entertaining dinner guests has made him curious. I'm too tired to argue. It seems to me he's making a lot of one caterer's van in the middle of the day.

It's seven fifteen and just about completely dark when we reach the pull-in where we parked this morning. Forrester has a torch, but he's reluctant to use it, so there are several stumbles as we climb the footpath to the vantage point we found earlier. The countryside feels different by night. I can't rid myself of the idea that someone's watching us, though there's no way anyone can be. We move cautiously and speak in whispers.

The lights are on in all the ground-floor rooms and several of the upstairs rooms as well. Through the binoculars I can make out the shapes of several cars parked in front of the house. The steps up to the front door are flanked by low-set lanterns.

I report what I can see to Forrester and he draws my attention to a glow of headlights between us and Morecote, marking the progress of another car in the direction of the house.

'Hexter may come out to meet whoever's in that car,' he says. 'Keep watching.'

I watch. The car slows, probably at the gate in from the road, then heads on at a lazy curve towards the front of the house. Maybe some sensor strip signals their arrival, because the front door of Morecote opens on cue and a figure walks out and descends the steps.

I recognize him. But it's not Hexter.

'It's Roger Lam,' I whisper. He's wearing a dark suit and tie. He looks slim and smooth and very much at home, as if this is something he's done before.

The car draws up right by the foot of the steps. There's a chauffeur, I guess. A man gets out of one of the rear doors, while Lam opens the other rear door. A second, bigger man emerges. There are handshakes and greetings. The faces of the three men are tinted red by the glow of the brake lights. Then the car draws away and they turn towards the steps.

'I know who the guests are,' I whisper, hardly able to believe my own words.

Forrester says nothing. He waits for me to continue.

There they go. Up the steps. The front door open ahead of them. A figure standing just inside, his face obscured by the porch, who might or might not be – but probably is – Clive Hexter. He's waiting for them. No doubt he's smiling. No doubt his guests are smiling too.

I'm not.

Billy Swarther, founder and chairman of Venstrom Computers, accompanied by Bruno Feltz, head of technical operations, are having dinner with Clive Hexter and Roger Lam and lord-knows-who-else at Morecote, while Forrester and I face each other across a corner table in a village pub some miles north. The conversation's no doubt flowing with the wine at Hexter's house. Forrester and I, on the other hand, seem unable to find much to say.

We're both thinking. Though our thoughts are probably not the same. I'm wondering what would have happened if I'd let Bernice persuade me to go into the Ritz with her yesterday morning. Would Billy and Bruno have mentioned their dinner date with Hexter? No. Of course they wouldn't. They'd have sold me some story designed to keep me quiet and reasonably content until . . .

'You're asking yourself where this leaves you,' Forrester says suddenly in a quiet voice, looking at me intently over his pint of beer.

'Indeed,' I respond.

'Better off than you were. You've seen now. With your own eyes.'

'But what have I seen, Duncan? What does it mean?'

'It means Hexter's buying Venstrom's silence – and their cooperation. What he's offering them I can't say, but it'll be enough to ensure they don't cause him a problem.'

'And what about me?'

'They've cut you loose, I'm afraid.' After a moment, he adds, 'I did tell you they would.'

Yes. He did. And I thought I believed him. But I didn't. Not really. I went on hoping Venstrom would somehow come to my rescue. But all that's changed now.

'Working for this company is much more than just doing a job. When we hire you we take you into our family.' That's Billy's videoed pitch to every new employee. That's the pledge the company makes to the likes of me. And I swallowed it. Whole.

It's quite something to realize all that warm, fuzzy, West Coast touchy feely togetherness is a big fat lie. But sitting here, gazing past Forrester towards the night-filled window, I do realize that. For the first time, I understand just how completely I've been cast adrift.

'Not a nice feeling, is it?' asks Forrester.

'No. It's not nice at all.'

'I'm sorry.' He sounds as if he means it.

'What can we do, Duncan?'

'Get Joe away from Hexter.'

'And then?'

'Then? The best we can, Nicole. And before you ask me if that'll be good enough . . .'

'You don't know.'

'No.' He smiles grimly. 'I don't.'

Friday October 18

I HAVEN'T PHONED MUM OR EVIE, THOUGH I REALLY WANT TO. But I can't risk any contact with anyone. Everything's riding on what happens this afternoon.

I look at myself in the mirror of the tiny bathroom at the Belmont Hotel. The bruise over my nose is a darkening yellow. It's still tender as I pat foundation over it. Could it be broken? I don't think so. My nail varnish is chipped, but I can't summon the energy to remove it. There's a fugitive look in my eyes. I wonder if it's as obvious to others as it is to me.

Forrester set out our plan last night.

I keep watch on the coffee shop, waiting for Martinek and Joe to arrive. Joe's unlikely to notice me, dressed as I am now – I hardly recognize *myself* – and I'll be doing my best to melt into the background anyway. I let the game get started, then I go in, sit down at their table and basically ask Joe to come with us. I assure him Forrester has a plan to unhook him from the Intelligence Service, then, as soon as he's got his head round the idea, I text Ready to Forrester on the second phone he's given me and he drives up to the loading bay behind the coffee shop, which we can reach in a few seconds as soon as we clock his car.

What if Joe doesn't come alone? What if he has minders with him to ensure the rendezvous is solely for the purposes of Go? Then I text Company to Forrester. He assures me he can deal with this contingency, but reckons it's best I don't know how.

Then there's Martinek. He's expecting a full-length game of Go and a further payment of £500 win, lose or draw – although I'm not sure you *can* draw at Go. He could become a problem if we just walk out on him. So, I've got his money to hand over if I have to. But will that satisfy him? I'm not sure.

And finally there's Joe himself. I don't know and neither does Forrester how he's been treated this past week, what assurances he's been given or what threats he's operating under. What will he do when it comes to the point? Maybe he won't want to come with us. We certainly can't force him to.

'He'll want to see me,' Forrester insists. I think he's counting on that. It's his principal reason for sending me in to talk to Joe. So that, to talk to Forrester, Joe has to leave the coffee shop and get into the car. Then we can explain everything to him he doesn't already know. And then . . . who knows?

We don't book out of the Belmont, but whether we actually return there this evening depends on what happens later. The course of events just can't be predicted.

The empty morning and early afternoon slide past me in a blur. I'm apprehensive and impatient all at the same time. This has to work. This has to lead to something. If not . . .

*

Forrester drives to a car park behind the Regent Arcade shopping centre. He stays there to wait for my text. I walk through the shopping centre and out into the Promenade, keeping an eye out for Joe. I don't see him anywhere. I cross the road and drift slowly towards Costa Coffee, hugging the shopfronts that I pass, head down, eyes scanning ahead from beneath the brim of my baseball cap. It's six minutes to three.

I reach a furniture shop more or less opposite Costa. I glance across and wonder if I should go in to see if Joe's already there. But I don't have to decide, because, at that moment, Joe bounces into view on the opposite pavement.

He looks just as I remember him from the first time I saw him in St Mawes, which is comforting somehow. It was only last week, though it feels more like months ago. Jeans, T-shirt, corduroy jacket, shoulder-bag. His curly hair is blown back by the breeze. He's moving almost jauntily, like he's relaxed and under no pressure at all, although he is smoking a cigarette.

I turn and gaze into the shop window in front of me. I see a reflection of Costa in the glass. And of Joe as he takes a last puff on his cigarette before tossing it away and swinging in through the door. He doesn't so much as glance in my direction. And, as far as I can tell, he's alone. No one swings in after him. No one follows him close behind at all. It looks like I'm never going to know what Forrester's contingency plan for Company is.

I turn round cautiously. I see Joe queuing at the counter. I cross the road and walk casually past the coffee shop, monitoring Joe out of the corner of my eye. He has his back to me. With a more decided glance I spot Martinek,

277

sitting at a table close to the rear door. He's got a full-size Go board in front of him, along with two bowls of stones and a clock, plus a giant cup of coffee. He's wearing a dark blue suit today. He's also wearing his white cotton gloves, for reasons known only to him. I don't think he notices me, but it would be like him not to show it even if he did. He's noticed Joe, though. The direction of his gaze makes that clear.

I browse in the furniture shop opposite Costa for ten minutes or so. Nothing changes at Costa Coffee. People are wandering in and out. Trade's trickling on through the afternoon.

Back out on the street, I glance around, wondering if I can see anyone who might be watching the place. There's no sign of anyone, though I suppose there shouldn't be if they're any good. Good or bad, though, they're not close by. That much seems certain.

I let someone else walk into Costa ahead of me and tag along behind them. They're big enough to give me plenty of natural cover as I stand in the queue. While they're waiting to order, I glance at Joe and Martinek.

The game's already under way. Martinek's stooped over the board, apparently pondering a move. The movement of his lips suggests he's muttering to himself. No surprise there. Joe's leaning back in his chair, gazing past Martinek's left shoulder.

I buy a *cappuccino* and sit down near the side door. Joe has his back to me. But Martinek could see me if he looked up. Except he doesn't look up. He goes on studying the board. Then he lays a black stone on one of the intersections. He presses his button on the clock and takes a slurp from a bottle of water stationed by his elbow.

Joe responds almost immediately, barely glancing at the board, presses his button on the clock and sits back again. Martinek stoops forward and resumes thinking. It looks like he's needing to do a lot more of that than Joe.

They attract a few curious glances from other customers, especially from children, but they seem to be playing in a bubble of their own concentration. It's as if their surroundings don't exist for them.

Looking around, I feel increasingly certain Joe really did come alone. Whether he told anyone where he was going or simply slipped away I don't know. But amongst the harassed mums with their children and the people whiling away an idle hour, only one person is watching him. Me.

Martinek makes another move. It's the same routine. Button-press on the clock. Slurp of water. And Joe responds as swiftly as before.

I can't wait any longer. I walk over to their table and swing a chair round from the empty table next to them. Martinek doesn't appear even to notice, staring fixedly at the board as he is. But Joe notices. He glances up at me. There's a split-second during which his expression changes from puzzlement to recognition.

'Nicole?' He frowns in disbelief.

'Hi, Joe.' I sit down.

I've got Martinek's attention now as well. He looks at me in obvious astonishment. 'What's going on?' he asks in a petulant tone.

'Sorry for the interruption,' I say.

'You two know each other?' asks Joe. The thought makes him only more disbelieving.

'That doesn't matter,' I reply, aware I have to vault over

a lot of explaining to get to what's really important. 'You did come alone, didn't you, Joe?'

'Why shouldn't he have?' demands Martinek.

'I came alone, yes,' says Joe.

'You're not supposed to be here,' says Martinek. He sounds genuinely aggrieved.

'Listen to me, Joe.' I face him directly, ignoring Martinek. 'Duncan and I are here to help you. We can get you out of Hexter's clutches. Now. This afternoon.'

'Duncan's with you?'

'He's waiting in his car. Just round the corner. Say the word and we can take you somewhere to talk all this through.'

'I don't get what's going on. Why have you and Duncan got together? And, like, what are you doing here?' Joe spreads his hands in bemusement.

'Who's Hexter?' Martinek cuts in.

'Would you mind staying out of this?' I instantly regret the sharpness of my tone.

'Well, pardon me for breathing.'

'I don't know what Hexter's told you, Joe.' I try to cut Martinek out of the conversation. 'But I'm lucky to be alive. And you're no better than his prisoner, are you?'

'Do I look like a prisoner? Where are the bars? Where are the jailers?'

'Did you tell anyone you were coming here?'

'No. But only because there might've been an objection to me giving up an afternoon to play Martinek here. But that's all it would've been. An *objection*. And what d'you mean about being lucky to be alive?'

'They tried to kill me, Joe.'

'*What?* Who tried?'

'Roger Lam.'

'That's crazy.'

'Let me call Duncan. He can explain everything. Wouldn't you like to speak to him?'

'Well, I . . .'

'Do you know this bloke she says tried to kill her?' Martinek cuts in again.

'Joe?' I press, ignoring Martinek.

'OK.' Joe pushes back his hair with his long fingers and gazes at me in what appears to be exasperation. 'Call him. Let's sort this out.'

I take out the phone and press *Send* on the Ready message.

'Are you feeling OK, Nicole?' asks Joe. 'I mean, Roger Lam tried to kill you? That's seriously nuts.'

'Talk to Duncan.'

'I will.'

'What about our game?' demands Martinek.

'I won't be gone long,' Joe replies. 'Have another coffee. And some strategizing time on me.'

'How do I know you'll be back?'

'You've got my word.'

'And what about my—' Martinek breaks off. The money isn't something he wants to mention in front of Joe.

'What about your what?' Joe frowns suspiciously.

'Forget it.' Martinek's expression suggests he *isn't* going to forget it. 'You'd better be back, that's all. Because there's no way you can win from here.'

Joe smiles. '*P-l-e-a-s e.*'

Martinek turns on me. 'Are you bringing him back, Miss Nicholson?'

I catch Joe frowning at me as he realizes I've given Martinek a false name. 'That'll be up to him,' I say levelly.

'Really? Not you and Mr Foster?'

Another false name clinches it for Joe. 'Did you set this game up, Nicole?' he asks.

'Just listen to Duncan, Joe. That's all I ask.' And, to my relief, the Land Rover comes into view at that moment. 'Here he is.'

Joe picks up his phone and takes a picture of the Go board. Martinek grimaces. 'Nice,' he mutters. 'Very nice.'

'Don't want any arguments when I get back.'

'Let's go,' I say, standing up.

We hurry out through the rear door. Forrester's turned the Land Rover round by the time we reach it. Joe gets in the front. I climb into the back.

'Good to see you again, Joe,' says Forrester.

'You too, Duncan. Though there was no need for you to come all this way.'

'I'm not sure you understand the situation you're in.'

'Tell me what I'm missing.'

Forrester puts the car in gear and we start away. 'You agreed to help GCHQ with research into artificial intelligence in return for the police dropping you from their inquiries into Conrad Vogler's affairs, right?'

'Basically, yeah. But it was a good deal in the circumstances. And they're an interesting bunch over there. They reckon I might have a particular aptitude for cryptography. I've enjoyed what they've had me doing these past few days. Maybe I've finally found the career I'm suited to. I reckon Mum'll be pleased in the long run. Zip too. There's no reason she can't join me here once I've settled in.'

'What about Vogler?'

'Well, I guess I may have to give evidence against him at some point. But—'

'He's dead, Joe.'

'*What?*'

We turn into Regent Street and head south. 'Hexter didn't tell you that, did he?'

'No . . .'

'Carl Hinkley's dead too,' I cut in.

Joe glances over his shoulder at me. Suddenly, he looks very confused. I don't blame him. 'How did they . . . I mean, what happened?'

'It looks like Marianne decided Conrad had to go to prevent him cooperating with the authorities,' Forrester replies. 'Carl just got in the way.'

'Nobody's told me anything about this. And why hasn't it been in the news? Mum obviously knows nothing about it. Otherwise she'd have—'

'They've hushed it up because it didn't go according to plan. The idea was to kill Nicole and tie me into the murders. But I stopped that happening. Something else I'm sure Roger Lam hasn't got around to mentioning to you.'

'That can't be right. Roger promised me my cooperation meant everyone I knew would be left in peace.'

We turn left, then right, still aiming south through the back streets. 'You can't trust Roger. He's Hexter's poodle.'

'But, Duncan, Hexter's only interested in intelligence applications for my particular abilities. Why would he want to frame you for murder? And why would he want to have Nicole killed?'

'Because his first loyalty isn't to British Intelligence. It's to China.'

'*China?*'

'I was in the Service myself, before I moved to Falmouth, before you were born. I've known Hexter's working for the Chinese for the past thirty years. And he knows I know. Which makes me a threat. Nicole too. And he deals with threats by neutralizing them.'

'Are you serious?'

Forrester glances round at him. 'I've never been more so.'

'You must've got it wrong, Duncan. The Chinese have no control over what happens at GCHQ. I'm working for the British government. I'm not exactly over the moon about that, but I'm willing to live with it if it means the police won't come after me on account of working for Vogler.'

'No. *You* have it wrong, Joe. Hexter has plans for you and you can be certain they won't serve the best interests of the British government. We know he's made some kind of deal with Marianne Vogler. Maybe with the Clearing House through her. I don't know what his exact intentions are, but you have to get away from him. A long way away. We all do.'

'Wait a minute. Where are we going now?'

'Not sure. But we should put as much distance between us and Hexter as possible. I think we should probably head for the Welsh borders. Find somewhere to lie low while I work out a—'

I see the other vehicle from the corner of my eye a fraction of a second before it slams into the side of the car. It's a chunky black Transit van powering out of a side street straight across the give-way lines. It forces the Land Rover up on to the pavement in a slewing, grinding skid. We hit a wall and come to rest in a crunching of metal and a gout of steam from the radiator.

There's a moment of immobility. Forrester has fallen against Joe, who has slid against the passenger door. I'm not immediately sure if they're injured. My guess is not. I think I'm all right too. There's no blood. It's lucky I was wearing my seatbelt. Fortunately, neither vehicle was going very fast. The other driver must simply have lost concentration.

Then I see three figures emerge from the van and I realize he didn't lose concentration at all. Scaddan's there, with two big, granite-faced men. And Scaddan's holding a gun.

The wing of the Land Rover is jammed against the wall we hit. Joe wouldn't be able to open his door if he tried. But the door next to me has been jolted open by the impact. Wide enough for me to get out. As Scaddan closes in on the car, I release the seatbelt, grab my shoulder-bag and scramble out through the door, crouching low.

There's a narrow alley between two houses a short distance away. Still stooping, I run towards it. I hear one of the Land Rover doors being wrenched open behind me and Scaddan's voice. 'Get out, all of—'

He breaks off, suddenly noticing, I suppose, that I'm not in the car. In fact, I'm in the alley, running hard. I don't know what's going to happen to Forrester and Joe. But I do know staying with them wouldn't make any difference and would mean that whatever happens to them will happen to me too.

I hear heavy, running footsteps behind me, but I don't look back. It flashes through my mind that these men aren't going to start firing guns in the middle of suburban Cheltenham if they can possibly avoid it. And I'm only a subsidiary target anyway. It's Joe they want. Everyone wants him. And some are prepared to kill for it.

There are back gardens either side of the alley and more

houses ahead, fronting on to the next street. An even narrower side alley crosses my path, threading between the gardens. On an impulse, I turn into it, hoping I can get into one of the gardens through the back gate. I see one a few along that's standing ajar and rush in through it, pushing it shut behind me.

The gate doesn't close properly, so I have to lean against it to keep it in place. I glance up the garden and wonder if I should make a run for the house. I can't see anyone indoors, so I don't know if I've been noticed.

Then I hear my pursuer. He's breathing heavily and he isn't light on his feet. He rattles a gate a couple of gardens over, sparking a burst of barking from a dog. He tries another gate that won't open either.

I'm not deliberately holding my breath. But still I'm not breathing. I can't move without the risk he'll hear me, even above the slowly less frequent barking of the dog. Eventually, though, he's going to try this gate. And I won't be able to hold it shut.

Then his phone rings. He muffles a 'Shit' and answers it. 'Yeah?' he whispers. 'No . . . Not sure . . . OK . . . See you there.'

He ends the call, mutters 'Fuck it' and hurries away. I think he turns right at the junction with the through-alley, which means he's heading for the next street. Maybe they're picking him up there and hoping to catch me on the way.

I hear a fence creak a little way off, which starts the dog off again. Wondering if my pursuer's hauled himself up on to a fence to see if he can spot me in any of the gardens, I drop to my haunches, with my back to the gate. A thick hedge to my left gives me ample cover, though. There's no way he's going to be able to see me.

*

286

I stay there a long time, listening to the snuffling of the dog and the ebb and flow of traffic noises and human voices in the area. Slowly, my breathing returns to normal. My heart stops pounding. I don't know what to do or where to go. Scaddan and his crew can't hang around waiting for me to show myself. I'm assuming they've transferred Forrester and Joe to the Transit van at gunpoint and driven off with them, destination . . . I haven't a clue. But the collision with the Land Rover will have attracted a lot of attention. The police will show up sooner or later. Maybe I should ask for their protection. Maybe I should tell them the whole story.

No, no. That won't work. Even if they believe me. Hexter's already shown he can tell the police what to do and what not to do. And Scaddan's working for Hexter. So this was done on Hexter's orders.

I begin to wonder if Hexter was happy to let us arrange to meet Joe, just so he could be kidnapped. Maybe they followed Joe to Costa. Then they followed us, until they found the right place to strike. But why? What purpose would that serve? Why would Hexter want Joe in Scaddan's hands? Or Marianne Vogler's? What's he planning? He's been one step ahead the whole way. And now he has Joe *and* Forrester.

He doesn't have me, it's true. Yet, anyway. But he doesn't fear me, as he probably does Forrester. I'm no threat. I'm just . . . a minor inconvenience.

What am I going to do? Where am I going to go? Who can I turn to? For answers there's only a void, a black hole where my future, short-term, medium-term, *any* term, used to be.

I hear police sirens in the distance. They're on their way. Scaddan and his crew – and Forrester and Joe – must be long gone by now. It's safe for me to move. But where am I moving *to*?

I walk along the alley to the next street. Behind me, I can hear the crackle of a police radio and a burble of conversation. The police are puzzled, no doubt, by what they've found. An empty Land Rover, jammed against a wall. The occupants? And the occupants of the *other* car? Witnesses will be telling them what they know. Did anyone see the direction the Transit van went in? And did anyone see *me*?

I head back towards the town centre. I move neither quickly nor slowly. I'm trying desperately to look normal and behave normally. I can't go back to the Belmont. That's too risky. And I have no transport now. I'm on my own. And I'm on foot. That's it.

I think back to what Forrester said I should do if he never showed up at the tea room in Hyde Park. Get out of town. Lie low. In other words, trust no one and think only of myself.

'That's great advice, Duncan,' I murmur under my breath. 'The recipe for a truly wonderful life.'

What are they doing to Forrester? He could be dead. I hope and pray he isn't. But it's a possibility. As for Joe, what are their plans for him? And what *were* their plans for me?

I'm alone. Utterly alone. Without Forrester, I have no one to tell me what the best thing to do is. I haven't the remotest idea what it might be anyway. I can't hurt Hexter. I can't defeat him. All I can do, if I'm very very lucky, is elude him.

But how?

It's started to rain by the time I reach Imperial Gardens, at the bottom of the Promenade. The rush hour's begun.

There's more traffic and more people on the streets. I'm wet and cold and tired. And I'm frightened. I've been frightened all week, of course. But this fear goes beyond that. It's like a choking weight on my chest.

I need to find somewhere safe and dry where I can just . . . think. But there's nowhere. And the only place where I can keep out of the rain at the moment is one of the bus shelters on the Promenade. I stand with several other people who are waiting for their bus. There are plenty of places to go. Swindon. Cirencester. Stroud. Gloucester. Places where people live and love and lead their lives. And there's nothing waiting for me in any of them.

My heart jumps when I spot a black Transit van the same size as the one Scaddan's using. It's moving slowly along the southern side of Imperial Gardens. Slowly enough to suggest the driver's looking for something. Or some*one*.

There must be dozens of black Transits on the streets of Cheltenham at any one time, but that thought doesn't make me feel even remotely safer. I shrink between the other people at the bus stop as best I can.

There's a bus approaching. Several people around me shuffle forward. I decide to get on with them. I don't care where the bus is going. I don't even notice. I just keep my head down, mumble 'As far as you go' to the driver and hand over the fare.

I climb the stairs to the top deck and head along towards the rear.

That's when I see him. And a second later he sees me.

'You are an endlessly surprising woman, Miss Nicholson,' says Martinek, moving his bag on to his lap so I can sit next to him. 'Take a seat.'

I sit down.

'I assume your name isn't actually Nicholson.'

'It's Nevinson,' I reply weakly. 'Nicole Nevinson.'

I can't think of anything else to say. There's no way I can explain myself to him. Part of me's actually glad to be with someone I know, though he'd probably find that the hardest thing of all to believe. In the end, just as the bus starts moving, I manage to get a few more words out. 'How'd you come to be on this bus?'

'I'm going home.' Of course. I'm on a bus bound for Gloucester. It makes sense, after all. 'I gave up waiting at Costa after a couple of over-caffeinated hours. I had a really enjoyable afternoon thanks to you and Mr Foster. Or whatever he's really called.'

'I'm sorry.'

'What for, exactly? Setting up a game you had no intention of letting be played to a finish? Making a fool of me? Or something else too subtle for me to comprehend?'

'I'm sure you don't think very highly of me.'

'That's a considerable understatement. Is there any chance you're going to tell me what this has really all been about?'

'I can't do that.'

'Well, maybe we could settle for some simpler questions. Why are you on this bus? Where's Mr Foster? And where's Mr Roberts? You haven't tucked him in your bag, have you?'

'I don't know where they are.'

'That's strange, considering you left Costa in their company.'

'We were . . . separated.'

'How did that happen?'

'You wouldn't believe me if I told you.'

'Are you going to Gloucester?'

'Apparently.'

'Do you have the rest of my money, by any chance? I think we can agree I've earned it.'

'Mr Martinek . . .'

'Yes?'

'Can I call you Lewis?'

He frowns at me. 'I suppose so.'

'I'm Nicole.'

'I know. You said. I'm just not much of a first name kind of person.'

'Could you try to be? Just for now?'

'All right. Nicole. Can I have the rest of my money? I did what you asked of me. It's not my fault Mr Roberts – Joe – abandoned the game.'

'It's not his fault either.'

'Why *are* you on this bus, Nicole?'

'Needs must.'

'When the devil drives. So, who's the devil in all this?'

'I'm in a lot of trouble, Lewis. I need help. Will you help me?'

He looks at me disbelievingly. I can hardly blame him. 'You're asking for my help? After manipulating me into enabling you and Mr Foster to lure Joe to that coffee shop? That was all garbage about giving him a chance to avenge his defeat in Bath, wasn't it?'

My answer sounds hollow to my own ears. 'Yes.'

'Who's Hexter?'

I lean towards him, lowering my voice. 'A dangerous man. We shouldn't be talking about him in a public place.'

'I'm not sure what to make of you, Nicole.' Martinek's lowered his voice too. 'You still haven't told me where you're going, by the way.'

'I don't know where I'm going.'

'*You don't know?*'

'That's right. I don't. Because right now . . . nowhere's safe for me.'

'What happened after you left Costa?'

I drop my voice still further. 'We were intercepted. Foster—I'm sorry. His name's Forrester, not Foster. He and Joe . . . were taken. I managed to get away.'

'Do you realize how crazy that sounds? The way you're talking is, well, either paranoid or . . .'

'It's true.'

'I'd hazard a guess Joe works at a certain doughnut-shaped complex on the western side of town. Would I be right?'

'Maybe.'

'And you? Do you work there?'

'No.'

'No?'

'Will you help me, Lewis?'

'Help you how?'

It's a good question. And looking at me, he must realize I don't actually have an answer.

Neither of us says much more until we arrive in Gloucester. Some way short of the centre, Martinek announces we're approaching his stop. When I get up to let him out of the seat, he says to me, as if the matter's already settled, 'If you're coming home with me, this is your stop too.'

I don't object. It's still raining. A damp evening is setting in. I've already admitted I have nowhere to go. I don't have any choices that sound like good ones. I have some money, but most of it's pledged to Martinek. I can't use a

292

cashpoint to get any more. And I can't use my credit card. There are a lot of can'ts. But as for what I *can* do . . .

Martinek's house is a semi-detached bungalow in a long road full of semi-detached bungalows. It looks less well cared for than most of its neighbours, with an overgrown front garden and peeling paintwork.

Indoors it feels cold and inhospitable. My host makes no move to turn on any heating. It doesn't look like the furnishings have been altered in thirty years. He asks me if I want any tea and I say yes. We stand in the kitchen next to a massive grime-encrusted range while the kettle boils and he ferrets around for biscuits.

'I'm not used to entertaining,' he says, as if that's what he's doing.

I sink into a chair at the kitchen table. 'It's fine,' I mumble.

'You look tired.'

'I am.' More tired than I can possibly describe.

'I've lived here alone since Mother died. She was very house proud. She probably wouldn't approve of the way I've . . . done things since.'

'It's fine,' I repeat.

'I'm not going to press you for an explanation, Nicole.' He gives me a cautious smile. 'You don't need to worry about that.'

'I wish I *could* explain.'

'All I will say is that I'd be inclined to write you off as a nutcase if it weren't for the fact that Mr Forrester struck me as sane if he was nothing else. And then there's Joe. Not to mention the mysterious Mr Hexter. And the man you claim tried to kill you. Roger Lam. Was that his name?'

'Yes.'

'You're obviously caught up in something beyond a bundle of personal neuroses. Quite what it is . . .' The kettle comes to the boil. He spoons tea into a pot and pours in the water. 'You may be glad to know complexity doesn't faze me. In fact, you have to love complexity to thrive at Go. Do you want milk or lemon with your tea?'

'It doesn't matter.'

'Really? It's always seemed to me to make a big difference. This is leaf tea we're talking about, after all. They use bags at the Records Office. Just awful, don't you agree?'

I gaze up at him. I'm not sure I've heard him correctly. 'Could I use your bathroom?'

'Certainly. It's just down the passage to your left. I'll take the tea through to the living room when it's brewed.'

'OK.' I heave myself out of the chair and follow his directions to the cheerlessly functional bathroom.

I splash some water on my face and try very hard not to stare at Martinek's toothbrush or the razor and shaving stick standing on the shelf beside it. What am I doing here? And what am I going to do if I leave? Is there any way out of the situation I'm in?

I can't think of one. I can barely *think* at all.

I'm just about to flush the loo when I hear the doorbell ring. It's just about the last sound I want to hear. Martinek can't have visitors. *Can he?*

I edge the bathroom door open and step out into the passage. I can hear voices from the direction of the front door, round the right-angled corner of the passage.

'Mr Martinek?'

Martinek agrees he is.

'DI Graves, Gloucestershire CID. This is my colleague,

DS Henderson. Would you mind if we asked you a few questions?'

The police. Shit. *Really?* What do I do now? Try to leave by the back door? Hopeless. It's in the kitchen, which is visible from the front door. A window, maybe? There's a closed door opposite me which probably leads to a bedroom overlooking the garden.

But if I make the slightest noise, they may realize I'm here. And then . . . I don't know. The question that really matters now is: will Martinek give me away?

'What sort of questions, Inspector?' he asks coolly. 'And who's your friend?' So, there are three of them in all.

'I'm Roger Lam.' Christ. It's Roger. With the police. 'I work with someone I think you know. Joe Roberts.'

'Perhaps we could step inside,' says Graves.

'Is Joe in some kind of trouble?'

'That's what we're hoping you may be able to clear up, sir.'

'You met him earlier this afternoon?' asks Roger.

'I did,' Martinek replies. 'May I ask how you know that?'

'He mentioned he was meeting you for a game of Go at Costa Coffee in Cheltenham.'

'Did he? Well, that's correct. We met there.'

'There's some concern about what's become of Mr Roberts since,' says Graves. 'We won't keep you long.'

'All right. Come on in.'

A shuffling of feet. The front door closes. The voices move into the sitting room and become slightly less distinct, though my senses are on high alert and I can still hear them well enough. I move cautiously across to the closed door and inch the handle down, alert for the slightest squeak.

'Would you like some tea?' asks Martinek. 'I've just made a pot.'

'No tea for us, sir,' says Graves.

'You live alone here, sir?' It's a different voice. DS Henderson, I assume.

'I do. Sit down, please. Mind if I fetch my tea? I don't want it to stew.'

Martinek comes into view along the passage. He doesn't move his head as he glances towards me. And his expression barely twitches. But he seems to be telling me to stay where I am.

I hear him pouring his tea. Then he reappears and heads back towards the sitting room. I gently open the bedroom door and peer inside. It looks like this was his mother's room. In fact, it looks like she's just stepped out to post a letter. There are brushes and cosmetics still laid out on the dressing-table. And in the dressing-table mirror I can see a pink quilted dressing-gown hanging on the back of the door. I can see my tight, frightened face in the mirror as well.

'I'm a little confused, gentlemen.' Martinek doesn't *sound* confused. Sceptical is what he actually sounds. 'I met Joe for a game of Go. An innocent Oriental pastime. Surely that's not a police matter.'

'We have reason to believe Mr Roberts may have come to some harm,' says Graves. 'After you parted.'

'Really?'

'We can't go into details of an ongoing investigation. I'm sure you understand.'

'How exactly *did* you part, sir?' asks Henderson.

'Joe left . . . with an acquaintance . . . before we finished the game.'

'Did you know this acquaintance?'

'I'd met her a couple of times, yes. Her name's Nicole Nevinson.'

My blood runs cold when I hear him name me. Christ. I get the feeling he isn't going to hold anything back. Except, I have to believe, that he met me on the bus and brought me back here and I'm standing a few metres away from them, listening to their every word.

They ask how he knows me. And he delivers the whole story. Me and Duncan Forrester showing up at the Records Office and subsequently asking him to challenge Joe to a Go rematch. Then me showing up unexpectedly at Costa and interrupting the game and spiriting Joe away.

Except it *isn't* the whole story. He doesn't mention being paid by us. He doesn't mention the names Hexter and *Roger Lam* cropping up in conversation between me and Joe. The way he tells it, all I had to do was say Forrester was on his way and Joe agreed to go with us.

I'm wondering why Martinek had to be quite as forthcoming as he's been when Henderson pipes up: 'The waitress at Costa said Mr Roberts didn't look best pleased at having to leave with Miss Nevinson.' Now I get it. Martinek realizes they've already been to Costa. He couldn't risk trying to edit me out of the picture.

'I wasn't pleased either.' He's surprisingly smooth. 'The game was developing quite interestingly.'

'But it was just a pretext, right?' cuts in Roger.

'A pretext?'

'Their plan was to lure Joe to a location where they could pounce.'

'*Pounce?*'

'We believe Nicole Nevinson and Duncan Forrester have kidnapped Mr Roberts,' says Graves.

297

'You do?'

'And they used you to get to him.'

'He went with them quite willingly, Inspector. I had no intimation anything sinister was afoot.'

'We're not suggesting you did.'

'Any chance I could use your loo, sir?' asks Henderson suddenly.

I freeze. What do I do now?

'Certainly,' says Martinek. 'The bathroom is at the end of the passage on the left.'

'Sorry about this, Mr Martinek,' says Graves. 'My sergeant seems to have a bladder about the size of a peanut.'

I hear Henderson lumbering in my direction, so I step into the bedroom and ease the door to.

A few seconds pass. I get the feeling Henderson's taking a good look round on his way. Then he looks closer. The door I'm standing behind is pushed warily open. Henderson's need for the loo's obviously a ploy. He can easily see the bathroom's on the other side of the passage because I didn't close the door. I shrink back behind the quilted dressing-gown and pray he doesn't come all the way in, though even as I do so I wonder whether he'll see me in the dressing-table mirror anyway.

'That's the wrong door, Sergeant,' comes Martinek's voice.

'Oh.'

'The bathroom's the door opposite.'

'Ah. Right. Thanks.'

I let out a relieved breath and hear the bathroom door close behind Henderson. The loo flushes a suspiciously short time later and then he's out again. But Martinek's obviously keeping watch from the kitchen to make sure he doesn't do any more prying. 'Sure you don't want any tea?

I'm just topping up my cup, but I can squeeze another out of the pot.'

'I'm fine, sir, thanks,' says Henderson. He sounds ever so slightly guilty.

A few seconds later, he and Martinek are back in the sitting room. I move into the doorway so I can hear what's being said.

'Did Nevinson or Forrester give you any indication of where they're staying, Mr Martinek?' asks Graves.

'None,' Martinek replies.

'Did Miss Nevinson mention me when she was talking to Joe at Costa?' asks Roger.

'No. I'd have said so if she had. Do you know her, then?'

'We've met.'

'Really? Have you met Forrester as well?'

'I don't think it's helpful to get into that, Mr Martinek,' says Graves. 'Suffice to say we're very concerned about Mr Roberts and we'd be grateful for anything you can tell us that may lead us to where they're holding him.'

'It's only a few hours since he left Costa with them, Inspector. If you're already so worried about him, I assume there must've been some kind of ransom demand?'

'I can't comment on that.'

'Right. OK.'

'What I need to emphasize is that if you hear from Miss Nevinson or Mr Forrester, or Mr Roberts come to that, you need to tell us straight away.'

'Of course I will, Inspector. But why would they contact me?'

'It's just an outside chance.'

'Well, you can rely on me.'

'Thank you, sir. Now, at some stage we'll need you to

come into the station in Cheltenham and make a witness statement about all this. I trust that won't be a problem?'

'None at all.'

'Right, then. Better make a note of Mr Martinek's phone number and email address, Sergeant.'

They leave a few minutes later. I stay where I am until Martinek appears at the corner of the hallway. 'They've just driven off, Nicole,' he announces. 'Want that tea now?'

I join him in the kitchen, where I find him hoiking my shoulder-bag out of a cupboard.

'Can't be too careful, can you?' He smiles lopsidedly at me, then fills the kettle and sets it to boil.

'Thank you, Lewis.' I'm surprised by the effort it takes me to say that. I don't really want to be indebted to Martinek. But I am. 'For not giving me away, I mean.'

'To that bunch? Why should I tell them the truth when they sit in my own home and lie through their teeth?'

'We didn't kidnap Joe. That was never our intention.'

'Clearly not. I don't like Mr Lam. I don't like him one bit.'

'Neither do I.'

'Well, you wouldn't like someone who tried to kill you, would you? I can understand that.'

The kettle comes to the boil. He tops up the teapot. 'D'you think they suspect you're sheltering me, Lewis?' I ask.

'No. Why should they? I'm a bit part player in this drama. The snooping sergeant with the supposedly weak bladder? Just nosing into other people's affairs like he always does, I suspect. To be honest, I had the feeling they wanted to test how much I knew. And I also had the feeling it was important I appeared to know as little as possible.'

'You're probably right.'

'So, your . . . reticence . . . has served me well, hasn't it?' He hands me a cup of tea. I sit down at the table. 'Biscuit?'

'Why not?'

He puts a shortbread on a plate for me. 'What are you going to do now?'

I shake my head. 'No idea.'

'You can stay here tonight. If you want. I could order in Chinese. I learnt Go from the father of the man who runs the takeaway I use. I'm one of their better customers.'

'Thanks.' There's nothing else I can say. I need to stay somewhere. And this, apparently, is where it's going to be.

Martinek sits down at the table opposite me. 'Are Forrester and Joe Roberts in danger?'

'Forrester is, certainly. Joe . . . is someone they have a use for.'

'*They* meaning GCHQ?'

'The Intelligence Service, yes.'

'What's this really about? Cryptography?'

'Sort of.'

'How did you get mixed up in it?'

'Bad luck. Bad judgement.'

'An unfortunate combination.'

'Yes, it is.'

'I'm not going to get my money, am I?'

'I promise you will. When this is all over. But just for now I need all the cash I've got.'

'You conned me.'

'I suppose we did.'

'I bet you never thought you'd see me again after leaving Costa with Joe.'

I can't find anything to say to that. I shake my head wearily and drink some tea.

'All in all, I have a lot to feel aggrieved about.'

'I'm sorry.'

He looks unimpressed.

'That's the best I can do for now.'

'Really? I see.' He says no more, but the expression on his face suggests this isn't the last I've heard on the subject.

I eat the Chinese food Martinek orders. I drink the Chinese beer he serves. I listen to a lengthy account of his playing record at Go. The evening passes.

I don't know what I'm going to do tomorrow or where I'm going to go. The emptiness of the immediate future looms over me as I lie in the bath, staring up at the ceiling through whorls of steam. I should probably be worried about Martinek, but there are too many bigger threats from other quarters for me to think about him.

He makes up the bed in his mother's room for me and asks me most particularly not to disturb any of her belongings. He doesn't say how long she's been dead or why he hasn't cleared the room. He has a capacity for not explaining himself that's mirrored by a tolerance for other people – like me – not explaining themselves either.

I'm exhausted, but I can't sleep. I keep thinking about how desperate my situation is. I really am at the end of my tether.

And then the phone pings.

*

It's the phone Forrester gave me in Cheltenham, before I went to Costa. The one I used to tell him he should come and collect me and Joe. Only when I hear its tone, muffled inside my shoulder-bag, hanging on the dressing-table chair, do I realize that, stupidly, I've left it on all this time.

I scramble out of bed and grab the phone out of the bag. Relief. It's just a text message from the service provider, offering umpteen free texts if I top up before Monday. I delete the message.

Then I notice there's one other message lodged in the system. I call it up. Package sent yesterday. That's all. No name attached. The origin's just a phone number. Time of message: today, 1611. Christ, that must have been almost exactly when the Transit van hit the Land Rover this afternoon. No wonder I didn't hear it.

I look at the sender's number. It starts 00358. An overseas code? France is 0033, the US 001. But 00358?

I think about turning the phone off for a second, then I realize there's no way I'm going to ignore the message. There's no Internet connection – Martinek must have one, but maybe he's deactivated it overnight – so I ring the operator. 00358 is the international dialling code for Finland. *Finland.*

I ring the number. It's a couple of hours later in Finland, of course, so it's the middle of the night. I'm not surprised no one picks up. An answerphone kicks in. Not surprisingly, the message is in Finnish. But I catch a name. Alvar Norrback.

I get so flustered trying to think what to say after the tone that I end up being cut off. I ring again. This time I'm ready.

'My name is Nicole Nevinson. I'm a friend of Duncan Forrester. Alan Travers, that is. He knows your brother.

I've got your message, but I don't understand it. I can't ask Duncan. We've been separated and the situation's become desperate. Please call this number six a.m. tomorrow UK time.' I'm calculating that'll be eight o'clock in Finland, so he should have got the message by then. 'Please respond to this call.'

That's all I can think of to say.

I turn the phone off and plug it in to re-charge. It's close to midnight. The safest thing to do, I know, is to keep the phone off until shortly before six o'clock tomorrow morning.

Six hours. That's all. Not long, really.

Why did Forrester give me this phone? This *particular* phone? Did he foresee I might need to get the message he was waiting for on it? Surely he couldn't have. Could he?

Package sent yesterday.

What package? Sent where?

I get back into bed. The message means something. That much I know for certain.

Right now, to me, it means something like hope.

Saturday October 19

I SLEEP FITFULLY AND WAKE UP HEAVY-HEADED. I'VE DREAMT I'm trying to hold a gate shut that's being slowly forced open from the other side. I know it's Scaddan doing the forcing. And that he means to kill me. When I start awake, it takes me several queasy seconds to remember where I am.

When I hear the clock in the sitting room strike five, I give up on sleep altogether. At half past, I turn the phone back on. There are no messages.

Six o'clock. Nothing. A quarter past. Still nothing.

It's dark outside. I can hear rain against the window. It's dark in here too. Waiting *is* darkness.

When the phone rings, I've actually fallen back to sleep. I grab it from the bedside cabinet and answer it.

'Hello?'

'Nicole Nevinson?' The voice is gravelly, old, Scandinavian-accented.

'Yes. Alvar Norrback?'

'No. He told me you'd called. This is his brother.'

Tahvo. I'm speaking to Tahvo Norrback. He's no longer in custody. 'Where are you?'

'I have a question for you.'

'What?'

'On my brother's twenty-first birthday, our parents gave him . . . what?'

Oh God. The question Forrester was primed to answer. But he never primed *me*. 'I don't know.'

'You should.'

'Duncan didn't tell me what it was. Only that he knew.'

'Maybe he didn't tell you because he doesn't trust you. And if he doesn't trust you, how can I?'

'You must. Please. I'm alone. I don't know what to do.'

'Where's Duncan, as you call him?'

'They have him. They took him. Yesterday.'

'But not you?'

'I got away.'

'Maybe.'

'Please don't hang up. I need your help.'

'Tell me something only Duncan could have told you.'

Christ. I scour my brain. Their meeting in Rome. What were the details? 'Rome. A Sunday in December, 1989. You played him the—'

'Don't speak of that.'

'Sorry.'

'Where did we talk? In Rome, that Sunday?'

'Ah . . . Piazza Navona. You, er, drank mulled wine.'

'Yes.' He thinks for a moment before continuing. 'I drank mulled wine.'

'Do you believe me now?'

A lengthy silence. Then: 'Are you in London?'

'No.'

'Can you get to London?'

'Sure.' Can I? I will if I have to.

'The package should have reached its destination by now. Only Duncan can collect it. Or you.'

'What's in the package?'

'What I tried to deliver to him three days ago.'

The tape? How is that possible? 'I don't understand. Is there more than one copy?'

'I made copies before I left Helsinki. I brought one with me. Another was sent later by my brother to an address Duncan gave him.'

'What address?'

'I can't risk saying it on a phone. But you and Duncan know the place. You've been there. I understand arrangements for the package to be sent there were made by a former colleague of Duncan's.'

A former colleague. That can only be . . . Colin Bright. A last favour before quitting the country? I suppose it must've been. But the address can't be his flat. He's not there. So . . .

Mavis Lane.

'Do you know where I mean, Miss Nevinson?'

'Yes. I think I do.'

'Go there. Get the package. Then we will meet. Phone me on this number. But not from the phone you're using now. A new one. Better still, landline. You understand?'

'I understand. Where—'

He's gone. *Call ended.*

I turn the phone decisively off. I remember what Forrester said to me. *Everything electronic is our enemy.* But not the only enemy. How am I going to get to London? How am I going to evade all those cameras?

I get dressed, struggling to think as I hurry into my clothes. Maybe if I leave now and get the earliest train possible, I can be in London before anyone starts monitoring downloaded CCTV images.

It's Saturday. The post will probably arrive early. But, with luck, the package is already there, awaiting collection. Surely Alvar Norrback will have sent it by some express service. Yes. It must be there. I can almost hear Colin's voice on the phone to Mrs Lane. 'For Mr Travers or Miss Nevinson only, Mavis. No one else. No one else must even know you have it.' It's *there*. All I have to do . . .

I tidy the bed, then open the door carefully, hoping not to wake Martinek. I head along to the kitchen, planning to scribble a thank-you note to him before leaving.

And there he is, fully dressed, leaning against the worktop and moving stones on his pocket Go set. He smiles at me. 'Good morning, Nicole. Popping out for a paper? Only it's a long walk to the nearest newsagent.'

'I thought it would be easier to, er . . .'

'Leave without explanation?'

'I was going to write you a note.'

'An *explanatory* note?'

'Not exactly.'

'Who were you talking to on the phone?'

'It's really better if I don't tell you that, Lewis.'

'I couldn't catch what you were saying to him.' I wonder if that's completely true? Not that it matters. He isn't going to tell me if it isn't.

'Good.'

'Where are you going?'

'London.'

'How? The train?'

'I guess so.'

'I wouldn't, if I were you. All those cameras. If GCHQ

are coordinating a search for you, using facial recognition technology in addition to everything else, then the police will have you off the train long before you reach London. By Swindon would be my guess.'

'What would *you* do?'

'Borrow a car. Take the back routes. Switch to a cab before I got too close to the congestion zone.' Christ. It's as if he's reading a script written by Forrester. And sticking to that script *is* the best thing to do, of course. If only I could.

'Got a car I can borrow, Lewis?'

'I'm afraid not.'

'Well, there you are, then.'

'*I* haven't got one.'

'What does that mean?'

'I'm going into the Records Office this morning to make up for missing yesterday afternoon. We keep a pool car there for staff to use for visits to potential donors of records. Donors are often elderly. Not able to get to Gloucester easily. It's quite a big county. Anyway, the keys for the car aren't very securely stored, to be honest. You have to know where to look, of course. But if you *do* know . . .' Martinek smiles. 'I doubt it would be missed before Monday. If it wasn't back by then, I mean.'

'Why are you doing this for me?'

'I didn't take to Mr Lam. It would be nice to play a *tesuji* against him. Even vicariously.'

I smile at him. 'What's a *tesuji*?'

'A particularly clever Go move. One that isn't obvious. One that's more beautiful because of that. *Tesujis* can be very satisfying. Although I must admit I do have another reason for helping you get the better of him.'

'What's that?'

'I want to go to Las Vegas.'

'I thought you didn't like travelling.'

'I don't. But Las Vegas is where the big money is in poker. And I'm rather good at poker. It's a piece of cake after Go. I'd want to travel in style, of course. First class flights. A five-star hotel. The full works. Including . . . a glamorous escort.'

'*What?*'

'Who'd pay all the bills.'

'*Me?*'

'Well, I suspect you could look the part if you wanted to. What you're wearing now is just a disguise, after all. I can sense your inner vamp itching to be freed.'

'My *what*?'

'And you do owe me some money. I'm sure Venstrom pay you quite generously. We'd split the profits, of course. Sounds like fun, doesn't it?'

'You're joking, aren't you?'

'No. I never joke about fun.'

In any other circumstances, of course, I'd tell him to get lost, or words to that effect. But that wouldn't be a smart move as things are. So, I just say, 'Great idea, Lewis. Las Vegas? Bring it on.'

And he looks delighted.

Half an hour later, we leave. We walk briskly through the empty streets of an early Saturday morning. There are so few people around that anyone following us – following *me* – would be unmissable. But there's no one.

There's no one at the Records Office either. Martinek has a key, of course. He leads the way in through the reception area and into a side-office. He unlocks a desk drawer, takes out some car keys and gives me one of his uninter-pretable looks.

'White Skoda parked round the side. Should have a full tank. Enough said?'

'I am grateful, you know.'

'Good. Because I intend to hold you to your promise.' He gazes at me quite seriously, as if, at least in his mind, his Las Vegas fantasy is far more important than any-thing else I have to contend with. 'Drive safely.'

I follow in reverse the camera-free route Forrester used when we drove to Gloucester from London on Wednes-day, though things go a bit wrong near Wantage and I end up heading south rather than east. It doesn't really matter, because I reckon my chances of finding Mrs Lane at home are better the later I arrive. I'm impatient to lay hands on the tape, of course, but as long as I'm doing something to achieve that, I can keep my anxiety under control. Just.

I finally reach London in the middle of a bustling Satur-day afternoon. Family life in the capital swirls around me. The shops are busy. So are the roads. It's grey and damp: anonymous London weather.

I drop the Skoda off in the privately operated car park in Brixton Forrester chose last Sunday. I get the feeling the man running it recognizes me, which is probably not a good thing. But there are too many other not good things for me to worry about, so I just pay him the deposit and set off on foot.

I'm at Mrs Lane's house an hour later. My heart's in my mouth when I ring the bell. She's just *got* to be in.

And she is.

'Miss Nevinson.' She greets me with a smile, then looks past me. 'Mr Travers not with you?'

'No, Mrs Lane. It's just me. Have you . . . received a package for us?'

I think I'll break down and cry if she says 'No' to that. But what she actually says is, 'Yes. It came this morning. From . . . well, from somewhere abroad. Just as Mr Bright said it would. Come along in.'

We're in her kitchen a few seconds later. It's as tiny and orderly as I'd expect. I spot the package at once. A Jiffy bag with a strip of colourful stamps on it. The address is written neatly in block capitals.

'Where's Suomi when it's at home?' asks Mrs Lane. 'That's what it says on the stamps. Suomi.'

'I think that's Finland in Finnish, Mrs Lane.'

'Really? Well, Mr Bright didn't say where it was coming from. Only that I was to take good care of it until you and Mr Travers came to collect it. And here you are. Is Mr Travers all right?'

'He, um, couldn't come to London, I'm afraid.'

'That's a pity. I was hoping he could reassure me that Mr Bright isn't in any kind of trouble.'

'What makes you think he might be?'

'Oh, something in his voice when he spoke to me.'

'When was that?'

'Thursday morning. Very early. Though I sleep so little these days early and late aren't very different to me. But it was certainly before seven o'clock. He said he was at the airport. He had to fly to Canada, apparently. Something to do with his mother.'

'I gather she's not well.'

'That explains it, then. Still, I—'

'About the parcel, Mrs Lane . . .'

'I'm sorry, my dear. Here I am, rabbiting on when you're probably in a hurry.' She picks up the package and hands it to me. 'There you are. Don't let me hold you up.'

'D'you mind if I open it here?'

'Not at all. If you don't mind me seeing what's in it, that is. Mr Bright was very cagey. Though I suppose that goes with his job.'

I struggle with the package for a moment. Alvar Norrback seems to have completely encased it in Sellotape.

'Use these scissors, dear.' Mrs Lane hands me a pair.

I cut through the Sellotape and tear the flap open. Inside, there's an object so swaddled in bubble-wrap as to be invisible. I pull it out, unroll the bubble-wrap and there it is.

An old-fashioned audio-cassette. On the label some one's written: *21.09.89.* I pick it up and stare at the reel of tape inside. It's strange to think so much could be riding on a few words recorded on its surface.

Then I notice Mrs Lane has a large, quite old-looking radio standing by the window. And it incorporates a cassette player.

'Can I ask you a favour, Mrs Lane?'

'Certainly, dear.'

'Can I play this tape on that?' I point to the radio.

'Please do. I still have a lot of tapes I listen to. Andy Williams is one of my favourites. I expect you've never heard of him.'

I'm so fixated on hearing what's on Norrback's tape that I fail to respond to the remark. I insert the cassette and press the *Play* button.

313

Two voices, speaking in what certainly sounds like Chinese.

Is one of the voices Hexter's? I don't know. I've never heard him speak. But there's something off about one of the accents. The speaker isn't Chinese. That's for certain.

The exchange is brief and rapid-fire. There's one word I catch that sounds slightly like *music*. I wonder if it's actually *Moscow*.

After I'm sure they're not going to say anything else, I rewind the tape and remove it.

'Did you understand any of that?' Mrs Lane asks.

'Understand? No. Not exactly.'

'But it's important?'

'Oh yes. It's very important.'

What I feel most of all in this moment is empowerment. Suddenly, for the first time in a week, I have something to hit back with, something to use against these people who think I don't matter, that I can be ignored until such time as I can be eliminated. I remember how angry I am. I realize my anger's actually stronger than my fear. *I'm just not going to let them get away with it.*

'One more favour, Mrs Lane?'

'Yes?'

'Is this the only cassette player in the house?'

'Well, no. There's another in my bedroom.'

'I wonder . . . do you think I could borrow one of them?'

'Borrow one?'

'I need to be able to play this tape to other people. Today. Tonight. I can't explain just how vitally important it is. You'll have to trust me when I say, without any exaggeration, this is a matter of life and death.'

314

She looks at me for a long time. She's probably asking herself whether I'm in full possession of my senses. The answer seems to come out in my favour. 'Well, actually, Mr Bright specifically said I was to trust you and Mr Travers. No one else. Just you. So, yes, you can borrow it. I'll want it back, mind.'

'Of course. One other thing . . .'

'Yes?'

'Could I use your phone?'

'*Hei.*'

'It's me.'

'What is your news?'

'I have it.'

'Good. What now?'

'We should meet.'

'I agree. I'm not far away. Where and when do you suggest?'

'Beau Brummell statue on Jermyn Street.' I don't intend to explain why I'm going to meet him so close to the Ritz. The surprise visit to Billy Swarther I'm planning will have to come as a surprise to Norrback as well. 'How soon can you get there?'

'Give me one hour.'

'OK. See you there.'

Mrs Lane gives me a canvas holdall advertising Lloyds Bank to carry the radio cassette player in and lends me an umbrella as well. She's clearly worried about the machine getting wet. I feel fleetingly guilty about more or less forcing her to let me have it. But if I'm to shame Swarther into some kind of cooperation, I don't have any choice in the matter.

'Take care,' she says as she sees me off.

'I will,' I reply.

I head for Hungerford Bridge. It's going to take me a lot less than an hour to reach Jermyn Street, but I can kill time in Fortnum & Mason if I need to.

My thoughts are already fixed on what Norrback and I are going to say to Swarther. I'm actually looking forward to the encounter. Maybe that's what makes me less alert than I should be.

I glance left and right when I reach Stamford Street, checking for a break in the traffic before crossing. That's when I see something – or, rather, someone – familiar out of the corner of my eye.

I whirl round. Roger Lam's only a few yards away. He must have been watching Mrs Lane's house. He smiles weirdly at me and makes some kind of *Don't worry* gesture with his hands. The road ahead, on the other side of Stamford Street, looks pretty empty. Was that where he was planning to stop me?

I don't hang around to ask. I dash across the street, forcing one driver to brake sharply. He blares his horn. I look back and see Roger dodging after me. I can't seriously hope to outrun him, weighed down by Mrs Lane's holdall as I am. What am I going to do?

I see a pub ahead and make for it. Safety in numbers is my calculation.

I rush inside. The place is about half full. Almost all of the customers are men under fifty. They're watching football on a large-screen television. No one notices me.

Except the barman. I order a G & T. Thoughts whirl in my mind. How long has Roger been on my tail? Since I left Gloucester? Has he just been waiting for me to collect the tape so he can take it off me? And what's he got in mind for me once that's happened? I try to think clearly and quickly about what my options are.

Then I realize what I have to do.

'Hi, Nicole.' He's standing right next to me. It can't be more than a couple of minutes since I entered the pub. 'Let me pay for that,' he goes on as my G & T arrives. 'Peroni for me.'

'There are a lot of witnesses around, Roger,' I say, virtually through clenched teeth.

'I don't see any. They're all watching the football, not you and me.'

'Leave me alone.'

'We're just standing here having a chat, Nicole. I haven't laid a finger on you. And I'm not going to.'

'What d'you want, then?'

'You know what I want. Hand it over and we can go our separate ways.'

'You must think I'm totally brainless if you think I'm likely to believe that.'

'Well, you've been behaving pretty brainlessly this past week.' His Peroni arrives. He pays for the drinks, then takes a swig from the bottle. 'Cheers.'

I'm going to go for it. 'How long have you known your boss is a double agent for the Chinese?'

'That's a ridiculous question. Now, what did you collect from that house back there? A copy of the tape, I assume. Just give it to me and we can forget all about this.'

'You tried to kill me, Roger. You think we can forget all about *that*?'

'A week's a long time in my line of work. We've got Joe and we've neutralized Forrester. Things are moving fast and delivering on a threat to you would be a needless distraction at this time. Provided you give me the tape.'

'Maybe there's another copy somewhere else. Thought of that, have you?'

'Like I say, things are moving fast. If Norrback has the original buried in a bank vault in Helsinki, so be it. My instructions are to prevent you causing any problems right now. That's all.'

'What are your plans for Joe?'

'None of your concern.'

'The kidnap was staged on Hexter's orders. Correct?'

'I'm not going to tell you anything about Joe, Nicole. You should be thinking about your welfare, not his.'

'But he's been reported missing to the police. So, officially, your lot have lost him. But they haven't really, have they? So, what's Hexter up to? And what deal have you done with Venstrom? I know you wined and dined Billy Swarther at Hexter's house in the Cotswolds on Thursday evening. What did you shake hands on at the end of that?'

'You're rapidly talking yourself out of all that slack I was intending to cut you, Nicole. My advice, my *sincere* advice, is that you should give me the tape and walk out of here. That really is the best I can do for you.'

'And Forrester?'

'Forget Forrester. Forget Joe. Forget everything.'

There's a thickset shaven-headed guy standing beside Roger, taking delivery of three pints of lager. It's a desperate move, but I reckon I'm only going to get out of this if I can involve other people. I launch myself at Roger as forcefully as I can, shoving the bag containing the radio cassette player into his stomach.

The impact's enough to knock him off balance. He cannons into the lager guy. Most of the contents of the pints slop on to the floor. One of the glasses slips from his grasp and smashes. 'Fucking hell,' he says. He sounds angry. He sounds drunk as well. Which all sounds good to me.

'Sorry,' says Roger, turning round to appease him. 'Didn't see you there.'

'Didn't see me? It's a fucking pub, mate.'

'Sorry again. Let me buy you some refills.'

'He does this kind of thing all the time,' I cut in. 'He brings me in places like this 'cos he says it's fun to slum it. Spilling drinks is all part of the show. I don't know why I put up with it. You should hear what he's been saying about you and your friends.'

The lager guy glares at Roger. 'What *'ave* you bin sayin'?'

'Nothing.'

'He calls you Neanderthals,' I say.

'That right?' He prods Roger in the chest.

'This is ridiculous,' Roger protests.

'Ridiculous.' The word's pronounced to mock Roger's accent. 'Fucking ponce.'

'I'd watch out if I were you,' I say. 'He carries a stun gun to get himself out of confrontations. He used it on me once.'

'You some kind of nutter, mate?' he demands of Roger.

'Ignore her,' says Roger. 'She's off her head. I'm happy to buy you replacement drinks. That's all I can—'

The hint of dismissiveness in his tone drives my new friend over the edge. He takes a swing at Roger, forgetting, I suppose, that there's a half-empty glass in his hand.

Roger's not expecting a fist wrapped round a glass to hit him somewhere round the left eye. But that's what happens. There's a crunching thud and a spray of blood.

Roger falls backwards. I dodge out of the way and hear his head hit the edge of the bar with a solid thump. He goes down on the floor in a crumpled sprawl, beer and blood pooling around him.

'Fucking hell.' I'm not sure who says that. The barman's hurrying out from behind the bar and other drinkers are gathering round, though most of the customers are still fixated on the football.

I'm at the door by now. This is my chance. I glance back at Roger, who isn't moving. I think he must be seriously injured. I wonder if he might actually be dead. If he is, who's to blame?

Roger Lam was the attractive man who gave me a beginner's lesson in Go and came across as a kind and cultured academic.

And Roger Lam was the man who tried to kill me one week ago.

So, he's to blame. And I'm slightly shocked by the fact that I'm happy for him to suffer for it.

I'm not trembling as I walk away from the pub. My mind isn't scrambled. I feel absolutely certain that what I'm doing is right. Whether I can pull this off I don't know. But I'm going to give it my very best shot.

Tahvo Norrback is waiting for me by Beau Brummell's statue at the end of the Piccadilly Arcade. I know it's him from some way off. Tall, lean and white-haired. He's wearing a raincoat that looks as if it's designed to cope with serious Nordic weather.

'Mr Norrback?' He doesn't see me coming and my words make him start with surprise. He's wearing hearing aids, I notice. Well, he's close to eighty, so that's no surprise. But there's no vagueness of old age in his gaze or in his voice. They're both firm and decisive.

'Miss Nevinson?'

'Call me Nicole.'

'I'm relieved to see you, Nicole.'

'Same here. When were you released?'

'Yesterday. After pressure was applied by the Finnish embassy. I'm glad the fall-back scheme worked. But still I was worried that . . .'

'Something would go wrong?'

'Quite a lot of things *have* gone wrong.'

'Not today. I made it here in one piece. So did you.'

'You have the tape?'

'Yes.' I hold up the bag containing the radio cassette player. 'And the means to play it.'

'Not necessary. I know what it says. I had it translated many years ago.'

'I think we may have to play it, actually.'

'Why?'

'There's someone who needs to hear it. And, with any luck, he's very close by.'

We walk into the Ritz at close to six o'clock. I'm gambling Billy will be in his room, probably getting ready to go out for the evening.

And we're in luck. The young woman at the reception desk calls his room. Sorry, his *suite*.

I guess he's surprised when he hears who wants to see him, but none of that registers in the expression of the young Ritz woman. 'Please go up.' She supplies the suite number and some directions.

During a slow walk round from Jermyn Street, I told Norrback all about how I was separated from Joe and Forrester and that previously Forrester and I had seen

321

Billy and Bruno at Morecote, Hexter's country house. He knows Billy's not to be trusted. What he doesn't know is exactly how I intend to persuade Billy to help us.

'If Hexter has done some sort of deal with Venstrom,' he comments drily as we go up in the lift, 'surely Swarther will just brush us off.'

'Venstrom has a reputation to protect, Tahvo. The other directors won't thank Billy for sullying it. That's where they're vulnerable. Corporate image.'

'And you think you can convince him their . . . image . . . is under threat?'

'That's the idea.'

'Well, I'll help you as far as I can. But this is your world.'

My world? I suppose so. But it doesn't feel like it. Not any more.

Billy Swarther's a big man, with a big personality. He generally laughs a lot and projects bonhomie. He likes large audiences and spacious surroundings. He likes, above all, to be liked. And that's relatively easy when you're fronting a successful multinational company with a large and adoring workforce.

Of course, I've never met Billy one on one. I've only ever been part of a group delivering glowing reports and optimistic forecasts. He loves that. He thrives on it. Expansion. Innovation. Growth. That's his domain.

He looks oddly different in the lavishly furnished and decorated acreage of his suite overlooking Green Park. He's wearing a dress shirt and trousers, which is quite a change from his Californian casuals. He also looks ever so slightly nervous, which I wasn't expecting. But then I've become a seriously unknown quantity and he probably

322

realizes he can't big-talk his way past whatever I've come to say.

It's probably even more significant that he's asked us up. He could have refused to see us. But he didn't. He's not sure what he's dealing with. I suppose that's why he hasn't called Bruno in to join us.

I introduce Norrback. There's a cautious handshake between them. Then Billy swivels his big blue-grey eyes to look at me. The trademark smile's in place on his broad, tanned face. But there's not a lot of warmth hovering around it.

'You could've come and seen me a few days ago, Nicole. But from what Bernice told me, you just turned tail and ran.'

'I'm here now, Billy.'

'So I see. But not alone. Who exactly are you, Mr Norrback? And what's your interest in my company's relationship with Nicole?'

'I'm a retired Finnish civil servant, Mr Swarther. I'm here to warn you against doing a deal with Clive Hexter. He's in the pay of the Chinese.'

'Who isn't? One way or another?' Billy laughs. It's not contagious.

'He's a Chinese double agent,' I state baldly.

'That's one of the craziest ideas I've ever heard.'

'Surely not. What about "When we hire you we take you into our family." Isn't that crazier still?'

'We've always supported you, Nicole. Does Mr Norrback know about your little crack-up in Palo Alto?'

I take a breath, determined to face down both Billy and the problems I had back then, which seem now unimportant as well as irrelevant. 'I fell in love with the wrong man

323

and I was stupid enough to believe he meant it when he said he was going to leave his wife for me and I didn't cope well for a while when I realized he'd been lying to me – and her – all along.'

' "Didn't cope well" is a hell of an understatement.'

'You all sided with Kevin so quickly, Billy. So quickly and so easily. You and the other men on your all-male board.'

'Maybe you—'

'Maybe *you* should concentrate on what really matters here and now, Mr Swarther,' Norrback cuts in. 'Your company is doing business with a Chinese spy.'

'That's horse shit. Where's Carl, Nicole? You told Bernice he's dead. But the police say they've no idea where he is. I reckon his "death" is just another of your fantasies.'

He's not going to rile me. I let him see that. 'Tell me where I figured in your deal with Hexter, Billy.'

'You weren't discussed. Why the hell would you have been?'

'What *was* discussed?'

'Ways in which Venstrom Computers could benefit from any AI breakthroughs Joe Roberts' work with British Intelligence leads to. Pretty much the best we could hope for after you screwed up so spectacularly.'

'British Intelligence don't have him any more.'

'Says who?'

'The police. According to them, he was kidnapped yesterday by me and a man called Duncan Forrester. Hasn't Hexter told you that? I suppose not, since the truth is he organized the kidnapping. He's paying the people who are holding Joe.'

'Why would he do that?'

'Probably because his Chinese handlers told him to.'

'You're out of your mind.'

'Will you listen to me, Mr Swarther?' Norrback sounds calm and oh so reasonable. 'I first met Hexter thirty years ago. You should know what happened then. Before you make any decisions, you should know that.'

'Are you going to let him tell you, Billy?' I ask. 'It'll go badly for you if you ignore this and then it blows up in the company's face. Reputations are hard to win. But you can lose one faster than you can blink.'

Billy slumps down petulantly in one of several plush Louis XVI-style sofas. 'Go on, then. What have you got to say?'

'Do you want to get Bruno in to hear this as well?'

Billy thinks about that for a moment, then says, 'No. Just give it to me.'

So Norrback does. The full story of the secret conference with Slavsky in September 1989; his subsequent assassination; the murders of Curtis and Bourdil, the attempted murder of Forrester; and the tape recording of Hexter's voice, ordering the hit on Slavsky and his team.

I can tell from the deepening frown on Billy's face and the draining of confidence from his gaze that he's worried by what he hears. He demands proof, naturally enough. I get out the radio cassette player and play the tape. Which is in Chinese, of course. Billy only has Norrback's word for what's said on it. Billy signals that thought with a sceptical shrug.

'Did you recognize Hexter's voice?' I ask.

'Maybe,' Billy admits. 'Maybe not. But *I* don't understand a single damn word.'

'Phone the concierge, then,' I challenge him. 'There are bound to be some Mandarin Chinese speakers on the hotel's staff. Get one of them sent up here to translate it for you.'

'That is a good idea,' says Norrback. 'If you don't believe me.'

Billy huffs and puffs a bit, as if we're putting him to some almighty inconvenience. But he can't think of a good reason not to take me up on the suggestion. He phones down.

The Ritz is the Ritz, after all, used to fulfilling stranger requests than this. He's told someone is on their way.

'You know Tahvo's told you the truth, don't you, Billy?' I ask as we wait.

'According to you, someone's been feeding me some big fucking lies, Nicole,' he growls in reply. 'So I can't afford to take anything – or anyone – on trust.'

There's no arguing with that. 'Did you make any serious attempt to find out what had happened to Carl? To me, come to that?'

'I put McKenzie on it.' Gordon McKenzie, Venstrom's Head of Security. No pushover. But not exactly an outside-the-box thinker either. 'He turned up nothing but dead ends.'

'And that's where you'd have left me? In a dead end?'

Maybe it's just as well that, before he can answer, the doorbell rings.

They've sent a sous-chef, kitted out in kitchen whites. He looks faintly puzzled. But he hides it well with an ingratiating smile. The guest is always right at the Ritz.

Billy tells him what we want him to do. 'OK,' he says.

I play the tape. He listens.

'You want every word?' he asks. Billy nods. 'Can I?' His hand hovers over the machine's buttons. He looks enquiringly at me. I nod too.

He rewinds the tape, then plays it again, stopping it at each change of voice, translating as he goes.

'First guy: *"White Tiger."* I don't . . . understand that. But it's what he says. *Bái Lǎohǔ.* White Tiger. Second guy: *"Report."* First guy: *"They've just left."* Second guy: *"I acknowledge."* First guy: *"You don't have long."* Second guy: *"We know."* First guy: *"They mustn't reach Moscow."*'

Billy interrupts. 'He definitely says that? Moscow?'

'Yes, sir. *Mòsīkē.* Moscow. He, cr . . . sounds worried.'

Billy puffs out his cheeks. 'OK. Carry on.'

'So, first guy: *"They mustn't reach Moscow."* Second guy: *"We know."* First guy: *"There mustn't be any mistake."* Second guy: *"Do you have anything else to report?"* First guy thinks for a moment, then: *"No."* Second guy: *"I acknowledge."* Then . . . clunk. End of conversation.'

'Well, thanks a lot.' Billy stands up and folds the sous-chef's hand round a fifty-pound note. 'We're casting for a film and wanted to check just how good these two guys' Chinese really is. This is kind of a confidential process, so . . .'

'I can't remember what was on the tape, sir.'

'Great. Thanks again.'

The sous-chef exits, still smiling.

Billy moves over to the window and gazes out across Green Park. Norrback looks at me. I signal we should give Billy some space to think. No one speaks.

Then Billy turns round and says, 'This proves nothing. It might be Hexter's voice. It might not. They don't mention the Russian you talked about by name. I don't see what you expect me to do based on something this . . . thin.'

'White Tiger is the known codename of a Chinese double agent active in the nineteen eighties,' I say. 'Slavsky's death and the deaths of Curtis and Bourdil are all on record. Duncan Forrester worked with Hexter and Hexter tried to have him killed. He tried to have *me* killed. What more do you want?'

'Proof. White Tiger is just two words that mean nothing to me. These other people? I've never heard of them. I've never met them.'

'You've heard of Roger Lam. You've met *him*.'

'Hexter's assistant? Yeah. I've met him. So?'

'Listen to this. It happened a couple of hours ago.'

I take out the phone and play the recording I made of what was said between Roger and me in the pub. I'm so glad now the idea came to me when it did. I had just enough time to set it up before he caught up with me.

I stop the recording before we get to the fight. Billy doesn't need to hear that. He's already heard enough.

'You'll notice Roger doesn't deny trying to kill me,' I say, breaking the silence that follows. 'Nor does he deny Hexter's responsible for kidnapping Joe. In fact, he doesn't deny very much at all, does he? But he mentions the tape. So I think we can agree the tape must prove something. Otherwise he wouldn't have been so desperate to get hold of it. And, like you say, he's Hexter's assistant. His trusted right-hand man.'

Billy looks warily at me. 'Where's Lam now?'

'I gave him the slip.'

He glances at Norrback. 'Was he right about the original never leaving Helsinki?'

Norrback nods. 'Yes.'

'Just so you know, Billy,' I add, 'I sent the recording of my conversation with Roger to another phone. It's in a safe place.' It's actually an entirely imaginary phone. But Billy needs to believe he really does have to listen to me.

'Where are you going with this, Nicole?' he asks, in a tone that suggests he doesn't think he'll like the answer.

'Something's going to happen soon, Billy. I don't know what it is, but it'll be bad for Joe and bad for Duncan. We have to act now. You're going to be tied in to a serious scandal if you don't disentangle yourself from Hexter. The media will make mincemeat of you when this all blows up. And then the authorities will probably come looking for people to charge with aiding and abetting espionage, starting with you. That's if Hexter gets away with whatever he's planning. Because you're the sucker who did a deal with him.'

'You want me to *un*do the deal?'

'No. *You* want to undo it. Because that's the only way you're going to survive this.'

Billy looks at Norrback. 'Hexter really is a Chinese double agent?'

'He is White Tiger,' says Norrback.

'Fuck,' Billy mutters. He can see Venstrom's precious reputation going up in smoke. And his with it.

'If we threaten Hexter with exposure,' I reason, 'he'll have to let Joe and Duncan go. You can guarantee maximum exposure of his activities through Venstrom's worldwide media outlets, after all. The days are gone when he can hide behind his chums in British Intelligence and other agencies. He'll realize there's no way out and give in to our demands. He won't have a choice.'

Billy looks unconvinced. 'He strikes me as the kind of guy who always has a choice.'

'He won't have bargained on you coming after him, Billy.'

'You're right there. Considering what a sweet deal I'll be kissing goodbye to if I do. Have you any idea what access to the Chinese market is *worth*?'

'Is that what he's offering you?'

'It's kind of on the table. It would give us a massive advantage over all our competitors. It's basically unheard of.'

'Then how come it's in Hexter's gift?'

'It isn't. Not exactly. But this other guy he introduced me to . . . Feng Jianjun . . . is some sort of middleman for the Chinese government. An expert in unlocking locked doors. That's how he put it.'

'What do you have to do for him to unlock these locked doors, Mr Swarther?' asks Norrback.

'Bottom line?' Billy smiles ruefully. 'What I'm told to, I guess.'

'And that would mean,' I go on, 'for me . . . and Joe . . . and Duncan?'

Billy shrugs, almost apologetically.

'No amount of door-opening in China will help you if the Hexter story breaks in the media and you're still part of it,' I point out.

'He's just throwing me a few bones to keep me quiet. Until he's got what he wants. Or his bosses in Beijing have. Yeah. I understand that.'

Billy lurches over to the desk and grabs his phone. He scrolls through some messages. 'Big numbers,' he murmurs. 'Big promises.' He tosses the phone down, heaves a sigh and looks at me. 'You should've come to me right away, Nicole.'

'And you'd have believed everything I said? Just like that? With no tape? With no evidence of any kind?'

'I'm not the asshole you're making me out to be.'

'Prove it.'

'OK.' Billy glances at his watch. 'It's too late now. This is a job for the morning. I'll settle this with Hexter then. I know for certain he's spending the weekend at Morecote. Feng Jianjun wants the full tweedy open-fire-in-a-village-inn English experience. If we leave here at six, we can be there before they've finished their breakfast.'

'Who's *we*?'

'You and me, Nicole. I want to hear you say what you've just said to me to his face. And then I want to hear what *he* has to say. After that, it'll be time to tell him what my terms are for letting him off lightly. And don't worry. Those terms will include Joe and your pal Forrester walking free. We'll take McKenzie with us to watch our backs. I suggest you stay in London, Mr Norrback. I'll leave Bruno here too. He'll be fully briefed by me, though. I'll make sure Hexter understands exactly how limited his options are.'

'You will be putting your heads in the white tiger's jaws,' says Norrback solemnly.

'Yeah, thanks for that. Thing is, I don't like being played for a sucker. And I have enough corporate heft behind me to make Hexter think twice about trying to push me around.' Billy looks directly at me. 'That's been your problem all along, Nicole. Yours and this guy Forrester's. Lack of fire power. Well, I'm not lacking in that department. So, are you up for this?'

He's as angry with Hexter now as I am. And anger drives out caution. In this mood, Billy Swarther is a force of nature. Norrback's right, of course. Confronting Hexter on his home turf carries risks. But what else can we do? If we catch him off guard, we can get the better of him. I believe that. I have to.

331

I wanted Billy to act. Now I've got my wish. It's as simple – and as dangerous – as that.

'Nicole?' He's still looking at me.

I nod. 'Yes, Billy, I'm up for it. One hundred per cent.'

Norrback's staying in a flat in Pimlico normally occupied by a member of the Finnish embassy staff, who's gone home on leave. He offers me a bed there and I accept gladly. We take a taxi straight there from the Ritz.

We barely speak during the journey. But once we're inside the flat, Norrback pours us both some vodka and asks me if I really understand the risks I'll be running by going to see Hexter tomorrow.

'He's ruthless, Nicole,' he says to me as we sit in the sparsely but stylishly furnished lounge of the absent diplomat. 'I thought he might have softened with age. But that wasn't my impression when he came to speak to me during my detention. He won't give in easily.'

'Picking off individuals like you, me and Duncan is one thing, Tahvo. Neutralizing Venstrom Computers, with its massive worldwide resources, is quite another.'

'I agree. But still . . .'

'We have to try this. There's nothing else we *can* try.'

'Again, I agree. But that doesn't mean I think your chances of success are high.'

'Are you going to give me odds?'

'No. I'm not. I'm going to give you some advice. Put yourself first. Let Mr Swarther do his best to get what you want. But if it looks as if it's going wrong . . .'

'Make a run for it?'

Norrback sighs and sits back in his chair. 'This isn't much help, is it?'

'Yes, it is. Because you have the original tape, safely locked away in Helsinki. That *is* true, isn't it?'

He nods. 'Yes.'

'Well, with that and the pressure Swarther can threaten to bring to bear, I think we have him.'

'I hope you're right.'

'Me too, Tahvo.'

'Of course.' He leans forward and clinks his glass against mine. 'We drink to that.'

Norrback cooks us some food. After our meal, I try to watch television, but I can't seem to take anything in. The outside world's become a strange, unreal place to me.

One day, I may be able to rejoin it.

That day could be tomorrow.

Or not.

Sunday October 20

I LEAVE THE FLAT AT DAWN. NORRBACK DOESN'T SAY ANYTHING as he sees me off. I don't look back as I head along the street, though I'm sure he's watching me from the window. He has a lot riding on what happens today. But I have more.

Billy's idea was that they'd drive me to Morecote. I didn't go for that. I said I'd drive myself. I'm not exactly sure why. I just want to control as much as I can.

I take a taxi down to Brixton and get to the car park while the night shift minder's still on duty. The morning's grey and quiet. London's Sunday-morning empty. I drive west, through Wimbledon and Staines. One way or another, this has to be the last of these furtive cross-country journeys.

I join the M4 at Junction 17, just east of Leigh Delamere services, where we agreed to meet. But I have to sit around nervously in the car park there for nearly twenty minutes before Billy shows up. McKenzie's driving him in a big, anonymous 4WD. They don't stop, just cruise slowly past.

McKenzie's bleak, grey-eyed glance rakes over me. He

335

has that weary but capable look that seems to go with his line of work. Rumour's always ascribed a dark side to him. Maybe I'll see that today.

I follow them across the motorway on the service road and back to Junction 17, then north to Malmesbury and out into the open Cotswold countryside, destination Morecote – destination Hexter.

A car's emerging from the driveway that leads to the house as we approach. The driver's a woman. I catch no more than a glimpse of her. Set grey hair, pale face, narrow mouth. Hexter's wife, maybe? Forrester mentioned her. Marjorie. That was the name.

Well, Marjorie or not, she isn't who we've come to see. We head slowly up the drive. I'm sure Hexter already knows who's on their way to his door.

We pull up in front of the house. There are three other cars there, two 4WDs, one mud-spattered, the other bigger and sleeker, and a grey Mercedes.

Silence greets me as I climb out of my car. Billy casts a glance in my direction. He looks less angry than yesterday and marginally less confident. He also looks as if he hasn't slept well. As I walk over to him, he says in an undertone, 'I'll do the talking.'

'Fine,' I say. 'Just as long as you say the right things.'

Gordon McKenzie gives me a narrow look. I have the strange feeling I'm impressing him. But it's hard to tell. Venstrom's security chief could be called ruggedly handsome. But his essential wariness saps any charm out of his expression. 'How are you, Nicole?' he asks gruffly, in that voice of his I remember now as always sounding like it didn't get enough use.

'As you see me, Gordon.'

He nods. 'OK.'

The front door opens and a short, thin, grey-haired Asian man looks out at us. He has an impassive expression and is wearing dark trousers and a waistcoat over a white shirt and tie. Is this, I wonder, the Chinese fixer, Feng Jianjun?

No, it isn't. 'That's Zhang,' murmurs Billy. 'He and his wife run the house, far as I can tell.'

'And they're Chinese?'

'Yuh.'

'So, Hexter has Chinese servants as well as Chinese masters.'

'Looks like it.' Billy smiles and raises a hand as he leads the way up the steps. 'Hi, Zhang,' he calls ahead.

'Mr Hexter did not say he was expecting you, Mr Swarther,' Zhang responds, in a tone that just manages to stay the friendly side of cautious.

'Sorry. Kind of an emergency. Not a bad time, is it?'

'I am sure he will be pleased to see you. Who are your . . . friends?'

'Two staff members I've brought along to help us . . . sort out a small problem. It shouldn't take long.'

'Please come in. I will tell Mr Hexter you are here.'

We enter the house. There's a lot of wood, oak maybe: beams, pillars and floors. The paleness of the wood and the height of most of the windows gives the place an airy, spacious feel, though the windows are mullioned, in a nod to tradition. There are a lot of rugs as well, with intricate patterns of writhing dragons, which takes us back to China again.

Zhang shows us into a big drawing room, looking out over the rear garden towards the wooded slope behind the house. There are sofas and armchairs, a vast coffee-table, a huge ceiling-suspended wood burner and loads of news-papers and magazines.

As soon as Zhang's left, saying he'll let Hexter know we're here, Billy stalks over to the window and stares out at the scenery. His hands are thrust deep into the pockets of his jeans. He's switched back into his cowboy casuals since I saw him at the Ritz. 'This is Hexter's stage,' he growls. 'He doesn't reckon anyone can out-act him on it.'

'This isn't about acting, Billy. This is about dealing with reality.'

'Yuh.' He doesn't sound completely convinced.

'I'm sure you've got the better of more formidable opponents than Hexter in the past.'

'Sure I have. But I generally enjoyed doing it. We're here to engage in damage limitation, not pull off a famous victory. I won't ever be able to brag about this day's work, will I?'

'No,' I admit. 'You won't.'

He turns away from the window and looks at me. 'And then there's the question of what your future in the com-pany's going to be, Nicole. We're going to have to talk about that at some point.'

'I look forward to the conversation.'

'Y'know, if I'd realized how . . . resourceful . . . you were, I'd have made sure you were better treated.'

Like hell he would. But I just smile and let him believe I believe him.

'So . . .' He puffs out his chest. 'We lay it on the line and, once Hexter's understood—'

'Understood what, Billy?'

The voice is soft and cut-glass accented, with a wispy hint of breathlessness. Clive Hexter walks into the room,

338

a tall, lean, white-haired presence. He's wearing a roll-necked sweater under a cardigan. His trousers have knife-edge creases. He looks like a man who concerns himself a lot with appearances. But I'm aware, given what he is – a spy, a traitor, an actor of a part – that his appearance is only one of many things about him I can't trust.

'Clive,' says Billy. 'Good to see you again.' They shake hands.

'You too,' says Hexter. 'And surprising, so soon after our last meeting.'

'Well, you said if I had any questions . . .'

'You shouldn't hesitate to get in touch. Very true. Though I imagined a telephone call rather than an unannounced visit in that event.' He sounds cool and unworried. He sounds as if he expects to be able to control whatever transpires.

Billy spreads his hands. 'I reckoned this had to be handled face to face.'

'Yet you brought with you two people who weren't party to our original discussions. That strikes me as odd. Where's Bruno, may I ask?'

'I left him in London. As for my associates here, Gordon McKenzie is the company's head of security.'

'Mr McKenzie.' Hexter nods in his direction. 'You anticipate some . . . security-related concern, Billy?'

'My concern will be clear to you soon enough, Clive. Nicole Nevinson—'

'He knows who I am,' I cut in. 'And he can guess why I'm here. Can't you, Mr Hexter?'

Hexter gazes at me for a moment with what looks like no more than mild curiosity, then looks back at Billy. 'Miss Nevinson is wanted for questioning by the police, Billy. Are you aware of that?'

339

'She's made me aware of quite a few things since Bruno and I dined here on Thursday, Clive. Is Feng still here?'

'Yes. You want to speak to him?'

'I guess not. What I have to say is just for you to hear. And maybe Roger Lam. Is he here too?'

'No. He's . . . unwell.'

'Just you and us, then.'

'As you say.'

'I'm here because of what's happened to Joe Roberts.'

'You should ask Miss Nevinson to clear that up. The police want to question her in connection with his suspected kidnapping.'

'You've no idea where Joe is?'

'I'm never short of ideas, Billy. I need to have them in my line of work.'

'Shouldn't you have told me he'd gone missing? It's kinda material to our understanding, wouldn't you say?'

'I was hoping he'd be returned to our care before there was any need to alert you. The man responsible for his disappearance is a renegade former intelligence officer named Alan Travers, alias Duncan Forrester. Miss Nevinson has been helping him. What she hopes to gain by misleading you, as clearly she has, I really can't imagine.' Hexter looks at me. 'Are you intending to give yourself up, Miss Nevinson? Do you want me to phone the police and ask them to come and collect you?'

'Shouldn't you be asking me where Joe is?' I throw back at him.

'Can you tell me?'

'No. But *you* can tell *me. Us*, in fact.'

'I have it on good authority *you* orchestrated the kidnap, Clive,' says Billy. He's sounding stronger now. He's hitting his stride. 'On behalf of the Chinese security service.'

'By good authority you mean Miss Nevinson here? Putting your trust in her would be extremely foolish.'

'It'd be extremely foolish to let you lead me by the nose, Clive. I can't put my company's name to a scheme that involves maltreating a young man and putting him to work for the Chinese government against his will.'

'Is that what you think I'm doing?'

'Yuh. It is. You've been a Chinese double agent for more than thirty years. That's what I hear. Which explains why you're in a position to offer my company unprecedented access to the Chinese market.'

'I arranged for you to meet Feng, who *may* be able to negotiate with the Chinese regulators to your advantage, as compensation for your company's loss of Joe's direct services. That's all there is to it. The idea that I'm a Chinese double agent is ludicrous.'

'Not when I hear your voice, Clive, on a thirty-year-old tape, triggering an assassination in pitch perfect Mandarin. It's very far from ludicrous then.'

'I know nothing about any tape. I've never denied being fluent in Mandarin. I've needed to be, as a matter of professional necessity. It sounds to me as if Miss Nevinson has taken you for a ride, Billy. You should stop this charade now. In your own and your company's best interests.'

'What's the plan for Joe?' I cut in. 'Is he going to be sent to China now he's so conveniently been kidnapped?'

'Ask your friend Forrester. Maybe *he's* a Chinese agent.'

'And then what?' I'm not going to be knocked off course now. I want to lay this on the line. 'Are Venstrom going to be blamed for Joe ending up in China working on

341

a government-backed AI project that promises to outstrip the Americans? Is that how you see it panning out? Venstrom as public enemy number one? Maybe accused of hiring the Clearing House to kidnap Joe when in fact it's you who's hired them for exactly that purpose? Leaving you as . . . what? An unacknowledged but richly rewarded servant of the People's Republic of China? Do they have an honours system? If they do, I guess you'll be in line for a top gong.'

'*Is* that how you see it panning out, Clive?' asks Billy, glaring at Hexter accusingly.

'She's talking nonsense,' snaps Hexter. The sharpness of his tone is the first sign we might be getting under his skin.

'I don't think so,' says Billy, with a shake of the head. 'I think she's right on the money. But I'm here to tell you, Clive, it isn't going to happen. The deal's off. And what I know about you only stays out of the public domain if Joe Roberts and this guy Forrester are freed right now and we—'

'There's something you and I need to discuss in private, Billy.' Hexter raises his chin slightly as he meets and returns Billy's glare. 'We can go to my study. It won't take long. Miss Nevinson and Mr McKenzie can wait here.'

'Whatever you've got to say you can say to me here.' I'm relieved by how adamant Billy sounds on the point.

'You don't want me to do that. This needs to stay between the two of us.'

'What does?'

'You have a tape. I have a tape.'

'What the hell's that supposed to mean?'

'It means what I suspect you're very much afraid it means.'

There's a long moment of silence. Is that a sheen of sweat I can see on Billy's forehead? What's Hexter getting at? I haven't a clue. But Billy has. I can see it in his eyes.

'You'll need to be satisfied I have it, Billy, which is why I suggest you come with me now.'

'What's this about, Billy?' I ask.

'I don't know,' he replies, without looking at me. 'I guess . . . it's simpler if I just go and find out.'

But he knows, of course. He knows exactly what this is about.

'Whatever it is, you have to stick with what we agreed.'

'Sure.' But he doesn't sound sure. 'You two stay here.'

Billy actually makes it to the door before Hexter. Then they're both gone, Hexter closing the door softly behind him.

I turn to McKenzie. 'What's happening?'

He lets out a slow, thoughtful breath. 'I don't know.'

'We can't let this be turned round on us.'

'I'm not in control of the situation, Nicole. I'm here to protect Billy. And to follow his orders.'

'What about me?'

'You don't pay my salary.' He glances past me, out through the window. 'There's a guy in the garden, watching us.'

I follow the direction of McKenzie's gaze. Sure enough, there's a man out there, walking slowly along a path bordering the lawn. And he's looking straight in at us.

He's wearing jeans, a leather jacket and a baseball cap. He's like a hundred other men. But there's a muscular set to his shoulders and a jut to his chin that suggests a seriousness of purpose.

'He's no gardener,' says McKenzie in an undertone. 'I saw him speak into a wrist mike a few minutes ago. Which suggests he's not alone. You mentioned the Clearing House, didn't you? Well, I've heard of them. And I've got to tell you, Nicole, that guy out there is just the sort of guy you get when you hire people like them.'

I can't stop myself shuddering. 'Christ, Gordon, Billy better not roll over on this.'

'He'll likely negotiate a favourable turn-out for you even if he doesn't get everything you and he hoped he would.'

'I wish I could believe that.'

'You must've weighed up the risks before you came here. You must have thought they were worth taking.'

'I had no choice.'

McKenzie nods dolefully. 'Then I'd recommend you leave with us, however it turns out.'

I'm frightened now. McKenzie can probably see that. The man in the garden. The mysterious tape. And why do I get the feeling Hexter knew we were coming? 'Do you know who Hexter's informant is, Gordon? Someone in the company fed him information about our interest in Joe Roberts. Billy must have asked you to find out who that was.'

'He has. But I can't get properly on to it until I'm back at HQ.'

'You think that's where the leak was?'

'Seems likely.'

'What if the leaker came to London with Billy?'

'You mean Bruno?' McKenzie mulls the idea over. 'That'd be . . .' His eyes narrow thoughtfully. 'That'd be seriously bad news.' Something like sorrow, or at any rate

344

regret, seems to drift across his face. 'There's nothing I can do for you, Nicole. I serve the company. So . . .'

'I'm on my own?'

The door opens. Zhang looks in at us.

'Mr Hexter and Mr Swarther would like you to join them in the study, Mr McKenzie,' he says quietly.

'What about me?' I ask, before McKenzie has a chance to respond.

'You can wait here, Miss Nevinson.'

'Like hell I will.' The prospect of being left alone in the drawing room while the three of them stitch something up in the study is deeply scary.

'Seems we're both coming,' says McKenzie.

'Very well,' says Zhang. 'Please follow me.'

We move at a stately pace down a narrow passage off the main hallway. The beams are lower here, the light thinner. I can hear a clock ticking somewhere in the background. I can hear my heart beating too, drumming in my chest.

The study's a big room, with a curving window that gives it the feel of a captain's cabin on some old sailing ship.

Hexter's sitting behind a broad desk scattered with documents. With the light behind him, it's hard to make out the expression on his face.

There's no sign of Billy.

'What's going on?' I hear myself ask.

Hexter ignores me. 'Billy's waiting for you in the car, Mr McKenzie,' he says softly. 'He's decided to leave.'

'We'll go join him, then,' says McKenzie.

'Just you, Mr McKenzie. Miss Nevinson is staying here.'

345

'Says who?' I demand.

'Billy.' I think Hexter's smiling. 'And me, of course. We've reached an agreement. Your remaining here is part of that agreement. Don't let me detain you, Mr McKenzie. Your employer wants to be back in London as soon as possible. I believe he's planning to fly back to San Francisco tonight.'

'I can't see any good reason for us not to give Nicole a lift, even so,' says McKenzie, with slow deliberation. 'Wherever she wants to go.'

'The good reason is that your employer and I have settled on a different course of action. Which I mean to ensure is followed.' Hexter picks up a phone from his desk, presses a button and says quietly, 'Come to the study, please.'

I look at McKenzie. 'You can't leave me here.' I'm imploring him with my eyes to say he won't. What happens if he leaves me with Hexter . . . I don't like to think.

But he'll leave me if he feels he has to. I can see that in *his* eyes.

'We all have to make judgements,' Hexter remarks, almost philosophically. 'Generally, in the end, they tend to be what we think will be to our personal advantage. Isn't that right?' He looks at McKenzie.

Who says nothing. And doesn't look at me.

Then I hear footsteps in the passage. Two men, tall and solidly built, appear in the doorway. They're slab-faced and every bit as dead-eyed as I might have feared.

'Billy's waiting,' Hexter says, still looking at McKenzie.

I hear the tremor in my voice as I speak. 'Don't leave me here, Gordon.'

He hesitates. Not for long, though. It only takes him a few moments to decide. Then he says, 'Sorry, Nicole,' and

346

walks straight out of the room. The two men step apart to let him pass, then move back together.

They won't step aside for me, of course. I know that. My breathing's shallow now. I suspect I'm visibly shaking.

'Sit down, Miss Nevinson,' says Hexter.

I lower myself slowly into a chair, facing him.

'It's disappointing, isn't it, to realize how unreliable most people are?'

'What do you want with me?' I manage to say. I look directly at him. I clench the muscles of my jaw.

'We have to arrive at a conclusion. You've made that unavoidable.'

'How did you get rid of Billy?'

'I showed him a possible future even less appetizing than having to fend off the scandal-mongering media should his company be accused of collusion with the Chinese government. I played him a videotape that came into my possession some time ago. Footage of an alcohol- and drug-fuelled sex party in a hotel suite in Malibu back in 1996. It happens to show, by accident, the death, due to a drugs overdose, of a young woman – a *very* young woman. Billy's on the video as well. The girl's never been officially pronounced dead. As far as her parents know to this day, she disappeared on her way home from that party. How her body was disposed of I don't know. I'm not sure Billy knows. It was arranged . . . on behalf of all those who attended the party, Billy included. He paid a lot of money a long time ago for what he thought was the only surviving copy of the tape. But there's never only one copy of such things, is there? As I happen to know from my own experience.' He sighs again. 'I'm afraid it was disastrously naïve of you to put your faith in Billy Swarther, Miss Nevinson.'

At that moment, his phone rings. He picks it up, listens for a moment, then nods in evident satisfaction.

'They've gone,' he announces after few moments' thought. 'In a proverbial cloud of dust. Leaving you . . . here.'

'You should think about the Norrback tape, Hexter,' I declare in as assertive a tone as I can summon. 'It won't stay hidden if I come to any harm. Nor will another recording I made, of Roger Lam shooting his mouth off.'

'Perhaps not. But Billy's already told me about the Lam recording. I think I can arrange to suppress that. What we're left with isn't quite damning enough for your purposes. Though I don't deny it could cause me a good deal of . . . difficulty.'

'Then let me go.'

'Maybe I will. If you convince me it would be safe to do so. Sadly, I doubt you can. You've already shown yourself to be much less tractable than the likes of Billy Swarther. You share some of Alan Travers' stubbornness, I'm afraid. Which severely limits our room for negotiation.'

'Where is Forrester?'

'Forget him. He's really not important.'

'Isn't he? Aren't you using his supposed link with the Chinese thirty years ago to claim he's kidnapped Joe in order to send him to Beijing when in fact it's *you* who's sending him?'

Hexter looks pained. 'You are right in so far as this is all about Joe. He *is* important. And I think it's time I took you to see him.'

'He's here?'

'No. Nearby. In a cottage I own.'

'But you are planning to send him to China, aren't you? That's what these men are here to arrange, isn't it?'

'I've no intention of discussing my plans with you, Miss

Nevinson. All you need to know for the moment is that Joe's safe and well – and I'm taking you to see him.'

'Why?' I can hardly believe he wants to reassure me about Joe's welfare.

'It's time we were going. I'd like to have you off the premises before Marjorie returns from church, if you don't mind.'

Marjorie. The wife. Could she be a lifeline? 'What if I do mind?'

'Then these gentlemen will convey you forcibly to the car. I'd urge you to spare yourself that indignity. Shall we go?'

We return to the hall, where Zhang is holding the front door open for us. One of Hexter's two goons walks a step ahead of me, the other a step behind. The way they hold themselves and the way they look at me suggests they'd easily and gladly carry me out like a piece of luggage if Hexter gave the word.

Or I gave them an excuse.

I'm boxed in as we descend the steps and move towards one of the 4WDs. My thoughts are whirling. I'm not sure I'm being taken to see Joe at all. Hexter may just have told me that to get me out of the house more easily. And why does he want me out of the house? Because it's neater – cleaner – to kill me somewhere else. He doesn't want to have to explain anything to Marjorie.

We stand by the car. Hexter gets into the driving seat and starts the engine.

'Get in,' one of the goons rasps in my ear. He puts his hands on my shoulders and pushes me towards the open door. His grip is tight and heavy. He's bruising me just by holding me.

He pushes me more violently. I half fall, half climb into the car. He gets in after me and the other goon jumps in on the other side. I'm sandwiched between them on the bench seat. The doors slam. The car starts moving.

As we head down the drive, I catch Hexter glancing at me in the rear-view mirror.

'Let me go, Hexter,' I say. My voice is hoarse and uneven. 'You don't need the trouble Norrback's tape can cause you. And I won't cause you any trouble at all if you let me go now.'

'In case you're interested, Miss Nevinson, Roger Lam's in hospital. Concussion and serious facial injuries. Is that the sort of thing you mean when you say you won't cause any trouble?'

'I did what I had to do to get away from him.'

'And no doubt you'll say what you feel you have to in order to get away from me.'

'I'm no threat to you.'

'If only that were true.'

We reach the end of the drive. Hexter turns out into the lane and accelerates, even as the lane narrows.

'Where are you taking me?'

'I told you.'

'I don't believe you.'

'That's your prerogative.'

'Why did you sell out to the Chinese?'

'You imply a financial motive which has never existed. I've simply acted in accordance with my assessment of the balance of historical destiny.'

'Most people would call that treason.'

'Some people, maybe. But China has existed for thousands of years. It's the summation of organized human society. The past *and* the future. What is Britain or any other Western state compared with that?'

'It's still treason.'

'You sound like Alan Travers.'

'What have you done with him?'

'Nothing. I left that to others.'

'Is he with Joe?'

'No. He's not *with* anyone. Any more.'

My God. He's saying Forrester is dead. Killed. On his orders.

'Alan had his chance thirty years ago,' Hexter goes on, as if reading my thoughts. 'He didn't deserve it. He certainly didn't deserve a second chance. He never had the breadth of vision to understand the logic of what I've worked for.' Never *had*. Past tense. Oh, Christ.

'The tape, Hexter. Remember the tape. Let me go and I promise it'll stay in that bank vault in Helsinki.'

'That isn't your promise to make, Miss Nevinson. And I don't believe you mean it anyway. Not that it matters. What matters is Joe. He's the prize. He has unique mental gifts: the potential to transform our whole approach to artificial intelligence. It seems he truly can out-compute a computer. Except that his brain doesn't use computational methods. He uses ... Well, that's the infinitely significant question. How does he do what he does? We need to find out.'

'You mean the Chinese need to find out.'

'The best researchers in the field are all Chinese, whether they're actually working in China or not. It makes perfect sense to put Joe where he can be of most use. Not here. And certainly not in the United States. But in the

351

country which is clearly going to dominate the world, economically, socially, scientifically and eventually militarily, in the century ahead.'

He slows as he finishes the sentence, then turns in off the lane through a gateway on to a rough track.

A short distance ahead, obscured by a heavily overgrown garden, stands a thatch-roofed cottage. The thatch and the timbered brick walls are both patched with moss. There's a tumbledown garage to one side. The place looks neglected, forgotten.

A big mud-spattered SUV and a dented black Transit van that looks like the one that crashed into Forrester's Land Rover in Cheltenham are parked in front of the garage. Hexter pulls up some way short of them and turns off the engine.

He turns and frowns at me. 'You shouldn't have come to Morecote this morning, Miss Nevinson. That was a grievous error. I always had the measure of Billy Swarther. And, actually, time was on your side. Delay would have served you better. You didn't know that, of course. How could you?'

'What do you mean?'

'I mean that I might have decided I had to live with the damage you could cause. As it is, you've given me the chance to put my affairs in good order. Not for the first time, I find circumstances conspiring in my favour. Norrback's tape will soon be irrelevant. You will be regarded as no more than Alan Travers' hapless dupe in his plot to spirit Joe out of this country. I didn't lie to you when we left Morecote, you see. Joe really is here. But I'm not sending him to China. I'm *taking* him.'

'What?'

352

'Delivering Joe is the perfect climax to my career. I'm retiring. And my retirement isn't going to be spent in Gloucestershire, but somewhere where my achievements will be better appreciated.'

'China.'

He smiles faintly. 'Exactly.'

A moment passes. I can't find anything to say. Why has he told me so much? The answer comes to me at the same time as the question. He wanted to tell *someone*. And he knew he could tell me . . . because he knew I wasn't going to be able to tell anyone else.

I can't find any way out of the trap I'm in. The end Hexter has prepared for me is closing in. I can sense it. I can feel it.

'Let's go inside,' he says quietly.

The goon on my right opens his door and starts to climb out.

Then he stops. A figure's emerged from the cottage and is striding towards us.

It's Marianne Vogler.

How different she looks now compared with the pushed-aside wine-tippling wife of Conrad Vogler I was first introduced to. But that wasn't the real her, of course. *This* is Marianne Vogler.

She's wearing a black tracksuit and trainers. Her hair's tied back. Her expression is sober – and deadly serious.

Hexter seems surprised to see her. He lowers his window and says to her as she approaches, 'I thought you were leaving this to Scaddan.'

'There's been a change of plan,' she announces, casting a fleeting glance at me.

'Not as far as I'm concerned.' Hexter sounds snappish. It's clear he doesn't like changes of plan. Unless he's the one doing the changing, I imagine.

'Sorry, Clive.' Marianne gives him a brief, tight little smile. 'I have new instructions.'

'And we have an agreement.' Hexter pushes his door open and steps out. He grasps the frame as he glares at her. 'I expect it to be honoured. In full.'

'No can do.'

'What the hell's that supposed to mean?'

'It's out of my hands. I'm sure you understand.'

'No. I don't.'

'It's been decided Joe's services are so valuable to the Clearing House that you can't be allowed to take him to China with you.'

'*What?*'

'Naturally, the rest of the agreement stands. Forrester's been disposed of and the plane's waiting at the field for the hop over the Channel. The pilot's a trusted operative. Every leg of the onward route to Beijing is secure, although I guess most of the precautions are actually unnecessary now Joe isn't going with you.'

'Are you mad? I've no intention of accepting this. I want to speak to Kremer.'

'Andreas won't take your call, Clive, I guarantee. Here's the thing.' She isn't smiling. But I get the distinct impression she'd like to. 'We're keeping Joe. And, since you contracted this whole operation to us, we're in charge. Leave now and we'll cover your tracks. Stay and your whole treasonable story, complete with the Norrback tape, the whereabouts of Forrester's body and an edited version of events we'll persuade Nicole to put her name to will be released to the media. I don't think you'll be able to weather that storm, do you? How long before Roger Lam does a deal to save his own skin? And how long after that before you become *persona non grata* in the intelligence community? Twenty-four hours? Or do you give yourself forty-eight?'

Hexter has no answer. He stands, supporting himself on the door-frame, breathing heavily. I can see his chest heaving. He's not as young as he was. He doesn't have the strength he once had. And, however quickly he thinks, I sense he can't think his way out of this.

In the end, he just murmurs, 'Bitch.'

'It wasn't my decision, Clive. But I have to live with it. So do you.'

Hexter pulls out his phone and stabs in some numbers. Marianne watches him with thin-lipped disdain. She glances in at me as Hexter holds the phone to his ear and, to my astonishment, she winks.

Then Hexter drops the phone back into his pocket. He hasn't spoken. Now he sighs audibly.

'Voicemail?' asks Marianne.

He says nothing. His thunderous expression is an answer in itself.

'We have to be moving if we're to keep to the schedule. The plane's waiting. We'll take the van. You and Nicole will have to travel in the back, I'm afraid. This journey needs to be as discreet as possible.'

'Where's Joe?'

'Inside.' Marianne nods back towards the cottage. 'And he's staying there until I've seen you off. Which is why Nicole will be coming with us. We can't have her and Joe cooking up some scheme together while I'm away, can we?'

'I want to see him before we go.'

'I don't think that would serve any purpose.'

355

'Well, I'm not leaving until I *have* seen him. How do I know you're not covering up for letting him get away?'

'We don't make slip-ups like that, Clive.'

'Then bring him out here.'

Marianne ponders his demand for a moment, then seems to decide she can't be bothered to argue. 'All right,' she says resignedly.

She turns and signals to someone I can't see inside the cottage. A moment later, Joe appears in the doorway with Scaddan at his shoulder. He looks rumpled and grey-faced. His mouth is fixed in a sullen line.

'I want to speak to him,' says Hexter.

'Joe's got nothing to contribute to this. It's a Clearing House decision.'

'*I want to speak to him.*'

'Why?'

'Bring him down here and you'll find out. The sooner you do that, the sooner we'll be done.'

Marianne gives a heavy, impatient sigh. She beckons to Scaddan. The meaning's clear. *Bring him here.*

The pair leave the doorway and start walking towards us. I notice they're handcuffed together, Joe's right hand to Scaddan's left. The short chain dangles between their wrists. Joe's ever-present shoulder-bag is hanging at his side.

'As you can see, Clive,' says Marianne, 'we're not taking any risks.'

Hexter waits until Joe's a few feet from him. Then he walks round to the back of his car, opens the rear door and lifts out a small suitcase. His going-away luggage, I assume. He's evidently not taking much with him. A spy travels light, I suppose. 'There's something I want to show you, Joe,' he says. 'In case we never meet again.'

356

'This is a waste of valuable time,' says Marianne.

'Humour me. It won't take long. Come over here, Joe.'

Scaddan and Joe move to where Hexter's standing with the case. Hexter slides the zip open and reaches in.

'This'll help you—' Faster than I'd ever have expected him to move, Hexter pulls a gun out of the case and jams the short barrel against Joe's temple. 'Don't move, Joe. Nor you, Scaddan. I'll pull the trigger if you take one step away from me.'

Suddenly, there's commotion. The goon on my left scrambles out of the car. The other one makes to follow him. But Marianne holds up a hand, first to them, then back towards the cottage, where there must be at least one other man.

'OK, Clive,' she says, raising both her hands as she looks at him. 'Let's not do anything stupid.'

Joe's gone white. He can feel the hard steel of the barrel pressing into the side of his head. Scaddan has a gun wedged in the waistband of his jeans. He was reaching back for it, but stopped at a glance from Marianne. No one's moving. There's utter stillness.

'If I can't take Joe with me,' says Hexter, coolly and calmly, 'I don't think it's in my interests to leave him in your hands, Marianne. So, I'll kill him, here and now, and his "valuable services" will be lost to your organization as well as to the Chinese government. Don't think I won't do it. I haven't led a double life for forty years without being able to shoot a man in the head when I need to.'

'This isn't my fault, Mr Hexter,' gasps Joe. 'You can't—'

'Be quiet, Joe,' snaps Hexter. 'I'm talking *about* you, not *to* you. You have a choice to make, Marianne. Let me take Joe with me or I kill him some time in the next few seconds. Your choice.'

'Clive—'

'Just make the choice. Now.'

I see Marianne bite her lip. No doubt she's as angry with herself for giving Hexter this chance as she is with him for taking it. Maybe she thought he was too old to pull such a stunt. If so, she was wrong.

'Time's up.'

'All right, all right.' Her hands are still raised. 'You can take him.'

'Thank you. Please tell Scaddan to transfer his cuff to my wrist.'

Hexter stretches his left hand towards Scaddan while keeping the gun pressed against Joe's temple. Joe's breathing through his mouth now, taking shallow gulps of air. Marianne nods to Scaddan, who unlocks the cuff on his wrist and locks it round Hexter's. He hands Hexter the key.

'Good,' says Hexter. 'You've got your passport on you, Joe?'

Joe nods.

'Show it to me.'

Joe lifts the flap of his shoulder-bag and pulls out his passport.

'All right. Put it back. Now, we're all going to move very slowly. Miss Nevinson will get into the driving seat of my car.' *Me?* Why is he involving me? 'Joe and I will get into the rear seat. Scaddan will load my case in the back. Then the three of us will leave.'

Marianne frowns at him. 'You're taking Nicole?'

'Someone has to drive us. I'm certainly not entrusting that to one of your people. I'll direct her. I know the way. Don't even think about following us. And when we get to the airfield, I expect the pilot to have been told to cooperate fully. Anything else . . . and Joe dies.'

'You won't kill him.'

'If I can't take him with me, Marianne, I arrive in China empty-handed. That's not what I've led my handlers in the Ministry of State Security to expect. Disappointing them wouldn't be a good start to my Chinese retirement. But they'd be even more disappointed if they knew I'd left him in the hands of a criminal cartel such as the Clearing House. So, you see, there are only two options. Either he goes with me. Or . . .'

I believe every word Hexter's said. And I can see Marianne believes it too. 'OK,' she says quietly. 'Have it your way.'

'Thank you. I believe I will.'

We all follow Hexter's orders. I get in the driver's seat. Scaddan stows Hexter's case in the back. Joe and Hexter get in behind me.

'Let's go,' says Hexter. 'Reverse out left into the lane.'

I start the car, engage reverse and immediately stall. 'Sorry,' I hear myself say in a panicky tone. 'I'm not . . . used to this.'

'Try again,' says Hexter, sounding remarkably tolerant of my mistake. He glances out of the car towards Marianne and Scaddan and the other two as I start up again and begin edging back, then swing out into the lane.

I look back at the cottage. Four stationary figures stand watching us. I can hear Joe's breathing. He can probably hear mine.

'Drive on,' says Hexter. 'Not too fast. Not too slow. And no sudden braking. It'll take us about twenty minutes to reach our destination. There's no hurry. It's going to be an uneventful drive.'

My hands are gripping the wheel so tightly my knuckles

are white. I try to relax as I shift the stick and move forwards, accelerating steadily.

We drive in silence for a few minutes, then Joe says, in a cracked voice, 'This is . . . crazy, Mr Hexter. Even if you get across the Channel, you can't take me all the way to China . . . in handcuffs . . . with a gun . . . held to my head.'

'You don't understand, Joe. By the time we reach France, there'll be no need for a gun or handcuffs. You'll be going with me willingly.'

'I . . . don't think so.'

'Yes, you will. Because by then you'll have come to appreciate that the continuing good health of your mother – and your girlfriend – depends on your cooperation. I'm actually doing you a favour. You'll be treated much better in China than you would be by the Clearing House.'

'But . . . I don't . . .'

'Have a say in this, I'm afraid. It's force majeure. Left at the T-junction ahead, Miss Nevinson.'

'Are you sure you should be going to China, Hexter?' My heart's in my mouth as I find myself stumbling into an attempt to dent his composure. 'What about the relatives of all those people you betrayed? Aren't they likely to catch up with you over there?'

I see him eyeing me in the rear-view mirror. 'You've no idea what you're talking about.'

'Do you ever think about them? All those people who died because of you. Do you actually know how many there have been?' I remember the estimate Forrester came up with and add: 'A hundred? Two hundred?'

'I've dedicated my life to objectives of which you can

have no conception. And I shall continue to do so. I can't be judged by the likes of you. You're not intellectually equipped to grasp why I've done what I've done.'

'Who is?'

'Joe, once he's had a chance to see the . . . historical importance of my work.'

'I'm never going to give you my . . . approval, Mr Hexter,' says Joe. He sounds calmer now. And quietly determined.

'Never's a long time. You'll see things differently once we're in Beijing. Meanwhile, remember what happens to people who try to obstruct me. Were you there when they killed Travers?'

'Yes.' The word comes almost as a whisper.

'If you want to avoid that happening to you – or Miss Nevinson – you'll do as I say. And that's all there is to it.'

Occasional, terse directions are all I get from Hexter for the rest of the journey. He lowers the gun from Joe's head as we reach busier roads and holds it at waist level. But the handcuffs ensure Joe couldn't run away from him even if we weren't in the car. And I'm not much better off myself. I've been frightened for so long the fear's become a leaden weight bearing down on me. It's so heavy I can't even think. *Our destination.* What does that mean for me? What *is* waiting for us at the end of this drive?

The airfield, when we reach it, looks at first sight deserted. Several hangars have been converted to light industrial use. But it's Sunday, so there's no one working in any of them. A sign advertises a local gliding club that doesn't appear to exist any longer. The boundary fence is in poor repair. The runway looks overdue for resurfacing. The grass around it is pocked with weeds and thistles.

But there's a plane, just one, standing at the end of the runway: red, single-engined, with the wings mounted above the fuselage.

'Get as close as you can in the car,' Hexter instructs me.

I obey, driving along a potholed service road towards the plane.

There's no sign of the pilot, but, suddenly, the engine of the plane kicks into life and I realize there's a figure at the controls. He's seen us and he doesn't mean to waste any time.

I stop where the service road ends in a turning-head. We're about thirty metres from the plane. The noise of the engine is muffled inside the car. Hexter's silence seems to make the air thicker.

Then he speaks. 'Take the key out of the ignition, Miss Nevinson. Toss it out of the window.'

What does he think I might do? I can't read his thoughts. I can't even read my own. I do as I'm told. As I lower the window, the noise from the plane invades the space inside the car. Out goes the key.

'Now,' Hexter continues, 'Joe and I are going to get out. Then you're going to get out and fetch my case. And then we're all going to walk over to the plane.'

'I'll go with you, Mr Hexter,' says Joe. 'As long as you don't harm Nicole.'

'How gallant. What are you afraid I might do to her?'

'You know what.'

'Individuals don't matter, Joe. The great sweeping longevity of Chinese history has taught me that. And it'll teach you that too, I promise.'

'We leave Nicole here, alive and well. Or you'll have to kill me.'

'Don't say that, Joe.' I look at him over my shoulder. 'Just do what you have to do to stay alive.'

He smiles faintly at me, as if reflecting on the irony of our situation. I went to Cornwall to root him out of his old life. And I succeeded. In ways neither of us could have imagined.

'I only need Miss Nevinson to carry my bag, Joe,' says Hexter gently, as if he's asking little from either of us beyond a few small favours. 'Don't worry. She can wave us off.'

But Joe's counting on nothing. 'I meant what I said.'

'Duly noted. Can we go now? I don't want the pilot to become impatient.'

They clamber out of the car together and stand waiting while I get out and unload Hexter's case. Hexter nods for me to go first. I set off towards the plane, dragging the case behind me, its wheels snagging in the grass we have to cross to reach the runway.

I glance back and see Joe and Hexter following me. Hexter's walking in Joe's shadow, judging, I guess, how to position himself so the pilot can't see the gun in his hand. *If* the pilot's looking. But maybe he already knows about the gun and has been told to do whatever Hexter says. There's a whole swarm of maybes around us. More than I can count.

We reach the plane. The pilot's clearly visible now, though I can't see much of his face beneath the brim of a baseball cap. He looks expectantly in our direction.

'Put the case inside,' shouts Hexter from behind me. The noise of the engine and the vortex of air thrown off by the propellers make it difficult to hear. My hair's blowing in my eyes as I reach for the handle to open the door.

In that instant my eyes catch a movement by the tail-plane. A figure emerges suddenly into view. And I look. Straight at him.

For a frozen fraction of a second, I think he's an hallucination. I can't really be seeing who I'm seeing. But I am.

Forrester has a gun in his hand. He raises it as he takes a stride forward and shouts Hexter's name. I look round and see Hexter raising his gun too, swinging it up and away from Joe.

There's a sharp crack of sound, then another, the first from Forrester's gun, the second from Hexter's.

Hexter jolts back, staggers and slowly topples to the ground, pulling Joe with him.

Only one of the bullets fired has hit its target. Forrester marches past me and kicks Hexter's gun further away from his hand. He stoops over his old enemy.

'Where's the key to the handcuffs?' I hear him ask, though who he's asking isn't clear.

Joe fumbles in Hexter's trouser pocket and pulls out the key. He tries to fit it into the lock, but his hands are shaking too much for him to manage it at first. Then it clicks in. A turn of the key and the handcuff falls open.

'Move away, Joe,' says Forrester.

Joe rises unsteadily to his feet and steps towards me. His gaze meets mine, a mirror of my own astonishment. But not my disbelief. Not quite. Somehow, I realize, Forrester's appearance wasn't as unexpected to him as it was incredible to me.

I don't have time to think about what this realization means, though. Forrester is standing over Hexter, who's gurgling and weakly flapping one hand at his throat, where I think the bullet hit him.

Forrester says something I don't catch, something directed only at Hexter. I guess they're looking at one another now. I guess their pasts are compressed into his words and the look that passes between them. Then Forrester points the gun at Hexter's head and fires again. And Hexter stops moving altogether.

The door of the plane's been pushed open. The pilot's standing on the sill, staring out, wide-eyed in dismay.

Forrester unloads the magazine from his gun and throws it down next to Hexter's body. Then he turns towards us.

'How . . .' I begin. It's all happened so quickly I can't adjust to the reality of it. I feel weak and shaky with shock.

'Joe did a deal with Marianne,' says Forrester, as if that's a complete answer to everything.

'I thought . . . I was going to have to go with Hexter,' says Joe. 'How did you get here ahead of us?'

'I took a different route. The story of my life. As for Hexter, I should have done what I've just done a long time ago.'

'I still don't . . .' I try to begin again.

'Joe can explain. I can't stay. Not after this.' Forrester gestures towards Hexter's body, from which blood is now seeping in a dark, spreading pool. 'Get Norrback to hand over the tape. I'll tell Colin to head back to London. With your evidence, his own researches and what the tape reveals, the powers that be will have to acknowledge Hexter's treachery. As soon as I've gone, call the police. Tell them everything. Except the identity of our kidnappers. Leave the Clearing House out of it. Marianne and Scaddan and the other two will have left the cottage by now anyway, along with all trace they were ever there. Say nothing that could identify this plane or the pilot. That's crucial if you want a clean exit from all this. And one for me too. OK?'

'OK,' says Joe. 'But . . .'

'There are no buts, son.' Forrester smiles at Joe. 'There's only whatever you want to do with the rest of your life.' Then he looks at me. 'You'll be all right now, Nicole. It's over.'

'Where are you going?' I manage to ask.

'France. To start with. Then . . . I'm not sure.' He glances up at the pilot. 'Are we still set?'

'Yeah,' comes the bellowed answer. 'But we need to get the hell out of here right now.'

'Let's go, then.'

Forrester actually looks as if he's going to shake Joe's hand. But Joe gives him a big hug instead. There's not much for me to do after that but hug him myself.

'Do you really need to go, Duncan?' I ask.

'Oh yes.' He nods. 'I really do.'

'*Get in*,' shouts the pilot.

Forrester gives farewell glances to both of us then and climbs into the plane, pulling the door shut behind him.

The plane begins to taxi forward.

A few moments later, the engine roars as it accelerates down the runway.

Then lift-off. And Forrester is on his way, up into the clear blue sky.

*

366

Joe and I stand together, watching the plane bank as it climbs, the drone of the engine growing fainter with every passing second. Neither of us speaks.

Hexter's dead. But Forrester's alive. So's Joe. And so am I.

And for the moment – this moment – nothing else seems to matter.

* * *

Joe used Hexter's phone to establish exactly where we were, then he rang 999. He didn't tell the operator much, except there'd been a fatal shooting and the gunman was no longer on the scene. He never even mentioned me, which I guessed was just in case I wanted to clear out before the police arrived.

But I wasn't going to do that. It was time to stop running. Because what I'd been running *from* had died with Hexter. I didn't feel as relieved as I knew I would eventually. I was still numb with shock. But the certainty that it was over had lodged in my mind. I was going to be all right. Everything was going to be all right.

We stood by Hexter's car and waited. Joe smoked one of his roll-ups and I smoked one too. He didn't seem to be in any hurry to explain the deal he'd done with Marianne Vogler. So, in the end, I just asked him straight out what it was.

Joe, it soon became clear, had never quite been the innocent he presented himself as.

'Truth is, Nicole, I'd known for a long time Conrad was a big-time money launderer for an international crime consortium. Hacking into files he thought I didn't have access to was easy peasy. So, I knew all about the Clearing House. But I enjoyed what I did for him and he paid me well for working pretty much on my own terms, so . . . I turned a blind eye.'

'I imagine there was quite a lot to turn a blind eye *to*.'

'More than you know, actually. Con's boss, Andreas Kremer, was skimming money off Clearing House funds and Con was stashing it away for both of them.'

'You mean *you* were stashing it away.'

Joe shrugged. 'If you want to be picky, yeah. Anyway, when Ursula Kendall turned up at Tideways, asking way too many questions about Con, I hacked into her files as well and discovered HMRC were seriously on his case. So, I reckoned it was time to move on, in my own best interests.'

'That must have made my offer of a job with Venstrom look more appealing than you let on.'

'Yeah. But I had no idea how far Con was prepared to go to hold on to me, did I? Things got way out of control after what he did to Mum. I pinned my hopes on your boss Carl coming to some arrangement with him, but that didn't exactly work out, did it?'

'And after you were arrested, Hexter made you an offer you couldn't refuse?'

'To work for him at GCHQ, yeah. I didn't have any choice really. I actually started to enjoy some of the problems they threw at me. But then . . . well, you know what happened then. Hexter hired the Clearing House, through Marianne, to arrange his – *our* – removal to China. Plus he wanted you and Duncan . . . rubbed out. Obviously, I couldn't let that happen.'

He couldn't let that happen. It was strange how, through

everything, Joe had always thought he was in control, even when he wasn't. Or maybe, on some level, he actually was. 'So . . . what did you do?'

'I had to think fast when Duncan and I were taken. I knew Con's share of the skimmed Clearing House funds was held jointly in his name and Marianne's. And I assumed she knew that as well. But I was wrong. He'd kept the whole thing from her. Anyway, I told her the details of the skimming operation would be automatically emailed to the Clearing House within forty-eight hours by a program only I had access to unless she let Duncan live and cut me free from Hexter. I'd set the program up as a precaution when I first realized what was going on. But I'd never initialized it, so, technically . . . it was an empty threat.'

'But she believed it?'

'Yeah. It seems a reputation for being a genius can be useful sometimes. She was furious with Kremer, reckoning stealing from the Clearing House was suicide. She used my threat to force him into agreeing to filter the money back in, so nobody would ever know it had left. And they both agreed to my terms.' Joe smiled at me. 'Result, you could say.'

'Marianne's claim that the Clearing House had decided to hold on to you was just a cover story, then?'

'She and Kremer calculated Hexter wouldn't want to admit to his new masters in Beijing that he'd left me in the hands of an international criminal organization, so he'd have to come up with some version of events that didn't involve the Clearing House. In that case, there'd be no danger of the Chinese coming after her and Kremer because they'd never know anything about them.

369

But Hexter wouldn't take no for an answer, would he? And Marianne had to do whatever kept me alive in the short term. So, she let him take me.'

'But she sent Duncan after us?'

'Seems like it. She must've let him use one of their cars. Otherwise, he'd never have got here in time. And she must've given him a gun as well.'

'How did he talk her into that, do you suppose?'

Joe let the question go unanswered. Eventually, I tried to answer it myself. 'Maybe she just trusted him to get the job done.'

Joe nodded. 'Yeah. Maybe that was it.'

'And he did, didn't he?'

Joe nodded again. 'Oh yeah.'

'What will you do, Joe? Now there's no threat from Hexter *or* the Clearing House?'

He shrugged. 'Not sure.' And he wasn't, of course. But the world isn't going to leave someone like him alone. He must have known that. Me, yes. But not him. 'What about you?'

I was still trying to come up with a reply when I heard a sound in the distance. Joe heard it too. The wail of a police siren. All I said in the end was, 'Here they come.'

I knew there were going to be lots of questions for me to answer in the hours and days ahead. But I also knew, even then, that the hardest one to answer was going to be the one Joe had just asked.

* * *

I'm not going back to work for Venstrom Computers, with or without Billy Swarther at the helm. Which would be without, from what I hear. So . . . what, then? I still owe

Lewis Martinek £500. And I promised I'd take him to Las Vegas if I made it through. God, I might actually have to deliver on that!

I don't know. A few days ago, I didn't seem to have a future. Now I've got one. And it's empty. A few *weeks* ago, that would have terrified me. Now it feels good. In fact, it feels . . . fantastic.

ROBERT GODDARD

WHERE WILL HE TAKE YOU NEXT?

1720

SEA CHANGE What are the contents of a mysterious package that could spark a revolution in England?

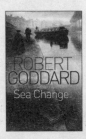

1880

PAINTING THE DARKNESS
The arrival in London of a stranger claiming to be a man long thought dead uncovers dark family secrets.

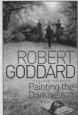

1910

PAST CARING Why did cabinet minister Edwin Strafford resign at the height of his career and retreat into obscurity on the island of Madeira?

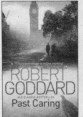

IN PALE BATTALIONS Loss, greed and deception during the First World War – and a murder left unsolved for more than half a century.

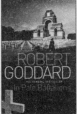

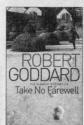

TAKE NO FAREWELL A murder trial forces Geoffrey Staddon to return to the Herefordshire country house that launched his architectural career – and to the dark secret it holds.

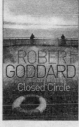

CLOSED CIRCLE On board a grand cruise liner, a pair of chancers are plunged deep into a dark conspiracy.

DYING TO TELL What happened in Somerset in the summer of 1963 that holds the key to a devastating secret?

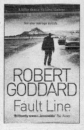

FAULT LINE A father dead in his fume-filled car. His young son alive in the boot. Not your average suicide . . .

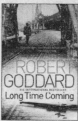

LONG TIME COMING For thirty-six years they thought he was dead. They were wrong.

1980

INTO THE BLUE   When a guest goes missing from his friend's villa on the island of Rhodes, Harry Barnett becomes prime suspect and must find her if he is to prove himself innocent.

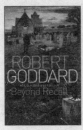
Into the Blue

HAND IN GLOVE   What long-buried secret connects the murder of a dead poet's elderly sister with the Spanish Civil War?

Hand in Glove

BEYOND RECALL   Dark family secrets are unlocked when a man seeks the truth behind the suicide in Truro of a childhood friend.

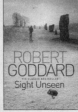
Beyond Recall

SIGHT UNSEEN   A trail of dangerous deceits connects eighteenth century political writer Junius with the abduction of a child at Avebury more than two hundred years later.

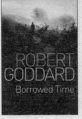
Sight Unseen

1990

BORROWED TIME   A chance meeting. A brutal murder. How far will one man go to gain justice?

OUT OF THE SUN   Harry Barnett must unravel a web of conspiracies if he is to save the son he never knew he had.

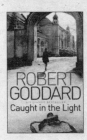
Borrowed Time

CAUGHT IN THE LIGHT
A photographer is drawn into a complex web of deception and revenge following an encounter with a beautiful woman in Vienna.

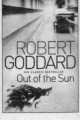
Out of the Sun

Caught in the Light

2000

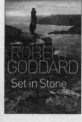

SET IN STONE A house steeped in a history of murder and treason exerts an eerie and potentially fatal influence over its present inhabitants.

DAYS WITHOUT NUMBER Five Cornish siblings are dragged into a deadly conflict with an unseen enemy as they confront their family's mysterious past.

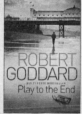

PLAY TO THE END An estranged husband becomes caught up in a dangerous tangle of family rivalries and murderous intentions while appearing in a play in Brighton.

NEVER GO BACK A group of ex-RAF comrades, Harry Barnett among them, uncover an extraordinary secret during a reunion in Scotland, which puts them all in mortal danger.

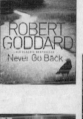

NAME TO A FACE When an ancient ring is stolen in Penzance, a centuries old mystery begins to unravel.

FOUND WANTING What connects a dying man's grandfather with the tragic fate of the Russian Royal Family, murdered ninety years earlier?

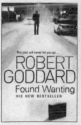

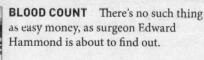

BLOOD COUNT There's no such thing as easy money, as surgeon Edward Hammond is about to find out.

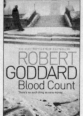

2010

BLOOD COUNT
Robert Goddard

Thirteen years ago, surgeon Edward Hammond performed a life-saving operation on Serbian gangster Dragan Gazi. Now Gazi is standing trial for war crimes at the international court in The Hague. After Hammond saved his life, Gazi's men went on to slaughter thousands in the Balkan civil wars.

Now, in exchange for keeping Hammond's dirty little secret, Gazi's family want a small favour: to find the man who knows what happened to Gazi's money. But Italian financier Marco Piravani doesn't want to be found. And no sooner has Hammond tracked him down than he disappears again. Hammond has no choice but to set off across Europe in pursuit.

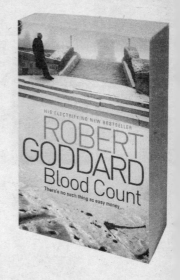

In *Blood Count*, every action has a consequence and every question must have an answer. Only then might Hammond be able to lay the past to rest . . .

'Ingenious'
SUNDAY TIMES

FAULT LINE

Robert Goddard

A search for missing documents in an international mining company becomes a voyage into dangerous waters.

It could be your average suicide. A man found dead in his car, engine running, parked at the end of a lonely track, a tube feeding deadly fumes from the exhaust through the window. Except for the seven-year-old boy still breathing in the boot . . .

For Jonathan Kellaway, the past is somewhere he chooses not to go. Dead friends, lost lovers and a family dynasty hell-bent on self-destruction lie buried there.

But if he is to uncover the truth, he must confront all the secrets which have consumed his life, and which may yet consume him . . .

'Brilliantly woven . . . irresistible'
THE TIMES

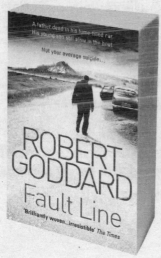

PANIC ROOM

Robert Goddard

High on a Cornish cliff sits a vast uninhabited mansion. Uninhabited except for Blake, a young woman of mysterious background, currently acting as house-sitter.

The house has a panic room. Cunningly concealed, steel lined, impregnable – and apparently closed from within. Even Blake doesn't know it's there. She's too busy being on the run from life, from a story she thinks she's escaped.

But her remote existence is going to be threatened when people come looking for the house's owner, rogue pharma entrepreneur, Jack Harkness. Soon people with questionable motives will be asking Blake the sort of questions she can't – or won't – answer.

WILL THE PANIC ROOM EVER GIVE UP ITS SECRETS?

'Is this his best yet? . . . Full of sinister menace and propulsive pace with twisty plotting'
LEE CHILD